COLOUR

For Julia,

Thanks so much

Ken Reynolds

Ken Reynolds

ISBN 978-1-68526-240-2 (Paperback)
ISBN 978-1-68526-241-9 (Digital)

Covenant Books
11661 Hwy 707
Murrells Inlet, SC 29576
www.covenantbooks.com

CHAPTER

ONE

Ed cradled the company's phone receiver against his cheek, running his finger around the rim of the mouthpiece. A shiver ran down his spine when she answered. "Bronson and Schubert's." Her voice. Gail's dulcet, shiver-inducing tones.

"Good morning, my one and only, my inspiration, my own true—"

"Again, Ed? It's only been three minutes."

"But you forgot to tell me when the order will be in."

"Riiight. I think you're just missing me."

"Well, of course I am. Shhh! Don't tell anyone."

There, the little giggle that made his heart loop the loop. Just one of those could see him through the day.

"Don't worry," she said. "It's our little secret, hey?"

He cupped the mouthpiece and blew a kiss into it.

"Your order," she continued, "will be in tomorrow morning by ten o'clock, via our courier. Will there be anything else, Mister Brent?"

"Why no, Miss Rabe. Not for at least another three interminable minutes."

Another musical laugh, warming him down to his toes. "Okay then, I'll be waiting with anxious anticipation for your next order."

Ed replaced the receiver and stared, unfocused, and straight ahead. He took a deep breath and got to work opening parcels. The morning proved slow, other than the usual few customers buying films or dropping them off for developing and a couple needing pictures for drivers' licences. Just as well. Concentrating was difficult

3

after any phone conversation with Gail. The memory of her laugh kept intruding, as did her anxious anticipation of his next order. Right. Sometimes, there could be days between orders from Bronson and Schubert's. That meant days not hearing her voice. Her laugh. Miserable days without Gail.

How long had it been? His almost affair with Gail. Six months? More, maybe seven or eight. Could he call it an affair? He'd never met her, never seen her, she was a voice only. He hadn't the foggiest idea of what she looked like. Every time he passed the telephone, he stared at it, willing it to ring. But will alone didn't produce a peep out of the soulless black instrument of torture. A more modern convenience, inadvertently making things worse. In former times, it would have meant countless trips to the letterbox, only to find it empty. Torture. This couldn't be healthy.

A couple of hours later, the phone rang and he snatched up the receiver. Mrs. Cahill, their boss, answered. The forty-something blonde, whom they all called Mommy, hardly ever came into the shop. "You did remember to order those Tri-X four-by-fives? I've got a wedding shoot on Saturday, and I'm running low."

"Of course," he answered automatically. But had he? He couldn't remember off hand, but they hadn't turned up in the mail. He'd cleared all of it. His gaze shot to the dial, his fingers itching. "Don't worry, I'll call them at once and check why they haven't arrived."

"Please, do that. I must have them. Bye."

Had he ordered them or not? His panic evaporated since they would have been from Bronson and Shubert's. His fingers were already dialing, they knew the number by heart.

"Gail, heart of my hearts, love of my life, pretty please, tell me I ordered twenty Tri-X four-by-fives."

"Sorry, Ed, no can do."

"You don't have them?" Panic gripped at his heart, not what his heart usually got up to while talking with Gail.

"I didn't say that. I only said I couldn't tell you that you ordered them—seeing as you didn't. They'll be on the courier van this afternoon."

He blew out a breath. "Phew! Thank you, my lifesaver. I can't imagine what I'd do without you, you always come to my rescue." He stared down at the receiver longingly.

"Right," said Gail. She laughed. One of his favourite sounds, he could listen to it all day. "Quite obviously you forgot again. You'd be lost, Ed, without your mommy, let's face it."

"Mommy! No, don't say that, oof! My image of you as a ravishing beauty just popped. Now all I see is my mom glaring at me. Besides which, that's what we call Mrs. Cahill around here. You really do know how to destroy the moment, don't you?"

Gail laughed again, and he savoured the sound for a few moments. It always started as a gurgle, rising in pitch before ending in a giggle. Pure music. He had, in fact, tried emulating it on his piano but gave it up as a miserable interpretation. It would take a maestro to come even close, and he never claimed such skills, so the solution was making her laugh as often as possible without it becoming painful to her.

He sighed. "Well, I suppose I better let you go back to your work. I've taken up too much of your time, as usual."

"Yes, typical, preventing a poor working girl from doing her job. All bluffs, Ed, not to worry, but I am kind of busy…sorry."

"Yeah. Me too. I'm holding you up. Thanks again, Gail, my favourite phone pal, love of my life. Talk to you soon," he said.

"Sure, love of your life, I bet. I love…" she hesitated. "Talking with you. Bye now."

"Goodbye, Gail." He stood for a while, resting his cheek on the receiver.

"Not Gail again?" Mark strode over and peered at Ed through his thick-framed glasses, which accentuated his bald head. He wore his customary grin. "What? Can you see her, something about the phone I'm not aware of?"

Ed sighed. "No, sadly not. Perhaps one day they'll make a phone where you can view the person on the other end of the line." He stared at the floor.

"Like in Dick Tracey? I'm not sure I'd want some people seeing my expression while I'm speaking to them. I wouldn't be able to pull faces at them."

"Yes, good point, but in this case, I would love to see Gail. Is she as gorgeous as she sounds? I wonder."

Mark grinned his wide grin, always looking like somebody had just told him a joke. "You mean, you never met her at all, old boy? You sound absolutely besotted when you're chatting to that woman. It's positively nauseating."

"That bad, huh? Mark...do you think it possible to fall in love with a voice?"

What if it were personality that mattered most after all? He'd always fallen for the most salubrious of women, and they hadn't all been that great. What about those with the pleasant personalities who had been invisible to him? Perhaps it made more sense getting to know someone intimately before ever seeing them?

Mark's voice intruded on his thoughts. "I would say no, old chap, but since you spend so many business hours chatting up Bronson and Schubert's order clerk, and spending even more mooning over her, then yeah, I guess it is."

"I don't talk to her that long, do I?"

Mark glanced at his watch. "Hmm, okay, only ten minutes this time. For a reorder." He winked. "But how many times have you called today, huh?"

Ed ran his fingers through his hair. Mark, though teasing as usual, had a point. How much of the business's time had he wasted talking to a girl he'd never met? What a voice though. What a cultured divine sound, something he could listen to forever. Gail was intelligent, witty, and shared the same interests and perfectly matched senses of humour. Then she had that flirty tone that sent shivers through his body. They chatted as if they were old friends, perhaps even a couple...and why not? If you liked someone so much on the phone, why wouldn't you in person?

Mark's voice interrupted his thoughts. "You all right?"

"I'm fine thanks. You ever seen her?"

"No, and I hardly ever get to speak to the woman. Fat chance, with you around, you've been hogging her all these months. But look here, you definitely ought to make a plan, Ed. I mean 'Maritzburg is not far from Durban. Fifty miles. You can drive down in an hour and chat in person, or take her out."

"Take her out?" Mark was right. Hadn't he been fantasising about such an event for months? He often drove down to Durban, so he could easily pop into Bronson and Schubert's. Talk to her for real. Ask her on a date.

He sat on a stool, feeling a bit dizzy. Why did his heart pound like that? Asking her on a date? It would be so easy—over the phone. Sure, he'd thought about it, more than once. Okay, lots of times. But what was she really like?

Mark winked. "Ah! As is obvious from your noticeable hesitation you're contemplating the idea. Great job. You're twenty-five, it's high time you got married, isn't it?"

Ed started. "That is a jump. I've never even seen her yet, and now you're marrying me off."

"And why not, pray? I hear being married is a wonderful life." He sighed. "Listen to me giving advice, here I am, a twenty-seven-year-old bachelor."

"That may be, but listen, how do I know she isn't a hag, one with a marvelous voice?"

"But you apparently like her. You're always on about her. This might be a match made in heaven. How bad could she be and what does her appearance matter? This is nineteen seventy. These days, ugly girls are as rare as snowflakes in Durban. They take care of how they look. Besides, even if she should have a face like the back of a bus, you like her personality. Anyway, what if she's a real hottie?"

Mark made sense, as usual. Still, Mark wasn't aware of his passionate fussiness. Appearances were everything. And he liked Gail so much. What if he met her and he was put off because it turned out she was hideous? Would things ever go back to the way they had been? Would their long phone romance be over? Could it just be a phone romance?

*****

Ed arrived, bleary eyed, at Cahill's next morning. What a night, tossing and turning, sheets rolled up and damp. He'd spent half the night dreaming of an enormous phone making faces at him, and the other half lying awake, imagining walking into Bronson and Schubert's and asking for Gail. The scene had played repeatedly in his mind, each with a different ending when Gail had appeared. Sometimes ordinary, sometimes gorgeous, but other times a hideous atrocity. His emotions had taken a roller-coaster ride all night.

It wasn't as though these scenarios were entirely new to him, Gail had often materialised in his daydreams, but Mark's words had turned the imaginings into a stark reality. His dreams had demanded he should make a move, but what if the result should damage their friendship? He couldn't do without it—life would be barren and meaningless without Gail.

Already he'd been affected. He'd entirely ignored Josiah, busy as usual sweeping the floors, flashing his pearly white teeth in a grin. Ed felt bad about it afterwards. Like all Africans, Josiah had to spend a couple of hours just getting there the Black location, miles from town, before doing all the dirty work. And all the time, he'd be treated as some sort of inferior human being. Josiah surely wasn't even his real name, merely a tag that Europeans could pronounce.

He'd also been abrupt with Mark, hardly acknowledged the Coloured girls who worked in the labs, and glared at Dolores every time she appeared.

Dolores was the typical complaining, middle-aged White Afrikaans-speaking woman, who'd had to flee from Black rioters in Kenya. He hoped his glare would dissuade her from starting on him this morning. He kept himself busy opening and unpacking boxes, keeping his back to the phone.

The front bell sounded and a customer walked into the shop. A middle-aged woman, dressed up to the nines and oozing money, sauntered among the displays of cameras, accompanied by an attractive blonde teenager in an extremely short miniskirt.

"Yours, lad," said Mark. "I'm in the middle of something."

Ed strode forward, greeting the woman and girl.

"Thank you, I wish to buy a movie camera. My daughter will be skating at a competition in Durban next week."

"Sure, I can help you with that." He slid open the glass door of the display cabinet behind him. "I suggest this Minolta, which has a fast f 1.4 lens, since there won't be much light in the ice rink."

"I haven't the faintest idea about that, just sell me the best for the job."

Ed demonstrated the expensive camera, which would earn him a good commission. She seemed satisfied and also wanted a startling number of high-speed films.

"Aside from this," she asked, while Ed wrapped up her parcel. "Could you tell me where I can buy ice skates in town?"

He shook his head. "I'm afraid you won't find any in 'Maritzburg, madam. We have no ice rink here."

The woman huffed and her daughter looked down. "I'm well aware of that."

Wait a minute! This could be his opportunity. Ed's pulse sped up, seeing another excuse for calling Bronson and Schubert's. "Perhaps I could find you some. Our licence covers nonphotographic goods, so I can order them for you, from Durban. One of our wholesale suppliers deal in almost everything." And they have the most charming of order clerks.

"Would they have Stubbs and Burts? My daughter needs professional skates."

"I can certainly check on that. I can phone them right away."

The woman pulled a tight mouth. "Well...we need them soon. She has to walk around in them for at least a week to break them in."

"Of course, if I ordered them for you, I might have them here by Monday."

"Oh! What time? Can you be sure they'll arrive during business hours on Monday?"

Excellent point. Ed knew the reliability of the courier services, and he couldn't put his firm's reputation on the line. Normally, he would forsake the sale even though a pair of Stubbs and Burt Professional would earn him quite a lucrative commission. Suddenly, all the scenarios of the night came back, together with a resolution, the possibility of killing two birds with one stone. What if he picked them up himself, from Gail? The very thought had his heart beating in jumps.

He tried to steady his breathing. "I may be able to ensure you get them first thing on Monday morning, madam. Please take a seat and I'll check if I can manage that."

The woman, apparently satisfied, sat with her daughter on the chairs provided. "Her size is a six, and we'll want them with the professional blades attached."

Ed entered the office and dialled the number. His breath caught at the sound of her voice. "Bronson and Schubert's, good morning."

"Gail."

"Ed. Already? Did you miss me so much these uh, twenty minutes since our last talk?"

He listened to the music of her laugh.

"Of course, I did. You knew I couldn't do without you." Again, the chuckle. He loved it. "Firstly—business. You do keep Stubbs and Burt Pro, white skates in stock, right?"

"Yes. All sizes. If I put them on our van, you'll receive them Tuesday. Wednesday at the latest."

"Well, uh, that's the thing…the customer needs them Monday. Tomorrow's my day off, so I thought of coming in and collecting them? In person." He held his breath.

"In person?" She sounded surprised. A pause followed. "Um. You could, but I'm sorry, you know we're closed on Saturdays."

"Yes. I…er, wondered…um…if at all possible…perhaps, if you might take them home with you, and if I…could pick them up there?"

A long hesitation ensued. She didn't want to see him. She wanted to keep this as a telephonic relationship. She…

"Uh. I don't know, I...um..." The wait seemed forever. "I guess."

"Or we can meet somewhere, like a café or a restaurant? How about one on the beachfront?"

"No." Her voice made him jump. "It would be better if you came to the house, I think."

Nothing more. A sudden doubt questioned whether this was the right thing to do. Perhaps he should simply put the customer off. She could pick up the skates herself in Durban. Obviously, Gail didn't want to meet in person.

"Are you still there?" she said.

"Yes. I only thought you didn't appear too willing. Is everything okay?"

"I'm fine. I suppose it was inevitable we would meet each other one day."

"Of course, are you worried?" Please say no.

"Frankly yes, I guess I am."

"Me too." He meant it. This wasn't going the way he planned. He thought she'd be as eager as him.

"Why are you nervous?" she asked.

"Perhaps because we're such close friends, yet we've never met face to face. What if meeting actually spoiled things?"

The joviality in her voice had gone. "Me too. I'm afraid you won't like what you see."

"Aw, Gail. I always love our chats. I'm sure it will be the same in person."

"I hope so. Well, you'll need my address."

He wrote it down since his memory was appalling and because he was unfamiliar with the area and not knowledgeable about suburban Durban. She gave him some basic directions, which he also jotted down and told her he thought he would find the house without too much trouble. After giving her the order details, he thanked her, but Ed's soaring emotions had crashed. The conversation had taken a disturbingly formal tone. He hoped he hadn't ruined everything.

Mark sauntered out of the office. "Best thing you can do, Ed. You're meeting your crush at last."

He glared at Mark. "You were eavesdropping, weren't you?"

Mark grinned back. "I figured out what you were up to, while chatting up your customers, the delightful Mrs. Point and her gorgeous daughter. I'm proud of you, old sport. Don't worry, I'm sure your young lady will be as beautiful as you imagine."

"I'm not sure I have a visual image, she's only a voice."

"Only a voice? A charming, seductive, cultured voice. I've spoken with her too, you realise, despite your nasty little habit of grabbing the phone every time you find a need to call Bronson and Schubert's. Do you mean you never formed a picture in your imagination?"

"Not actually, nothing tangible. Only a voice, as you say, beautiful and cultured. Just as well, I think. No actual imaginary image to shatter tomorrow."

"Well, take a camera with you, because I also want to know what she looks like." Mark leaned forward and elbowed him in the ribs. "I bet she's a stunner."

"Maybe so."

"Who's a stunner? Who y'oll talking about?" Candy, the Coloured assistant who worked in the darkrooms at the back of the shop, appeared, carrying some boxes.

Mark chuckled. "He's got a date with Gail tomorrow."

"A date? With Gail? Y'oll saying Mr. Brent's asked her out at last?" Candy opened her mouth wide, revealing missing front teeth.

"No, I have not got a date," said Ed, folding his arms. "This is a business order, nothing else."

"Ja, suuuure. Just business." Candy winked at Mark, who grinned back.

"Well, when y'oll finished with your business. Are y'oll askin' her out?"

"That is my affair, Candy. You should keep your little nose out of it."

Candy tossed her head and shrugged, but curiosity evidently kept her from completing her errand. She was very short, cute, with thick black hair that waved down over her shoulders. She had a darker complexion than usual for her race and a bad case of acne, not unusual for a sixteen-year-old. Both the men had a congenial,

12

friendly rapport with her and her coworker, Pamela, also a Coloured, with lots of banter between them.

"Where y'oll going on y'oll's date?" Candy asked, always curious.

"We never made any plans for a date. I am merely picking up some skates from her at her house."

"Then y'oll going skating at the ice rink?"

"We never arranged anything over the phone. Like I said, it's business, not a date."

"'Kay, best of luck." Candy squinted at the notepad Ed had put on the counter. "This Gail's address?"

At Ed's nod, Candy suddenly departed with her boxes toward the darkrooms where she worked. Mark and Ed stared after her.

"Rather an abrupt exit, wouldn't you say?" Mark said.

CHAPTER
TWO

Gail slowly pressed the button to hang up but kept the receiver in-hand, caressing her cheek with it.

Janet, one of her coworkers and best friend at Bronson and Shubert's, strode over, a frown accentuating the wrinkles in her brow. "Your boyfriend again, Gail? If you could only see your adorable but silly expression."

Gail sighed and shook her head. "Ed is not my boyfriend."

Janet's greying eyebrows shot up. "Not your boyfriend? Well, excuse me, why not? You're so soppy about him. You should hear yourselves when you chatter. Are you telling me you two are not dating?"

Dating? The idea sent a thrill down her middle. Anyone hearing some of her conversations with Ed might certainly be excused for misunderstanding. For a moment, she imagined going out with Ed, a thought as familiar as an old and constant friend. Yet a perverse and unwelcome one at the same time, so why did it keep returning?

She replaced the receiver and stared at the floor. "No, Janet, I've never even met him. He's only a phone friend."

Janet's jaw dropped. Hands on hips, she leaned toward Gail, peering through her bifocals. "A phone friend, huh! Excuse me, but you sound like lovers when you're talking to him. On company time I might add." She winked, tapping her watch.

Gail stared ahead, eyes unfocused. "Do you suppose it's possible, falling in love on the phone?"

Janet grunted and ruffled her graying hair. She studied Gail, her eyes magnified twice their size by her glasses.

Was it possible? Gail didn't expect Janet would have an answer, yet she meant her question seriously. She'd always appreciated the older woman's advice.

Janet chewed her lip, as if considering the idea from all angles. "Sure, I believe it's possible. Think about it. You've been speaking to this gentleman for ages, having long conversations each time. That doesn't happen without a definite rapport. I'm sure you know everything there is to know about each other by now. I confess I'm surprised he hasn't already made a move."

Gail's heart hammered. Was it surprising that Ed hadn't made a move? She'd always assumed his flirtations weren't serious, he just liked to tease and joke. But what if they were? They had shared some rather personal things with each other. Some of his embarrassing moments he had never told anyone but her. She knew his parents lived in Mossel Bay, what schools he had attended, and where he worked. He'd had only one serious girlfriend, Jenny. They'd had near identical tastes in books, films, and music. But he wasn't going out with anyone now. And he knew all her background, her fancy private school, and the fact she'd never had a steady boyfriend. Could she handle it if he wanted more from their friendship?

She should call back and tell him what he needed to know. What she should have told him months ago but hadn't had the courage. She reached out a hand, picked up the receiver, then replaced it, wincing.

Janet looked puzzled, then both her hands shot up over her mouth and her eyes widened. "You can't be telling me he doesn't know."

Gail shook her head and swallowed. "I doubt it. No, he couldn't. I would know."

Janet reached out a friendly arm and grasped Gail's shoulder. "In that case, I suppose you'd better trust he doesn't get interested."

She sighed. No fear of that, one look at her and Ed would lose all interest. Sad, but something she needed to face. She turned away from Janet's well-meaning but sorrowful expression. "Anyway, I must get back to work."

She resumed filling orders and packing them for mailing. Something to take her mind off Ed, but taming her thoughts proved difficult. She dumped a camera case into a box, stuffing straw all around it, slamming the box lids together, and drawing the tape machine forcefully across. She brushed the address label with water and slapped it on the top.

At the next ring, Gail whipped the receiver off the phone and all but yelled, "Bronson and Shubert's, good morning."

"Gail."

Again, so soon.

Her irritation and worry flew away at the sound of his voice. The familiar, sweet voice that cleared her mind of any dilemmas. However bad her mood, Ed always cheered her up. He only had to utter a word.

"Ed, already?" she said.

"Hello my precious, favourite order girl. How are you?"

He wanted skates. No problem. He wanted to pick them up himself. Huh? Problem.

Her throat dried up. He wanted to meet her, he was just as curious as she. Terror gripped her heart. What should she do? She'd never planned for such a remote possibility. He carried on talking, suggesting meeting at other places, like restaurants. It was getting worse, how might she put him off? This simply wouldn't do. What should she say?

Her terrified no came out snappy and loud. What must he think of her? Very rude, that's what. But an icy hand clutched at her heart. She had so often wondered what she'd do if Ed wanted to take this further, and now that moment had come. She had to stop him.

Ed didn't say anything for a long time. The phone remained stubbornly silent. Had she offended him? Perhaps made him mad at her? Afraid? She asked if he were still there. Yes, he'd cottoned on to her, saying she didn't seem too willing to meet. Talk about understatement. Ed understood her too well. He sounded anxious, asking her if she were worried.

If only he knew. Thinking it best to be completely honest, she admitted it. Then he confessed to being a bundle of nerves, too.

Maybe he suspected, he might even realise the truth. No, probably he only worried he wouldn't like what he saw. Privately, she knew, positively, that he wouldn't.

"Aw, Gail. I always love talking to you. I'm sure it will be the same in person."

Yeah, sure. Normally, when he spoke like this, her stomach fluttered with excitement. Now she just shivered with anxiety. But there was no going back. She gave him her address and hung up, leaving her hand still gripping the receiver.

"Goodness!" Janet shuffled over, eyes wide. "My dear, are you all right? You look like you saw a ghost. Whatever is the matter?"

"It…it's Ed."

Janet's face paled, and she gripped Gail's hands in her own. "What's the matter? He had an accident? Is he okay…is he…dead?"

"No," she said and paused. "He's not dead. I am."

Janet's eyebrows rose higher. "Huh, what do you mean? Tell me what happened?"

"He's coming to my house, Janet. Tomorrow." Gail sagged her shoulders and her jaw trembled. Tears forced their way out.

Janet pulled her into a close hug. "There, there, my dear girl." She stroked Gail's hair behind her head. "Tomorrow? He can't wait, hey?"

Gail sobbed into Janet's shoulder. The end of a beautiful relationship. Her words came out in a torrent of anguish. "As soon as he arrives, he'll find out. It'll all be over, the special bond we had, gone." Her sobs became louder as the pain stabbing her in the heart increased.

Janet put her arm around her. "I don't know what to say, you poor thing! Please don't cry." She drew closer and rubbed her back. "Gail, think. Since he's such a wonderful friend on the phone, why wouldn't he be in person?"

Gail sniffed, took the tissue Janet gave her, and blew her nose.

Gripping Gail's shoulders, Janet stared into her eyes. "It isn't against the law to be friends, you're aware of that, aren't you?"

She made no reply but gave Janet a piercing stare.

"Oops!" Janet bit her lip. "You don't just want to be friends, do you?"

"I do want to be. Of course, I do." Gail dabbed her eyes with a second tissue. "Only, I'm sure he's not coming to meet me just to be friends."

Janet grimaced. "Probably not, he is a man after all, dear."

*****

Mrs. Rabe sat with Gail on the sofa, her mouth tight. She shook her head. "Tell him no, he mustn't come here."

Gail's tears ran over her cheeks while she rested her head on her mom's lap. "But, Mom, I couldn't stop him. You don't understand how he talks. It's so hard to say no. The brutal fact is he is coming, and there's absolutely nothing I can do to prevent it."

"Oh, my girl." Her mom smoothed Gail's hair. "There, there! I know this must be painful, but you can't trust young men like him, dear. They only want one thing, and then they'll disappear from your life forever."

Gail raised her head and glared into her mom's face. "Mom, quit that right now. I don't believe for one-minute Ed is like that. Don't forget I've known him on the phone for the best part of a year. He's coming only as a friend."

"Sure." Mrs. Rabe pulled her mouth yet tighter. "I think I understand men better than you, dear."

Gail gritted her teeth. How dare Mom judge Ed, knowing nothing about him. She hadn't ever met him. Her attitude wasn't fair. "Just because you made a wrong choice and ran away… Mom, I'm sorry. I didn't mean—" Too late, she had already said it.

Her mother pushed her away from her lap and rocketed off the couch. "How dare you bring that up again, Gail. I'm only trying to protect you from making the mistakes I made. Phone him now, at once, and tell him. You realise perfectly well what he is. Don't pretend you don't."

Gail's nostrils flared, and she stood, tears stopping instantly. "Really, Mom, there's no need for this. You know nothing of his heart, nor his motives, you don't know him at all."

Mrs. Rabe muttered. "All of those don't change what he is, you can't deny it."

"No, perhaps not, but neither does it alter the fact that he's coming tomorrow, whatever the outcome, and you had better behave, Mom. Do you hear me?"

She heard all right but grumbled as she left the room.

CHAPTER

THREE

Ed exited the freeway and navigated from the open map of Durban on the front seat. Someday they'd probably make some device that told you how to find an address, but he sure would like it now.

After making several wrong turns, he found the right road at last. He drove through some questionable areas. He was now south of Durban, passing an industrial area. Had he got the address right? But shortly, things appeared better. While waiting for the green light at the next robot, he studied the map. Yes, this led directly there. As he got nearer, it became obvious it was a poor neighbourhood. Well, possibly she didn't earn much as an order clerk at Bronson and Schubert's.

Ed made a right turn onto her road and counted the numbers. The houses were small and rather close together. Some children played in the streets, real ragamuffins with shabby clothes and no shoes. As he neared the right number, he began to understand her apparent reluctance for him to pick up the skates at her house.

Twenty-four, here it was. He parked and took a look in the rear-view mirror. He ran his comb through his all too long hair. Maybe he should've had a haircut yesterday; those long sideburns were sticking out again. Licking the fingers of both hands, he tried to smooth them down. He blew out a breath into his hands. Not good.

As he got out the car, he wondered if she was watching him through the light floral curtains. Just in case, he remembered to check his feet from splaying out as they always did. He walked down the few steps from the front gate. The house was small but neat, painted white, with a green tin roof, window frames and front door. Vines grew all around the windows, adding more colour.

Ed paused at the door, raised his hand to knock but hesitated. This was it, the moment of finally seeing her. Gail, the sweetest voice in all the world. Would her face and figure match that beautiful music? He rapped a couple of times and held his breath.

The servant smiled and opened the door wider. "Good morning, sir."

"Hello, I'm here to see Miss Gail," he said, amazed that they could afford a servant while living in such a tiny house. She was a small woman, with a tight smile on her pleasant, brown face. She wore no apron, no uniform and no head covering.

"Gail is expecting you, Mr. Brent," she said, but the smile faded. "She is in her room. I'll fetch her. Please come in and have a seat."

Ed did so, wondering at the servant's well-enunciated speech. He looked around the small but tidy lounge. There were two armchairs, a couch with a low coffee table in front of it, a full dining suite and a sideboard with framed photographs on the top. Surprisingly, one of them showed the woman he had just spoken to. She must be a well-loved servant, probably been in the household since Gail was a child. Another picture stood beside it, of a man, and he—

"Ed." He heard the voice behind him. Her voice. Hearing his heart galloping, he almost didn't want to turn around.

"Gail," he said, turning at last. He stopped, his mind freezing. She was beautiful. He hadn't anticipated such beauty to go with that wonderful voice. His jaw dropped. Quite unable to speak, he wondered if that was because he had not expected her to be so gorgeous from her flowing black hair framing a heart-shaped face of classical beauty, with reddish brown lips parted in a hesitant smile, to those stunning long legs ending in blue canvas shoes…or whether possibly…it was because she—was a Coloured.

Or was she? His mind flew into denial. Impossible. Though she was talking, she had no trace of the Coloured accent. Maybe she had a heavy suntan, she was a Durban girl after all. She had none of the dark complexion both Candy and Pamela shared. Her hair hung long, smooth and wavy, jet-black, yet a little of what Candy would call kroes at the edges. Surely, she couldn't be. She stood right next to the servant who had let him in, holding her hand. Unless the servant…

"This is my mom, Ed," said Gail. The woman with her smiled and raised her hand in a wave. There could be no doubt, Gail's mom had much darker skin, almost as dark as an African. No way would she pass the "pencil test" he had read about, where they would try to pass a pencil through the hair of people suspected of being Coloured. Gail's hair would obviously pass, but since her mother was most clearly of that race, it meant Gail was, too. She was off-limits.

He turned back to Gail. "Oh, sorry, uh. Pleased to meet you, Gail, at last."

"Surprised?" She looked him in the eye, a question hanging in the air, beyond the single word she had uttered. When he said nothing, she dropped her glance. Her lips didn't form a smile but were partly opened, forming a delicate cupid's bow, the corners slightly down-turned. She glanced up again, straight into his eyes. "No need to answer." Again, her eyes dropped.

"Surprised?" he said. "I half expected you'd be plain, but you're beautiful."

Her eyes came up again, moist, and her mouth had opened more.

"Thank you. You're not so bad yourself. In fact, I imagined you exactly like you are."

"Honestly? You did?"

"Yes, no surprises…for me." She blinked several times. "Anyway, take a seat. I'll bring you your skates." She turned and left the room.

Her mother remained behind. "Can I make you some tea, sir?"

"Thank you, yes, I would like that indeed. Thanks so much."

She turned to go.

"Mrs. Rabe." He cleared his throat and clutched his tie. "I'm sorry."

"Sorry, why?"

"I didn't realise you were Gail's mother when you answered the door."

"Oh! No problem. You thought I was a servant, didn't you?"

Ed couldn't tell whether she was amused or sorry or both. He bit his lip but didn't answer as she left for the kitchen.

He sat down again and waited several minutes, his mind in a whirl. This was South Africa. It was illegal to have any sort of romantic relationship with a non-White. Even if it were possible for him to take her out, how would people react? What would his friends say? He visualised Mark's derisive giggling. He would never hear the end of this. The girl he was pretty much in love with turns out to be a Coloured. All that time, the hours spent on the phone and flirting, yes, decidedly flirting with her. Oh yes, he pictured the moments when he would introduce her to his friends. Perhaps they wouldn't say anything, but what would they think? Could he even get permission to visit them? Would they let her into their houses? And, oh yes, "Mom, Dad, this is Gail, we want to get married and have children." Sure, that would go down well. Then there would be the secret police breaking down the door at 2:00 a.m. and hauling them both off. Great!

The tea arrived at the same time Gail returned with the skate box.

"How do you like your tea?" Gail asked, settling gracefully on the sofa a fair distance from him, knees together, stretching her long legs out to the side.

Ed tore his eyes away from them. "Lots of milk, no sugar, thanks," he said. Why did the hateful racist expression "two coffee one milk" even enter his mind? It didn't belong there.

"Well, I'll leave you two with your business," said Gail's mom as she left the room.

"You'll just have to sign this, and here is your invoice," Gail said in a businesslike voice, sounding unnatural for her. "I hope your customer knows there are no returns allowed as the blades have been screwed onto the boots already, but we do have a list of people looking for discounts on such expensive boots, so she may be able to sell them if there should be a problem."

"Oh, right," he replied vaguely, sipping his tea.

"It's nice to finally meet you," she said, leaning back on the couch, her hair flowing down the seat back in graceful patterns. She appeared more relaxed, but this wasn't anything like the electric tension that always existed between them on the phone. Something had short-circuited their relationship.

"Yes, putting faces to the voices at last," He cringed at how lame it sounded. This wasn't them. The magic had gone.

Silence prevailed as they both sipped at their teacups.

"Oh, sorry. Biscuit?" She passed the tray over. He took a Marie biscuit willingly. It would be good to have something to nibble on, since saying anything was so awkward.

Gail was the first to break a rather long silence. "I'm sorry."

"Huh! Sorry for?"

"For not telling you before. I wasn't sure how. I always wanted to figure out some way to bring it up. After we'd become such firm friends, I mean."

"Okay. It's not a problem." He gulped at his tea.

"When you said you wanted to come here, I didn't know what to say. I'd been wondering lately if you were thinking of bringing our remote relationship to a more personal level but dreading what your reaction would be when you found out."

"Oh."

"I wanted to tell you yesterday but couldn't find the words." She stared into her teacup.

"I understand. Not to worry."

"I never knew. That is, if you realised I was a—I wasn't White."

"No, I never had a clue." He paused and gazed at her. "Please, I hope I'm not rude, but you have no accent, none at all. I mean, I work with Candy and Pamela. You probably know, I'm sure I told you about them..." Gail inclined her head. "I mean, their accents would give them away at once, but yours is about the most cultured accent I ever heard."

"My mom, she's had a hard life. She wanted something different for me, a better job, respect. I think she was very unrealistic." Gail grimaced. "She worked several jobs and sent me to a private boarding school. My White father helped by investing money in it on the proviso that his daughter would be allowed to attend in spite of her race. Even then, they had to inspect me first before they reluctantly agreed. It was a small school, and progressive, I suppose you'd call it. Most of the girls were friendly, the teachers too. So just call me Eliza Doolittle."

Ed laughed. Something of the humour between them sparked again. "Just don't call me gov'nor, Eliza."

They both chuckled, like they often had on the phone. But the laughter died away. Ed broke the brief silence. "They did an excellent job," he said earnestly.

She smirked. "They made me a lady in a flower shop, they did," she said in a Cockney accent.

Ed smiled. "Perhaps they did. You got an enviable job in your firm."

"There were some benefits, I suppose." She dropped her head and the smile vanished. "Some. Eliza became a lady, but I didn't become a White."

An oppressive silence ensued. Neither one seemed to have the power to break it. Awkward.

"It was jolly good of you to do this for me, Gail. Thanks so much."

"Don't mention it. It must be a significant commission for you, enough to pay for your petrol to drive down here, I presume."

"Yes, of course." He dropped his gaze and chewed on his lip. "Gail, I have to confess that it wasn't commission nor the desire to please the customer that made me decide to do this. I had to."

She beamed. "Well, I'm glad you did. It's really good to see you in person, and to get this…secret off my chest."

Another thorny silence.

"I'd better be going."

She rose, taking the hand he offered her, shaking it silently. Her fingers trembled against his. "Very pleased to have you visit." She filled in the brutal void, holding on to his hand longer than necessary.

It was he who eventually broke the connection. "Well. I'll talk to you on the phone. Thanks again."

Ed took the skate box and walked out the door together with Gail. Gail's mother waved to him from the kitchen. "Goodbye. Nice to meet you."

"Yes, me too. Goodbye."

"I'll walk you to your car," said Gail.

She stood aside as Ed put his hand on his door handle. Why was she so beautiful? His eyes focused on the cupid shape of her mouth, just a little open as before. Gorgeous, tempting. Her face turned up, eyelashes blinking rapidly. He imagined his head moving on its journey heavenward, tasting those lips.

His head jerked up. Those lips indeed. They were not for him. What did he think he was doing? He was looking at her through bars. Dirty black bars. Were they on his cell or hers? Or both. Of course, they would never be able to see each other through the bars, they'd separate them forever, not even allowed to talk through the phone line.

"Well." He forced his voice to behave. "I better be off. Thanks again, Gail."

"Goodbye, Ed." It seemed so final. It was. The end of the story. Nothing more here. He drove off. Were those tears that had welled up in her eyes? Those tears had been bullets, striking his heart directly. He blinked rapidly to avoid his own from running down his cheeks. He slapped his forehead with such force he had to spin the wheel to avoid hitting the curb. A solid brick wall faced him at the next corner. Should he just put his foot down and aim the car at it?

*****

Gail lay face down, crying into her arms. She raised her head only to wipe the wet patch on the sofa.

Her mom patted her shoulder and placed a teacup in front of her. "Please stop, Gail," she said. "Here, drink this. You'll feel better."

As if she ever would. Not in this lifetime. She tried to answer but choked, unable to produce any other sound.

Her mother sighed. "You knew the man was White. I mean, what did you expect? Did you assume he would hold you tight and tell you he loves you?"

She shook her head and sniffed.

"It's your own fault, you should have told him right from the start. Now he knows your little phone affair is over. I must admit he did behave nicely though, considering?"

Gail sat up, her feet tumbling to the floor. "I suppose so." She wiped her eyes and took the cup, stirring the tea slowly. "Mom, things changed immediately. So...so...formal."

"Why would he be anything else for a business transaction, love?"

She took a sip of tea. "Yes, but this is Ed. I can't face it, Mom, I truly can't." She banged the cup on the saucer, spilling some tea on her dress, the brand-new blue one she'd bought for his benefit, his favourite colour. She didn't care. "Ed...he's my phone boyfriend. I care for him. We had an affair by phone. I'm convinced he felt the same. Just because it came over the wires doesn't mean it's any less sincere."

Her mom scoffed. "Affair by phone? There's no such thing, only your fantasy. Loving you is impossible if he never met face to face."

"Well, people in olden days had relationships by letter without ever seeing each other. Anyway, you can't understand, you've never heard our conversations."

Her mom brought a wet cloth from the kitchen and wiped Gail's dress. "Well, if you're lucky, you'll still have them. Nothing's changed, dear, he has to phone you to order from Bronson and Schubert's. He can carry on imagining he's talking to that White-girl image he carries in his mind."

She sat up straight. "You think so?"

Her mom left the room, cloth in hand, without answering.

Maybe things would stay the same. Her mom was right. Ed did still need to phone through those orders. Surely, it wasn't a forlorn hope he would continue flirting the way he always had. That would be better than nothing. After all, she had never expected to meet him, hadn't wanted to in fact. But now that they had...how would things change?

She had liked what she saw, yes indeed. So much. His eyes, blue like a winter sky, a startling contrast to his jet-black hair, looking her over with breathless surprise, hardly blinking. His handsome face outlined by thick sideburns and marked with that dark shadow of a beard that some guys had no matter how clean-shaven. She'd had to look up to see his wide-eyed, open-mouthed stare, several inches higher than her own. The intensity of his sweeping gaze had made her heart pound so hard that he must have heard it across the room. He had a sturdy build, with strong arms a girl wouldn't mind getting lost in. At least, she wouldn't mind, not at all. She'd imagined such a thing a couple of times during long drawn-out orders that turned personal, when he'd shifted from laughing and flirtatious to soft and compassionate.

Out by his car, during that horribly awkward goodbye, his eyes had repeatedly dropped to her lips. She'd seen longing in them, hadn't she? If he had tried to kiss her, would she have let him? She'd often imagined them kissing, when his affectionate teasing had caused the fluttery sensation of a kiss. His voice would sometimes become low and intimate, like a caress. "Aw, Gail," he'd say, and she'd melt. Yes, it would have been very natural for him to kiss her. She wouldn't have stopped him.

But then he'd jerked his gaze away, evidently having second thoughts. Realising he'd be kissing Coloured lips, no doubt. No, it wasn't prejudice—she couldn't believe that of him—but probably fear. And rightly so.

She grabbed a cushion from the couch and hugged it tightly. Who had the right to decide who should kiss whom? A foul, odious abhorrent government, that's who. They pick their own chosen ones, some of whom are even less White than her Coloured friend, Elaine. Elaine could pass as White anywhere and did. She played White, going out solely with White guys. Some of them knew she was a Coloured, but did that stop them? No. They'd probably marry her if she wanted. *But I can't marry Ed.* What exactly was the difference between Elaine and her? They were the same race. A slightly different skin tone, that's all.

She threw the cushion on the floor and dragged her nails up her arm, hard, leaving white streaks. If she could only get rid of this darker skin, she could have whatever she wanted. She drew a deep breath, then groaned. It was illegal even to date a White guy in this country. So having a White boyfriend definitely wasn't an option. Yet for nearly a year, she had yearned for him. Would those calls ever be enough, now that she'd seen him, looked into those sky-blue eyes? Sensed his appreciative gaze on her?

Her mom returned and interrupted Gail's thoughts. "You must stop moping, my girl. A phone affair, as you call it, is safer than a real one, I guess, but any relationship with a White man is out."

"Why not, Mom, you had one yourself?"

Her mom's jaw set and her brows ruffled. "It was different back then. We got married in church in 1945. We had you the next year, and he ran off a couple of years after that. In any case, four years later, the Nats brought in that awful new law, the prohibition of mixed marriages act, making all mixed-race ones null and void. Not merely new marriages mind you, but fully legal ones like ours were suddenly prohibited." She swallowed and stared down, eyes vacant. "It meant the breakup of so many families." She frowned at Gail. "And that horrid law is still valid, in case you believed it possible to marry Ed."

"I know, Mom, but I believe we have something real and special between us. I feel it in my heart, and I'm sure he does, too. Don't we deserve a little happiness? I'm not giving up. Before leaving, he stood so close and looked at me as if—"

"That," her mom said, folding her arms up high, "is not love."

CHAPTER
FOUR

After battling with the decision whether to come to work, Gail arrived at Bronson and Schubert's two hours late on Monday. She thumped her handbag onto the small desk in her cubicle, sat down heavily, and supported her head with hands cupped under her chin.

"Oh, dear!" Janet made her way over.

Just what she needed. Why couldn't everybody leave her alone?

Janet peered at her face. "Your eyes." She pursed her lips and shook her head. "I've never seen those beautiful eyes of yours look like this, Gail. You poor dear. I suppose he took one glance at you and hightailed out as fast as possible."

"No." She couldn't truthfully say that had been the case. He'd been nice and pleasant. Nobody would accuse him of being rude, but...she involuntarily let go a sob.

Janet massaged her shoulders. "But he wasn't like he was on the phone," she finished for her.

She leaned her head onto Janet's torso, and her tears flowed again as Janet's arms closed around her. She had lost count of the number of times she had wept after Ed had left. Her red and swollen eyes were the reason for her tardiness.

Thankfully, Janet remained silent, squeezing her shoulders gently. It soothed her enough that after a few minutes, Gail sat up straight. Perhaps she should talk with someone. She had long since given up talking to her mom, who acted like a judge and treated her as the accused. Besides, she could do with a different perspective and Janet was White.

She sniffed and wiped away some tears. "I realise he must have had a shock, but he was still civil, though nothing like he used to be on the phone. We were friends for ages, and now it sounds like we've just met. Oh, Janet, what will I do? Things will never be the same. He'll likely never phone Bronson and Shubert's ever again."

"Come now, Gail. Cahill's is a steady customer of ours. Mrs. Cahill will never let him quit ordering from us. Things may be a bit awkward at first but will soon return to normal, I'm sure."

"You think so? He knows what he's talking to now."

"Now you stop that right there, Gail," she snapped. Gail had never once heard Janet speak in anger. "I won't let you call yourself a what. You're not a thing. You're one of, if not the most decent human being I ever had the pleasure of meeting. Friendly, intelligent, funny, and above all, cultured. Your Ed obviously thought the same while he chatted you up on the phone. Why would he change? You surely don't believe he's prejudiced?"

"No. I don't, not at all, but he is realistic. White guys can't have Coloured girlfriends, not in this country."

"Perhaps, I can't argue about that. It does seem impossible, doesn't it?" She sat on the corner of the desk. "I wonder. Do you suppose if you lived some other place, England or Australia for instance, Ed might have reacted differently?"

Gail stiffened. "Janet, when we were together at his car, saying goodbye...well... I imagined he was about to kiss me. I mean, I can't be sure, probably I was only fantasising."

Janet grinned and clapped her hands together. "Nonsense! I'll bet he was the one fantasising. Of course, he wanted to kiss you, what man wouldn't? And it's a hundred to one you hoped so. See, what a beautiful blush, Gail. You did. If you two lived almost anywhere else, you'd be going steady by now, be engaged in a month or two, married soon after, and be having..."

"Whoa, stop, Janet." Gail's blush deepened. "My entire life is flashing past too quickly." She giggled.

"Sorry, but no. Actually, I'm not sorry. The thought has cheered you up."

"Maybe, but not for long." Her smile faded along with her humour. "You're forgetting one thing."

"Yes." She breathed in deeply. "You actually live in South Africa."

Janet had cheered her though, and she got down to some work. She had orders to make out, filing, and, of course, answering the phone. At every jangling ring, her heart fluttered, followed by bitter disappointment. How she longed to hear Ed's voice again, but by late afternoon, she'd realised just how silly she was being. Ed had never called every single day.

True, he had called at the least opportunity, always checking up if a parcel was a trifle late. Once he'd called to purchase a new car, knowing perfectly well Bronson and Schubert's never dealt in cars. She chuckled as she remembered the time he called in for flowers. Things had been especially busy, and she'd become as irritated with Ed as possible, for her. Reluctantly, she'd agreed to order the flowers and asked him for the delivery address. He'd told her to send them to Bronson and Schubert's for attention Miss Gail Rabe. The memory brought on a fresh attack of tearful chuckling. How could she ever be mad at him?

The day finished with no calls from Ed.

*****

Candy accosted him as soon as he walked into the lab area on Monday. She leant against the darkroom wall, arms folded.

"Hi, Mr. Brent. She's one of us, hey?"

"One of you?" Ed gave a start. She knew! Amazing how fast news travelled in this place. He'd mentioned nothing about Saturday. They couldn't possibly have heard. "Okay, how'd you guess?"

She chuckled and slapped her fist into her palm. "I saw the address you wrote down. I know Durbs, hey! I got family living there." Then the grin vanished. "Sorry, hey!"

Yeah, sure. "Well, why didn't you tell me?"

"Ag, no. It isn't for me to tell, hey. Sorry, Mr. Brent."

"That's okay, Candy." He sighed. The entire staff must have heard the news already.

"Do y'oll still like her?"

"Yes. Yes, I do. Why wouldn't I? I like you, don't I? You and Pamela."

"Yes, Mr. Brent, we have fun, but y'oll never talk to us like y'oll talk to her. No way, admit." She giggled, her cinnamon brown cheeks darkening with embarrassment.

"I guess not." He coughed.

"So y'oll didn't ask her out?" Candy's left eyebrow reached into the solid mass of her thick black hair.

Quizzy as usual, that Candy. He frowned at her. "Ask her out? Do you want to see me in jail?"

"But she fooled you. She made you think she was sommer a White girl, hey? Does she play White?"

So much for sympathy from this quarter. "I sincerely doubt it."

"Does she look like me and Pamela? Or could she pass?"

"You two are darker. Still, dating would be too dangerous, specially for her." He frowned, could Gail pass for White? On the beach, with sunglasses? "Possibly she'd pass as a White girl who spends all day, every day in the sun."

"Come on, Mr. Brent. If y'oll took her out at night, they won't notice."

She looked eager, like she wanted him to date Gail. He didn't answer. Candy was only sixteen after all. What would she understand about it? The idea had crossed his mind though, as had a hundred others, but he'd pretty much dismissed them all.

"Would y'oll like to? Hey? Was she pretty?"

Talk about youthful enthusiasm. "Pretty?" His mind reverted to Saturday, the first moment he'd laid eyes on her, ever. "She sure was, Candy. Certainly, the most beautiful girl I've ever seen."

Candy squealed, startling him. "Wow! You're hooked, hey? You're falling in love with somebody who's on our side of the line?" She clapped her hands together and grinned broadly, her youthful charm marred only by her lack of upper front teeth.

"Do you know anyone who plays White, Candy?"

"Of course, there's lots of our kind who do but mostly women. Most cops arrest the girl and let the White man go, but if a Coloured oke chanced his arm with a White girl, he'd be taking a hang of a chance, as true's Bob, hey!"

"Well, anyway, there's no way I'd do that. Even if I believed it perfectly safe to take her out, I would never put her at risk. Never." He pictured her sitting opposite him in a restaurant and something stirred in his gut.

"Ooooooh. You love her." Candy's eyes grew enormous. "Ag, shame man, you seriously love her. What you goin' to do?" Genuine concern showed on her wrinkled brow.

"Nothing, there isn't anything I can do. I simply need to forget her." He blew out a deep breath.

"No, you can't. What when y'oll talk on the phone again? Y'oll always talking to the woman, man."

Ed shrugged. "I don't know, and I don't want to—forget her—I mean." He bit his lip and frowned.

Mark made a bee line for him when he returned. "Well, old sport? Was she half as good as she sounds? Did you go out? Tell me all the disgusting details, old chap."

Dolores, the office clerk, appeared suddenly from nowhere. "Didn't you hear? Turns out his dream voice girl is a different colour." That was Dolores, always direct and to the point, never a worry about what she said. Not to mention flapping ears that clearly heard everything. A lopsided smile had replaced her usual tight mouth, and something in her tone indicated disgust.

Mark looked from one to the other. "Different colour? A voice? What do you mean? Hey, wait a minute! You don't mean…" His guffaw echoed throughout the shop. "She's a Coloured? You got yourself involved across the colour line? Oh! That is funny. Oh glorious!"

"Well. Thanks, Mark. Glad to have your support."

"I'm sorry." He continued chuckling. "Truly, I am. So it's all off, is it? I suppose I'll have to make the calls now. Not that I object, you realise. She has that backbone tingling voice. I won't mind a bit."

"I'm sure you won't." Ed busied himself opening a package from the post.

Mark sobered. "Well. Are you truthfully not going to call her again?"

"I dunno." He ripped at the paper wrapping. "I'll order from elsewhere for a while." He took in a huge breath and expelled it in a deep sigh. "I suppose I'll still talk to Gail if she calls."

"Flirting over the phone is not exactly illegal," said Mark.

"What? In this country? I'm not so sure." He ripped more of the wrapping that refused to give way, with far more violence than necessary.

"You'll get over it, Ed," said Dolores. "She isn't worth all the fuss."

Ed stopped and scowled at Dolores's retreating back.

"Don't let her bother you," said Mark, his hand on Ed's shoulder. "Listen. Don't worry, I'll take Gail's calls for you for a while if you'd like."

"Fine," said Ed, still glowering tempestuously Dolores's way.

FIVE

Tuesday was such a busy day Gail wondered if all of Ed's calls had been transferred to someone else. They hadn't. Wednesday was no different. She stared at the phone in quieter periods, willing it to ring. The stubborn instrument just sat there, its dial grinning at her, mocking her. She prepared to go home, feeling as if she never wanted to return. Why look at that miserable phone yet another day?

Janet clearly read Gail's mood and made her way over, but Gail didn't feel like hearing her commiserations. It was over. Ed had found some way to avoid her forever and would likely never speak with her again.

"Still nothing?" Janet looked at her intently, as if seeing into her soul. "Okay, the time has come, Gail. You're quite distraught, so unlike you. Do you still have those feelings for Ed?"

Gail realised with surprise she'd been glaring at the older woman. Janet meant no harm, she wasn't even a busybody.

Janet frowned. "Hmm. I thought as much. You hate him, don't you?"

Gail gaped at her. Hate Ed?

"That will be a 'no' then," said Janet. "So let me rephrase it, you love him, don't you?" Not waiting for an answer, she carried on. "This is the moment for a strong woman like you to take things into her own hands. You'll be the one phoning. Tomorrow, you will phone Cahill's."

Goose bumps invaded her skin. "I will?"

"Certainly. He's such a skellum for leaving you in anticipation this way. Whether or not there is a reason for Cahill's calling our firm, he should have spoken to you. He hasn't. Shows lack of character. Let him see what character looks like. Phone him, before you leave home."

She gripped the handle of her bag with both hands. "Me? phone him? But what'll I say?"

Janet rolled her eyes. "Didn't I mention something about character? It isn't my business to tell you what you should or shouldn't say, Gail. Pick up the phone and talk. You two have done that for ages. Sure, there's always been a purpose for either one of you to call, but you never planned what to say. Don't start now."

Her fingers relaxed, the weight lifted from her shoulders. Yes, why worry about it? She would call, there'd be no need for a script.

"Thank you, Janet," she said and wrapped her arms around the older and definitely wiser woman.

*****

On Thursday, when Ed arrived at Cahill's, a grinning Mark held up the phone, pointing to it and nodding vigorously. "Better take this," he mouthed.

Fine. He couldn't even get inside the shop before he needed to take calls. One more thing adding to his whole week of irritability. He snatched the receiver from Mark's hand.

"Hello, this is Ed," he barked.

"You haven't phoned me once this week."

"Gail." Ed didn't know what else to say. Normally, his heart would have somersaulted after hearing that voice. No matter what his troubles, Gail had always had a calming, pleasurable effect on him. Now...

"Yes, Gail. Remember, we used to be best friends on the phone?"

Ed found himself at a loss for words.

"Does this mean we're no longer friends?" she asked.

"No, n-n-no. Absolutely not. Please, don't think that."

The edge in her voice softened. "It must've been a shock, Ed."

Shock? It was full-on electrocution. "I've been trying to sort things out in my head."

"I understand what's at stake, I always did. But all this time I loved talking to you, never thinking we would ever meet. We'd be phone pals forever. I never imagined you actually wanting to get together. But now we have, I'm like the proverbial hot potato that's been dropped. Can't we go back? Before Saturday? Just friends... Nothing else—Ed? Are you still there?"

"Yes, I'm here. I'm trying to process what you're saying. Can't we go back to before Saturday, you ask—but now that we've met, I'm not sure I can."

There was a pause. A long one. "I can't believe this. This isn't you. I never believed it possible you're prejudiced. I can't." Her voice dropped, becoming a muffled sob.

He gripped the receiver but simultaneously heard a click. She'd hung up! He banged the receiver down and his panicked fingers spun the dial. He opened and closed his free fist as he waited for her to pick up. It took forever, till at last he heard her emotionless voice. "Bronson and Schubert's..."

He almost shouted into the mouthpiece. "Prejudiced? No! No, no, Gail. My feelings might have changed but not the way you think. This has nothing to do with race. I don't want to break our friendship. Please don't believe that." Ed clawed at his hair, wanting to pull it out.

"Then why didn't you call? You could've phoned to tell me the skates had been delivered, that the customer was happy. Anything. I was worried about your reaction. I mean, I always knew you were White. It was no shock to me. The shock was all yours. I felt awful, as if I was dropped like a burning coal. That is true, isn't it? I'm like coal, and I am burning now."

"Stop, Gail. That isn't true. Not at all. I admit to being petrified to find out you were ugly, or fat, or ten feet tall. But even if you were all those, I would still want to be friends and still have asked you out, but—"

"But being a Coloured is worse than all of those things?" The edge had returned. A dangerous edge.

"No. Never. The brutal fact isn't that I'd gone off you because I'm racist. After seeing you, I thought, and still do, that you are indisputably the most gorgeous girl I've seen anywhere in my entire life. I wished for so long that I could speak with you in person, but five minutes after setting my eyes on you, I wanted to be real friends more than you can possibly imagine. This isn't a case of not wanting to see you anymore, rather of wanting what I can't have."

"Oh!" She became quiet.

"Gail?" The hairs rose on the back of his neck. Had he blown his chances?

"What can I say?"

"How about saying you want to see me again," he said, "even half as much as I want to see you."

There it was, the laugh. Only, the feeling it produced in him was far more intense now that he was familiar with her face. Was he being absurd? Did she believe him? Was she relieved? Did she feel the same way?

"I do."

Two little words, said in a matter of milliseconds, yet those two miniscule words evidently had the power to wash away all the doubt, the tension, the misery that had plagued him continually for five days. He sighed, his whole body relaxing. The process must have taken some time. He heard another word—his name.

He stopped breathing. "When?"

He heard her quick intake of breath. "As soon as possible. I assume I can persuade Mom to invite you here for dinner. Would you like that? Of course, I'll help cook."

"Anytime. I would love to."

"Hold on." He heard the receiver clattering down, and her voice, talking to her mother. The conversation became louder and perhaps angrier, not close enough for him to catch the actual words. Then he heard footsteps returning.

"Can you come for lunch on Saturday? I'm sorry, that's the earliest we can manage."

"Of course, you bet. I'll be there. What time?"

"My mom said about twelve o'clock, but I'm sure she won't mind if you come a bit earlier. We can probably find something to talk about."

He grinned. "About eleven?"

"I was hoping you might get here about ten?"

"I'll be there at nine then."

There was that giggle again. He enjoyed it, running his finger gently around the mouthpiece of the phone. But then he heard a voice in the background, raised in anger. Momentarily, the sounds on the other end were muffled.

"Ed. Better stick to eleven. Mom's having a cadenza."

"All right, Jolly d, eleven it is." He blew a kiss into the receiver, said goodbye, and hung up.

A spontaneous clapping from behind abruptly brought him down to earth. Candy and Pamela were the culprits.

Mark joined them with his infectious laugh. "Well done, old sport. We understand you've got a date."

Ed grinned. "Your hearing is remarkably good, all three of you."

"Not at all, not at all. You were just so eloquent, and, ahem! Loud, on the phone."

"We put two and two together," added Pamela. "Congratulations, Mr. Brent."

"Yes, congrats," Candy agreed, grinning ear to ear.

"Thanks, you little eavesdroppers, now get back to your den and do some work." He shooed them off with his hands. They ran off, chuckling.

"So." Mark's smile turned into a purse of lips. "I'm glad for you, Ed, but you be careful with this, hey. Watch out for the boys in khaki. I hate visiting friends in jail."

"I'm only going to lunch at her house. Is that also illegal?"

"I won't check. If it is, it's too absurd." His face turned serious. "I'm hoping you won't get into this too far. It can be dangerous."

SIX

Gail rushed to snap up the phone. "Hello, Elaine?"

"Yes, Gail. Howzit? My roomie said you wanted to speak with me. What's up, hey? I haven't heard from you in donkeys' years. It must've been what, six months?"

Probably more. Elaine had been a constant playmate when they were kids but had grown apart of late. "Yes, I'm sorry. We should talk more."

"I'd like that hey, we must. But I bet there's something on your mind."

Gail paused, how could she put it? "I need your advice—about dating a guy."

"Hah! A guy hey!" She broke into song, "If you're looking for trouble, you came to the right place. If you're looking for trouble, just look in my face."

"Woah, Elvis!" Gail had to chuckle.

"Right, spill the beans. It's rumoured you've been chatting up a White guy for months. Anything to do with him?"

What? How on earth did she know? She'd told no one about Ed. Nobody but her mother. Wait! Her mother and Elaine's were friends, weren't they?

"Gail?"

"Sorry."

"So I'm right." Elaine made an elated sound. "I knew it. You've got yourself involved with a clip, hey. Man, my song was spot on. You are looking for trouble, but no worries, man. You have come to the right place for advice. What is it you need to know?"

"Look, Elaine, I don't want to say the wrong thing, but I do know you've been out with some White guys, and…"

"Some? Excuse me! I only date White okes. They treat you well on a date, hey! But listen, those okes want one thing you know! That's why it's some, okay, lots of them. With Whites, it's one date per man only, ending in a fight. Knowing you Gail, I'm sorry, but they aren't for you. Though wait a minute! I forgot, you're a jiu-jitsu fundi."

"I'm not worried about Ed that way, and I won't need my jiu-jitsu on him. I'm scared though. He's coming on Saturday, and I think he'll expect to go out with me. I don't think he knows how impossible it will be. That's why I'm turning to you, because you made it possible."

"Sure, it's easy."

"Easy for you maybe. Nobody can tell you're not White."

"Until they speak to me, then it's obvious. But you, Gail, you've got a cultured accent hey, from that larney White school."

"But nobody will believe I'm White if they look at me."

"Hmmm. Okays. Like I said, you've come to the right place. A bit of hair straightener, lots of Super Rose and some makeup. I'll get you into the Edward Hotel even. But wait! Saturday? That's a bit of a problem, *ek sê*. It'll take time."

She knew it, too soon for any effects. She'd be on her own on Saturday if he did take her out. Oh well, it would probably be over after Saturday. Permanently.

"You still there?" said Elaine. "Why not drop in to my place this evening and let's check what we can do, okay?"

She agreed and replaced the receiver. Why not? If by some miracle the first date was a success, she might well need Elaine's assistance for more.

*****

She was there at the gate as Ed pulled up, dressed in a sleeveless blue shirt and a pleated blue skirt, ending a few inches above the knee. Perfect! Cool, casual but smart, and tasteful. Her smile triggered in him an immediate inner glow, which pushed away the anxiety he had carried all the way from 'Maritzburg. Her broad smile dispelled any doubts left inside. At least for now.

He waved as he locked his car. Force of habit, he always did, but now that may have given Gail the wrong impression, as if he might be afraid to leave it unlocked in her neighbourhood. So he unlocked it again. Too obvious? Never mind, he'd forgotten to take out the flowers, anyway. He reached inside for them and slammed the door with a flourish. At least he thought it was a flourish, probably more boorish.

She had come through the gate looking utterly entrancing and stood peering up at him. He reached for her hand but pulled back immediately, looking over his shoulder to see if there were any rubbernecks present. There was nobody, and he hastily gave her the flowers.

"Oooh. My first." She took the flowers and nestled them against her cheek, like the brides he had posed while photographing weddings. Immediately, he visualised a white veil covering her head, with a beautiful wedding gown flowing toward her feet, enhancing her beauty. The overall whiteness disturbed him, not so much the idea of her as his bride, but rather that she wasn't White, so couldn't be his bride.

He brought his thoughts back to the present. "Nobody ever brought you flowers before?"

"Never."

His eyebrows shot up. "I can't believe that."

"It's true though, I've never had a boyfriend." She lowered the flowers and looked down at them in another bridal pose.

He managed to stop his chin dropping. How was it possible such a beautiful woman had never had a boyfriend?

She frowned, tilting her head at an angle. "What?"

He closed his mouth. Was she having him on? She was incredibly good looking. A real prize. Where had she been hiding?

"The school was girls only," she said, as if reading his mind.

No surprise, most schools were single gender. "Still, that was some years ago, I guess. Did you go to university?"

"No, that cost way more than Mom could afford. My dad got me into the private boarding school, but Mom still had to scrape and slave to pay the fees. If I go to Varsity one day, I'll pay my own way."

"So where've all the guys been since you left school? Are they all blind?"

She took in a deep breath and let it out slowly. "No, thank you, but don't blame them. It's mainly my fault. I'm not proud of it, but the school spoiled me. It turned me into a spoiled White brat." She fingered one of the flower's petals, rubbing it between her fingers and letting the pieces fall. She looked at him again, with tears in her eyes.

"Do you mean…?"

Gail turned and walked through the gate. "I mean, I simply don't fall for the guys I meet." She spun round. "In this neighbourhood, hardly any have as much as a junior certificate. I've never met one with matric yet, and there's no chance of meeting anyone with a degree."

"A degree? No chance for me in that case?" He followed her along the path to the door.

"Nonsense!" Again, she turned her eyes downward. "You're doing pretty well on the phone, remember?"

Ed lifted her chin gently and wiped a teardrop from her cheek. "This last week has been an eternity, Gail, especially since your phone call on Thursday."

She opened the door and slipped through, pulling him inside. They walked into the lounge. "Are you sure? I told you I'm a White brat, but I'm also a Coloured version of a White brat. Did you really want to be friends with me?"

"Yes, I did, and I'm going to pretend you never called yourself a brat."

"Fine." She grabbed his hand and held it against her cheek, peeking up at him. "Get used to it, I believe there'll be a lot of pretending between us."

"I don't believe so." For a moment, he fought the compulsion to kiss her. What wouldn't he give to press his lips to that heavenly mouth?

Even if he had been that reckless, the chance escaped. Gail left to look for a vase, and her mother stepped in from the kitchen, greeted him a little stiffly, then excused herself to make tea. He had another look at the photos on the sideboard.

Gail reappeared and placed the vase of flowers on the coffee table before sitting on the couch, patting the seat beside her.

"I was looking at your photos here," he said. "There's no evidence of brothers or sisters."

"No. Just me."

"And your dad?"

"I don't remember even meeting him." She furrowed her brow. "He was White. But he disappeared without trace, leaving my mom to bring me up on her own. Other than my boarding school, she never got a penny out of him. No support, not so much as a postcard."

"But they were, uh…"

"Married? Yes. But then such marriages became illegal, so they had to live apart or risk jail. Apparently, that suited him, seeing as she never saw him again. Not once. Mom blames herself, she thinks no ill of him. I, on the other hand." She clenched her fists. "I'd like to…"

"I'm sorry, I hope you…you, that is, you don't uh…"

"No. I'm quite aware there are good people and skellums in every race. I would never tar you with the same brush."

"Thank you for that," said Ed, relieved.

"My mom has been through the works. She's always working like a slave for me. I'm forced to imagine she wanted me all White rather than half. That will not happen. It messed me up. Here I am, not one nor the other, Ed. I want you to understand this and also to see that I'm not my mother and definitely don't want to date anyone like my dad. You're the first guy I've really liked, and we couldn't even have a legal relationship."

He sat by her side and took her hands in his, squeezing them tightly. Their future together was impossible. He would never do what her father did to her mom. In the back of his mind were images of men in khaki uniforms and bars on his jail cell. Still, he was pretty sure he wanted to share some form of future with Gail.

Gail's mom entered with the tea, and Gail poured out a cup for him. Mrs. Rabe returned to the kitchen and the meal preparation, or so she said. The clock showed just eleven fifteen. Gail sipped her tea, frowning into the cup.

Ed sipped his. Parts of the conversation with Candy echoed in his mind. You love somebody on our side of the line? Of course. There's lots of our kind who play White. They're just careful. Most cops will arrest the girl and let the White guy go. He'd answered he would never put her at risk, but was it true? Even being here may be risky for her. Neighbours might talk or call the police. So long as he had any sort of relationship with her, she would be at risk. So would he, but what was the alternative? Not seeing her at all? Romancing her purely on the phone? In his imagination, he was back talking only through the phone, with a mental thought bubble showing a picture of her in all her beauty.

No! That wasn't enough, he'd never accept it. An imaginary image hovering above him while he chatted with her over the phone. No chance!

"You're right." Rapidly standing, he banged his cup onto the table, spilling some tea. "I'm not your dad, and I will not be like him. Somehow, you and I will find a way. I want to date you, bring you flowers and presents, take you out, go dancing with you, introduce you to the staff where I work, bring you to meet my folks, make sure you're friends with my sister."

"Whoa there." She was chuckling, flushed, turning a darker tan, a beautiful colour. "Perhaps you're getting too far ahead, mister. Being courted is something I fancy, but I'm part of this, too. Small steps, Ed, especially for us," she ended soberly.

He sat, taking up his teacup. "Of course, sorry."

"Nothing to apologise for. I loved every part of what you said, I did. Only, let's take one step at a time."

After a sip of tea, he sighed. "Very well. One step at a time." A momentary silence reigned. One step at a time? No problem if she were a White girl, the steps would be a well-defined staircase and though it may be long, at the top would be the altar. With Gail, it wouldn't be a staircase, more a rickety ladder from which one of them, or both, could fall into a pit of uncertainty. Many steps were broken or missing altogether. He shook his head to dismiss the image. At the top, for him at least, there was still the altar. "All right then, what's the first step?"

"Now then, Ed. You're the guy. I'm not one of those modern women's libbers. You're the one to decide what's the next step."

He plunked his cup on the table and shifted closer.

"However." She cleared her throat loudly. "I am the one who decides on how appropriate that next step is."

She leaned her head back on the couch and folded her arms. Ed hesitated at her mixed signals, especially when her lips parted a fraction. The opening of her cupid's bow lips hypnotised him. He moved a little closer, his right arm inching across the back of the couch. Her gentle eyes focused on his own. He sighed and moved up yet closer, till there were mere inches between them. His mind shifted into neutral, yet imagining the softness and the warmth, the—

"Oops! Sorry." He heard a voice, and with one eye, he noticed Gail's mom backing out of the room.

*****

Gail switched on the hi-fi to play the record she'd placed there earlier. She'd chosen "Swinging Safari," because Ed had mentioned it was a favourite, during one of their many phone conversations. She almost closed the kitchen door but couldn't help but peek through the remaining gap. He sat, hands clasped together, a frown on his face.

She wondered what he was thinking. Their lips had not quite met, yet the spark was beyond imagination. Her heart had hammered so loudly she imagined he could hear. His lips had been so close, she'd imagined how soft and tender they would be, how strong the passion. They'd been on the point of kissing when her mom came into the room. Her timing must have been deliberate.

Ed turned suddenly and his eyes found hers. His mouth opened into a wide grin. After giving a brief wave with his right hand, he used it to blow her a kiss. She caught the kiss on her lips and returned it. Behind her, Mom was evidently having trouble with her throat. Heaving a sigh, she wiggled her fingers through the opening at Ed and pulled the door till it clicked.

Too elated to stay annoyed for long, she crossed the floor and took her mom's hands in hers. "What do you think of him, Mom?"

She pulled her hands away. "What do I think of him? I suspect he's nothing but trouble. Oh, he's pleasant enough, but what does he want with a Coloured girl? He can't take you out."

"I can't say what his plans are. All I know is that I care for him, and he likes me. That makes me happy now, whatever the future throws at us."

Her mom slapped a ball of dough on the counter and kneaded it. "Well, our immediate future is making 'koeksusters.' I'll roll this out, and you can cut out the strips and plait them together."

They worked in silence until her mom had rolled the dough flat. She held the roller in one hand and shook it at Gail. "You want somebody that will stay with you. There are plenty of nice Coloured boys around."

"Oh! Where?"

"Well, how about Nick? He lives a few houses away."

Gail, slicing the strips, nearly cut her finger. "Nick! He already asked me out, and I told him no. He's a thug, Momma, you're not serious."

"Nick may have been in some scrapes, but if you give him a chance, he'll settle down. He'd be just right for you."

Gail gathered her last few attempts at cutting the strips, squished them into a ball, and slammed it on the surface. "Right for me? Clearly, you haven't heard him talk."

"Well, you can't be fussy. Not many Coloured boys attended your kind of school."

"Then why did you send me? If I'd gone to his, perhaps I'd use the same kind of words. But I didn't, and if you suppose I would put up with…"

"Okay! Okay, but surely some decent boys live in the neighbourhood. You could go to a dance."

Yes, sure. Obviously, Mom didn't know what went on in local dances. She'd gone once shortly after her own matric dance. Drunk bodies, a loud racket, couples locked together in groping matches, the smell of vomit, all before she got through the door. No thanks.

Once she'd tried the nearby fleapit cinema and had hardly settled in a seat by herself before a train of would-be admirers swamped her. They'd made it perfectly clear what they wanted from her.

She faced her mom. "If there's a respectable boy in the neighbourhood, don't you suppose he would've found me by now? Going anywhere around here is plainly not an option. Forget it, I'll stick with Ed, even if we only sit and talk in the house."

"You imagine just sitting and talking will satisfy him?"

"Well, talking is what we do, remember? Only now we can be face to face instead of mouthpiece to earpiece." She stared into space. "We have identical interests and sense of humour and love the same music, films, and literature. And he'll treat me well."

Her mom shook her head sadly. "Yes, literature, that sounds like courting in those books you read. I doubt Ed enjoys those old ones."

"Ed is old-fashioned and very romantic. Of course, he likes them."

"You fancy he's your Mr. Darcy?"

"Mr. Darcy from *Pride and Prejudice*? No, he's too pompous for me. I'm more Jane than Elizabeth. I prefer Mr. Bingley. He's friendly, agreeable and much more fun, unlike his stuck-up friend. Also he's…"

"White."

She folded her arms and glared. "Well, if we're looking for literary parallels, there are classics dealing with lovers who are different."

"Yes. Romeo and Juliet. Is that how you see yourselves?"

"Wrong again. That was two families feuding. Besides, it's too old. Remember the film we watched in the church hall last year? *West Side Story*. I can relate better to that one. Tony was a White American, and Maria was Puerto Rican. He didn't care that she was different either. I still get the shivers when I remember the scene where they noticed each other across the hall."

Her mom took some of the finished plaited pieces and put them into the sugar water bowl. "Come on, Gail, you do remember how both those stories turned out, don't you? Correct me if I'm wrong, but didn't everybody end up dead?"

"Fine, poor example." Yes, that had crossed her mind, and consequences for her might be yet worse. The Whites didn't take kindly to non-White races snatching up their own. She and Ed were taking a risky turn. Was it fair to put him at such risk? Maybe she should break this off, now. "Still, the point is she was falling for him. We should still be able to do stuff, even though we can't marry."

Her mom slapped her forehead. "It can't end any way but badly. I've been there and done that. Perhaps you can simply be friends. Visit each other now and again."

Possibly that was the answer. Friends. They'd always had good times on the phone. There was that time he told her he'd forgotten her name. She'd fixed him. She'd said, "Who's speaking please?" Then he gave some stupid fictitious name, and she pretended she knew him and chatted him up. They were always doing some silly, childish nonsense, but each time it brought them closer, more intimate, more...

She chuckled at her reminiscence, yet there were also memories of the sober times like discussing their likes and dislikes. Gosh. How much of their firms' time had they wasted?

CHAPTER

SEVEN

Ed sat on the couch again, alone with his thoughts. Sure, he had offered Gail and her mom his help while they prepared lunch, but they'd insisted he wait in the lounge. He'd argued to the point, he supposed, where he turned obnoxious. Gail had put her palm on his arm, stared into his eyes, and told him he would spoil the surprise she was making. Defeat!

Here he was, on his first date with Gail. Lunch? But why at her home? Because she was a Coloured. The thought made him sit upright. Why should that matter? It didn't, of course, but that was the rub. Personally, he was in paradise. Unfortunately, he was also in South Africa. He stood and paced the floor. What problems lay in store for him? And her, of course.

Still, he was happy with his thoughts. Bert Kaempfert's music played gently, and he tapped his foot, but as he couldn't remember the name of the number, he checked the record jacket. "Black Beauty." *I get the message.* But Gail was not a Black, she was a Coloured, so he'd ignore it. She was beautiful, though. Somehow the music reminded him of her, and he stood dreamily watching the record go round and round till the number ended.

He flipped through her collection after removing the disc and replacing it in the jacket. It might well have been his own. Not surprisingly, her choices coincided precisely with his. He stopped at one, "Elizabeth Serenade," the Günter Kallmann Choir. He was lucky enough to have seen them in 'Maritzburg's city hall on their 1966 tour. For a while, he stood, eyes closed, remembering watching them from the side gallery, not more than ten yards away. The bells had sounded so clearly. What an experience. As he pictured the scene again so vividly, he wondered if Gail had seen them. He slapped his forehead. Stupid jerk! It was impossible. She wouldn't have been allowed in.

The thought worried him. Supposing he'd known her back then, like he did now. What a chance, what an amazing opportunity, taking the girl of his dreams to the event of his dreams, only to be turned away at the door.

He hung his head, paced the floor, hands behind his back.

"Don't wear out the rug, please," Gail said on her way out of the kitchen with a tray of cold drinks and snacks. "I'm sorry to leave you on your own, Ed. Shame! You'll be pleased to hear the main dish is in the oven. Meanwhile, let's have something to eat."

Ed pouted. "Lonely and bored and banished from your sight."

She put on a suitably chagrined expression but winked. "Sorry, Ed. Never mind, we'll get plenty of time together today." She lifted a plate from the tray. "Would you like a koeksuster?"

"Ah, one of my favourites," he said, taking one. The koeksusters were small and greasy, exactly the way he liked them. Then again, she probably knew that.

She confirmed his conjecture. "I know you love them, and they're freshly made. Lots of work, but you deserve it."

He took a bite. Deliciously sweet and still warm. The syrup squeezed out over his fingers and Gail passed him a serviette.

"Delicious. Oh yes. This has got to be the best koeksuster I've tasted. Is this a special recipe? Are koeksusters by any chance a Coloured food?"

"Coloured food?" She swallowed a mouthful and frowned. "What's Coloured food?" It wasn't actually a question. "You English Whites, you make British food, don't you?" He nodded. "But the Afrikaners have their own food dishes."

"True," agreed Ed. "Some derived from the Dutch, others from the French, but mainly their own."

"Yes, and we're eating one of them now. And Indians have their specialties and the Blacks have theirs, and they're all very different."

"Right, and so I presume there are Coloured dishes?"

"We're a mixed race, unlike the Whites, Blacks and the Indians. We're liquorice all sorts. Our food is everybody's. We have different tastes. In one house, they may eat curry and samoosas, others mielie-pap and wors, another steak and kidney pie or fish and chips. Some like nothing better than bunnychow. We never came from other nations. We are South Africans."

"That makes so much sense, choosing the best dishes in the country." Ed took a bite of his koeksuster and licked the syrup from his lips and fingers.

She breathed in deeply and let it out in a long sigh. "Wouldn't it be nice if every citizen also shared our country?"

They sat in silence for a while. Ed savoured the sweetness of the koeksuster, and he watched her select one for herself. Juices oozed from her lips, her tongue caressed her top lip and heat flooded his body. He ran a finger under his collar, wishing he could loosen his tie. She slowly wiped her lip with the tip of her forefinger.

"It's hot today," he ventured. Oh no! Let's not talk about the weather. He asked her if she liked vetkoeks. She did, and then the conversation veered off, diving into new subjects and bantering in their usual, comfortable way.

Gail's mom entered with a pot of tea and rusks. Ed jumped up and took the plate from her hands. "Thank you, Mrs. Rabe. You're going to make me fat today."

She laughed and informed him she'd made the rusks herself.

"Homemade, yum! In that case, I'll definitely get fat."

She laughed again. "Thank you, sir."

Ed paused. "Sir? Oh please, Mrs. Rabe, call me Ed. Don't make me feel like a schoolteacher." He dipped his rusk in the Rooibos tea Gail had poured for him.

She murmured something and poured a cup of tea for herself. Putting a couple of rusks in her saucer, she started for the door.

"Mom." Gail arched an eyebrow. "What did we talk about?"

Her mom paused and perched on a stool. Ed looked from her to Gail. He guessed Gail wanted her mom to be friendlier. Apparently, the older woman didn't trust him. He understood, though, she wouldn't like her daughter being too fond of a White guy. How could he get Mrs. Rabe to trust him, that he could never do what Gail's father had done?

Gail sipped her Rooibos. She turned to look his way, her expression softening into a warm smile. He melted. Whatever this girl wanted, he would willingly give her. Being on friendly terms with her mother was fine by him.

They did their best to include Gail's mom in the conversation, though she didn't add much. After she'd left again, Ed believed he'd made a tiny step toward winning her over. Many steps of the ladder were still to come.

On his own again later, while Gail helped prepare the meal, he perused the several photograph albums she'd given him. They were mostly of Gail. A tiny bundle in the arms of a younger version of her mother. He couldn't see evidence of her dad anywhere. A little toddler. A cute little girl grinning at the camera. She showed more signs of her race at that age, her lips somewhat thicker, her skin slightly darker. Perhaps it was just the photo. It was monochrome after all and maybe underexposed. Why should he even notice her colour? Her race was completely irrelevant. Race? She didn't even belong to a race, she was a mix. Half her genes were of the same race as his. None of that mattered, anyway.

He turned the pages, filled with the cute little girl growing, becoming an attractive teenager. Many girls lost their cuteness and good looks as they went through puberty. Not this one. Every page revealed a growing beauty. There was a photo of her graduation from the private school and one of her Matric class. Every other face in the picture was White.

There were a few from her work. Apparently, she'd worked at Bronson and Schubert's from the start. One picture showed her talking on the phone. He wondered if it had been during one of their conversations. She did look happy and flirty.

At last, Gail and Mrs. Rabe invited him through to the dining room, not actually a separate room, adjoining the small kitchen. It had enough space for a full table and four chairs. A thick, white tablecloth covered the table, set with a pretty Willow Pattern crockery set and sparkling cutlery. Gail pulled out the chair at the head of the table for him, and her mother sat opposite.

Gail served, placing a shallow seashell in front of him. It contained shrimp in a pink sauce, resting on finely cut lettuce. A delectable starter. Ed expressed his delight.

"Gail made it herself, from her own recipe," said her mom, and Gail glowed.

"All the things you are, Gail, and now a superb cook to boot," he said. "Absolutely perfect in every way." He narrowed his eyes. "You're not Mary Poppins, are you?" It was one of their mutually favourite movies.

"Enjoy it while you can, Ed. One day, when I'm not needed and the wind changes direction, I'll be off on my umbrella." She smiled as she said it, but Ed put a spoonful of the shrimp in his mouth and frowned. That picture was disturbing.

*****

Gail passed Ed another dish as they stood at the sink, shoulder to shoulder. Ignoring her and her mom's protests, he had taken off his tie and rolled up his sleeves. It was cosy washing up together, she could easily get used to it.

"Only a few more, Ed, and we can relax." She passed him another bowl, and he dried it with more vigour than necessary. Her eyes kept darting toward the muscles rippling in his forearms.

They packed the crockery away, and Ed began rolling down his sleeve.

She placed a hand on his forearm. "Don't, this is relaxing time."

Ed followed her into the lounge and sat beside her, stretching his right arm along the couch behind her head. "That was, without doubt, the best bobotie I ever ate," he said, rubbing his belly with the other hand. "That was only a serious meal, hey?"

"I'm glad you enjoyed it." It was the first time she'd made it. "Mom showed me how, but she only helped a little." She grinned, holding up her hand with thumb and forefinger almost touching.

Her mom, sitting opposite, also smiled. She was much friendlier now that they'd broken the ice and perhaps less suspicious of Ed's intentions. Gail was glad she'd thawed so much during the day and happy she sat with them, but was she going to stay there the whole afternoon? Patience, Gail.

As if reading her mind, or Ed's perhaps, her mom rose and stretched. "Ja well, no fine," she said, "I think I'll go for a lie down." She gave Gail a pointed look as she left the room.

Gail crossed to the hi-fi cabinet. "Let's put on some music." It wouldn't matter what record she chose, Ed's choices aligned almost perfectly with hers. She selected one of his favourites, pressed the button and returned, to the strains of Viennese music.

Ed immediately swayed to the music, keeping the waltz beat. He sang in that rather tuneless monotone he had crooned sometimes over the phone. He wouldn't receive any prizes for singing, but he'd told her she was the only person he ever sang to. That, for her, turned it into the best singing she had heard.

He stopped and shrugged. "Sorry, I only remember the first words of the chorus. *O komm mit mir, ich tanz mit dir ins Himmelreich hinein.*"

Gail nodded with a grin. "Oh, come with me, I'll dance with you into the kingdom of heaven."

Ed's chin dropped, then he clicked his fingers. "Oh yes, you took German at your school." He grabbed her hands. "Come, let's sing the chorus together this time."

She happily obliged, after which they collapsed on the couch, laughing. "I sure hope the neighbours won't complain about that horrible caterwauling."

"Not to mention your poor mother trying to sleep."

He was still holding her hands when the next waltz began. "The Blue Danube," with a slower tempo. She kept in time with his swaying, hooking elbows together. Her eyes locked on his, as blue as the Danube, at least the way she imagined it.

"Let's dance," she said, gripping his fingers. She remembered he had taken a course in dancing almost a year ago but hadn't kept it up.

"There isn't exactly enough room here for doing a Viennese waltz," he remarked.

"Oh, come on, we can shift this coffee table away. We don't need that much space."

Ed gave in and effortlessly moved the table into the kitchen. When he came back, he took her into his arms. Her breath left her as he pulled her close. They moved with the music, bodies swaying as one. She glanced up at his face, always locked on hers while they turned and twirled. All too soon, the music stopped. During the pause before the next track they stood, faces anchored together, breathless with both exertion and excitement. Ed was panting just as hard. The next one was fast; they both knew the pace was beyond them. He removed his left hand from hers and placed it on her waist. Her right hand, deserted, dropped to his shoulder.

After several seconds of standing still, she lowered her gaze and sensed his face snuggle in her hair at the top of her head.

"Thanks for dancing with me," he said, still gripping her hand, though his tone had turned serious.

She gave his hand a squeeze, too overwhelmed with emotion to get out any words. After a brief silence, she asked a few questions about his dance lessons, but his answers were short, to the point, abrupt. Fine, animals then, she knew how he loved animals. "Are you fond of lizards?"

"Of course."

"Snakes?"

"Yes."

"Mosquitoes?"

"Huh?"

She tapped him playfully on the shoulder. "Is my constant chatter boring you, Ed?... What?"

He twisted round to face her directly. "Never, you couldn't possibly bore me. I'm sorry, you're not bored, are you?"

She giggled at his outrage. "No, just curious. Sorry, but you seemed so far away."

He pulled her closer and rubbed his cheek on her hair.

"And I didn't mean that," she snapped playfully.

He sighed. "Well, what's on your mind?"

"I don't know. It's just…well, even though I've never had a boyfriend, I'm sure couples don't sit around the house the whole day."

"Oh. Sorry. Yes, of course. We should go somewhere."

"But where? I thought you believed it impossible for a White and a Coloured to date each other." She winked, bringing her right arm around his neck. "Are you feeling reckless?"

"You've no idea," he murmured into her neck.

"Stop. That isn't what I meant."

He inched closer. "I know. You're suggesting we might do something we're not allowed to do."

"It seems to me, if we didn't go out, you'll be attempting that in any case," she said, pushing him away.

"Sorry, you're right. Why not? Let's go out, try at least. You've never had a boyfriend, so you deserve your first date. Where do you want to go?"

She shrugged. "I haven't the foggiest idea." It was true. It was a nice idea, but an impossible one. Unrealistic.

"Well, we could try the Edward. It gets crowded in there so you might go undetected. Their smorgåsbord is perfect."

"Smorg…what?"

"Smorgåsbord. Scandinavian. Oodles of fish dishes, cold and hot, and cold meats, hot too, and loads of the finest desserts you can find anywhere. You can eat as much as you want."

"Eish! Ed. Didn't we feed you enough? I'm stuffed full after the koeksusters, shrimp appetiser, babotie and dessert. Not today, thanks."

"Ja, that's true. Sorry." He stopped for a moment and frowned. "Well, I suppose we can go for a coffee or drinks?"

Sure, that's going to work out. But what was that proverb? Nothing ventured, nothing gained. She jumped up. "Right. Let's go." Might as well get Ed's lesson in realism over with. And at least they'd get away from Mom while in the car.

"Just like that? You're ready?"

She paused only to put on her white raffia beach hat. "Uh huh. I spent a lot of time getting ready for you today, you realise. Didn't you notice?"

"Didn't notice? Of course, I did. It blew me away. Didn't I mention that?"

"Hmmm. I think you said something to that effect," she teased. "Let's go."

She called out to her mom and stopped to listen. A whistling. Her mom was whistling to the tune of "Be back soon." In spite of her annoyance, she had to admit that her mom was probably right. Ed had some lessons to learn in the interracial world.

CHAPTER

EIGHT

Lines of worry creased Ed's brow as he drove into Andrew's parking lot. He'd chosen the smallish café because Andrew was a friend. Still, the problem remained; would they let Gail in?

Gail was silent, something he wasn't used to. On the phone, and since he'd met her in person, one or the other was always talking. What was she thinking? Everything became quiet when he switched off the engine and lifted the gear selector up into park. He waited a moment with his hands on the wheel, but when she reached for her lap belt, he hastily got out and rushed to open the door. She'd beaten him to it, already unbuckling, and opening her door by the time he got there.

"Gee, thanks," she said. "It's nice to see gentlemen still exist."

"Really? Don't your boyfriends usually open the door for you? Slack!" He grinned.

She climbed out, straightened her skirt, and took his offered hand. "Yes, sure. We know how overwhelmed I am with all those boyfriends. But the guys I work with aren't exactly what you'd call gentlemen." She grimaced.

"Do they make passes at you?"

"If that's what you'd like to call them."

He decided not to ask. Keeping a hold of her hand, they hastened toward the entrance, where a man with a badge and wearing a long apron greeted them. He peered at Gail, turned to Ed, then did a double take back to Gail. His jaw dropped.

He recovered and addressed Ed. "Can I help you, sir?"

"We'd like a table please, somewhere quiet."

"Of course, sir. Er...one moment if you will." He walked off quickly into an office, leaving Ed and Gail exchanging looks.

An older man in a suit hastened out, with the first young man following behind. He gave Gail a penetrating stare and frowned, then grunted. "Hawkins, I'm the manager. Could I see you a moment in my office, sir?"

The invitation was for him alone, of course, but he wasn't about to leave Gail all on her own. A few men sat at their tables, staring at her. He hooked her arm through his and followed the man, who turned at the office door, his eyes flicking to Gail.

"Oh! I...um, wanted to see just you, sir."

"Whatever you have to say, you can say to both of us," said Ed.

The man squirmed and looked so awkward that Ed felt sorry for him. Beads of sweat covered his brow, his face beetroot red.

"You see," he said finally, tugging at his tie. "There are laws, certain laws. It isn't me that writes them, you know. But there are laws... do you know which ones I mean?" He gave Ed a meaningful look.

"Do these laws, by any chance, have anything to do with my lady friend here, perhaps?" Ed narrowed his eyes.

The man was now openly sweating. "Er...perhaps I might trouble you for your ID, miss."

Gail, looking flustered, told him she didn't have it. Sure, she wasn't required to carry it at all times like the Blacks had to. She looked at the man directly. "Is it my age you're worried about?"

The drinking age was eighteen. No way did she appear younger than that.

The manager shook his head. "No, miss, sorry, no. It's only that you, um...you look..."

"Coloured?"

He sucked in a breath through his teeth.

"Surely, there's nobody here who would object," Ed broke in. A couple of the men at the tables nodded. One of them muttering that it was no problem at all.

"If it were just them and me," the manager continued, "I wouldn't have the least bit of trouble. But you have to understand, it's against the law for any race other than White to dine here. We could lose our licence."

"Oh, come on." Ed blew out a breath. "How likely is it they'll raid this place? Do the police go around actually looking for non-White people so they can fine you?"

"They can also arrest her for being here." He pointed toward Gail. "You wouldn't like to see her in jail, would you? And by the way, they could also throw you in jail. You would both be guilty on account of the law. The Immorality Act."

"Come on, are you serious? We're only here to have a drink." Ed rubbed the back of his head with his free hand. He looked at Gail. Her eyes dropped and her cheeks flushed. He turned back to the man. "Let me speak with Andrew? He's a friend of mine. I'm sure he'll let us stay."

"Perhaps, but I doubt it. There's too much at stake here. Anyway, he's away on a three-week holiday in the Seychelles."

Ed raised both eyebrows. "The police are really likely to raid this place, solely to catch interracial couples eating together?"

"Perhaps, perhaps not, but there are a lot of police who eat here. It's very popular with them." He hesitated. "Some of the police, certainly not all, but some of them are very racist." He seemed sympathetic.

Ed could feel Gail tugging at his arm. "C'mon, let's go," she said.

"I'm sorry, hey," said the manager.

In all honesty, Ed thought, he did seem apologetic. There was nothing more Ed could do, he shrugged and turned.

As they walked toward the exit, two police officers entered, as if their sole purpose was to prove the manager's words. Ed squeezed Gail's hand and kept walking. Gail's eyes focused straight ahead.

Ed stopped breathing while they passed. One of them gave a quick glance at Gail, blinked twice, and turned to face the front. The other hardly looked their way.

"Quick, let's get out of here," Gail gasped. She breathlessly raced to the car.

"Go on, go on!" She shooed him after he'd unlocked her door. "I can get in by myself. Hurry."

Ed darted to his side, alarmed by her expression, fumbled with the lock, then almost fell onto the seat and drove out the lot without putting on his seat belt. "I'm so sorry for putting you through that," he said.

"It's not your fault, Ed, it's the government's." She patted his hand on the steering wheel. "I do appreciate your trying."

There was an unusual silence as Ed drove along Smith Street. He should have the right to date any girl he chose, with her permission only, not some stupid government from the dark ages. He was not going to give up, but it could mean severe trouble for him. So what? Things would never change if nobody questioned them. Silence wasn't the answer. Few spoke out in Germany while they were burning Jews. He glanced at Gail. She faced forward, her lower jaw sticking out. Her eyes were closed.

He wasn't quitting yet but had no idea whether she'd willingly share the risk he was contemplating. He glanced at her. "Let's try the beachfront. We could take a walk on the beach."

She rolled her eyes. "You're not ready to give up?"

Exactly, he wasn't about to give up without a fight. "It'll be lots more crowded there, I'm sure no one will notice." Okay, the north and south beach were off-limits because of her race, but all the Transvaal tourists were in town, and the beaches would be packed with tanned young bodies. Lots of skin even darker than Gail's. "Could you reach into the cubbyhole and find my sunglasses, please?"

"Of course." She reached for the case, then raised an eyebrow. "You blue-eyed people, you're so sensitive to the sunlight," she said, with something of her teasing manner returning.

"They're for you," he said. "Put them on."

"But, Ed. I don't even own a pair of sunglasses. I don't need them at all. And why are you so concerned…? Oh. I get it." She put on the sunglasses, peered into the vanity mirror on the back of the sun visor, then grinned. "A disguise."

"It will cover part of your face anyway, and you'll be like a Transvaal chick chasing a tan, hey?"

"Perfect."

Ed pulled into the diagonal parking in Lower Marine Parade at the beachfront and looked around. "Quite a crowd! No one will ever spot us. See all those tanned bodies." Ed gazed at them till a punch landed on his shoulder.

"Stop checking out those chicks, Ed, you only have eyes for me, remember?" She winked.

"Sorry. I was only thinking what inferior sights they are, in comparison."

"Izzit? Sure you were, you skellum."

Ed smirked as he opened the door for her. She got out and he thought how lucky he was, in spite of their worries. She was a real prize. With her large white floppy sun hat and his own huge sunglasses there was little of her face left. The song "I've Got My Sunglasses" played in his head. I've got my sunglasses, mmm mmm to hide behind. Perfect. But were the sunglasses such a good idea? She resembled a superstar now. She'd probably get more attention with the sunglasses than she would without. Or was he just being paranoid?

"Well. 'Taking-out-Gail,' test number two," she said, adjusting the sunglasses and smoothing down her dress. "Let's go."

CHAPTER
NINE

They walked along the pavement, and it wasn't long before Gail spotted a large notice board on the beach side of the low brick wall separating the beach from the parking.

CITY OF DURBAN
UNDER SECTION 37 OF THE DURBAN BEACH BY-LAWS.
THIS BATHING AREA IS RESERVED FOR THE SOLE USE
OF MEMBERS OF THE WHITE RACE GROUP.

That's a fine start. Shouting it out in all capital letters, like they really meant it.

Ed's sunglasses were rather big for her, covering a substantial part of her face, but exactly how much would they serve as a disguise? Her bare arms and legs made her feel naked. Perhaps she should have taken the time to change before leaving the house.

As they neared the swimming baths, she became well aware of the looks she got from the White guys. Was it because of her colour, or were they simply ogling her? Did they suspect, or did they just think she had a good tan? Or maybe she was merely being paranoid?

Gail was fascinated by all the activity and things to do. The beaches she was allowed on had nothing like this. Just a beach and rather stark. They passed by the large swimming pool, surrounded by a brick wall, but Ed led her up steps to a covered walkway from where they could look down at the pool. On the far side, there were green slopes, covered with tanning bodies lying on their towels. Right below them was the long pool. They watched divers gracefully somersaulting into the pool, where others swam, played games or sat on the sides dangling their feet in the crystal-clear salt water. How she wished she could join them.

All the women and girls sported bikinis, making her feel over-dressed. Still, she couldn't help being aware of the stares from almost every man she passed. Were they staring from admiration, or did they suspect?

They descended the stairs at the other end and returned to the road. Shortly, they came to a place that had little gondolas sailing along a curvy channel route in the concrete.

"Come on," said Ed. "Let's take a ride. It's like a date, isn't it?"

"Sure," she agreed. "Let's, it looks a lot of fun."

Ed bought tickets from the man in the booth, who merely glanced at her and handed them the tickets. Ed helped her in and followed.

"You drive," he said, leaning back with his head resting on his hands. "I've done enough driving today."

She took hold of the wheel and put her foot on the accelerator. The boat couldn't even make a walking pace, but it was fun. This sort of thing was lacking in her life. She knew no equivalent in her world.

She pointed ahead to a brick enclosure. "Look, we're going into a tunnel."

Ed grinned. "Why do you think I got you on one of these?"

"What do you mean?" The boat entered the tunnel. It was pretty inside, away from the sun, away from the noise, and away from people. She took her foot off the accelerator and the motor idled, the boat slowed to a gentle creeping.

Ed leaned back and pulled her with him. "Ed, stop! I can't steer."

"Look, there's bumpers all the way around. The boat will carry on right through without you."

His arm crept all the way round her shoulders as he stared at her with his intense blue eyes. She didn't stop him. His head contacted the rim of her hat, which fell behind her, the string dropping to her neck. She faced him squarely, focusing her eyes on his. The intense blue stood out, even in their relative darkness. Her gaze dropped to his lips, coming closer and closer. She shut her eyes. His left arm curled round her shoulders, pulling her tightly and their lips met. She felt their delicate softness before they firmed up, and she let go of all her tension. There was nothing but their lips.

Yes, there was—reality returned, together with the bright sun. She sat up straight, reaching behind her for her bonnet and in the process the sunglasses fell onto her lap. She reached for them and looked up, straight into the eyes of an elderly woman.

"What the…" The woman's eyes widened as she stared at Gail. "You're Coloured. I know one when I see one." She shifted her gaze to Ed. "What? You're bringing a Coloured girl to a White beach?"

Ed put his foot onto the accelerator and their boat picked up speed a little. "What's that got to do with you?"

"I'm reporting you," said the woman, and she immediately hobbled toward the ticket office.

Gail replaced the sunglasses and her hat. "Well, now we know the disguise works, but I need it."

"Let's get out of here." Ed got off the accelerator and steered up against the channel edge. He climbed out over the back of the seats and held out a hand to her. She took it, and a moment later, they were racing back the way they'd come.

After no signs of pursuit, they returned to the car and climbed in. She removed her sunglasses, whipped off her hat, and fanned herself with it. "Let's have some of that air-conditioning."

Ed paused with his keys in his hand. "Wait. We've had no troubles when you've had your hat and sunglasses on. Are you game to try for a drink or snack in that café?"

She was game, why not? She felt hot after their little run. Hot enough to test her confidence in the disguise.

Still. "But what if they do twig?" she said. "How'd you feel if they threw us out because of me?" She would certainly be the only Coloured in the café, in the entire beach area in fact. It would need only one person to detect her, maybe a child. She heard a little girl's voice in her mind. "Look, Mommy, that woman, she's a…a Coloured." Everybody around would turn, following the direction of her pointing finger. What if they didn't just stop at throwing them out? The management might as easily have her arrested. Perhaps both of them.

He didn't respond, looking conflicted.

"I'm sorry for not thinking of you, Ed. You must be thirsty, and now you're trapped here because of me." She lowered her eyes, running her hands down her skirt. "You go on. I'll be fine."

"No way. I won't leave you here alone." He sounded adamant, but his next words were softer. "You're quite right. You should be scared. After today's lunch at your place, I won't exactly starve, and we'll soon cool off when I turn on the air conditioner. Don't you worry about me, they only serve rubbish here, anyhow."

"Aw, thanks, Ed. You're sweet." She smiled, and Ed squeezed her hand before reaching for the ignition.

It wasn't a little girl after all. This one was a boy, around seven or eight, and he was knocking on her window. He had black hair neatly combed and wore a huge grin. He looked so appealing she didn't think and at once rolled down her window.

"Hello," he said, beaming at her.

She greeted the little fellow with a smile. "Hello. How are you?"

"I'm Luke. I think you're pretty."

"Well, thank you."

The lad smiled open-mouthed at her. He carried a tub from which he shovelled popcorn into his mouth. His face and expression were appealing. Nevertheless, his presence meant there was at least one adult nearby.

"But." The boy shoved in another fistful of popcorn. "Are you White?"

Gail became rigid. Luke continued chewing his popcorn, not seeming in the least hurried for her answer—and apparently not overly curious.

"No, she's not." The man materialised out of nowhere and grabbed Luke by the hand. "Come away from her at once."

"But, Dad, she looks awful nice."

"She's a Coloured. We don't mix with her sort. Now, back to the car, right now!" He thrust the boy away, watching him scurry to their own car, and then faced Gail. "What're you doing here? This beach is for Whites only. You expect you can come here and talk to our children?"

Ed retorted over her shoulder. "It was your boy who knocked on our window, you know. We didn't start the conversation."

The man peered through the window at Ed. "You're White? What are you doing with a Coloured woman? Can't you find yourself a White girl? How dare you bring a Coloured here just because they're easy."

Ed snatched at his door lever, but Gail grasped his arm. "No, Ed, stop. Please, don't make a scene."

At Ed's reaction, the man backed away and into his car and pulled off leaving rubber marks on the road.

Ed glared after him, she had never seen him so furious. He squeezed her hand and looked at her, the anger in his face transformed to concern. "Should we leave?"

Her mind was screaming yes, let's go! But her rebellious side took over. Should they run off because a bigot told them to leave? She looked into Ed's eyes. Why let this ruin their first date? Suddenly, she saw the funny side of the entire scene. She opened her mouth in mock horror. "What? Never. This is like watching a movie. I want to see what happens."

Since it was a sunny, pleasant day, every seat outside was occupied.

"Hey, here's a seat free, baby," a male voice called, but she couldn't figure out where from. Ed squeezed her hand against his arm. Only some guy chancing his arm, trying to flirt. She stared straight ahead when they entered the café itself.

She pointed. "Look, a free table over there." It was against the wall in a corner, and one of a crowd of tables occupied by young people in various types of beachwear. A loud chattering filled the room, which smelled of suntan lotion and fried fish and chips with lots of vinegar.

"Great," he said, hastening toward it and pulling a chair out for her.

A waitress hurried up, order pad at the ready. The attractive young blonde pointed her enormous eyes at Ed. "Good afternoon, sir—ma'am. Would you like a menu?" Without waiting for an affirmative, she plunked one in front of Gail and handed him another with a flutter of her long eyelashes.

Ed smiled at her. "Thank you, let us have a few minutes."

The waitress smiled at him and set off. At least she didn't give the impression she suspected anything and had hardly glanced at Gail. The waitress may have been a little flirty, but she was sure Ed wasn't interested.

Gail stared at the menu for a long time, then raised her head. In the dark café, the mirrored sunglasses made it difficult for her to read. "I'm taking these off. It'll be suspicious to have them on, and I imagine it's dark enough here." She continued to read the menu.

He glanced up from his. "Anything you fancy?"

"I'm not exactly starving yet, but I may manage a bowl of fruit salad and cream. That sounds yummy, and a lime milkshake."

"Of course. Why not? I'll have the same."

As Ed tried to catch the eye of their waitress, Gail spotted a man sitting alone at an adjacent table giving her the once-over. Not an appreciative one, nor an ogling. In fact, it was more a dark frown. He was middle-aged, portly, and had a substantial nose, down which he stared at her with rising consternation.

Ed finally attracted the waitress's attention, and she trotted over with surprising speed, again fluttering her clearly false eyelashes. Ed gave her the order, looking at the menu rather than her face, and she wiggled away with a backward glance. The nearby man grabbed the waitress's arm.

Gail tried to hear what he said, but all she caught was the word *Coloured*, which the man uttered as an epithet.

Ed spoke, but she shushed him. By this time, the customer was making such a racket that Ed turned his head to see what was happening. The man scowled pointedly at them. The waitress shook her arm free and stared straight at Gail, perhaps seeing her for the first time. Her mouth dropped into an elongated "O." After a few moments, she turned and hastened through the office door.

Gail sighed deeply. "The sequel begins."

A worried, red-faced man, evidently the manager, swept out of the offices. He glanced at the man who'd been making a fuss, then came over to their table.

"I am sorry, miss," he said, addressing her. "So sorry to trouble you. Please may I see your identity document?"

With a sense of déjà vu, she told him she didn't have it.

"I'm afraid someone has made a complaint." He fingered his collar, and his face turned a few shades redder. "Might I ask, um, could you tell me if you are of the White race?"

Gail shook her head calmly. "No." She left her answer deliberately ambiguous.

"Oh, well." He paused. "You realise, this beach is for Whites only?"

"Yes," Ed said, "but we're not going to the beach, we came here for a snack and drink. There's no sign on your door."

"Oh, um, yes. That is true. That is an oversight. You're quite right. The meaning is understood, though. This cafe is part of the beach."

Gail stood with a heavy sigh. At once, Ed jumped up and squared off with the manager, but Gail stopped him. "Don't make a fuss, Ed. Let's go."

Ed's mouth opened and closed. He glared at the customer who had complained.

"I really am sorry," said the manager, wiping a hand on his jacket. "My hands are tied. If that man had not complained, I would never have asked you to leave. It is just that…"

"We know," said Gail. "You'll lose your licence."

Ed interrupted. "But you don't sell liquor here, surely?"

"No, we don't. The problem is not the licence. The police can make trouble for us." He beckoned the waitress. "Judy, prepare the order for this lady and gentleman as a takeaway please. Quickly." He turned back. "There will be no charge."

Ed opened his mouth, but Gail read his expression and pursed her lips. It was better to remain calm and friendly. If they made a fuss about their treatment, it would reflect on themselves. She'd give no reason to be accused of any sort of bad attitude or behaviour, nothing at all besides the colour of her skin.

"Thank you," she said, facing the manager. "That is kind of you. I am a bit peckish and thirsty, and I'd love a milkshake. Thank you."

They didn't have to wait long before the waitress returned with their takeaways. Gail took the box and said, "Thank you." Ed must have got the message, he offered to pay for the order. The manager shook his head with some violence, holding his hand up. However, Ed tipped the waitress a couple of Rands.

As they walked out, the complainer glowered at them, his face redder than ever. Gail ignored him and walked past his table, but instinct told her the man was preparing to stick his foot out in front of her. No longer content with embarrassing her and having her removed, he now wanted to trip her. She passed by with no change of expression but left him gripping his shin and gasping in pain. The self-defence course at her private school sure came in handy at times.

Ed caught her up outside. "How did you do that, whatever it was you did?"

She grinned at him. "Wouldn't you like to know? I may not be experienced when it comes to having boyfriends, but I have learned how to take care of myself. Coloured guys are not always the perfect gentlemen, you understand, and sometimes, White guys take an interest and think Coloured girls owe them." She glanced back at the café. "I imagine he'll be limping for days."

Ed laughed as he put his arm around her shoulders and pulled her in. "Bully for you," he said, adding with a raised eyebrow. "Also, thanks for the warning."

Ed couldn't drive while eating fruit salad with a little plastic spoon, but he started the engine and switched on the air conditioner. She was thankful, not many cars had them. The cool air blew out the vents below the dash, making this—their first date—pleasant enough.

Ed scratched his head after a few minutes of eating silently. "Let me see, how about…"

Gail held her fist against her forehead. "Enough! I can't take any more. For today, at any rate."

Ed's jaw dropped. "I'm so sorry, Gail. I absolutely wanted to take you out on a proper date. Why not try…"

"Forget it, Ed. I've had it up to here with your White world. Let's leave it for another day."

Gail finished her fruit salad just as Ed wiped his mouth and hands on the paper serviette. He shifted the gear selector lever. "Fine, I'll take you home."

C H A P T E R
TEN

"Well, thank you for trying, at least," said Gail, as he opened her door.

"Why are you mad at me, I tried?"

She winced and put a hand on his forearm. "Oh, please, Ed. I'm not mad at you but at apartheid. Can you see how hopeless this is?"

They walked toward her house in silence. He held his hands behind his back and looked down till they reached the door, then he raised his eyes to meet hers. "I want you to know that I enjoyed going out with you. Honestly."

She nodded. "I did too. Hey, at least it was an adventure, and I got a glimpse of your world." She let out a deep sigh. "That isn't part of my world, unfortunately. Sorry, Ed, I never believed you'd get me into any White place, but I didn't want to dampen your hopes."

"But I really do like you." He squeezed her hand. "I'd better be going."

"What do you mean? Aren't you coming in? I like you too."

"Thanks, but your mom has probably seen enough of me today. Tell her I said goodbye."

"But—"

He glanced at his watch. "I suppose I better hit the road."

"It isn't even five o'clock. Please come in. Listen, I'm sorry I've been so quiet on the way back, but that doesn't mean—"

"That's okay. I'll talk to you on the phone then, tomorrow."

She forced a smile. "Back to being phone friends."

"Ja, it was always fun talking to you on the phone." He sighed and took her hands. "Bye, Gail."

"Goodbye, Ed."

His head moved toward hers, but he stopped, squeezed her hands again, and walked away. That was it. He was walking out of her life. What just happened? There'd been something powerful between them which had been extinguished somewhere on the road home. It was all over. Was the kiss on the little boat rendered meaningless? Ed turned to wave from his car, got in, and drove off. Her hand froze in the wave. She backed into the house, watching his car out of view, then closed the door. Immediately, the tears flowed over her cheeks.

She turned to find her mom staring at her, wearing her smug expression. "Told you."

She ran to her bedroom, slammed the door and fell face down on her bed, sobbing.

*****

Ed thought of calling in sick on Monday morning. Two sleepless nights had left him feeling less than human. Still, he dragged himself to work. May as well be miserable there as at home. At least he'd be earning his salary, though what for he didn't know. Life without Gail was scarcely worth living.

He busied himself with the mail and opening boxes of film and other photographic equipment, trying to think of something other than last Saturday.

Mark put his head round the corner of the cubicle. "Mommy called, and she's coming in today."

Great, just what he needed. Their boss was okay, but on those days she came into the shop, she spent a lot of time looking for faults. Dust here, dust there, this needed straightening, the window display needs changing, have you checked all these films for expiration dates? He had no time for such nonsense today. Let Mark take care of them.

"Oops, customer," said Mark, and he departed from the doorway.

Ed carried on with his work, every now and again poking his head round the corner to check for customers but hoping for none. He was in no mood for them. Gail occupied his mind constantly. So she was a Coloured. What of it? She was beautiful beyond words and hardly anything about her features and skin was that different. There were scores of young White girls on beaches with tans far darker than Gail's skin. It wasn't as though she were a Black girl, a Zulu girl.

She'd been there with him all night long, at least in his mind, and he hadn't been able to think of anything else. He'd been off-hand and cruel. Maybe he ought to phone her, but what would he say? What do you tell the girl you love more than life when going out with her is hopeless? He would give anything for another date attempt. Why not? It could have been just an unpleasant experience. After all, that boat ride in the tunnel...

He took another peek. Mommy had entered, sporting her latest new hairdo, her long blonde hair twisted into a huge bun with long waves running down her back. Her makeup was overdone to extremes as usual, but what worried him was her talking to Mr. Nzimande and his delightful wife. Two of his favourite people, always so friendly, polite and respectful. Damage control. He dashed toward them.

Too late! Mrs. Cahill was already talking. "Hello, Ed, can you help this boy please. He wants to look at projectors."

Ed cringed. He stared at his friend, a gentleman in an expensive suit, whose countenance had changed from his normally appreciative smile. He stood straight, scowled at Mrs. Cahill, and tugged at his tie. "I am not a boy, madam. I am a man, a banker with an excellent reputation, as has my wife." He turned to her with a softening of his features and squeezed her hand. "We have spent a lot of money in your business, as Mr. Brent will confirm. We have not come here to be insulted."

Ed shifted his weight between his feet. Mrs. Nzimande, despite being Black and older, was a woman he admired immensely. Now she hung her head, embarrassed either by her husband's rant or Mommy's words. Anybody could see Mr. Nzimande would be offended, proud as he was of his Zulu race and himself and what he'd achieved in this White economy.

Mrs. Cahill half muttered an apology, saying she didn't realise. Realise what? She hurried off, leaving Ed to placate his customer. "I

76

do apologise, Mr. Nzimande. Mrs. Cahill had no right to call you that."

Mr. Nzimande glared after Mrs. Cahill for a few moments, his already wide nostrils flaring. "No, she has no right. And she doesn't have a right to call any of us African men, boys."

"No indeed. I'm sorry."

He turned to Ed. "It isn't for you to apologize, Mr. Brent. You have always treated me well, like a human being. I am sure you don't use that label to any Black men."

Well, as to that—he was saved from having to answer when Mr. Nzimande discussed the outrage with his wife. She stood with not an ounce of malice on her face, smiling at her husband. When Ed looked at her, she turned her smile on him. She truly was a sweet woman.

He had often used the common term "boy" himself. When using third person, Whites used "boy" or "girl" to refer to African men or women. Why? They were adults, not children. Perhaps a way of belittling them? He never wondered about the topic before, not until Mr. Nzimande had called Mrs. Cahill out on it. Why was calling him "this boy" demeaning, but not when applying the term to countless others? Perhaps because they dressed in shabby clothes, and they ponged to high heaven. Was that actually so surprising? If Ed had to walk all the way from home on a hot day and couldn't afford new clothes and deodorant, would people call him "boy?" Sometimes much worse. What about the fact it was more than likely there was no bath at home? Pictures flashed in his mind of Black families sharing one outdoor tap. How was it possible people lived this way in one of the richest countries in the world? He knew South Africa produced almost all the world's gold, platinum, and diamonds. South African Whites enjoyed one of the highest standards of living in the entire world, yet the Indians and Coloureds fell far behind, and the Blacks generally lived as if they were in the third world.

Mr. Nzimande's voice came through his thoughts. "Oh! I beg your pardon, Mr. Nzimande, my mind was on Mrs. Cahill's rudeness. How can I apologise?"

"Not to worry, Mr. Brent. It is fortunate that you work here in this shop. Otherwise, I would go somewhere else, but you understand, they would most likely treat me the same."

Ed sighed. "I'm afraid you're right. One day, I hope that we'll be able to be friends, and that I'll be able to invite you and your wife to visit me at home."

Mr. Nzimande grinned, and Mrs. Nzimande smiled prettily. "Thank you, Mr. Brent," she said, "it would be lovely to have you at our house, too."

Grateful they'd cleared the air, Ed took the couple through to the projector demo room behind Mrs. Cahill's office.

Ed's forefinger dialled the number with practiced rapidity. "Hello you."

"Ed."

As usual, the sound of Gail's voice turned him to jelly. "You sound surprised," he said.

"Of course, I wondered. You were a real bear when you ran off."

"Well, what do you expect when you just told me you wouldn't ever go out with me again?"

"What? Peer closely through the phone, do you see my jaw dropping? I told you I'd never go out with you again? My memory must be failing me, Ed. I could've sworn it was you who said that."

"Me. I said no such thing. Fact is..." Ed swallowed, his finger wandering around the dial. "I want to try again. I mean it. What you said was, that unfortunately, it wasn't part of your world. I realise it isn't, but I don't want to accept it. There are lots of things wrong in our country, and I don't want to spend the rest of my life regretting. I have an idea for a date I believe might work."

"No."

This wasn't possible, he'd bet his life on this. She—

"I mean, going on a date, yes. I absolutely agree, but this time I decide."

"Huh? Well, where?"

"Not any more of your White-prejudiced establishments. Do you fancy Indian food?"

"You bet I do." His eyes glimmered. "Do you mean…?"

"I do. Why should we try more of your places who won't…or can't accommodate us? Let's try Indian Town. I remember a place I went with my mom. It has curry to die for."

"The kind that leaves sweat on your top lip?"

She smiled. "If you prefer your curry so hot, tell them."

He toyed with the idea. Indian Town in Durban, he should have thought of that. Indian men didn't have the same hang-ups as White men.

"Excellent," he said. "It's a date then?"

CHAPTER
ELEVEN

Elaine answered her call almost immediately. She came with a box of products under her arm. "Right, Gail. Let's get to work. First off, this stuff is good. I don't actually need it, but this Super Rose lightens the skin of Africans."

"Wow! Really? To white?" Could it really be that simple?

"Well…actually, no. Some of them have turned yellow or red. You've got to be careful. Less is more, we don't want to ruin your skin. But we do want it whiter, your Ed isn't gonna know you." She swirled a sheet around Gail's shoulders and pushed her onto a chair. "And I've got something they call 'the perm' for your hair. By the time I finish with you, Ed will think you're a White, hey."

Gail sat and listened to Elaine gabble on. She had transformed Coloured girls much darker than Gail, who had gone on to date White men. "But don't get your hopes too high. There's always someone in the crowd who will know. It even happens to me, hey. But look, even if it gets you one date in five, it's worth it."

She started to work on Gail's hair. "The main thing is confidence. This change will make you feel whiter. With enough confidence, you'd pass for White even if you're Black. Don't look around all nervous like, that makes them look at you. Hold onto your fella. Look afraid and you'll be hauled off in a Black Maria chop chop, hey. Just believe you're White. Like you've got every right to be there, wherever you're going."

Elaine chatted and gave nonstop instructions, culminating in the procedures she had to do for the rest of the week. "Good luck,

Ed's going to be one lucky oke on Saturday. Let me know how it goes." She waved and walked to her car.

"Thanks, Elaine," she said. Perhaps, if she had a small part of Elaine's confidence come Saturday, it would work.

After a week of agonised impatience, Saturday arrived at last. She catapulted herself through the front door and flung her arms around him in a bear hug. They remained that way for some time, until she realised he only had one arm returning the hug, the other held flowers out of harm's way.

They parted at last, and he handed over the bouquet. "You look stunning, Gail."

"You too. My, you're probably overdressed for Pillay's, but I don't mind."

"What about you?" He swept his gaze from her head to her toes. "There's something different. I can't quite figure it out, but whatever it is, you're more beautiful than anyone I've ever seen."

She glowed and smiled. Elaine's work was evidently showing some results, but that would be her secret.

She put the flowers in a vase and told him to take a seat, but he refused.

"Let's go," he said. "I hope you're hungry. Maybe this time we'll be able to sit down and enjoy the full meal."

"And hopefully, I'll have no need to fight with obnoxious White men."

He peered at her through lowered lashes. "I hope you don't mean me."

She winked. "Not unless you're still suffering from a very sore shin bone."

They set off, and Ed navigated out of her suburb to West Street, when he asked if she knew the way.

She covered her grin with a hand. A man asking for directions. She directed him to turn off after the railway station. They drove past crowded flats, interspersed with marketplaces, beautiful mosques, temples and churches. It could have been India. They arrived at Pillay's, and Ed pulled into the parking area. This time, she waited for him to come round to open her door, and the two walked to the entrance. The alluring aroma of curry and strong spices hit her nostrils the moment Ed opened the door.

Ed greeted the waiter. "Good afternoon, a table for two, please."

The waiter greeted them, gesturing toward a couple of chairs, and told them to wait for a few moments. He walked past the many tables crowded with Indians and disappeared through a door at the back of the restaurant.

Gail looked around. Everybody's plate was full of delicious yellow-coloured food. Suddenly, the desire to eat left. Perhaps it was because of the powerful smell of curry and spices, or maybe it was because every dark face was turned towards them. The noise of happy chatter had stopped. When she returned their gazes, they resumed their eating and their conversations. She waited patiently with Ed for several minutes before the waiter returned with the manager.

"Good evening," the newcomer said. "You wanted a table?"

"Yes, please."

"I'm sorry, sir, but we're having a problem here."

"Problem?" Ed's eyelids started closing.

She knew he had the same thought, the feeling of déjà vu.

The manager shook his head sadly. "It is like this, sir. They are not allowing us to serve White people here."

"Oh." Ed closed his eyes, his grip on her hand tightened.

Gail broke in. "But I have eaten here before with my mother. We're not Indian."

"With you, that is not a problem. They are permitting us to serve Coloured people, but we are not allowed to have White customers. The government is not allowing it."

Gail's shoulders sagged. She glanced at Ed. The irony of it struck her; Coloureds were welcome, but not him. His whiteness counted against him. Abruptly, she spun round and strode towards the door. "This can't be happening."

The Indian manager followed them both through the entrance. "If it were only me, I could let you in, but some of my customers are not liking Whites inside. They might be telling the police. I am losing my licence."

Ed closed the door of his car while the man continued uttering his apologies.

Gail sat tight-lipped as Ed drove out of the lot.

"Are you ready to give up?" he asked.

She sighed heavily. "I suppose so. At least for now, the sun's going down. We'd better go home, assuming my mom isn't going to throw you out for being White."

Ed peered through the blue tint at the top of his windscreen. "The sun's setting? So it is. Don't give up yet, I think it's time for my idea."

Gail asked what he had in mind, but he told her it was a surprise. "I'm still determined to take you on a date. Maybe not such a romantic candlelit date, but that's denied us. So this will be the next best thing."

That did it. Her mood changed. She tried guessing what it was, but he refused to tell.

"How can you be sure they'll let me in?" she asked. "They'll simply turn me away."

He smirked at her. "I don't believe they will."

*****

It was fully dark by the time they arrived at the Durban Drive-In Cinema. Ed pulled up at the ticket office, where a blonde girl smiled at him.

"Two please," Ed said.

"Two adults, that'll be one rand twenty, thank you." She beamed at Ed, scarcely glancing at Gail. In any case, the darkness made it unlikely she'd perceive her race.

Ed paid and drove off to select a space.

"At last," said Gail. "Somewhere we can go together. What a fantastic idea, Ed, thanks. Do you realise, this is my first time at a drive-in?"

"Honestly? I know you said you haven't been dating, but didn't you ever go with your mom?" He winced. "Sorry, I suppose you weren't allowed."

83

"I don't know about that, but while I was growing up, we never had a car. My mom couldn't afford one. After paying for that private school, she didn't have money for such things." Her eyes darted everywhere, taking it all in, "This is really cool."

Ed chose a site in the back, calculating they'd be safest there. He adjusted the car's position for an unobstructed view of the screen, well aware that the large American van in front would obscure some of it on her side. He rolled down his window and fitted the speaker on it.

"Hmmph." Gail folded her arms and stared ahead.

"Hmmph, what?" He folded his own and peered at her from the corners of his eyes.

She scowled at him. "You never asked me if I can see the whole screen, Mister Inconsiderate Parker."

Ed grinned and jerked his head to the right. "I have a perfect view."

"Hmmm, but you didn't even ask if I did." She tightened her folded arms and pouted.

Ed, noting the twinkle in her eye, rested his left arm along the seat back and gave her a sly grin. "So are you going to sit way over there all night?"

"Oh! I'm the one who has to move? Why can't I sit on this side anyhow?"

He patted the seat beside him. "You'll find it far more comfortable over here."

"I'm quite okay here, thank you." She peered at him through lowered lashes. "By the way. What makes your side more comfortable?"

"For one thing, there's an extremely comfortable head rest."

She frowned. "Headrest? These seats don't have any."

"Right here." He stroked his left shoulder.

"No. I don't want the loudspeaker too close."

"I can turn it down."

"Well, I don't see why I should be the one to move." She turned and looked out her window.

84

Her words didn't fool him. She was only teasing or, at any rate, he hoped she was. He harrumphed. "You know nothing about drive-in etiquette. Do you?"

"I told you I've never been. Oh all right." She huffed and shifted over. "But if this headrest is too hard..." After snuggling into a comfortable position, she leaned her head on his shoulder. "Or if anything attached to this headrest starts doing something it shouldn't—"

He lowered his arm around her shoulders and pulled her closer. "Don't worry," he murmured into her hair.

She purred contentedly for a few seconds, then lifted her head. "So what's on tonight? I spotted lots of posters on the way in, but I didn't know which was which."

"*Airport*, a disaster movie. I hope you like them." In his desperation, he'd hardly spared a thought for the film, what if she hated it? "It's got really good and famous actors in it, Dean Martin and Burt Lancaster and Jean Seberg."

"Is there a plane crash?"

"I'm not sure."

"Well. It's not as though I'm planning any air flights. It might be interesting."

Mmmmm. He inhaled deeply. "I love the smell of your hair."

"Thank you. Herbal Essence Clairol."

He took in another long breath. "I'll remember that." Her birthday was a long way off, so was Christmas. Was this the kind of thing to give a girl out of the blue? He'd have to consult his expert, Candy.

She interrupted his thoughts. "I adore the fragrance of your aftershave."

"Mennen." He was sure his voice sounded muffled, buried as it was in her hair. "And your perfume is heavenly. What is it?"

"American Girl, something or other." She chortled.

"What's funny?" he asked, backing his head out of her hair to look at her face.

"Sniffing each other like dogs." She wiggled a bit, getting more comfortable.

Ed approved. This was heaven. The girl of his dreams, in his arms at last after a year of yearning. Was this their place? The anonymity of the drive-in cinema, the comfort of his car. It was completely dark, nobody would see them, and even if they did, they'd be hard-pressed to tell her colour. He was hers, she was his, and nobody could change that. Could they?

They sat and idly watched the advertisement movies for a while. A Caribbean-type jingle advertising Joko Tea. A Peter Stuyvesant cigarettes one featuring jet aircraft, ironic, considering the feature film. Another for South African Airways, "We fly your way, SAA." Seriously? Before a disaster movie with airplanes? Was this planned or coincidental? While the commercials droned on, Ed's attention returned to Gail's hair. He should have been studying the movie trailers, since they'd most likely spend every future date here at the drive-in; apparently, the only safe place they could be together.

The feature film finally started, a typical disaster movie character lineup. The essential problem surfaced quickly, engrossing them both for a long time. Ed had never felt such deep contentment as he did, sitting there with Gail.

At one slower point in the film, she looked up into his eyes. Her eyes sparkled, reflecting the light from the screen. She laid her left hand on his chest and sighed. Those enticing lips opened slightly, tempting him. He lowered his head slowly, pausing a couple of inches away. She didn't pull back. Her breath warmed his mouth a moment before their lips lightly touched. The softness of her skin sent a shudder all the way to his ankles. He deepened the kiss and caressed her cheek.

*****

Abruptly, lights from both sides flooded the car. The word *interval* displayed on the screen. She jerked up and scooted back across the seat, leaving her whole side exposed and cold.

"Can I get you something to eat or drink?" Ed offered, his hand on the door handle.

"Ummm." She frowned as she stared at the people getting out of their cars and heading toward the concession stand. "I'd rather you didn't leave me alone here."

"Well, come with. It's fairly dark. You can stand behind me while I buy."

"Yes, but what if they twig? How'd you feel if they threw us out because of me?"

She cuddled up again, close and cosy, keeping her head low and towards him. When the film resumed, he pulled her even tighter against him, making her feel snug and secure.

What was happening on the screen was getting exciting, and she soon forgot her worries. She gripped Ed's arm several times tightly, but apparently, he didn't mind.

*****

"The end" slid onto the screen and everywhere engines started: the drive-in Grand Prix. Ed had joined in on other occasions. His big Rambler Rogue boasted solid, protruding bumpers. Few drivers had the courage to challenge him while he merged into the exit lanes. He was always one of the first out. This time, however, he didn't see any need to compete.

"Probably best to wait until they thin out a bit," he said.

They waited a while and discussed the film, agreeing it had been a reasonably good one and exciting. She liked the humour, chuckling over how the priest, while crossing himself, smacked the panicky passenger sitting by his side after he reached "amen."

Ed laughed. "I loved the hilarious old lady stowaway and the tension when the Jumbo jet, with over three hundred people on board, had to land on the only open runway, which just happened to have an airliner stuck in the snow on it."

"Which they managed to clear in the nick of time."

"Imagine if they hadn't though." He bit his lip. "So many people killed. Everybody here demanding their money back."

Her laugh pleased him, tinkling like tiny silver bells. How wonderful that their first movie together was one they'd remember forever. How could he ever forget?

They sat in silence for a few moments, Ed surveying the lineup of cars, timing their own exit. Not yet, but soon. He glanced across at Gail back on her side, but she hadn't yet fastened her lap belt. He hummed quietly.

"What's that tune?" She frowned. "Unless you're out of tune, which you most likely are..." She wrinkled her nose at him. "It must be that song with Frank and Nancy Sinatra, what's it called? Man, I can't remember."

"'Something Stupid.'"

"Yes, I agree, but do you remember the title?"

He opened his mouth to repeat the title, and she giggled.

Okay, she's teasing again. "Yes. The name of the song is actually *Something Stupid.*"

He tried to remember the words, but only a little of the chorus came back. He never sang in front of anybody, but now, surprising himself, he began, softly singing the words. He paused, forgetting the next line. She jumped in with the following lines and sang it for him.

"Ah yes, thanks," he said and took over the refrain, finally getting to the very last words in the song. Instead, his throat tightened, he couldn't finish, too embarrassed by the tears flooding his eyes.

Once more Gail came to the rescue.

"I love you."

He eased her gently back to his side and nuzzled her hair.

"Ah, Gail. I love you."

CHAPTER

TWELVE

Gail peered through the door of her house, watching till his rear lights disappeared from view.

"So you decided to come home." Her mom switched on the light, and Gail closed the front door. "Where've you been? I've been worried sick."

"Sorry, Mom. We ended up at the drive-in, and there was no phone."

"The drive-in? They let you enter?"

"It was the only place dark enough."

"This isn't smart, Gail, and I hope you're over it now. You had your little White man fling and now you'll forget him."

Forget him? After that kiss?

"Well?" Her mother peered into her face, as if trying to read something there.

"I suppose that's his decision to make." It really was. After Ed had taken time to consider the problems with their 'dating,' he would probably want to go back the way they were. No more face-to-face dates. Just as well, it was far too dangerous. Even though they succeeded in finding a place at last, they could have been exposed. It was madness.

Her mom started the kettle and took down a couple of cups. "It's up to you, not him. He's White, you can bet he'll get off lightly. You're the one who they'll throw in jail."

Gail sighed, dragged herself into the lounge and collapsed on one of the armchairs. "I am well aware of that, but somehow I doubt only talking by phone will satisfy Ed anymore. I tried telling him, but when he looks at me with those eyes..." No, he definitely wouldn't want just a telephone romance. *And nor would I.*

"Don't let him take advantage." Her mom paused as she spooned tea into the pot and frowned. "He didn't try anything, did he?"

Gail looked down.

"Gail?"

She breathed in deeply. "We may have kissed."

"We? I can understand if he tried it on, but you! You kissed him back?"

"I couldn't help..."

Her mom cut her off with the lecture Gail knew was coming. You know the dangers. What were you thinking? Do you realise someone might have seen you? Men only want one thing. White men are dangerous.

Finally. "Are you finished, Mom?"

"Well?"

"I realise the dangers, but there was no harm in what we did. I'm sure Ed will forget me. He'll drop me when he faces the worst of the difficulties. He's an intelligent man." The one she'd always hoped for, but somehow something always dashed her hopes on the rocks.

Her mom hmmmphed, snatched the kettle, and commenced pouring the tea, muttering all the while.

Next morning, Gail trudged into her work building, her head thick with lack of sleep, eyes red, and lips sore from constantly biting them. Janet was waiting by Gail's desk, tapping her watch and frowning. *Here comes part two.* Gail dumped her handbag on the only space left on her desk not covered with parcels and invoices, and whipped off her jumper, not bothering undoing the buttons.

"My, my." Janet's eyes bored into her.

Fine, her mom had been on her case all morning and now it was Janet's turn. She frowned and thumped down.

Janet peered over her glasses. "Care to talk about it, dear?"

"No."

Janet strode away after stretching her mouth into a tight line.

Gail called her back. "Sorry, Janet."

With lips pursed, Janet paused, shuffled back but said nothing.

Gail picked up some mail and wielded the letter opener on a large envelope like a sword.

Janet's eyes widened and chased up her eyebrows.

"What?" Gail snapped, holding the opener firmly, pointed up.

"I didn't say a thing, dear," Janet said, backing away.

Gail pointed the opener at her. "You want to know what happened yesterday."

"I do?"

"Fine!" She yanked the contents out of the envelope, a large order. "We had a date, at the drive-in. We had a wonderful time, and he kissed me. Okay?"

Janet nodded. "I thought so."

"But it'll be over. He won't want me anymore. I'm Coloured, why would he? What could he do with me? Even the drive-in was dangerous. Why did we bother?"

"So you're going back again?"

"He said he'll pick me up on Monday. Janet, what'll I do?"

Janet sat down beside her and wrapped an arm round her shoulders. "There's only one thing right now that you can do: go with him to the drive-in. Had you contemplated saying no to him?"

Tears sprouted and flowed onto her cheeks. "I can't say no."

"Then all I have to say is que será será."

Gail stared. "A song?"

Janet winked. "Whatever will be, will be. Let's see what Ed does first. He may well change his mind after he considers the consequences. You're both so much in love that I fear the two of you are facing a dangerous and rocky ride. But if anyone can weather it, it's you."

Gail's eyes blurred. Janet's arms pulled her into a full hug.

*****

Mark stopped cleaning the lens of the Kodak Reflex he'd taken from Cahill's window. Carefully, he replaced it on its stand. He looked appalled as he paraphrased Ed's statement. "You actually told her you were in love with her?"

"Indirectly, kind of in reference to a song, she could take it ambiguously. But I am, Mark, utterly. And I want to marry her."

Someone squealed loudly behind them.

"Candy," Ed scolded. "Eavesdropping again."

"Aaaaw!" Candy gaped wildly. "Y'oll really want to marry her? Yeslike! Y'oll brave, man!"

Mark shook his head and scratched his bald patch. "Brave, but incredibly naive. Look, I worried you'd want to do something stupid like this, so on Saturday, I paid the library a little visit. I've got some things for you, old sport. Wait while I get them." He strode off.

Candy pressed her fists together and bounced. "Do we get to meet her?"

Before he managed an answer, Mark was back. "Here you are," he said, waving a stack of papers at him. "My research."

Ed frowned. "Research?"

"You said you wanted to marry this girl, right?"

"I do."

Mark licked his forefinger and flipped through the tops of the pages. "Here you are." He slapped a pile of stapled Roneoed copies onto the counter next to Ed.

The title was: Prohibition of Mixed Marriages Act. Amendment 21, 1968.

"It's long," said Mark, "but the point of this one is it invalidates and forbids any marriage between a White male citizen and a woman of any other group. Naturally, some versions also apply to White women."

"Fine!" Ed snapped. "So I'm sure there's a church somewhere where we're able to marry, even if it isn't strictly legal in South Africa."

Slap. Another paper hit the counter.

"Unfortunately, you wouldn't be able to consummate your marriage. This is the Immorality Act, which forbids 'any adultery, or immoral or indecent acts between White people and anyone not White.'"

"Okay, maybe, but we'd be man and wife in the eyes of the church, committing crimes, but not sins. We could still live together."

"Oh? You think so, hey?" Another paper joined the others.

Group Areas Act.

Mark read from the page heading. "'Forbids people of one population group to live in a residential area reserved for another.' Now, precisely where would you live, Ed?"

"We'll find somewhere, we must. Couldn't we have Gail reclassified as White?"

"Here's one on that." He added it to the collection on the counter. "Virtually impossible, I'm afraid."

"Then, what if I change? Aren't there ways to darken your skin? I read this book, *Black Like Me*, about an American guy, what's his name? Somebody Griffin, a journalist. He had his skin temporarily darkened to pass as a Black man. If he could do that surely I might pass as Coloured, if I tried."

"What about your *Book of Life*, that little thing with all your info that everybody is supposed to carry with them? Does it say you're Coloured? No, it states distinctly that you're White. You're simply clutching at straws, Ed."

Ed took a deep breath and let it out slowly. "I don't approve at all, but we could just live together? In her house perhaps."

"And what would her mother say about that? What about Gail?"

Ed put his hands deep into his pockets and frowned. Mark was right. There was no way he would put her through that. He sighed. "I still love her. I guess we'll just go on dating."

Mark chuckled. Typical of him! This was serious, but Ed knew it was just his way.

Ed pulled his hands out of his pockets and placed them on his hips.

Mark stared at him. "Dating? My dear boy, you told me how that worked out for you, didn't you? Not too well. What, are you going to Durban Drive-In with her every night?"

"Ag! Mr. Sanders," Candy broke in. "Leave him alone, man. Shame!"

"Well, someone's got to talk sense into him. The best thing he can do..." He turned back. "The only thing you can do is back away from this. Come on, I've had dozens of girlfriends, and I was in love with them all. Well, most of them at any rate, couldn't live without them, but I did."

Ed sighed heavily. "I tell you, Mark, this is the real thing. I must do something."

"That's another thing. You had a pleasant date at the drive-in, one of many more, no doubt at all, and I wish you the best. Honestly, I do. But as you become braver, you'll want to try other places, take chances. I wouldn't put it past you to try some disguise, even as you suggested, to make you look like a Coloured. You can certainly mimic their accent. Right, Candy?"

"Right, Mr. Sanders." Candy giggled. "He's good."

"Perhaps, and pretty soon you'll attract attention. They'll watch you. The cops may rock up at your flat late one night. Do you realise they can arrest you just on suspicion of breaking the Immorality Act?" He flipped through his remaining papers, frowning.

"Never mind, I believe you." Ed snapped. He ran his hand through his hair.

"And what about your girlfriend?" Mark spread his arms. "They can arrest her on suspicion, too. Ninety days without a warrant. Do you want some male correspondence-course doctor inspecting her body for contravening the Immorality Act? Would you like that?"

"Of course not." He frowned at the growing pile of odious laws on the counter. He felt like burning them. Giving Gail up? He'd sooner cut off both arms than remove her from his life.

As if Mark's rant about the dangers Ed was facing and how perilous it was for Gail wasn't enough, Dolores was approaching the group, no doubt to add her own two pennyworth of advice. Dolores was a know-it-all, she'd have a lot to say.

"Listen to Mark, Ed," she said. "For once, he's talking sense. You must drop this—girl. She's not worth the risk. Nothing but a lot of trouble. I've seen it, Ed. She'll take you for all your money and then run out on you. These people have no morals."

Candy glared at Dolores and stomped off. Ed wanted to follow her. Dolores was always telling them her experiences in Kenya, "When the Blacks took over." Everyone in the shop avoided her as best they could, never agreeing with her racist opinions. Now it was personal. Too difficult to ignore.

He glowered and pointed at her. "Don't. Ever. Say anything about Gail like that again. Gail is a decent woman. She was not responsible for your losing your home in Kenya, and you have no right to make assumptions about her. Keep your racist opinions to yourself."

Mark had his hand over his mouth, and Dolores turned the colour of beetroot. She humphed and hastened back through her office door. Out of the corner of his eye, he saw Candy creeping back, a smile on her face.

Mark uncovered his mouth and grinned. "Ed, I'm impressed. You well and truly told the old baggage off."

CHAPTER

THIRTEEN

Ed sighed audibly as the closing credits came on the screen. "Are you certain about this, Gail?" He caressed her ear with his lip. "This is Thursday, the fourth night this week at the drive-in. We even watched the same film twice."

"And?" Gail murmured.

"You're not bored?"

"Of course not, how could I be when I'm with you?"

He edged his mouth along her cheek toward her lips. He couldn't say how long the kiss lasted, but by the time they parted for air, the screen had gone dark. Ed reached for the window handle to replace the loudspeaker.

"But, Ed…"

Uh oh! Here it comes.

"I am worried about you. You drive here every night from Pietermaritzburg and back after the show, over a hundred miles a night. You're getting home after midnight."

"So?"

"So I worry about you, about your health. You must be getting tired. What if you had a crash going home?"

"I'm always exceptionally careful, on account of I wish to be back with you the next night."

"But your health, and you have your job. You start at eight."

"Oh, stop! Everything's worth it, as long as I can see you every night, speak with you, kiss you."

Another long kiss, after which few cars remained. Ed started the engine. It wouldn't do to be the last car out, drawing attention.

He exited the drive-in and headed for her home. Another half hour getting her there, who knew how long to say goodbye, followed by another hour home. He had to admit it was tiring, but he was not about to drop his new habit. Unless. Maybe she was the one getting tired.

He pulled up outside her house and switched off the lights. The moon illuminated Gail's tiny white house. They conducted their last farewells for the night. They both agreed it wiser to complete farewell kisses in the car than spending too much time at her door, but staying too long in the car was also inadvisable. Lots of houses were close by, and they didn't want any gossip. After one more lingering, sweet kiss, the memory of which would serve him on the long drive all the way home, he got out, opened her door, and escorted her home.

"Thank you so much for a wonderful date, again," she said.

"Only a pleasure, as always. Till tomorrow, Gail."

Lines of worry wrinkled her forehead. "Are you sure, Ed?"

"Sure, and spend all Saturday with you. I thought perhaps we might try Pietermaritzburg together."

"Fine. We'll discuss it tomorrow. Goodnight, Ed." She opened the door and slipped in, giving him a coy smile and a cute little wave.

Ed sighed, walked slowly away, and unlocked his car door.

From nowhere, a hand closed over his wrist. "Wait, ou. We want to talk to you."

He made out a tall, shadowy figure, with two others behind him in the dark.

"Who sez you can joll with our cherries, ou?"

Ed squinted at him. "Your girls?" His chest tightened as he perceived two more join the others.

"Gail's one of us, ou. You got your own cherries. Why y'oll jolling with Gail?"

He shook off the man's grip on his wrist. "What business is that of yours?"

"We don't want no White okes like you messin' with our girls."

"I'm not messing with her, and she's not your girl."

"Maybe not, but she isn't y'olls." The figure intertwined his fingers and twisted his palms outward with a loud crack. "Clear off now and don't come back."

"Shouldn't she be the one who decides whether she wants to go out with me?"

"No. We decide." He stepped sideways. "Jerry!"

"Okay, Nick." Jerry stepped forward, holding up a rock the size of a rugby ball, with sharp points.

"This is for now, and all the other nights y'oll been jolling with our cherry."

At his nod, Jerry took another step and whammed the rock down on the Rambler's bonnet.

The metal crunched and crumpled, visible despite the dark. He winced.

"Next time it'll be you, ou."

Jerry raised the rock again, Ed lunged, but somebody grabbed him by the collar and yanked him back. He twisted around and knocked the arm away. Its owner propelled a fist toward him, but Ed ducked and swung a punch at the speaker's face. Pain shot through his wrist and fist, then a sharp, searing blow met his face, and all went black.

*****

Mom was standing in the kitchen, arms folded, wearing her "tight" mouth. Gail rarely raised her voice, but now she felt like screaming at her. "I did try to stop it, Ma." Why couldn't she leave her to sort it out herself, in her own time?

"Oh, really? You told him to stop coming here?"

"Well. Not exactly. I suggested he should give it a rest. He's got a long drive home every night."

"That's telling him you want to call it off? Doesn't sound like it to me."

"I don't want to be rude. I'm sure he'll get tired of the same drive-in night after night." That was precisely what she was afraid of.

98

"Sure he will. He'll figure he'll get nothing else, and he'll drop you like a sack of mielies. But by then, you'll be so smitten it'll break your heart."

"Then I'll worry about my own heart—what was that?"

Something had crashed, like some sort of metal drum. Loud voices, angry ones. Gail rushed and peered through the curtain gap. Ed's car was still there. In the dim street light, she could make out the shapes of some men. One of them lifted his arms and brought them down on the Rambler's bonnet with a sickening crash. She heard Ed's angry yell and unlocked the door.

Her mom stepped up behind her. "I'll phone the police."

She grabbed her mom's arm. "No, we shouldn't call the police. Ed will get in trouble. Wait here." She swung the door open and ran toward the disturbance.

Sickening thuds echoed, and she heard a body fall. Ed's. She knew it, crying out as one of the men prepared to strike him while he was immobile.

"Stop," she screamed. As the man spun toward her, she recognised his face. "Nick!"

"Gail." Nick lowered his arm. "Stay out of this."

She dropped beside Ed and gripped his shoulders. "Ed, speak to me. Are you all right?" Hot tears ran down her face. This was all her fault. What if he were dead?

"No, Erick!" At Nick's shout, she jerked her head up. Another of the gang glared at her, drawing his fist back. She caught a glint of light reflected from his fingers. Knuckle dusters. Instinctively, she rose, grabbed his arm, rolled her body against it, and fell down in one swift movement. The result was the satisfying crack as his arm broke under her.

Erick screamed in pain, and she sprang up and whipped round to face Nick, who backed away. The others in the gang gaped at the writhing figure on the road.

"Mom," she yelled. "Call the police, quick."

Nick waited a few seconds, staring between his writhing friend and her. "Okay yous, let's waai." He hauled Erick up by his good arm, and they all scuttled away.

Gail waited long enough to see them vanish into the darkness before dashing back into the house. "Mom, forget the cops. We don't want them here. Call the hospital for an ambulance. Hurry."

Gail rushed back to where Ed lay, putting her ear against his heart and hearing a beat. She put her cheek to his mouth and felt his breath. Hopefully, he was only knocked out, not in a coma. She placed her hand on his forehead and jerked it away immediately. Something sticky dripped from her fingers. Blood, a growing patch, dark against his light skin.

Terrified, she sprinted inside, wet a towel under the bathroom tap, and gathered an armful of others. Sudden panic hit her. She needed a torch. There, on the hand basin of all places. She ran back and snapped on the torch, studying Ed's face. A wide jagged gash ran across his forehead awash with scarlet blood flowing toward his eyes. The gruesome sight had Gail's stomach lurching. She blotted the wound with the wet towel. His forehead cleared, but in a few moments, it filled with blood again. Did her efforts cause even more bleeding?

As she wiped away the fresh blood and put a dry towel on the wound, her mom banged out the front door, and her footsteps echoed across the courtyard. She panted, gasping out. "Addington Hospital refuse to come to a Coloured area."

"But he's White. Bother these stupid laws. Did you try our hospital?"

Her mom ran off again. Gail resumed nursing Ed, easing the towel away. The blood gushed out as much as before. Ed needed urgent attention. Ambulances were notorious for taking ages to respond—Ed might bleed to death before they came. And what if they wouldn't admit him because he was White?

Acting on a sudden thought, Gail held the towel with her right hand and patted Ed's pockets with her left. It didn't take long before she found them—Ed's car keys. She whipped them out and jangled them. After fixing a fresh towel on his wound, she tugged at the backdoor handle. Locked, but the front was unlocked. Reaching through, she lifted the rear door lock and swung the door open. She grabbed Ed's shoulders and pulled, but he was too heavy.

Her mom returned at the run. "They said they can't take him to Addington, but they'd try to get him in theirs."

"Try? They don't know?"

"That was only dispatch, not admittance. They weren't sure but estimate a delay of an hour before they can come. Should we ask our neighbours with cars?"

"Never mind, there's no time to waste. I'll take Ed's car. Help me lift him."

Struggling between them, they raised Ed's head and shoulders onto the cushion, then Gail zipped round the other side and pulled till Ed's body lay sprawled on the seat.

"Should I come with?"

"No, Mom, you stay here in case I need help with anything else." She turned the key in the ignition. She hadn't driven for ages, but thankfully, Ed's Rambler had automatic transmission, and it was fast. She gasped when it pulled off with a wheel spin.

A red robot forced her to stop, drumming her fingers on the wheel. She glanced left and right before flooring the accelerator. Why wait when there're no cars? At each red robot after that, she slowed, accelerating again if it was clear, but she never realised just how long West Street was. Most of the lights were green, and she drove as fast as she dared, noticing seventy miles per hour on the speedometer. Jail time for certain if she were caught, though surely they'd let her off, since this was an emergency. Perhaps they would escort her.

At last, Erskine Terrace came into view and the lights of the multistoried hospital building. She swung off the main road into the grounds and floored the accelerator, with one hand leaning on the hooter ring. The resulting blare echoed all around her, and some startled people jumped aside when she pulled up as near the entrance as possible, tyres squealing. She pressed the ring for several sharp blasts, and three men ran out the entrance.

Gail jumped out and swung open the car's back door. "Quick, he's unconscious and losing a lot of blood."

One of the men, in a white coat, shone a torch and inspected Ed's wound. He signalled the team who rushed through the doors with a rolling stretcher. "Quickly, get him to emergency."

They transferred Ed onto the stretcher and the man turned. "Don't worry, they'll take good care of him. Come with me, if you don't mind. My name's Jimmy Hean. We need you to fill in some paperwork."

She followed him across the brightly lit hall to a desk where a receptionist in a green dress frowned at her. Jimmy turned round and gave a start, but he blinked, shook his head, and gestured to the lady. "Mrs. Nagel will take down his information and then you may wait here. I'll return as soon as I hear something." He touched her shoulder briefly and left.

Mrs. Nagel stared at Gail above her bifocals. Gail recognised the stare. The "you're Coloured, what are you doing here?" look.

"You know this hospital is for Whites only?" The woman's words and accent confirmed Gail's thoughts: fifty-something White Afrikaner, with greying hair. Gail expected she'd be turfed out the building in next to no time.

"I'm sorry, but he…is White."

The woman sniffed. "Very well, complete this form. Do you have any identity papers?"

Gail shook her head. "Perhaps they're on him."

"Go there." The woman indicated several writing desks attached to the wall.

The form was long and wanted considerable information. Her heart sank. How would she be able to fill in all the details about him? But she soon realised she knew almost everything about him from their phone conversations, and more recently, their dates. Next of kin? Middle name? Address? No problem. Next came a large space for the nature of accident/illness. She filled it in, including the attack, because he'd been visiting a girl in the Coloured area, but left out her name.

Gail returned the form to Mrs. Nagle, whose left eyebrow rose. Her eyes dropped and scanned the form. "You missed out parents' address."

"I'm sorry, I filled in everything I could."

"What is your relationship to the patient?" Her eyes bored into Gail's.

"We…we're friends."

"Friends." She scribbled something on the paper. "Will Mr.—" She peered at the form. "Brent, be paying for this?"

"Yes. He has Medical Aid insurance."

"Hmm. Very well. Here is a card. You may phone this number if you want. Good night."

"Oh! but that gentleman, Mr. Hean, said he would come back with information about him. He told me to wait."

Mrs. Nagel sniffed. "This is a White hospital. We do not have a waiting room for non-Whites."

Gail turned, walked out, and parked Ed's car in a proper parking spot. She returned and strode toward a row of chairs against the wall and sat down with arms folded, determined to wait for news of Ed. They would have to throw her out. She returned Mrs. Nagel's stare with narrowed eyes.

About forty minutes later, Jimmy rushed back, breathing hard. He wiped his brow with a handkerchief. "Thank you for waiting. Mr. Brent is still unconscious, but his vitals are satisfactory, and the doctor sewed up his wound. It could be a while before he regains consciousness, but Dr. Spence is confident he'll be okay."

Gail sighed. "Thank you. Could I see him?"

He stared at the frowning Mrs. Nagle. He shook his head and fumbled in his pocket. "Here, this is my card. You can phone me tomorrow about your friend. At this stage, I don't know whether they'll allow you to…er…see him, but I'll keep informed of his condition for you." He smiled, reached out with his hand, hesitated, withdrew it, his face reddening.

Gail thanked him, then slowly strolled out to the Rambler.

CHAPTER

FOURTEEN

Next morning, Jimmy called with no good news. He told her Ed was
still unconscious, though his vital signs were sound, and he was sorry
she couldn't visit him, but the administration were being very hard-
nosed about it. He advised her against coming in.

Her mother, who'd been hanging around during the call, faced
her. "Of course you can't visit him, Gail, what were you thinking?"

Gail rested her hand on the receiver, frowning. Ed had been
unconscious more than seven hours. What if he were in a coma? She
remembered Ed telling her about his ex-girlfriend, his very first girlfriend, who had lain in hospital a whole week after a car accident and
never recovered. But Jimmy had mentioned nothing about a coma.

She thought of the information she had filled in at admissions.
Not knowing his family's address or phone number, she hadn't left
them much.

Lifting the receiver, she dialled the number she knew off by
heart, Ed's work. The infamous Dolores Pieterse, the White Afrikaans
woman Ed all but despised for her racism, answered. She told her Ed
had had an accident and was in hospital.

"Thanks, I'll tell the others. What happened?"

She preferred to keep that bit of information to herself. Ed
beaten up by Coloured boys. That would be precisely what Dolores
would want to hear. More ammo for her arguments against racial
integration. But Mrs. Cahill, Mark and the others would want to
know. "I'll call with the details later. Thank you, bye."

It was a long day. Gail stared at the phone, willing it to ring,
but it obstinately refused, just sitting there with its dial grinning at

her. She pulled out a book at random from the bookcase. *Cry the Beloved Country*. Indeed. She opened it up and read the first two pages, at the end of which she realised she remembered nothing but the first few words. There is a lovely road that leads from Ixopo into the hills. She snapped it shut and tried the radio. A soap opera. She spun the dial through all the stations and finally settled for some music, tucking her legs under her and leaning against the end of the couch. The night's activities were catching up with her. She yawned and stretched out her legs.

*****

Light, dark, intense pain. Again. It kept repeating. How many times? Ed lifted his hand and felt his forehead. Another flash of white light hit his head, but something soft took hold of his hand and moved it away.

"Hello." He heard the voice but saw only a blob. The blob gradually came into focus, but the searing pain in his head made it blur once more.

Something wet passed over his brow. He opened his eyes once more, and the blob slowly cleared. Two smaller blobs materialised, and he focused on those. Like a photograph developing, two eyes eased through the fog. Dark hazel mixed with brownish spots, slight upturn at the outside ends, now in sharp focus.

"Gail?" He tried sitting up but couldn't move.

"Sorry no, I'm not Gail." A mask covered everything below the eyes, and above them, a white mass. A hat? A nurse?

"Chantal Breyers. I'm your nurse. How are you feeling?"

"Where am I?" Ed asked.

"You're in Addington Hospital. I'm afraid you took a serious beating. Right now, I'm trying to patch you up, and whoever's responsible did a poor job of stitching you up. Too much of a hurry. So unprofessional."

"Addington? How did I get here?"

"Someone brought you in a car. A bunch of Coloureds attacked you, but you were in their area." Chantal frowned, tutted and shook her head as she continued doing whatever it was to his forehead. "This will hurt a little…"

Ouch. She was right about that.

She held a needle in her hand. "That was the twelfth stitch. That should do it." She peered closely at him, giving him a closeup of her bewitching eyes. But they were Gail's eyes! If she took off her mask, would she look like Gail? Was he imagining the likeness?

Her eyes bored into his, then wandered away as they examined his forehead. "Almost like new again, if I don't say so myself. Not a bad job at all. I fixed up the mess they made last night."

"Thank you, thank you very much," he said, wishing she would take off the mask.

Chantal threw the needle and thread in a bin, took a cotton ball, and returned her attention to his forehead. "Seems the Coloured boys didn't like your taking out one of their girls," she said, with a matter-of-fact air.

"Apparently."

Her brows knit together. "Why were you taking out a Coloured girl, anyway?"

He remained silent.

"I'm sorry," she said, averting her eyes. "It isn't any of my business."

"I just happen to have fallen in love with her," he replied, raising a hand to his forehead, but she stopped the movement.

"No touching." She sighed deeply. "You fell in love, oh dear, that sort of thing happens. Still, this could have been lots worse than it was. They might have killed you, you know?"

She got that right.

"Isn't it difficult? I mean, dating a Coloured girl. I imagine they wouldn't allow her in most places."

"Eh…ja! You're right about that." His many body aches reminded him of what had happened. Those Coloured guys would be waiting for him when he called for Gail again. A whole gang of them. Next time could be a lot worse.

Chantal wiped his face gently while fixing him with a concerned stare through Gail's eyes. "A nice White girl is a lot safer. You could take her anywhere you like, you should think about that." She continued stroking his face with the wet cloth. She winked. "You could ask me out if you like. I would go out with you in a heartbeat."

He forced a smile. "Thank you, Chantal. A couple of weeks ago, I would've jumped at that chance. You're delightful, but since then, I met Gail, and she's the one. Somehow, we'll make it work."

"Well. Don't say I didn't try." She dipped the cloth in water and resumed wiping his cheek. "It is rather sweet that you're so loyal."

"You have her eyes, you know, almost exactly, identical colour and shape."

"I do? Really? There you are. I thought I might have something you like. I'm halfway there." He could tell she was smiling from the way her eyes pinched. Just like Gail's.

"How long have I been here?"

"It happened late last night. They brought you in this morning, very early. It's now six o'clock in the evening. We'll be feeding you soon if you're up to it."

"Six o'clock! Did Gail come and visit me at all today?"

"Gosh, I'm not sure. I'm positive they wouldn't have let her in, though. That is, if she looks Coloured. They don't allow non-Whites here." Her eyes showed sympathy. "Tell you what! I'll make enquiries. If anyone did try, I'll let you know. Hullo, here's your dinner coming. I'll be off and see what I can do." She squeezed his hand, smiled again with her eyes, and left him.

Ed tried some of the hospital food but had little appetite for a dry hamburger with carrots and peas. A Black woman in a standard housekeeping uniform removed his plate later, and now he had only his thoughts, all involving Gail. Did she even know what had happened? Would they let him phone her? How would this affect their dating, their relationship? He waited in agony, till at last Chantal came back, without a mask this time. She bore a distinct resemblance to Gail, quite apart from the almost identical eyes. An undeniably beautiful girl, however, she wasn't Gail.

"Hullo," she said. "Your young Coloured lady friend brought you here. You might like to hear she did want to see you, but the administration just wouldn't let her in. I'm so sorry."

107

Ed wrinkled his brow. How had Gail brought him here, a White hospital, and what must she be thinking about it all, wanting to visit him yet being denied?

"Now I'm going to give you some Mogodon, which will help with the pain and make you sleep. It's pretty powerful." She frowned and pursed her lips. "But, regrettably, not the pain in your heart. I'm truly sorry, Ed."

*****

Briinng Briinng.

Gail woke and sat up, startled. What was happening? The phone. She dashed into the hall and snatched it up. "Hello."

"Is this Gail Rabe?" It was Jimmy.

"Yes."

"Your friend woke up. He's okay."

A shiver ran down the length of her body, freezing her voice. Ed was fine.

Jimmy's voice crackled in her earpiece. "Hello. Are you there?"

"Yes. Yes, thank you. Can I visit him?"

"Sorry, he won't be getting visitors today, through tonight."

"So I can come tomorrow then?"

There was a brief silence. "Uh. You know how it is." He sounded grave. "You won't get past Mrs. Nagle."

"Oh."

"Look, I know his nurse. Her name's Chantal. I might ask her to take Ed for a walk downstairs or something. Maybe get some sunshine. She'll figure out something."

"Thank you, Jimmy, you're the best. I appreciate that."

"You're most welcome. If I do manage it, I'll call this number with a time."

*****

The Mogodon worked only too well. He woke up for breakfast, which he ate with somewhat more appetite than his supper. Chantal hadn't come in. Possibly it was her day off.

Compounding his dismay, another nurse entered the ward and approached him. This one was stout, much older, and didn't wear a mask. "The doctor checked you this morning while you were asleep. We're keeping you at least another day. Someone will be in some-time, asking if there's anybody you want us to contact, and so on. In the meantime, here's another pill, doctor's orders, for pain."

He grunted. Would they let him phone Gail? He calculated it was Saturday, so they had better call Mrs. Cahill in case he couldn't get there on Monday. "Is Nurse Breyers not here?" he asked.

"Yes. She's in surgery ward now. You'll probably see her later."

Ed took the medicine, which had an immediate effect. His eye-lids grew heavy almost at once.

When he raised his heavy lids again, his vision was blurry. At least it was light, it had to be Sunday morning. He made out the fig-ure of a nurse standing over him. After his eyes focused, he became aware she was wearing a mask, but those eyes were Chantal's. Eyes totally like Gail's. Remarkably like Gail's. She'd come back. Maybe she had news of Gail. The eyes stared at him with even greater inten-sity, sending a shiver throughout his body. Looking into them, it was startling to think it possible to fall in love with them just as he had with Gail's. From their sparkle, he knew she was smiling again, smil-ing broadly. She held a forefinger in front of where her lips would be, behind the mask. Strange.

"Ed," was all she said. It was enough. Behind the mask, wearing a uniform like Chantal's, was Gail herself.

He opened his mouth to call out, but she held her fingers against his mouth. "Shhh, it's me. I got in here at last. Thanks to your nurse."

"Chantal?"

"Yes, she's been marvelous." She bent down and inspected his stitches with a worried frown. "She told me she redid your stitches and all, say..." She winked. "You're not getting fresh with her, are you?" She raised an eyebrow.

He shook his head. "But I did believe she was you at first. She has your eyes. But you say she got you in here, how…"

"When she heard I was trying to see you, she smuggled me in. She met me outside and smuggled me through the non-White cleaners' entrance, where I changed into her spare uniform with her badge and mask."

"I'm so glad she did this."

"Me too. Oh, Ed, I'm so sorry about what happened. It was Nick. He's been after me for years and just won't take no for an answer."

Ed raised his body on one elbow and grabbed her hand. "What about you? Are you in danger?"

"I'm not sure. Probably not, but I'd like a change of scenery for a while. I was considering staying in 'Maritzburg."

"Pietermaritzburg?"

"Yes. So I can be nearer you, and where I'm not known. It'll be safer for you." She paused, and he perceived the concern in her eyes. "That is, if you still want to go out with me after what happened."

"Of course, I do. It hasn't changed how I feel about you. But that's great. 'Maritzburg has far more possibilities to take you on a date than just the Highway Drive-in Cinema."

"I talked to Candy on the phone," she said.

"Candy, from my work?"

"Yes."

"I didn't realise you knew her."

"Well, you sometimes mention her, and I knew she was a friend of yours. I asked her if she knew a suitable place for me to board, and she insisted I stay with her and her family. I'm using all my annual leave, eighteen working days, and some more I had left over from last year."

Someone knocked, coughed, and the door opened. Gail's eyes widened, and she stepped quickly back from the bed, arms behind her.

A cheerful face peered through the opening. "Good morning, Mr. Brent. I'm seeing you awake for the first time." He held out his hand. "I'm Dr. Spence. How have you been feeling?"

Ed shook hands with him. "Much better, thanks."

Dr. Spence glanced at Gail, arched his eyebrows, and turned back to Ed, flashing a crooked smile. "Splendid. Flirting with a pretty nurse is always a good sign of recovery. Well then, let's look into the possibility of discharging you."

The doctor pressed his stethoscope against Ed's chest for several seconds, then peeled back the bandage and inspected his stitched forehead. He looked approvingly at Gail. "Excellent work, Nurse Breyers."

Gail was the picture of discomfort and only managed a bob of her head.

He handed her some equipment. "If you don't mind taking Mr. Brent's blood pressure while I fill in this report."

Ed watched Gail as the doctor wrote on a pad. Her eyes filled with terror. She put in the earpieces, then paused. Did she have a clue what came next?

Ed furtively pointed to the rubber cuff and made a circular motion with his finger on his forearm, hoping she'd understand his signals. She took the cuff and wrapped it around his arm successfully. He placed the diaphragm against his arm and opened and closed his fist. After a momentary puzzled look, she pumped the bulb.

When the pressure reached pain level, he held up his right hand in a stop sign, swiftly changing it to scratching his head as Dr. Spence's eyes flitted towards him, then back to his notes. Ed tapped his forefinger and thumb rhythmically, conveying the beating of his heart. Her furrowed brow cleared, and he peered toward the gauge, hoping she would note the number. He continued beating with his forefinger, then sliced his hand side to side when he wanted her to stop.

He squeezed his eyes shut. How would she ever figure out what he meant? In a few seconds Dr. Spence would expose her as a phony nurse. Chantal could face severe trouble for this, perhaps they'd even fire her. And it was all his fault. None of this would be happening if he'd just had the ice skates delivered in the normal way.

His panic increased when Doctor Spence spoke. "Well then, that about wraps it up. What's the reading?" He turned to Gail, pen poised above his paper.

Ed held his breath, waiting for Gail's response. Two tense seconds passed—four seconds—ten. When would the security officers come and drag her out, or arrest her for impersonating a trained nurse? Besides, he couldn't even imagine what difficulties Chantal was in for.

"One twenty," said Gail finally.

"Over?"

"Eighty," she gasped, the lines showing on her brow.

Ed started breathing again.

"Excellent. Well done, Nurse Breyers, commendable job." He smiled. "Well, there's no reason for keeping you any longer, Ed. You are well enough, and there's no apparent problem with your mental faculties. The stitches will dissolve on their own. I'll arrange for your discharge. Keep well now and be careful in future, Mr. Brent." He shook Ed's hand again. "Nurse Breyers, good stitching, and that was an incredible job of taking blood pressure."

He paused at the door. "I shall congratulate the real Nurse Breyers when I see her." He gave Gail a broad wink and strode away.

"He knew all the time!" Gail, wide eyed, let out an explosive breath. "That doctor saw right through me. I must get out of here before I get arrested, and Chantal…"

"Relax, Gail. I'm sure the doctor didn't want to make trouble for you at all. Wait for me to be discharged, please."

Gail hesitated. "You're right, and besides, I'm meeting Chantal again for my clothes. You won't have to fetch your car from my place, since I drove it here. I'll meet you in the front parking garage."

"Sure, and I'll give you a lift back."

"No, absolutely not. I'll take the bus. I'll also be taking the railway bus to Pietermartizburg in the next few days. Goodbye now."

She removed her mask and kissed him long and tenderly before she walked out the door.

CHAPTER

FIFTEEN

He'd climbed behind the wheel at the first sight of Chantal's Triumph Spitfire sports car. Naturally, he'd only had to plead with her a little to let him drive. Now he exited the hospital grounds and pulled into Erskine Terrace, thrilling at the throaty roar from the exhaust.

He stopped at the first robot in Smith St. "I wanted to thank you for swapping places with Gail. That was so nice of you. You might've got into a lot of trouble."

"Only a pleasure," Chantal answered, patting his hand on the steering wheel. "There were no problems for me at all."

"Obviously, Dr. Spence didn't report you. He caught on, you know. He told us so as he left, after forcing Gail to take my blood pressure."

Chantal giggled. "Poor girl, he must have terrified her."

"For sure, she was frantic he'd figure out she was a Coloured."

"As he did. No, Dr. Spence is a real sport and especially active in the Progressive Party. Luckily, you didn't get Dr. Swanepoel. He's a National Party follower who'd have her arrested on the spot."

A shudder travelled through Ed's body. "So Doctor Spence didn't care?"

"Heavens, no. He believes in change. If he got his way, he'd eliminate apartheid in the hospital." She sighed. "If only the progressives could gain control."

"Fat chance of that! With the Nats being in for over twenty years. Even the United Party has no chance."

"Hmmm. True, I don't suppose the UP is likely to change things, not immediately at any rate." She shook her head at the floor.

Ed slowed the car, scanning the shop windows. "Here we are. Sterns. Let's hope we find a parking spot."

"Quick, someone's moving out there. Grab it." Chantal urged.

Ed drove straight into the parking bay, easy in the little Spitfire, and rushed round to open the passenger door for her. "There is a little time on the meter, but I'll add ten cents. I suspect this will take quite some time."

Hooking her arm through his, they walked back toward the shop.

"Thanks, Ed. You're a proper gentleman."

A portly, elderly gentleman in a tuxedo greeted them as they stepped through the entrance. "Good morning, sir, ma'am. What can I help you with today?"

Ed exchanged a glance with Chantal. "We'd like to look at some engagement rings, please."

"Certainly, sir. I can assist you, and may I say congratulations to the happy couple?"

"Why, thank you so much." Chantal winked broadly at Ed.

Ed grinned, and she gave him a ravishing smile in return, tightening her hand in the crook of his arm.

"You are more than welcome. My name is Tom Hammersley, and here at Sterns we like to match every couple with the perfect ring for the lucky bride. Er…of course, we have a broad range of prices to suit every pocket." He paused, lifting a brow while looking at Ed.

"Oh. Actually, I hadn't thought much about price." Now he thought about it. He didn't want to be a cheapskate, but neither did he want to become bankrupt.

"Of course, sir, we could discuss that matter in my office while your bride-to-be looks around…"

"No worries." Chantal waved at him as she walked ahead. "You choose whatever price you like, Ed. I'll be sure to tell you if you dip into the tacky range." She wrinkled her nose and grinned smugly.

"Well, let's see." He earned around four hundred a month. "Um, how about around five hundred rand?"

"Absolutely, sir, follow me." He headed toward a glass cabinet, withdrew a set of keys from his pocket, and inserted one, frowning.

"Do you think it isn't enough?"

Tom smiled. "Not at all. Quite generous, in fact, and should get you at least a half carat, maybe more. No girl could ask for more from a working man." He produced a tray which displayed a varied assortment of rings.

Chantal returned, her chin resting in her propped-up palm on the counter, her eyes ever widening.

Ed had no clue how to select from the vast array of sparkling diamonds. "Well? What's your opinion?"

"This is reeeally hard." Chantal frowned, her hand hovering over several. "Say! Wait a minute. Oooh yesss. This is the one. Oh, Ed. This one is perfect! This will suit her—um—me, to a T. No contest, it's divine."

The one she selected had a sizeable round diamond in the centre of a circle of smaller diamonds, with four blue sapphires inset symmetrically at the top, bottom and sides. He reached for the ring and studied it close up. Yes, this was more than beautiful—exquisite. How could she not like one with such allure? Chantal entwined her fingers under her chin, her mouth open, scarcely breathing.

"An admirable choice if you don't mind my saying so," Mr. Hammersley enthused. "The little sapphires add a touching accent to the central diamond. Your bride made an excellent choice indeed."

Ed held Chantal's hand. "Why don't we try it on?" he said, slipping the ring on her finger.

"This one's superb, truly. Unquestionably. You wanted me to choose, I have, end of story." Her eyes glinted as she stared at the ring. She peered back into Ed's face. "This will warm any bride's heart."

Tom cleared his throat. "I should mention this piece is slightly above the price you suggested, sir, but it's a bargain at only six hundred and forty-nine rand. Would that suit you?"

Ed swallowed. Nearly two months' salary, but Gail was worth every penny.

"I'll take it," he said.

"Oh, Ed. I'm so happy." Chantal squealed in delight.

*****

Another huge secret. Ed wasn't giving her any inkling of where they would be going, but she gathered it was somewhere special. He had advised her to dress up in something appropriate. Typical Ed. What was appropriate for a place she knew nothing about?

Early Saturday morning, Candy, bubbling with excitement, took her shopping. Candy held a dim view of the shops in the Coloured and Indian areas, insisting they go to the large White stores.

They entered one named Regal Gowns. The electric door closed behind them, shutting out the traffic noise. Gail couldn't even hear her own footsteps on the thick red carpet. Beautiful, lifelike models stood on elevated pedestals at every corner of the aisles, adorned with flowing dresses. Sales ladies, possibly outnumbering customers, gazed at them as they passed.

Gail stopped in front of a reasonable-looking long gown, red and velvety, and fingered the price tag for a few moments without daring to peek at the amount. "Candy, couldn't we rather go to Woolworth's or the OK Bazaars?"

Candy's gaze shifted between Gail and the gown and sighed. "Man, that would only look so larney on y'oll."

Finally, Gail glanced down at the amount. She whistled softly and shuddered. "Hmm. I'm sure something from Woolies will be every bit as nice. No amount of money is going to change my looks."

"Ag, no ways, Gail. Y'oll be beautiful in anything. 'Kay, let's joll to Woolies and see what they got."

They hurried out past the expressionless sales ladies, who ignored them. One of them called out, "Thank you for shopping at Regal Gowns."

Well, that had worked out well. Those White women doubtless had plenty of spending money. Undeterred, they set off for Woolworths, a long walk, past the city hall, from which point all the businesses were White-owned. Here, it didn't matter what you were—Coloured, Indian, White or Black—as long as you had money to spend. You could stand shoulder to shoulder with a White person and, as Candy so cutely put it, none of your colour would rub off on them. Yet if you set foot inside a cinema, theatre or restaurant, you'd be promptly arrested. Here they were walking among Whites, yet they ignored you. Well, most of the time perhaps, she thought, noticing the high school boy in his rugby uniform, giving her the once over.

Candy covered her mouth. "He's only checking you out, hey?"

They entered Woolworth's and strode to the escalators. A White guy arrived at the same pace but from a different angle. Watch this. She prepared to stop, but, wonder of wonders, he stood aside and gestured. She flashed him a smile as she and Candy entered. This was a confusing world.

There it was, right at the beginning of the ladies' department. Perfect. A royal blue evening gown on a window dummy. Slim fitting, down to the ankles, with a broad, matching belt. A conservative V-shaped neckline and half-inch choker showed off the model's graceful neck. Its translucent, powder blue sleeves billowed down into snug, dark-blue cuffs at the wrists.

She fixed her gaze on the outfit. "I want that, whatever the cost."

A middle-aged saleslady in a dark suit materialised at her side as if summoned by a spell. "That will suit you perfectly, miss. Would you care to try it on?"

She hesitated for a fraction of a second. It looked too expensive. Maybe she'd ask the price after trying it on. The saleslady clasped her hands and observed Gail's figure with one eye closed. "I'll fetch one in your size."

She returned with the dress, and Gail headed into a change booth with Candy.

"Ag, why y'oll bothering. Of course, it'll fit, hey. Y'oll got a window dummy figure."

The fit was perfect. Gail twisted and turned as she observed the gown. Ed would love this. Candy certainly did, staring with big eyes, palms against cheeks, mouth open.

"Yeslike, Gail," said Candy. "Y'oll so gorgeous. Ed's gonna freak, ou."

CHAPTER
SIXTEEN

Gail answered the door later that afternoon. Ed's hand remained frozen after its second attempt at ringing the doorbell, yet his eyes were darting all over her.

She reached out her hand and tugged him over the threshold. "Oh my! I like that," she said, stepping back, taking in his three-piece suit. It was different. This one was medium blue with a waistcoat. Judging by the crisp look and "new" smell, he'd just bought it. "You do clean up so nicely, I must say. And you brought flowers? Proteas, they're beautiful…thank you." Leaning forward, she planted a kiss on his lips. "Though, isn't that overdoing it a tad for the Highway Drive-in?"

"Is that what you think? I planned something else for tonight."

She searched his face. "Really? That is fantastic, but is it legal?" she said, pulling her mouth tight.

"Most likely not, but very secure."

She opened her mouth, but he put his index finger on her lips. "No, no details. It's a surprise."

"But, Ed, did you seriously believe I'd pack something to wear that goes with your spiffy outfit?"

Ed's eyebrows jumped up and his smile vanished.

"Relax. If you could see your face." She giggled. "I got something appropriate, with Candy's help. Would I want you to date a frumpy girl?"

His body relaxed. She peered closely at his wound. "Your stitches, I only notice them now I'm close. What an outstanding job Chantal did. When will they take them out?"

"Seems they simply dissolve on their own or something. Chantal told me all about them, but being me, I didn't pay much attention."

She punched him playfully on his shoulder. "That better not be because you were paying her too much attention. She is kind of beautiful."

"Her eyes are exactly like yours."

"No bluffs! I know. Isn't it amazing? The moment she met me, she realised she could smuggle me in, posing as her."

He laughed. "I'll never forget the look in your eyes when the doctor made you test my blood pressure. Who knew he was aware of Chantal's switch?"

*****

They walked into the living room together, where Candy introduced him to her mother and father. Her mother, Ria, as pretty as her daughter, had short, dark brown hair. Her father, Leonard, contrasted starkly with tiny Candy, by being well over six feet tall and almost as broad, and three hundred pounds if he were an ounce. He gripped Ed's hand tightly, and Ed was more than relieved when he didn't crush it. All of them were completely welcoming, but would he ever have met them if not for Gail's presence?

"Please," said Ria. "Sit down. I'll bring the tea."

"And I," said Gail, pointing to her slacks and T-shirt, "had better change into something that will match my well-dressed boyfriend. I assume we'll be leaving soon?"

Ed glanced at his wristwatch and pursed his lips. "I'm so sorry about that. I realise I'm early for a dressy date, but my hands were tied as to the time. I do apologise."

"Not a problem. I can't wait to know what you've got in store for us." She waved a hand as she hurried into a bedroom.

Ed enjoyed his time waiting; Candy's parents were delightful.

Candy sat and eyed him with barely hidden glee. "So where y'oll going?" In fact, she looked as if she'd bust if he didn't tell her.

"That," he scolded, "is my secret, and there's no way you'll dig it out of me, Candy, so don't you try."

She pouted, though her eyes twinkled. "Mr. Brent, you can tell me. I won't tell her." She winked as she tilted her head towards the door Gail had passed through.

*****

Candy's prediction was evidently correct, judging by Ed's expression when Gail stepped through the bedroom door.

"Gail, that's…it's…" His mouth clammed shut.

"Strange?… Flashy?… Tacky?… Hideous?"

He blinked. "*Exquisite…magnifique…éblouissante.*"

"Huh? You're a Frenchman now? *Mais, que signifie éblouissante?*"

"I don't know. English is inadequate to describe what I'm seeing. There are no words…"

She reached up and entwined her fingers behind his neck. "Well, Ed. I'm wondering…why bother putting it into…words." By this time, his mouth was mere inches away, his fiery breath on her lips as they inched closer, her own lips parting as—

"What d'y'oll think Ed? She's sommer smashing, hey." Gail opened her eyes and saw Candy's grinning face.

Ed pulled back, still watching Gail with an intent gaze. "She most definitely is, Candy. Sommer smashing."

"Yeslike, ou. Y'olls made for each other, hey?"

Gail couldn't argue with that, though the sentiment had broken the mood. Apparently for Ed, too.

It was early for a conventional date. The sun hadn't yet set, and Gail wondered for the umpteenth time where they were headed. Ed drove along Church Street, remaining mum despite her pleading. He slowed the car as they reached the ill-defined area shared by Indian and White entrepreneurs. She peered all round to see what their destination might be.

"Ah, here's one," said Ed, manouvering into a parking space, looking over his left shoulder as he spun the wheel.

Impressive, he got it first time. She always had trouble with parallel parking.

He walked round and opened her door. A green bus hurtled past, and an African man ran towards the bus stop ahead. Without waiting, Ed took off ahead of the car, shouting at him. What in the world? Had he stolen something? It took only a few moments for him to reach and slap the shoulder of the man, who skidded to a stop and swung round, panic crossing his face.

Surely, Ed had seen the man picking a pocket or shoplifting. Instead, Ed held up something resembling a big wallet. Of course, the man's passbook, he must have dropped it. The man's face showed a series of strong emotions; surprise, disbelief, heartfelt relief and intense, passionate gratitude.

"*Hauw! Ngiyabonga Mnumzane.* Thank you, *baasie,* thank you."

"*Kulungile,*" Ed answered. "Okay. Lucky I saw it."

"*Hauw!* How can I thank you, *Mnumzane?*"

Of course. It was nearly sunset, being caught in town at night without his passbook would mean immediate jail time. And who knew for how long? She could imagine the relief he must be feeling.

Ed patted the man's shoulder. "No problem. Now you must hurry, or you'll miss your bus." He pointed at the quickly diminishing queue of passengers boarding. It was probably the last one he could take. "Go well, *Mnumzane. Hamba kahle.*"

"Yebo. Stay well, *hlala kahle.* Thank you, sir, thank you." He backed away toward the bus, waving and repeating his thank-yous. Just in time, he rushed through the door, still waving. The bus pulled off in a cloud of black diesel fumes.

Ed jogged back. She sighed as she looked at him. She knew White men, and Coloured men, who would've ignored the passbook, or kicked it into the gutter, or checked for money and thrown the rest away. Clearly, Ed was a gentleman.

He opened the door fully and extended his hand. "Sorry about that."

"Sorry? Why? Are you sorry you saved him from arrest and abuse?" She took his arm as he shut the door. "I'm so glad you're what you are, Ed. Gentlemen like you are few."

He broke into a grin. "A diamond in the rough, that's me hey, Mary Poppins?"

They both chuckled as she placed her hand in the crook of his arm, and he led her along the pavement.

*****

"Here we are," Ed announced in triumph when they reached a storefront. A very ordinary front, with shop windows covered by boxes piled high and tables covered with fruit and vegetable displays. The aroma of Indian curries and herbs wafted from the interior.

She stared at him, one eyebrow raised, the cute little upside-down smile indicating she thought he was insane.

Ed waved his hand toward the displays and the mess. "Okay, it doesn't look like much yet, but just you wait."

"Ah, Mr. Brent." Ed's Indian friend met them as they passed through the door. He looked uncustomarily smart in a double-breasted suit with matching bowtie. Obviously, he had taken the trouble to comb his unkempt bush of jet-black hair with a lot of gel.

"Howzit, Naidoo?" Ed greeted him with a warm handshake. "How are you doing? Long time, no see."

"Yes, indeed, sah. Please come in. I have an exceptional room for you to dine in. Impeccable, only for you two."

Ed put his hand on Gail's waist. "Gail, meet my good friend, Naidoo. He likes to be called by his surname. He's always giving me the best offers of whatever he sells, and tonight, the store is ours. Naidoo, meet Gail."

"Good evening, Miss Gail. You are very much welcome. A friend of Mr. Brent's is a friend of mine. Please come in." He stepped back, bowing and gesturing with a sweep of his hand.

"Pleased to meet you," she said, looking around the room with interest.

"As am I, Miss Gail. I am happy to meet you. I hear much about you from Mr. Brent."

Gail fixed Ed with a faux frown. "Not bad things, I hope." She winked at Ed.

"Of course, of course." Naidoo nodded briskly. "Only the best things."

He led them through his shop. "I am hoping the two of you will be happy with the room."

Naidoo held aside part of a curtain of hanging, multicoloured bead strips, and stood aside to reveal a small but cosy room, bright with yellow and orange pompom strips hanging in graceful arches on the rear wall. At its centre stood a small table, covered with a white tablecloth already set with two places opposite each other. Tall candles were burning in elaborate brass candlesticks on the table.

Ed scanned the room. "This is decidedly romantic, isn't it, Gail? Naidoo's done a fantastic job for us." He watched her eyes darting all around the room, taking in everything. Her wide, open-mouthed grin told him what he wanted to know.

Naidoo bowed, his grin revealing bright white teeth. "Nobody will be disturbing you here, except for the waiter. Anything you need, anything at all, and you only have to be ringing this bell." He pressed a button in the centre of the table, and a buzzer sounded in the main shop. Ed thanked him and tucked a twenty into his palm.

"Thank you, Mr. Naidoo." Gail beamed one of her brightest smiles.

Naidoo bowed and exited backwards while Ed pulled a chair out for her. Gail regarded him with warmth as she sidled onto the chair. "What a surprise! How on earth did you arrange this? Are you sure we're safe, though? What if the cops raid this place? Can we trust Naidoo?"

"Whoa!" Ed raised his hands. "One question at a time, please."

She sat down as he pushed her chair in for her. "On second thoughts, forget the questions," she said. "I don't want to worry. This room is perfect."

"I put a lot of business Naidoo's way," he explained. "And vice versa. I'm quite confident we'll be safe here tonight."

Gail leaned forward with her chin resting on both fists. He loved when she did that, especially now that her eyes sparkled in a tension-free way he'd never seen on their other dates.

He reached forward to take her fists in his hands, bringing them to his lips. "This is what you deserve, not fighting to get you into places that won't let you in, nor sitting in my car, watching a film at the drive-in. You deserve so much more."

Whenever she smiled, her eyes narrowed and curved gently up at the outer ends. What wouldn't he do to make that smile materialise? How long they kept looking into each other's eyes he didn't know, but he never wanted it to stop. If only he might do so whenever he wanted and forever. It was she who broke the moment's magic. She coloured a little and lowered her eyes. Embarrassed, or maybe something else? Doubt, maybe.

"We should order," she said.

Ed hit the button. At once, a waiter popped up, neatly dressed in proper attire. It was clear Naidoo had gone the extra mile, even procuring his outfit specially for tonight.

"Good evening, sah. Good evening, madam. My name is Bobby. Here is our menu and drink list."

Gail scanned her menu with a frown. "Ah, here it is." Her expression lit up. "Biryani. I had that at an Indian wedding once. I love it, don't you?"

"You bet I do," he answered, studying her instead of the menu. "Could you bring us two of those please, Bobby?"

"Yes, sah. Thank you, sah," said Bobby. "And to drink?"

Gail shook her head. "I don't drink alcohol, a ginger beer for me, thanks."

"Certainly, madam, and do you like your curry strong, medium or weak?"

"I haven't the faintest idea. How strong is your strong?"

Ed broke in. "Enough to make your mouth produce steam."

The waiter laughed. "That is true. The curry can be a bit too much if you are not an Indian, madam. I suggest mild."

"Agreed," said Ed. "Mild is still plenty strong for us." Was he doing the right thing by lumping the two of them together as "us?" But it sounded right. Just two people in love, no us or them.

"Fine, I'll take the mild. I'm sure it will be just right." She smiled at Bobby, who exited with a spring in his step.

One glance at the waiter's smiling face told him she had an effect on him too. One smile made him happy. Indian, White, Coloured,

Black, she could charm everyone with a mere glance or word. He held her hands across the table.

Ed scarcely paid attention to the meal; Naidoo's food was always delicious, it was a given. He concentrated his attention on Gail, her delight and the way she exclaimed over each dish. She finished the last spoonful of the delicious Indian ice cream, reached for his hand, and beamed. "Ed, you're a genius."

Ed chuckled. "It took you this long to reach that conclusion?" But he relished the compliments that followed on the meal, Naidoo and Bobby, and of course, himself.

"Are you really having an enjoyable time?" he asked, looking straight into her eyes.

She laughed. "Of course, I am. Didn't I make that quite clear?"

"I can't tell you how much I enjoyed it all, but specifically your company, Gail. There is no person on earth I'd rather be with, and right here, in Naidoo's shop, in this little room."

She said nothing but merely glowed. A light leading him on his path. A warmth to confirm his true desire. The moment had come.

"Gail," he murmured. "I love you with every thought I have. I can't bear being without you. Life could never be complete." He got on his knee and withdrew the box, opened it, and tugged at the ring. "Will you please accept my proposal?" He lifted her hand and held the ring up. "Will you marry me?"

*****

Never had Gail imagined such a ring. Her eyes widened, so did her mouth. "Ed, this is so…beautiful. I've never seen anything so wonderful. This must've cost you a fortune." How could he spend so much money? On her. She bit her lip. *He actually wants to marry me.*

"Um. Is that a yes?"

She blinked, aware of how long she stared mutely at the ring. "No. I mean, yes…no. I'm not sure." She tore her gaze from the ring back to Ed's face. "Ed, what were you thinking?"

"Well, having you as my lifelong partner in marriage is the general idea," he replied, still on his knee.

She looked from him to the ring, which she studied for a while, then back to his face. She frowned. "Tell me, in marriage, what is the first thing that comes to your mind? Now."

He didn't hesitate. "House. That is, home, sharing a home."

She blinked rapidly and a tear spilled onto her cheek. "That sounds like the correct answer. But now…where will this house be?"

"Gail." He breathed in a deep breath. "I realise this marriage won't be normal right away. I don't have a clue where we'd live. But I want you to understand that this proposal is my commitment. Somehow, somewhere, sometime, I am determined we'll live together as a married couple, in our own home."

Gail's blinking couldn't stop the flow of tears over her cheeks. Ed really wanted to marry her. He had accepted it as a challenge. He had thrown his gauntlet down at apartheid's feet. Should she let him do such a thing? On his own? No, they must share the gauntlet and meet the challenge together. "Ed, of course, I will. I accept and echo your commitment."

She allowed him to slip the ring onto her finger. It fit as if made for her. She faced him with a frown. "How come you know my size?"

He smirked. "A simple phone call to your closest relative."

"Mom? She never said…"

"A simple threat that if she didn't agree…" He paused and grinned. "No, all bluffs. She took it extremely well when I explained, and she promised to keep mum about it."

Gail moved her hand, observing the ring from every angle. "I'm most impressed that you chose such a perfect ring on your own, being a man and all." She fastened her eyes on his. "You got help from a woman, didn't you?"

He coughed but made no reply other than a grin and a wink.

CHAPTER
SEVENTEEN

Mark shook his head and peered at Ed over his glasses. He sat down on the stool behind Cahill's film counter.

"I was afraid you'd take that approach, Ed," he said. "You do realise, of course, that what you're planning is plainly and simply illegal."

"I know. It's against the law. We couldn't even marry in a registry office. So we're going to marry in a church."

"A church? Dear boy, what's the difference what building you use? It's still against the law. What is it about the word you don't understand?"

"It means in the eyes of the law we wouldn't be married. There's nothing at all we can do about that, but if we married in a church, we'd be recognised by the church. We're both okay with that."

Mark leaned against the counter, holding his head in his hands and pursing his lips. "But where on earth would you live? Somewhere other than South Africa, I assume."

"We'll figure out something." Ed gazed at the floor.

Mark stroked his beard. "And in the meantime, you'll be living apart. What kind of a marriage is that?"

"It's our commitment to each other, that we are intended for each other, and someday, somehow we'll be together. I can't explain it any other way, Mark. I know you think I'm crazy."

Mark held up one hand and surreptitiously lifted a finger to his lips. Too late!

"Crazy isn't the word." It was Dolores again, sticking her nose in where it wasn't wanted. From her position squatting at the photo albums while taking stock, she'd evidently heard the conversation. "This will end badly. I've seen it!"

Ed glared her way. "You haven't seen something that hasn't happened yet. And it's my wedding, not yours."

"Fine, have it your way." Dolores pencilled in something on her clipboard and shook her head. "It's your head. This will end in trouble, I tell you. You mix with that kind and you'll see. They're troublemakers. She's after your money. They're not like us."

"What money? I work in a retail photo shop. Salary and commission, I can barely support myself. I'm hardly a prize catch for a gold digger."

"Just leave him alone, Dolores," Mark broke in, frowning. "It's his own neck. And hers, of course. If he wants to get married and still live alone, let him do it."

"Then I'll take that as your blessing, Mark." Ed smiled, in spite of the gnawing in the pit of his stomach.

"Yes, take it. I can't talk sense into that head of yours anyway." Mark scratched his beard and stared solemnly for a moment. "Well then, if you're going through with this wedding, when do you plan on having it?"

"Gail and Candy have talked to Candy's minister. Saturday next week." He had to grin at Mark's open-mouthed expression. "I take it your disapproval of my wedding won't stop you from being my best man. I can't do this alone."

Mark gave a start and broke into a huge grin. "Thanks, old boy, I wouldn't miss it for the world." He held his thumb up as he added. "I'll borrow one of the Graflex cameras and take some pictures. I think Will is all booked up for weddings next Saturday."

"Great. Pictures are important," Ed said soberly. "They might be all we'll have for a while."

Mark grinned. "And what delectable piece of female pulchritude will be standing next to me, might I ask?"

Ed chuckled. "That would be Chantal, the gorgeous nurse who sewed me up and brought me back to life. And before you look askance at me that way, you should know it was actually Gail's idea. Chantal is the one who managed to get her into the hospital. They're friends now. Of course, Candy and her parents will be there, especially since she persuaded the minister to do this White man's wedding at her church in spite of potential problems. Also, Pamela will join us. But other than you and Gail's mom, that's all."

"What about your folks?"

"They live in Mosell Bay and, well, let's just say they declined the invitation and leave it at that." Ed twisted his mouth and looked at his feet.

"Oh. Like that hey? Sorry, Ed."

*****

Panic rose in Gail's chest. She shouted into the receiver. "Mom, tell me exactly what happened."

"Nick threatened me, Gail. I'm scared. That boy is dangerous. I'm afraid for you."

"Never mind that now, Mom." Gail raked a hand through her hair, then gripped the phone tightly. "What exactly did he do?"

"He wanted to find Ed. Nick threatened he'd do awful things if I didn't tell him where he was. But I don't even know where Ed is."

A quick huff escaped her. "Good. Does he know where Ed works?"

"I don't think so. He asked me that question, but I don't know either. But, Gail, it's you I'm really worried about."

"Why, Mom? Why me? You don't mean…"

There was no reply. Gail shouted into the mouthpiece. "You told him where I'm staying, didn't you?" Still no response. She could visualise her face, tearful, nodding, red eyed…"Okay, look, Mom. You're coming to our wedding next week. I'll speak with the others and see if they can put you up earlier. Otherwise, I'll book you into an hotel. You can't stay home right now. It's too dangerous."

"You'll come and get me?" Her voice was barely audible.

"No, I want you gone from there as soon as possible, and I don't think I could arrange for a car. Now listen. Pack a suitcase with some clothes and the things you'll need for next week and call a taxi immediately. In fact, call the taxi first, then pack. They take ages getting there. Go straight to the station and catch the next train for 'Maritzburg. Phone me from the station the moment you have the details. Get it?"

"Got it."

"Good. We'll pick you up from the station when you arrive."

"What about you? I'm scared for you. What if Nick comes and tries to bully you about where Ed is?"

"You just get here as soon as you can, Mom."

*****

Ed replaced the phone with a bang, his hair bristling at the back of his neck.

Mark hurried over. "What's wrong, Ed? You're as white as a sheet."

"That was Gail," Ed replied, pursing his lips. "That character who beat me up with his gang, he knows where Gail is staying. He's looking for me."

"What? Again? You'd better get the police onto him, quickly."

"No. Not a chance! Those boys in khaki will be far more interested in what I am doing with a Coloured girlfriend. No. I'll have to handle this myself."

Mark looked at his wristwatch. "Quarter past one," he said. "You want the afternoon off?"

"I sure do. Do me a favour, Mark, phone Mommy and tell her I had a family emergency, or something."

"No problem, old sport. I'll fix that. You shoot off now and go protect your fiancé."

Ed was already at the door. "Thanks, Mark." He ran to his car and stomped on the accelerator immediately. After screeching to a halt in front of Candy's house, he tried to make sense of the scene in the front yard. Candy's father, all three hundred plus pounds and six and a half feet of him, stood outside the front door. Halfway between him and the gate stood Gail, arms folded high against her chest. And at the gate, he recognised Nick, the Coloured man who had confronted him that night outside Gail's house, now with red eyes, his

130

mouth hanging open, and his right arm hanging limply at his side. Blood was pouring from his nose. Ed's gaze flicked from him, back to Gail, and then to Leonard. Ed tipped his fingers in a salute.

"No, it wasn't Leonard." Gail looked back at him. "He's a Teddy bear."

Leonard shook his head rapidly. "Yes, not me," he said, holding his palms out in front of him. "I couldn't believe how that ou came short, hey. Gail's sommer like lightning. One two three and the ou doesn't know what hit him, *ek sê*." He grinned from ear to ear.

Gail smiled her crooked little smile. She rubbed her right-hand fingernails against her chest, then blew on them. "Jiu-jitsu, remember?"

Ed sidled past Nick, who at that moment collapsed on the pathway, and circled his arms round Gail. "You didn't even need me," he said, his left hand cupping the back of her head. He kissed her long and hard, savouring the taste of her lips. The kiss was more for his own reassurance, and it worked, dispelling the anguish he'd been experiencing ever since her phone call.

EIGHTEEN

Loud raps sounded on the door of Candy's house, approximating the tune of "Here Comes the Bride."

Gail ran and snatched the door open. "Chantal, bright and early."

"You bet." Chantal held an armful of packages. "So much to do, so little time. It'll take hours getting you looking halfway decent." She grinned, wrinkling her nose. "This must be Candy, if my guess isn't wrong."

Candy held out her hand, grinning. "Hi, Chantal. Pleased to meet you."

"Me too, but just a sec, till somebody takes this stuff from me."

"You made the dresses? Oh, Chantal, you shouldn't have," said Gail. "But thank you so much. They'll be thrilled. Or do they already know? One of them must have given you their sizes." Pamela joined the others at the door, and Gail frowned at both of them.

Candy ignored her. "Yeslike, ou!" She took the dresses from Chantal's arms. "They're only beautiful, thanks hey!"

They were indeed. Straight, with a high belt, all in a delicate baby blue shade, but with white lace sleeves that would fit loosely around the arms with another ring of the same blue securing the wrists and a similar piece at the neck. A white lace frill spread in a loop from shoulder to shoulder.

"Don't mention it. Now hurry, I might need to make alterations."

The two girls dashed off with the dresses, and Gail hugged her new friend. "I'm so glad you're doing this, Chantal, there was really—"

"No speeches, save that for later. Let's get to work on you."

They walked through to the bedroom, Gail introducing her to Leonard and Ria on the way.

Chantal rushed her into the bedroom and plunked her down onto the chair in front of the dressing table. Pamela got straight to work applying base makeup, enhancing her lips and cheekbones and brightening her eyes. Gail admired Pamela's skill as she touched up her eyelashes with black mascara, added a hint of colour to her eyelids and a gentle rose-coloured blush to her cheeks. She blinked. Pamela had transformed her face in a matter of minutes. Gail leaned forward to inspect herself. "That's beautiful, Pamela. I actually look pretty."

Candy snorted. "Y'oll always beautiful." She inspected Pamela's work from up close. "But ja, she knows what she's doing, hey?"

Chantal had been working on the wedding gown and now held it in her arms. "She sure does, thank heaven for that. My makeup skills are limited to smearing on a bit of lipstick and then spending a lot of time on wiping most of it off with a tissue. But let's get you into this dress now." She helped her fit and adjust her dress and veil.

The modest, silky-white dress clung to her figure, then swept down in a puddle around her feet. Its gauzy, luminous sleeves billowed at the shoulders and tapered like flowing water to her wrists. Gail couldn't see the whole dress in the mirror, but Candy and Pamela oohed and aahed enough to let her know it would more than pass.

Chantal seated her on the chair again and started work on her hair. She tried not to frown as Chantal twisted up the thick locks into a loose bun on top, leaving the bangs straight, but curling two trailing wisps around her face. She placed a broad white ribbon just below the bun to help hold her veil. "There it is, Bob's your uncle!"

Gail stood and moved back from the chair. Candy clapped her hands, then held her cheeks, and Pamela stood grinning with both thumbs up. Chantal stepped back, hands on hips, frowning. "I think that will do. It was a heck of a job getting you looking passable, Gail." She winked. "Seriously though, you look absolutely gorgeous."

As she studied herself in the mirror, Gail had to admit her hair and makeup were beautiful. She felt beautiful. *I hope Ed will think so.*

Gail stared out the window of the dressing room of the church. The afternoon had turned cold and rainy, not exactly what Gail would have dreamed for her wedding. Still, not everything could be perfect. Like having no friends or relatives, apart from her mom, at her own wedding. There had been so little time. Besides, there was no knowing how they would take to a mixed-race wedding. She knew Ed thought the same. His parents lived in Mossel Bay, and they'd said they were unable to come at such short notice.

Or perhaps there was another reason they didn't want to come. Mossel Bay, she remembered being there once when she was little. A lovely little town, perfect. A nice place to spend some time, perhaps with his parents later. Or maybe sooner. Ed had said nothing about a honeymoon, and she'd dismissed the idea as impractical in the circumstances, but what if Ed planned to go there. A honeymoon, a huge beach, a lagoon, a room to stay in his parents' house. How perfect that would be.

"Mom, please stop fussing with my veil. It's fine." Were the butterflies flying around in her stomach normal, or reserved only for those brides who were marrying illegally? "I'm sorry, Mom. I didn't mean to snap at you."

Her mom continued messing about with her hair. "I just want you looking your best, dear, even if it's a pretend wedding."

Gail suppressed a sigh of relief when Mark entered the room with a large camera with attached electronic flash. "I'll take care of her from now, Mrs. Rabe," he said. "Gail, you look stupendous. We'll get some splendid pictures. A pity outdoor shots won't be possible today if this rain keeps up. It's really hosing out there."

A blinding flash startled her. Mark chuckled. "I couldn't resist your expression while you fiddled with your veil."

She supposed he knew what he was doing.

She pulled Mark to the others and introduced him to Chantal, whose eyes widened as they shook hands.

"More than delighted," Mark said, with his special grin that made him seem he was laughing. He held onto Chantal's hand far longer than was necessary.

She smiled, while her eyes darted all over Mark. "Charmed. Pleased to meet you."

When their handshake broke apart at last, Mark got back to work. Gail allowed him to boss her around. "Tilt your head a bit more, so. Pleasant smile now, that's it. Beautiful!" Flash. "Now with your mom, let's hold hands together, that's it! Perfect." Flash. She watched in fascination at the speed with which he removed and replaced the dark slide in the film holder and turned it around for the next picture. "Now, same again, this way, both of you. Yes."

He took several more pictures of Gail with her mom, then turned to Chantal. "And now with the bridesmaids, let's have you here, next to Chantal. Aren't these ladies gorgeous? Lovely dresses."

Candy looked from Mark to Chantal and back. "Chantal made them."

"Really?" Mark returned his gaze to Chantal. "That's serious work. I'm impressed. And it looks delightful on you."

Chantal smiled and tilted her head down, her cheeks reddening. Flash.

Gail grinned. These two could make a good pair. How delightful if the four of them could do things together. Mark had Chantal by the window, posing her, and taking photos lit by the window only. But now it was Gail's turn, and, with apparent reluctance, he parted from Chantal. He led her to the window for a series of close-ups.

Gail's mom hurried up from the doorway. "I think everybody's here. Your friend, Jane, and Janet from your work, all of Candy's family, Mrs. Cahill and her kids, some guy I imagine is Pamela's boyfriend, and finally, a friend of Pamela's. Will is doing another wedding, and Dolores declined the invitation."

Gail shrugged. "Not much of a crowd, hey?"

"Well, what do you expect with such short notice?"

Quite apart from the fact that Gail wanted this wedding to be small. Mixing a large number of Whites and Coloureds together under one roof to celebrate an illegal wedding wasn't perhaps the wisest plan. Yes, the tiny congregation would look silly in this church, much bigger than the church they usually attended in Durban.

Mark was all finished after not more than a quarter of an hour. He bowed to them, his eyes wandering again over Chantal. "Well, ladies, if you'll excuse me, I must get ready for my part in this. I'll see you in a bit. Cheers for now."

"Oooh, yes." Chantal kept her eyes fastened on his retreating figure. "The balding head on such a young guy, it's fascinating, especially with the beard, not bad at all. I could go for him, Gail, as true as Bob, hey!"

Gail grinned at her. "Maybe you'll be the bride next."

"Huh! About time! Do you realise I'm twenty-seven and still no ring?" She lifted her left hand and wiggled her fingers.

"Well, you could do a lot worse than Mark. Go for it!"

Pastor Hendricks knocked and popped his head round the open door. He was a dark-complexioned Coloured man, greying at the temples. "Good morning, ladies, is everybody ready?"

A shiver ran down her spine and something like an icy hand gripped her heart. This was it. She inclined her head.

"Excellent. Now, it's my duty to remind you, Miss Rabe, that your marriage will not be legal in South Africa, and I'm afraid I can't register it as such, though anywhere else will accept it."

Gail bit her lip, would this mean she would be living in sin, like some other couples she knew of? She held her breath.

"However, let me assure you your marriage will be valid in the eyes of the church. There will be no sin in living together."

She released her breath in a long sigh.

"It is also my unpleasant duty to warn that there will be dangers for both of you from the police and government. Some segments of the police force are specifically required to root out all illicit interracial relations."

She nodded continually while he spoke.

"I assure you that, though it's such a small wedding, I shall use the full version of the service. And finally, though you both know your lives together will be difficult, if not impossible in the near future, I find the proclamations of the World Council of Churches and our own South African Council, together with their support, very encouraging. There will come a time when you and Mr. Brent will be able to live legally and free. My sincere hope is that it will be sooner rather than later.

It was time. She stood out of sight with her mom and the others in the vestibule, peeping through the gap in the door which gave them an unrestricted view of the church entrance. Her heart galloped as Ed walked with Mark into the entrance lobby, dressed in a neat and new three-piece suit. His blue eyes stood out, matched by the blue of his suit, and contrasting with his black hair. For once, he'd put something on it to control its unruliness. *My, but he's so handsome.*

Mark stopped to adjust Ed's tie. Gail could just make out the words, "This is it, old chap." The two men walked down the aisle and out of their sight.

Chantal took Gail's hands and gave them a near painful squeeze. "Gail, you are so lucky." She beamed, her eyes twinkling. "At least for being his bride. I do hope you two will find a way, but now's not the time for that. Love will look after such an adorable pair."

"Thanks. I believe that." She couldn't help the tears running down her cheeks.

"Oh, Gail, you're ruining your mascara." Chantal found a tissue from somewhere and dabbed it on her eyes and cheeks. "We can't have that now. If you're going to be miserable, there's still time for us to change clothes and places." She raised an eyebrow.

"Not on your life." Gail punched her playfully on her shoulder. "Hands off. He's mine."

Chantal inspected her repair work on Gail's face and grinned. "That's the spirit! Anyway, I've changed my mind. You can keep Ed after all. I've set my sights on the best man."

Gail smiled at the apparent growing chemistry between the two.

"Time to go," Pamela said, knocking her fists together under her chin. Her teeth chattered. "Good luck, Gail."

They heard the organ start playing. "That's our cue," said Candy. The three girls wished her well, got into a line with Candy in front, and shuffled out to their places at the top of the aisle, from where they would glide down to the altar. Gail's mom hugged her tightly. Gail took several deep breaths and gripped her bouquet as if she were afraid it would be torn from her grasp.

At last they stood at the top of the aisle, Mendelsohn's wedding march played on the organ and Gail stiffened. Slowly, arm in arm with her mother, they glided down the aisle. The entire wedding party had their eyes fixed on her. She concentrated on steady, even steps, it wouldn't do to trip or stumble on those high heels. Her eyes focused on Ed's face, and she was calmed by his encouraging, expectant gaze, giving her the courage she needed to finish the long, nervous journey down the red carpet. With a tearful kiss on Gail's cheek, her mom departed and sat in the front pew with Candy's family.

Ed's face held a warmth she had never seen as he stepped down from the chancel and offered her his arm, which she gladly took, and they climbed up the steps together to face Pastor Hendricks.

He smiled and started the service. "Dearly beloved, we have come together…"

Gail watched the pastor while he spoke, but every time she stole a glance at Ed, he was staring at her with a smile. "Into this holy union, Gail Anna Rabe and Edward Heddwynn Brent now come to be joined. If any of you can show just cause why they may not lawfully be married…speak now or else forever hold your peace." He paused briefly, then took a breath to continue.

A sudden loud cough from behind them interrupted the proceedings. Everyone turned. Her heart jumped into her mouth, an immediate sensation of dread caused a shiver that spread all the way down her body. A man in the familiar khaki uniform of the police was striding down the aisle, tapping his baton into his hand.

"Sergeant Van Greuning, SAP." The man was tall, moustached, and spoke in a gravelly Afrikaans accent.

"Can I help you, sir?" Pastor Hendricks stared at him.

"Yes. You said I should speak if I knew just cause why these two should not…"—he coughed—"lawfully be married. Well, you do understand it isn't—uh—lawful in this country for a White man to marry a… Coloured woman."

CHAPTER

NINETEEN

Gail's heart stopped, and the blood drained from her face. The guests murmured loudly as they turned around and glared at the officer.

"Yes, I understand, as do the couple," Pastor Hendricks replied, his voice calm. "I have explained that this is a marriage with the blessing of the church only, not the…government."

Van Greuning frowned.

"Will you allow me to continue with the service, sir?" Pastor Hendricks continued.

Sergeant Van Greuning scowled at the three of them. "Fine," he said at last. "Go ahead with your…ceremony…but I will be speaking to this couple afterward."

A glance into Ed's eyes revealed he shared her worry. Her heart raced, not only with fear, but from her overwhelming love for him.

Pastor Hendricks turned his gaze back to them. "Do you, Gail Anna Rabe, of your own free will, take Edward Heddwynn Brent as your lawful, wedded husband, to love and honour as long as you both shall live?"

So he had kept his promise to do away with the "obey" clause. "I do indeed," she said.

Then it was his turn, he answered, "Most definitely, I do." Whatever he was feeling inside about the waiting police officer, she knew for certain he had his entire attention focused on her. A warmth crept over her heart, a strong calming influence. Whatever the consequences, she knew she had his complete love.

Trying to ignore the police officer who remained standing in the aisle, they managed getting through the vows and the rest of the ceremony, ending in, "You may now kiss your bride" from the pastor.

She barely heard the clapping and cheers from the small congregation, aware of nothing else beyond Ed's passionate kiss. The kiss told her they belonged together for better or worse despite the small voice in her head insisting it might very well be for worse. For much worse.

There were a few moments of happy congratulations from the wedding party at the altar before the wedding march started to play on the organ. She placed her hand in the crook of Ed's arm, and they set off up the aisle. The sergeant remained standing in their way, but Ed led them straight through without pause, forcing the officer to step aside.

At the curb, the guests sprinkled confetti and clapped and cheered, everyone ignoring Sergeant Van Greuning, who repeatedly edged closer. Mark, an experienced wedding photographer who knew how to deal with disruptive guests, shoved ahead of him and took more pictures, glaring at the officer whenever he tried pushing his way in.

Only when they sat on the back seat of the car, ready to drive off, did Sergeant Van Greuning succeed in reaching them. He yanked Gail's door open. "Let me make this quite clear, hey. I don't care if you got married in church, marriage between races is still illegal. Let me warn you, the Church won't stop the law. Even if you think you're married, remember this, you cannot live together. That is also against the law, and no religion will change that. I'll be watching you. Watch out, hey!"

The car moved away before he could say more, and Gail slammed the door. The fury on the officer's face triggered a sense of dread and sent her into Ed's comforting arms.

*****

Ed kissed Gail, leaned forward, and spoke to Mark in the driver's seat.

"Could you head to my place first? I have a few things there I need." Such as checking the post for a letter from his parents. He hadn't heard from them since he'd written and told them everything. It seemed he'd been plaguing them forever to get a phone. This was his last chance to check if they'd agreed to his honeymoon plans or hopes. He could see Gail, his wife, lying on the beautiful white sands of Mossel Bay, catching a tan.

"No problem at all," Mark said. "Carry on snuggling your lovely bride. A pity the weather spoiled the chance to take pictures at the park, isn't it?"

Ed agreed. A photographer himself, he appreciated not getting photographs in the best setting was disappointing. Still, it was not topmost in his mind now after the police gate-crashed his wedding. Unease crawled around in his solar plexus, even when Gail's lips fastened firmly on his once more.

They pulled up in front of his flat. On his way to the door, Ed spotted a man standing a short distance away, scrutinising him. When Ed shifted his gaze to him, he turned away. Another man stood on the other side of the road, smoking a cigarette. Plain-clothes police. Before he left, he peeked out a window. The one over the road was staring directly at the flat. One thing was evident—if he brought his bride into his home, there would be a raid. He sifted through the post—no letters, just bills.

"Did you observe our little flatfooters?" said Mark when Ed returned to the car.

"Yeah. I'm not completely blind," Ed answered.

"Well, I take it you weren't planning on spending your wedding night in your flat in any case. Better persuade Candy's folks to put you up at their house for the night."

"Candy would move out her room for me, I'm sure," said Gail.

Ed's mind wandered. It wasn't as if he'd been expecting any wedding night bliss in the circumstances.

When Mark parked in front of Candy's house, Ed noted two men walking together on the sidewalk.

They watched the two men continue down the pavement. "What are the chances of that?" said Mark. "A Black man with a White man in a Coloured neighbourhood."

Gail frowned toward the two men. "The police are not known for their brains, are they?"

Ed put a hand on Mark's shoulder. "Let's wait a bit, I want to make sure."

"Good idea."

The two men continued to the next intersection, where the Black man glanced back over his shoulder, then hurried on. They turned into the other road, and the White man looked toward them before being hidden from view behind a house.

"That confirms it," said Mark. "Candy's place is also being staked out."

They walked into the house where the guests instantly gave them three loud cheers. A surprise reception. Someone had decorated the house, moved the kitchen and dining room tables together, and loaded them with food. The bridesmaids whisked Gail away, supposedly for repairing any damage her makeup had suffered, and for changing into her "going away" outfit. Small chance. For them, there was no place to go.

Mark, Ed and Leonard took turns watching for the stakeout cops' return. They didn't have long to wait. Leonard called them to the curtains. "That them?"

It was. They were still together watching the house when they turned the corner.

Chantal joined them at the window. "Gail told me about the plain clothes cops staking out your flat and this house, Ed," she said. "Listen, it wouldn't be fair if you guys spend your wedding night apart." She held her hand out. "Here are the keys to my flat in Durban. I want you to use it."

"Thanks, Chantal," Ed held out a hand, but Mark interrupted him.

"Wait, I wouldn't chance it," he said. "Those goons will see you leave and follow you."

"I can shake them off in my Rambler," said Ed.

"Great, all they need is the chance to arrest you for speeding and add other charges. You'd be in custody. I'm not so sure Gail would escape arrest either, a Coloured woman in your car. Also, if you don't shake them off, they'd follow you to Chantal's flat and stake it out. Then if they catch you together, that's it."

Ed bit his lip, hard.

Mark continued. "And what about Chantal? She would be an accomplice and join the party then, wouldn't she?"

Ed guessed he'd be sleeping alone tonight.

The reception, though small, was extremely enjoyable. It had everything, Mark's speech, cutting the cake, throwing the garter… caught by Mark, throwing the bouquet…caught by Chantal, dancing to music played on Leonard's small but adequate hi fi set, and of course, giving his speech.

Small crowd or not, a speech was a speech. When he held his glass of champagne, Ed's hand shook, and his throat turned dry. He hadn't expected a speech, and therefore his words were unrehearsed. "Ladies and gentlemen, if there are any of the latter here," he began, to cheers and laughter. "I would like to thank everyone for setting up this unexpected reception. To Leonard and Ria, for all you've done and for opening up your house for Gail and me. Candy and Pamela, bless your hearts, for being not only work buddies but proving yourselves loyal friends. Mrs. Rabe, for having the best daughter imaginable and for bringing her up as a lady beyond compare and a wife out of my wildest dreams."

A big round of applause.

"Then there's Mark, of course. Where would I be without you? Thanks for everything, all your help, for taking the photos, being my best man to hold me together, and being my mentor, guide and best friend. Chantal, a brand-new friend, for literally putting me back together, in fact, sewing me back together."

Loud laughter and applause.

"You have proven yourself a staunch friend both for Gail and me, and I honestly hope we can return the favour someday."

Chantal blushed amid loud clapping and a couple of hoots.

"Gail. Words fail me. Outside of this house, at this moment, I feel the entire world's against us."

Murmurs of assent and of disapproval.

"Here's my promise—I will fight all those odds against us until we are truly together, as one, like it should be. How can we fight it? Well, there is one weapon, Gail. One thing that will win in the end, and make us husband and wife for all time, till death do us part... my love for you, Gail."

The speech ended to applause, surprisingly loud from the small group. Gail fell into his arms and raised her mouth to his, giving him a deep lingering kiss. When they broke apart at last, she said, "And you can count on me fighting, too, because I'll always love you."

The party eventually died down but without the traditional going-away ceremony. No guests lining up with hands joined in an arch, forming a tunnel for them to pass through. No saying their farewells to the music of "Wish Me Luck as You Wave Me Goodbye."

In any case, there weren't enough guests to perform it, and the couple would not be leaving together.

CHAPTER

TWENTY

Gail bit her lip as she added an X to the calendar. The first day of the new month. Day eleven of her annual leave, meaning seven more days plus the weekend. What then? She would need to go back to work, and there'd again be over fifty miles between her and her new husband.

Not that it made much difference, she would scarcely see much more of him than if she stayed here. She blinked back tears. In any normal civilisation, she'd be living with Ed as husband and wife. She sighed. Now she had to be satisfied with a date tomorrow night at the drive-in. The one place they could feel relatively alone.

Talk of being alone. Both Candy and her father were at work. Chantal had gone back to her hospital job in Durban, so the only person left in the house was Ria, who now sat glued to the radio listening to a soap, something she had no inclination to share. Gail took a break after helping her with the housework.

Wait. There were no laws against visiting Ed at work, all races were allowed in retail shops. Her heart beat faster at the thought of seeing him at work. She knew all his habits from their long phone relationship. For instance, he often spent his lunch hour in the little office behind the studio. She glanced at the clock on the wall. Nearly lunchtime. Why not drop in and pay him a visit?

She changed and put on a little makeup—Ed didn't like it over-done—then left the house and caught a bus into town.

Her heart fluttered immediately she caught sight of Ed. Though busy with a customer, he glanced her way and looked ecstatic when he saw her. Mark, also with someone, waved at her with a huge grin.

While she browsed through a collection of 8mm movie titles, she heard a voice behind her. "Have you been served, madam?" An older woman with a tight mouth held a sheaf of papers and a pen and showed every sign of impatience.

"No, I am waiting for Ed, thank you."

"Mr. Brent is busy. May I help you?"

"Thank you, but no, it's personal."

The woman frowned. "Personal?" She tilted her head and pursed her lips. "You wouldn't be Gail Rabe, would you?"

"Yes, I would. That is, I was. My name has changed to Gail Brent since Saturday." Her heart skipped a beat. This was the first time she'd told anyone this news.

"Well, Miss Rabe, if you would wait here, Mister Brent will be here when he's finished." She turned briskly and walked off back to her office, leaving Gail gaping after her.

Well. So sorry I don't fit your expectations! Though no stranger to rudeness from shop employees, given her race, she hardly expected it at Ed's work. Clearly, the woman was Dolores, of whom she had heard much. Still, Gail had developed an extremely thick skin. Growing up Coloured made that vital.

A few minutes later, another older woman with long, neatly groomed blonde hair approached from the offices. Rather overdoing the makeup. This had to be Mrs. Cahill, the widowed owner of Cahill's Photo. Ed had often mentioned her. She walked right up to Gail with a broad smile.

"So you're Gail," she said, hand outstretched. "You work at Bronson and Schubert's, I'm sure we've spoken on the phone. Pleased to meet you."

"Oh, thank you." *She's more civil at any rate.* She took the offered hand. "Mrs. Cahill?"

"Yes. Ed must have talked about me. Not very complimentarily, I suppose."

Gail opened her mouth in protest, but Mrs. Cahill grinned. "Anyway, I believe I must congratulate you on becoming Mrs. Brent."

"Thanks," Gail breathed. Recognition at last.

146

"It's clear why Ed fell for you," continued Mrs. Cahill. "You're certainly a good choice. Not the wisest perhaps." She grimaced. "I do hope you two can come to some arrangement, but you know…"

Gail nodded. Mrs. Cahill was realistic, apparently frank, but pleasant, especially compared to Dolores.

Ed, finished with his customer, hurried over. He grinned. "Do I need to make any introductions?"

"Too late," said Mrs. Cahill. "Well, I'll leave you lovebirds. Nearly your lunch time, Ed? Why don't you take off now?"

"Well, thank you. I certainly shall," Ed answered, offering Gail his arm.

That was a surprise, she hadn't foreseen he would choose to walk with her, but Ed said he needed to speak with Naidoo, and they headed that way. Now they were outdoors she fully predicted he'd drop her arm, but instead he held her hand firmly in the crook of his.

"Either they're going to accept us or they're not," he told her. "And if they don't, I don't care."

She smiled and moved closer. "Well, if you don't, I don't."

A few people stared as they passed, some even turning around for another look, but most didn't look at them at all. On the way to Naidoo's, the number of Whites steadily dwindled, to be replaced by Indians. Their faces looked less judgmental than those of the Europeans, but some were even more shocked. Gail tightened her hold on his arm and held her head high. This was enjoyable.

"Here we are," Ed finally announced.

She recognised the rather shabby exterior of Naidoo's market, but no place could compare with it. A tingle travelled all the way down her spine. The memory of the most intense pleasure of her life came back. This was where Ed proposed to her a lifetime ago, but it had only been two weeks.

Inside, they were met by the waiter who had attended to them that day. He bowed dutifully and fixed his eyes on Gail.

"Is the boss around?" asked Ed.

"Um. Mister Naidoo is, uh very busy, sah. I am thinking he will not see you today, sah."

"Not see me? Nonsense, of course he will. Tell him Ed is here, with his wife."

"His wife?" His eyes were still locked on her.

She cuddled up to Ed.

"Go on," he urged the waiter. "Tell him Ed is here and wants him to meet his wife."

The waiter vanished through a doorway.

"Ed," she whispered, looking around. "This place brings back the best memories. I shall never forget it. I hope we can come back here often."

Naidoo entered the room after a while, but he didn't look altogether happy.

"Are you okay?" Ed studied him intently.

"I am sorry, Ed. Normally, I am being happy for you to visit and, of course, for your lovely wife. Congratulations, Mrs. Gail. I am delighted for you."

"Well, come on, Naidoo, you don't seem overjoyed. What's the matter with you?"

"Ah, Ed. You are knowing me too well. You see, Ed, it is like this. I am no longer allowing you to come here together."

Gail's heart sank. Not Naidoo, too? Not the Naidoo who made things especially agreeable for them, so that Ed could propose in the perfect setting. She glanced at Ed, who stared at Naidoo with his mouth open.

"No longer allowed? But I came to ask you if we could come on a date tonight to celebrate our wedding. This is the one place I can count on. What do you mean?"

Naidoo looked down at the floor and shook his head. "It is not possible. This policeman, he came this morning. He said he would close me down if I let you and your, your—wife dine here again. I am being so sorry, Ed. You are my friend, but he would come here if I let you eat here again. I think he is watching the place."

"Who told you this? What is his name?"

"Sergeant Van Greuning. He is not nice, this man. He would do it."

Gail's mind whirled. That horrible officer. How did he learn about this place, about their engagement? Naidoo probably wasn't to blame, and it couldn't have been the waiter. Were they under suspicion before the wedding perhaps? Maybe it was Nick who had set this detective onto them. She was aware of no law preventing them eating together, if they could find a place that permitted it. But this infuriating sergeant had managed to track down the cosiest, warmest, memory-filled place in her world and shut it out for them. And Naidoo was Ed's friend. Could Sergeant Van Greuning wreck that close interracial friendship, like he tried to destroy their marriage? It was too much. She rushed to the door, wiping the tears from her eyes.

*****

Gail evidently had recovered from her depression by the time Ed picked her up. They had a date at the drive-in. In fact, she became overjoyed when he told her the name of tonight's feature film, *They Call Me Mr. Tibbs*. Sidney Poitier, a Black man, had the lead role. However, when Ed explained Poitier's role was a police lieutenant, she was not so sure.

"Why couldn't it be *Guess Who's Coming to Dinner?* He starred in that one, too." She pouted. "That would be more suitable for us. Like when you eventually take me to dinner at your parents' house." She gave him a sideways glance.

"I like that idea, maybe we could rent it sometime on 16mm." He conjured up a vision. Sitting and snuggling with her in the dark.

He drove up to the ticket office. "Two please."

"Sir, could I ask you please to drive up alongside that building. Just turn left here." The young lady gave no reason.

Ed followed her directions. What now? Sounds like more trouble.

Less than a minute later, a man stood beside his door. "Good evening, sir. Sorry about this, I am standing in for the manager tonight," he said.

Ed put his head out the window. "Good evening. What seems to be the trouble?"

"We had a report to watch out for your car—make, model and number plate," he said, bending down and peering at Gail.

"Oh, why?" Ed said, though he knew what was likely coming up.

"A police report actually. A certain Sergeant Van Greuning. Apparently, he has an issue with whomever you were bringing in as a passenger."

"Oh. This is my wife, Gail," Ed answered.

"Your wife? He didn't mention that."

"He should have. He even came to our wedding," Ed said with a wry smile.

"I can well imagine he did," said the manager. "Did he give you grief?"

"Yes, but since it was a church wedding, there wasn't much he could do except keep his nose out of our business."

He gave an answering chuckle. "And on that note," he said, "I better keep mine out as well. Sgt. Van Greuning's issues are not mine. You two go ahead and enjoy the show. I'm pretty sure you must have been here before. Just don't attract any attention, okay?"

"Thanks, man," said Ed, holding out his hand.

"I'll see what I can do to remove the report on your car," the manager said, shaking Ed's hand. "After all, we did stop you and warn you. Bye now, I hope you'll like the show, Gail."

"I will," she said, beaming at him, "Thank you so much."

"You're welcome, just don't tell Van Greuning I let you in."

*****

Mrs. Cahill wasn't in when Ed returned from lunch. But the next day, she called him to her office with, "I'd like a word." He faced her across her desk. He half-expected bad news after the shock they'd had at Naidoo's. Would he be fired for marrying a non-White? He couldn't believe that. Mrs. Cahill had genuinely been enchanted with Gail.

"Did you enjoy your walk with Gail yesterday? Where did you go?" she said.

It was best to tell her all. Get it all behind him. He told her about Van Greuning, how he had shown up at the wedding, staked out their homes, and how he had threatened Naidoo.

Mrs. Cahill's brow wrinkled while he told her. But when he finished, to his astonishment, she was smiling.

"So you couldn't get near your bride after the marriage? Well, cheer up, Ed. What I wanted to talk to you about had nothing to do with her, but now I think it may kill two birds with one stone."

He answered that one with a raised eyebrow. "If you mean I should kill Sergeant Van Greuning..." he said with a grin.

She smiled in return. "Nothing that drastic. The thing is, I am having a weekend away with the kids, and we're departing on Thursday."

She paused. He waited.

"My nighttime security guard is ill in Edendale Hospital. I was worried about leaving the house, and I thought I might ask you to keep an eye on it. Now I have the perfect plan for both of us. Why not stay in my house till Tuesday, when I come back?"

Stay in a six-bedroom house on the hill, with en-suite bathrooms in each room and pool and hot tub.

"Of course, I'll pay you extra."

And get paid for it.

"Naturally, you can invite your new bride to stay with you."

"Um, let me think about it," he said.

Mrs. Cahill's waxed and shaped eyebrows shot up.

"I thought about it," he said with a chuckle. "I can't come up with any objections to that."

She laughed, then told him the details and how to disarm the door and window alarms.

"Here's the spare key to the house and garage and the car keys. Please use my car while you're there, your own car may draw attention. The fridge is well stocked, don't let it go to waste, and you're welcome to all the things in the kitchen. Take my room, the biggest. I'll see to it you'll have clean bedding. Make yourself at home anywhere."

"Thank you, that is most generous of you, Mrs. Cahill. I'm sure Gail will be thrilled."

No more than I am. He left the office in a dreamlike state.

TWENTY-ONE

Mark smirked. "So tonight's the night."

"Right. It sure is," Ed said.

"Imagine, all that luxury. Have you seen the rooms in that house of Mommy's?"

"No, I've only seen them from outside, all six bedrooms in a row, upstairs. Makes you wonder what on earth they keep downstairs, doesn't it?"

"Well, for one thing, I did see an enormous lounge with attached bar. I haven't ever seen upstairs, though." Mark shook his head. "I take it you won't be using said lounge."

"We won't be doing much entertaining during our stay there, Mark. However, I'm sure Gail would love a visit from you."

Ed turned at a clucking noise behind him. "Dolores," he said. "Have you taken something for that?"

Mark chortled but Dolores ignored the remark.

"Does Mrs. Cahill realise you're taking that Coloured girl to her house?" She pulled her mouth into a tight line.

"I believe she does. Actually, she's the one who suggested it."

Dolores clucked again and left.

Mark stared after her departing figure. "I think there goes someone who won't accept an invitation."

"Mark," he said. "I'm sure you know that I'm wary of inviting anyone around to the house, just in case a certain unwelcome guest shows up."

"Of course, old chap, you're quite right. Mommy wouldn't like it if you held any parties. Ruins the wall-to-wall carpeting, I believe."

"I would appreciate it if you could give me a lift to the house this arvie, Mark. I need to collect my things and take them to Mommy's house, and then I'll pick up her car."

"My my! Her car, too. Good idea. We learned from your trip to the drive-in last night that your car is hot and not in the right way. Be sure you don't transfer that adjective to Mommy's big flashy American car. Come to think of it, it's not the first choice of cars if your idea is to be inconspicuous."

"True enough. I'll only use it to drive to work. We won't be going to drive-ins or anything this weekend."

"I'm sure you won't." Mark winked.

*****

"Ooh! Ed. What a larney car." Gail stared at it in awe. "But so big. Everybody will be staring at us."

Ed winked but shook his head. "Sorry, Gail, Mommy doesn't have a Volkswagen Beetle, so we're stuck with this."

Gail smiled, refusing to worry too much. She was sure White people didn't stare at the people inside their fancy cars. In any case, she and Ed wouldn't use it much. She was sure it would be safe enough.

Ed took her suitcase and some packets full of her stuff and placed them in the enormous boot. Or should she say trunk, plainly it was an American car. Ed held the door open for her and she climbed in. She had to laugh when Ed got in the other side.

"Hello over there, can you hear me?" she called out.

He laughed. "Only just, but there's an echo."

"And you say the house is also big? I suppose you could put my mom's whole house in the entrance hall."

Ed didn't reply so she looked across at him. Maybe he'd taken her seriously. Just how huge was this house? It crossed her mind that she hadn't yet been in any house owned by a European. Surely, she couldn't be the only Coloured who hadn't? She imagined it must be the same for almost anyone living in South Africa. When Ed first visited her, it was the only Coloured home he'd ever set foot in. Now she was about to enter a White one for the first time. Would Ed carry her over the threshold, like all new husbands did? Still, it wasn't his house, and they'd never dare while Sergeant Van Greuning may be spying on it.

Ed drove in a part of Pietermaritzburg that was completely new to her. The higher up the hill they drove, the bigger and fancier the houses grew. By the time they entered the road where Ed said the house was, she felt completely overwhelmed, like being in another country. Did people genuinely live like this? Mrs. Cahill probably wasn't even close to being one of the richest residents. Where were their homes?

He looked across at her. "You're very quiet."

"Are you looking forward to being on our own at last?" she asked. She sure was.

"Gail, you can't imagine how happy I am. I'm so grateful to Mrs. Cahill and to Mark and the others. They're all envious, you know. Staying in this lovely enormous house, which has everything, with my beautiful new bride."

Suddenly, her tummy churned. She turned to Ed and studied his face, hoping the sensation would go away.

He shifted to look at her. "What's the matter?"

"You were talking about this in the shop?"

"Of course, we were. Like I said, everybody's happy for me… and you."

"Everybody?"

He nodded.

"Who?" she insisted.

"Why, Mark, of course, and the girls, Mommy, and me."

Okay. The troubling sensation in her stomach untangled a little, and she took a deep calming breath.

"Why, even Dolores is jealous. She would love to stay in that house," Ed continued.

The feeling returned, this time multiplied a hundredfold.

"Dolores? You told Dolores where we'll be staying?"

Ed's head snapped around and he fastened his eyes on hers. "What are you suggesting? Do you mean…?"

"Where did you first see Van Greuning?"

"At the wedding."

"And weren't you telling Mark all about the wedding at the shop?"

"Yes."

"So Dolores would've known." She frowned at him.

"Well, yes, but so did everybody there. By the way, she declined the invitation."

"Precisely, she didn't want to go to the wedding because she didn't want it to happen."

Ed repeated her words.

How could he be so…dense? "Oh, Ed. You Whites are so naive. She absolutely hates that you married me. She is racist to the core."

Ed stared at her as if this was news to him. Really!

"What about Nick?" he said.

"Nick wanted you, not me. I don't believe he knew about the wedding. I think he's given up."

Ed folded his arms. "Perhaps."

"And if Nick likes me, he wouldn't do anything that would put me in danger, I'm sure. The police staked out your place. Dolores knows where you live."

"Yes, but I doubt she would be familiar with where Candy lived, and her place was watched, too."

Gail clutched at her head. "Oh, come on, Ed! She works in the office. How hard would it be for her to look up Candy's address?"

Ed slowed the car and pulled to the side of the road. He turned to face her directly. "Are you sure Nick couldn't get that information?"

"Nick tracked me down, yes, by threatening Mom, but how about this? When we dined at Naidoo's, we found out Van Greuning had threatened him, too. How would Nick know about Naidoo?"

Ed shook his head.

"And I don't believe Nick had any idea where you were taking me on dates. He only spied on you picking me up and dropping me off at my house. I'm pretty sure he didn't even know about the drive-in dates in Durban. Yet what happens? We go to the 'Maritzburg drive-in and find out Van Greuning's already posted a lookout for your car there. Was Dolores aware of the drive-ins?"

Again, Ed nodded, biting his lip. "I presume it would be difficult not to have heard about it in the shop, with Mark and the girls nattering about it."

"Exactly, she hears everything. The moment she hears what you're doing or planning, she's on the phone to her cop buddy. So much is obvious, Ed. Surely, you accept that."

Ed looked thoughtful but also miserable. Her feelings softened.

"I'm truly sorry. I know you were looking forward to our stay in Mrs. Cahill's house. So was I, trust me. But I just can't. I'm scared, Ed, scared for my life. You can't imagine what happens to my insides any time I even think of this man."

She moved across the vast seat space into his waiting arms. "Mrs. Cahill made a contract with you, so you'll need to stay in her house but alone. I'm sorry. They can't do anything to you if I'm not with you."

He sighed deeply. "I expect you're right. I don't like it, but I have to think of your safety. You're the most important—you're more precious to me than anything."

"We're onto Dolores, Ed. Don't worry, we'll keep everything a secret from her from now on."

"You bet. Her policeman boyfriend won't ever get any more info about us."

He sealed his vow with a kiss, then, reluctantly, he took her back to Candy's house.

"So what do we do about it?" he asked her between kisses.

"About what?" She kissed him again.

He gasped for air. "About Dolores."

"I thought that was your department." She ran a finger along his lips and down his chin.

"Hmmm. Come here."

She laid both hands on his chest and pushed him away. "No, Ed. What are we thinking, sitting in this car right outside where I'm living? I must go."

He sighed. "Fine, I'll see you to your door and then return to that enormous house, where I'll be all on my own."

TWENTY-TWO

Ed stretched his arms as he exited the walk-in shower room. He had never experienced anything like that. Certainly luxurious. Jets of water coming in from the sides, back and top. He was enjoying his boss's huge house, but...he put on the thick towel-like dressing gown and pulled the knot tight. How dare he enjoy it when Gail should be sharing it with him.

He rubbed his hair vigorously with a towel as he made his way to the bed. This was his first night at the Cahill house, but the sixth since the wedding, and still he was sleeping alone.

The thought didn't make him feel the least bit sleepy. He set off to explore the house after stepping into his slippers. He'd already explored all six bedrooms that lined the top floor, but not much of the ground floor, other than the large entertainment lounge. The bar stocked a wide variety of drinks, making him almost wish he weren't teetotal. Next was a kitchen with everything imaginable built in. He opened a cupboard door and smacked his lips at the range of breakfast choices. That would be first-rate tomorrow, but at the moment, he was not in the least hungry, so he passed on to the next door.

Wow! Two 16mm movie projectors stood on a platform inside an enclosure the door of which stood open. The front had cutouts for the projectors' beams. Opposite this were red velvet curtains, obviously covering a CinemaScope screen. Three rows of cinema seats filled much of the space in between—a home-cinema. That would be an excellent way to pass the time, considering.

His gaze scanned the room for the films. Perhaps they rented them. Then his eyes fell on a cupboard on the far side. It held some metal cans. Carefully, he lifted one. *Mannix.* Some sort of detective show. *Bewitched. Mission Impossible.* Obviously, American TV shows, he didn't know them. The film library at work had lots of two hundred ft films from British and American TV shows, but silent, they didn't handle 16mm colour sound films. These clearly could be worth watching. If only they had television in South Africa. That was a sore point with him, last year he had to listen to the moon landing, while the rest of the world watched it on their TV sets. He imagined there was no TV service because there were things the government didn't want anybody to see.

He moved on. There were more rooms, one for storage, another a little library, and apparently a family room, albeit a small one. This house was more for entertaining guests than family. Delightful, but not what he and Gail would want. That thought snapped him back to reality. Gail should be here and sharing his own flat, not a small bedroom with Candy in her parents' house. Soon, she would be returning to her mom's in Durban. He slammed the door of the family room and stomped back up the stairs.

For the fifth time since he had arrived, he peered out the window of the main bedroom, looking up and down the road for any sign of the house's being under observation. All clear. He repeated the checks after brushing his teeth. Nobody to be seen. He climbed into bed.

Ed's troubled mind kept him awake, as did the thought of Gail being in Candy's house. Was she having difficulty falling asleep, too? Thinking of Gail eased his mind for a while, then the worry retuned. Were they still watching outside the house?

Another thing keeping him awake was the modern alarm clock. Every minute, there would be a loud *kulunk* when the tumbler turned to the next digit. An especially noisy clunk would be coming up at the turn of the hour. Three o'clock. It was a pity he was such a nice guy; otherwise, that alarm clock would have landed somewhere in the garden, if not on the pavement. Infernal thing. Why couldn't clocks just tick? There it was, the extra noisy movement of three cylinders moving into place at once, announcing that he had made it all the way to three in the morning without sleeping a wink.

Then he remembered the home cinema. Why not? He drew on the comfy dressing gown and stumbled downstairs to the home cinema. He inspected the few titles in the cupboard. *Mannix: A Penny for the Peep Show.* That sounded interesting. He threaded it on one of the projectors, found the button for the screen curtains, and started the show, settling into one of the comfy cinema style seats.

The plot was interesting, and he watched with full attention as it developed. All these people held hostage in a room. All of a sudden, he looked around him in confusion. A flapping noise had woken him up. He sat up straight, finally noticing the film fluttering from a full reel on the projector. Jumping up, he hurried to turn it off. So he must have slept after all. He considered rewinding the film to review what he missed but shook his head and decided to try bed again. Everything was quiet without the whirring noise. Or was it? He heard something. A clanging bell in the distance. A bang. Voices. Footsteps. The door flew open.

"*Hier's hy.*"

Ed stared in bewilderment at the silhouette of a man and squinted as the room lights were switched on. The room was abruptly flooded with light revealing two more men, all dressed in the uniform of the police. A thumping came from the stairs, and before long, Sergeant Van Greuning appeared in the doorway.

"Ah so. You are here," he said with a smirk. "I was worried you wouldn't be. He turned to the tallest of the three men. "*Boei hom,*" he growled.

Ed stared at him, still blinking from the sudden light, as the tall man forcefully pulled him around and handcuffed his wrists behind his back. "What are you doing?" he said.

"Making sure you don't run off while we look for your girlfriend." Van Greuning's lip curled in a sneer. "Your so-called wife."

Two more uniformed men entered, and Van Greuning turned toward the door.

"*Waar is sy?*" he snapped at them.

The men explained that they had searched all the rooms on both floors and had found no trace of "the girl."

"Have you looked outside the house?" he yelled at them. "She's here. Find her!"

He glared at the retreating men a few moments, then turned back to Ed, his gray eyes forming slits. "Why isn't she here with you? And why are you watching movies at nearly four o'clock in the morning? Did you have a fight with your little Coloured girlfriend?"

"She isn't here. I'm looking after this house for my boss while she's away, and I don't think she'll take kindly to police breaking into her house."

"We do what we have to do to catch your sort. Why exactly wouldn't your—wife—come here? This would be a golden opportunity for you, hey?"

"We are living separately by choice. We haven't committed any crime."

Van Greuning prodded Ed's chest with his baton. "Getting married to a Coloured is a criminal act."

"Our marriage isn't registered. It can't be against the law," said Ed.

"We'll be the judge of that." He turned to his men. "Frans, *bring hom tot die slaapkamer.*"

Once in the bedroom, Van Greuning whipped the top sheet off the bed. He pointed to some folds in the bottom. "It looks to me like she did sleep here."

The cuffs cut into Ed's hands behind his back. "I'm a restless sleeper, especially tonight. I couldn't sleep, which is why I was watching movies."

"*Nouja.* We'll see about that." Switching to Afrikaans, he shouted at Frans, "Take all the sheets for evidence."

The men who'd been sent to look for Gail entered, their nervous faces betraying their lack of success. Van Greuning turned purple, yelling words at them that made Ed clench his fists in rage. He'd like to beat the man to a pulp for calling Gail an exceptionally crude racist epithet.

The handcuffs cut into Ed's wrists. He hated feeling helpless, especially when Van Greuning issued instructions to Frans to contact the men assigned to surveillance on Candy's house. Van Greuning turned back to Ed.

Ed scowled. "What has Gail done? She hasn't been here. We haven't touched each other. She's innocent."

"Innocent until proven guilty? For your information, Mr. Brent, we have the right to detain anyone without trial, just on suspicion, for as long as we like. We want to inspect her bedding, too. We will get evidence against you. You better believe it." He sneered at Ed and called one of the uniformed men to take him to the Black Mariah.

*****

"Still no answer." Gail furrowed her brow, panic rising in her breast. "Why doesn't he pick up the phone?"

"Maybe y'oll got the wrong number," Candy suggested. "Are you sure y'oll copied it right?"

"Of course, I'm sure," she said, trying her best to be patient with Candy. As if she would make a mistake like that with the most important number. For the fourth time that morning, she dialled the number, to be rewarded with the same monotonous, never-ending ringtone. She almost shouted, "Oh, Ed. Please pick up the phone."

Candy reached for her hand. "Gail, he may be busy. Getting ready. Maybe he drove to work early."

"Gone to work without phoning me first? Never."

"Okay, okay. Come, let's eat breakfast. Y'oll can call just now. Okay?"

What else could she do? Reluctantly, she took Candy's offered hand and the two walked to the kitchen.

"What y'oll eating?" said Candy.

"Oh, I'll just have some Weet-Bix, please. I'll do it." Perhaps if she kept busy she could bear the suspense. She poured milk over her cereal.

"I'll make you some coffee," said Candy.

"Please. I need it."

The coffee did taste good after her sleepless night. At times, she had wanted to ring up Ed to talk but waking him up from his deep sleep would have been unfair. He was probably snoring soundly on some expensive inner-spring mattress, with oodles of padding and surrounded with luxury. She remembered the hard coir mattress she had slept on and momentarily regretted not having joined Ed. She gave her head a quick shake. What was she thinking? She had turned down Ed's offer to be with him in Mrs. Cahill's luxury house in case the police raided it. Possibly, they had. *Ed's been taken.*

"Okay." Candy interrupted. "Y'oll finished your breakfast and coffee, why don't y'oll phone him again?"

Gail started. "Yes. Let me get to the phone." She glanced at her wristwatch. It was a quarter to eight. Ed would probably be on his way to work. *I'll try anyway.*

Still nothing. Absently, she held the phone for several minutes.

"Come on," said Candy, gently tugging the receiver. "Give him time to get there, then y'oll call him at work."

"Sure." Gail allowed her to remove the receiver from her hand.

Ria marched into the kitchen with Leonard and pulled back the curtains. "Look y'oll. The nosey police are still watching the house."

Leonard joined her at the window. "Well, I must go to work. Y'oll keep an eye on them, will you?"

"Of course," said Ria and gave her husband a peck on the lips. He waved to Gail and Candy, then left the house.

Gail and Candy spied on the policemen outside for a while. One of them was smoking a cigarette, the other hidden behind his copy of the *Natal Witness*. Other than occasional glances toward the house, they didn't seem particularly interested in their job.

Gail kept an eye on her wristwatch, and when it read eight o' clock, she returned to the telephone and dialled Ed's number at Cahill's.

Mark answered immediately. "T. J. Cahill's, good morning."

"Hello, Mark, this is Gail."

"Gail." Mark's sing-song voice, as usual, made her feel like royalty. She couldn't help smiling but got straight to the point, not wasting any time on pleasantries.

"Mark, has Ed arrived yet?"

"Actually, no," Mark replied at once. "He's late. No doubt he overslept in that sumptuous bed, and he's still in a dwaal."

"Oh, dear. I'm worried. I have a bad feeling about this. I've tried calling for ages, and he doesn't answer. He's always picked up straightaway before. I'm really afraid."

Mark's tone turned serious. "Gail, I'll give him a few more minutes. It wouldn't be the first time he's been late. But more than that and I promise I'll go and fetch him myself. Don't you worry."

"Thanks, Mark. Only I can't help worrying. I think—"

Candy yelped as Gail broke off.

"There's more." Candy, still at the window, looked petrified. Gail turned to see what she was looking at. Four uniformed men had joined the other two and now strode toward the door. One of them rapped loudly on it while another ran off toward the back of the house. Ria and Candy stood transfixed.

There was more banging. Both Candy and Ria were too petrified to open the door. An earsplitting crash accompanied a splintering of the lock, then it swung inward off its hinges.

"What was that?" Mark yelled through the earpiece.

"The police have come for me," Gail squealed and dropped the phone.

The men rushed directly toward her. One of them was shouting orders in Afrikaans, commanding the others to find out where she slept and to collect all the bedding. A man gripping a sack headed straight into her bedroom.

Another addressed her. "Miss Gail Rabe?" Without waiting long for a reply, he clicked a handcuff on her wrist, spun her round roughly, and snapped its mate on the other. "I arrest you on suspicion of contravening the Immorality Act and the Prohibition of Mixed Marriages Act. You may be detained for up to ninety days without trial."

And with that, they whisked her away into the waiting van; the phone receiver still dangling at the end of its line.

CHAPTER

TWENTY-THREE

Gail shuddered as the cell door clanged shut.

She held the bars and stared at the young female guard who twisted the key in the lock. "I know it's the law that anyone arrested has the right to at least one phone call."

Her guard peered up from the clipboard she held and removed the ballpoint pen from her mouth. "Not for criminals who break the Immorality Act."

Gail had overheard the jail manager call the guard Susanne. She was Afrikaans, young, Gail guessed in her early twenties, still bearing the scars of acne on her pale face. Straight, straw-coloured hair hung down all round her neck, emphasized by the way she hunched her shoulders, holding her head forward. The frumpy-looking brown guard's uniform hung loose on her body and sent a whiff of body odour to Gail's nose. She was recognisable as a "poor White," a working class without any special skills or education, yet having a superior status to anyone of a different race.

Gail hung onto the bars with both hands and surveyed her surroundings. The cell was approximately the size of her bathroom at home, with nothing but a flat bench supported by a chain from the stone wall. A hard coir mattress was the only covering on the bed, apart from a thin blanket folded at the base. On it was a copy of a *Huisgenoot* magazine. Serving as the toilet was an iron bucket covered by a wooden board, and by the stench, she assumed it hadn't been cleaned after the previous occupant departed. The only other furniture was a small table next to the bed, with a basin of water and a cake of that awful red soap they'd used in the school toilets. The sole window was high on the wall opposite the bars, so narrow that a single bar sufficed, and it was devoid of glass. She knew there was another cell just around the corner to the right. The entire front of the cell consisted of metal bars, each about an inch thick.

Physical escape was out of the question, but maybe there were other weaknesses. Gail held the bars while she pleaded with the woman. "Don't I have any rights?"

"You should've thought of that before. I can't help you." She looked away from Gail, yet her eyes kept returning to her face. She pursed her lips and lowered her eyes to the clipboard again.

There might be something going on in this girl's mind, but what? Gail softened her voice. "Can't you tell me anything? What happened? Is my husband all right? Did they arrest him, too?"

Susanne sniffed. "Sorry, I've no idea. Your fault, you should leave White okes alone." Again, her eyes regarded Gail, before focusing on the bars.

Gail tried to fasten her eyes on the girl's, to arrest their continual scanning. Susanne's attitude fell somewhere between fascination and scorn. Why? Perhaps she might gain information by making casual conversation with the woman. "Are you married, Susanne?"

"Huh! Yust look at me, hey! Who do you think'd marry me?" She focused her eyes slightly above Gail's head.

Why wouldn't Susanne face her directly? There was something going on here. Was she suffering from a lack of confidence? Susanne's answer to her question made that probable.

"Why not? Don't you fancy men?"

"Ja man, of course I do. I'm not like that, noways! But men sommer don't like me." Her gaze dropped.

This could be an opportunity. The girl was clearly troubled, and she had a complete lack of confidence. Well, Gail knew from her own experience growing up Coloured that confidence could make so much difference. She smiled at Susanne, whose answering smile, Gail was sure, was also genuine and made her appear appealing. "Susanne, you realise, don't you, that you are quite attractive? You just need to draw some attention."

It could be true. With a bit of work on Susanne's face, she wouldn't be that bad.

"Ag no man. Don't joll me, that's nonsense." Susanne turned at once and stormed out through the door to the offices.

Gail took a seat on the hard mattress and her hand fell on the *Huisgenoot*. With nothing else to do, she leafed through it, finding little to interest her. Mostly fashion articles, all for White Afrikaans women. Maybe this would be the only thing to keep her from going insane after being locked up here for…just how many days might they keep her here? Her mind wandered to the articles she'd read about political prisoners. It could be months. Her mind closed to further depressing predictions. She folded the magazine and put it aside, but a caption on the cover caught her eye. *Make-up idees vir jong vroue.* Her grip tightened on the magazine. Perfect, make up ideas for young women. At once, she read the article.

Though she had no clock and they'd taken her wristwatch from her, Gail calculated it was about three hours later when Susanne showed up with a tray. "Dinner." She unlocked the cell door and handed the tray to Gail, who murmured her thanks but nothing else.

Susanne lingered, gripping a bar with one hand. Gail ignored her and sat down on the bed, with the tray on her lap. While she ate, Gail ignored Susanne's constant stare and busied herself eating.

She barely heard Susanne's voice.

Gail looked up from her tray. "I beg your pardon. Did you say something?"

She looked directly at Gail for once but with a frown. "Yous sommer jolling me, hey?"

Gail stood. "Whatever do you mean?"

"You said I'm mos quite attractive." Her frown deepened.

Gail smiled. "I mean it. I think, under that uniform is a nice, curvy body and men find that alluring. You just need to draw some attention. A nice hairdo…a little bit of makeup to show off your pretty eyes, a new outfit. You watch. The boys will suddenly see you."

Her eyes widened, and she rubbed one arm. "Me? Boys? You scheme so?"

She had her hooked. "Have you been out with any men?"

167

"No, I'm mos too ugly. You said my eyes were pretty, but they're squif, hey."

Gail looked closely and shook her head. "I never even noticed, it's just a slight squint, you're not cross-eyed, and not ugly at all. You just imagine you are."

Susanne made a noise with her lips and walked away.

There was no more sign of her till she came and put a fresh jug of water through the bars. She looked over to Gail, seemed about to say something, then decided against it.

"Are you okay?" Gail asked.

Susanne looked up, her mouth twitching. Her lips briefly formed a narrow smile, and she nodded. Then she walked away.

Gail finished her food then rested her head against the wall.

*****

Ed had never before been behind bars. He was now. Overcome with the night's sleep deprivation, followed by the raid, arrest, and being thrown into a holding cell, he'd passed out.

The clattering of a key turning in a lock woke him. When his eyes focused, he saw a Black guard at his cell door lock, a uniformed officer waiting further off, and a man in a dark two-piece suit carrying a briefcase.

"Mr. Brent." The man with the briefcase said, holding out his hand. "Stuart Albright." His thin moustache twitched as they shook. Ed couldn't help looking down at his own rumpled prison uniform.

"Your work buddy Mark called Mrs. Cahill's lawyer, Alan Whittaker, in regard to your arrest. Unfortunately, he is not a criminal lawyer and so he contacted me."

Ed blinked. Lawyers were expensive.

"Let me say at the outset," Stuart continued, "that you are going to walk out of here a free man, and it won't cost you a cent. I feel strongly about these stupid apartheid laws, and I do what I can to help."

Ed perked up. Good news so far.

"Your case will be easy. Your wife's..." Stuart bit his lip and sucked in air through his teeth. "May be another matter."

A sense of unease gripped Ed's heart. "My wife?"

"Yes. Mark was on the phone to her when it happened. He heard everything and phoned Alan at once."

"When what happened?" Ed's heart hammered so loudly he could hear it.

"After they arrested you, another group picked her up at your work colleague's house. She is in the Coloured correctional prison."

"What? On what grounds? We weren't together. She's been at Candy's house, never with me."

"Correct. The police vice squad are assigned the task of catching, trapping, and arresting people suspected of interracial relations, the operative word being suspected. Offenders might be liable to prosecution of a maximum of seven years."

Ed's blood drained from his face. "Seven years?" he almost shouted. "Listen, please don't worry about me. See to it she's freed, whatever the cost. Annul the marriage if you have to, please."

"Don't fret. Your marriage is valid only in church, and the law criminalises only the solemnisation of mixed marriages, not the actual marriages. I can demand concrete evidence that you two had been together at Mrs. Cahill's house last night. If not, they will be required to release you at once. Therefore, forgive me, but I have to ask you, were you together?"

"Absolutely not, but what if they fabricate evidence?"

"Relax, I've done this many times. Their so-called evidence rarely stands up in court. Sad to say, most accused don't have the benefit of a lawyer to demolish the evidence in court and end up jailed even though they're innocent. In this case, you have me."

At that moment, the door banged open. Sergeant Van Greuning stood in the opening, glowering at Stuart. "You!" he said.

Stuart faced him. "Yes me. I order you to release Mr. Brent forthwith."

Van Greuning, red in the face, shifted his glare between Stuart and Ed. "I didn't check the evidence yet."

"Too bad," said Stuart. "You're aware of the procedure." He placed his hand on Ed's elbow and marched him towards the door.

Van Greuning stood in their way, finally stepping aside and glaring at Ed. "I'm not finished with you yet."

Stuart stopped next to him, his eyebrows nearly meeting. "Uh. Are you making a threat?"

Van Greuning grunted and stood with his arms crossed while Stuart and Ed passed.

After changing back into his clothes, Ed walked with Stuart to his car. Freedom was walking outside in the fresh air and unexpected. "I'm not sure how I can thank you," he said.

"Save your gratitude till I've got Gail out. It isn't so easy when it comes to the other races."

Ed bit his lip.

"No worries," said Stuart. "I'll use the full power of the law. It's what we do, our raison d'etre, especially when the laws themselves are flawed. We just need to outmanoeuvre the lawmakers." He paused outside and looked both ways along the pavement. "I will tell you something in confidence, and…when a lawyer says that, you'd better believe he means it. My interest in these cases is personal. I'm separated from my wife, but we're not yet divorced, and I still live in our house. I have taken a mistress, but she happens to be"—again, he looked around to see if all was clear—"Black."

Ed turned his head back to the jail to hide his surprise.

"We use their own rules to get around it. Black women are not permitted to live in the city, and I'm not allowed a Black mistress, but I can have servants. In fact, it's only expected from a lawyer living in a big house. She lives in the servant's quarters, of course." He winked at Ed.

*****

Gail's eyes opened, and she realised it was morning and she'd been lying on the bed. It must have been the clomping noise that heralded Susanne's return that wakened her.

170

"Could you really do my hair?" She lifted up some of the strag-gles and peered at them.

"Perhaps, but how? I'm locked up. How could I?"

"If you could, can you do makeup, too?"

"Sure." She had Susanne hooked. A plan was forming in her mind. It might work. "But it takes a lot of time to learn, and you need a lot of cosmetics and tools. If we only had those, I'd be able to do it for you. I do a great job with makeup."

Susanne inspected Gail's face, bringing her head closer, and frowning. "But you're so pretty. Do you honestly think the okes will like me?"

"You're blonde. Why wouldn't they? All the men I know love blonde girls."

Susanne pursed her lips. "But the men you know are... Coloured?"

"Not all. I'm married to a White guy."

Susanne frowned for several seconds, then. "You like White men?"

Gail shook her head warily. She wasn't about to fall into any traps. "No, as a matter of fact. The Coloured guys are so much nicer."

Susanne lapsed into silence, but Gail knew she'd caught the woman's interest.

Susanne sniffed. "Coloured guys won't want me, anyways. I'm White." She hung her head.

"Coloured men will think you're irresistible. You're blonde, and you're not full of yourself the way most White girls are."

Gail let her digest this for a while. She didn't think for a moment that Susanne would actually dare to go out with a Coloured guy, but that was not her goal. Alternate thoughts, that was her aim. Have Susanne question things. She needed Susanne to be confused and to have her on her side.

Apparently, Susanne wasn't ready for alternate thoughts. She spun on her heel and walked off. "I yust don't want no Coloured men."

Gail heaved a sigh, returned to the bench, and lay down on her back, hands linked behind her head.

There was a soft cough. Gail blinked and sat up. She must have dozed off.

Susanne stood gripping the bars, focusing intently on Gail. "Please could you do my hair and makeup?" she asked in a soft voice.

Now that was what Gail wanted to hear. A plan took shape in her mind. She laughed. "In a jail cell? What did I just tell you?"

Her eyes pleaded. "I can buy all the things you need."

Gail waited in silence, slowly reeling her in.

"Please, come on, man. I can pay you," said Susanne.

Gail folded her arms across her chest. "I don't want your money."

"How then? How can I pay you for it?"

"Information. I want to know everything that happened. Was my husband also arrested? Is he in jail? And I want to communicate with him." Gail looked straight into the woman's eyes. "Then I'll do your hair and makeup. And if you can get me out of here, I'll do such a fantastic job on you, the boys will queue up to go out with you."

Susanne grinned broadly, demonstrating that Gail's beautification scheme was already starting to show results.

*****

For three days, Ed had heard nothing at all about Gail. He found it very hard to keep his mind on his job at Cahill's. He tore open the incoming parcels with ferocity.

Mrs. Cahill had come back from her trip, expressing gratitude to Ed for his job in looking after her house; though if it hadn't been for Stuart's help, Ed would've failed. Happily, her lawyer had ordered the damaged door fixed and the bed linen returned, and Ed had fulfilled his commitment without further problems.

"Oh, Ed." Mark put his head through the doorway to the small mailroom. There's a lovely lady waiting for you."

A woman with thin, straw-coloured hair stood near the film counter. She hardly fit Mark's description. She wore clumpy black shoes, a much-dated straggly dress hung on her body, and she had unskillfully smeared red lipstick on her mouth.

"You are Ed Brent?"

172

"That's me, how may I help you?"

"I have something for you," she said, pulling an envelope from her bag. "No questions. No names. Don't try to find out anything about me. Or else, I'll never come back."

Ed lifted an eyebrow. Was this woman all there? Why should he worry if she never returned?

"I'll return this time tomorrow morning if you have something for me. I won't answer any questions. You won't try to follow me. I am yust the messenger. Understand?"

Ed muttered that he did, and she turned and tromped out the shop, leaving the envelope in Ed's hands.

TWENTY-FOUR

Ed steered up the long drive of Stuart Albright's massive house. Though single story, it had that architect-designed air, obviously even more expensive than Mrs. Cahill's.

He gazed around, admiring the huge, kidney-shaped pool. Set well back to the right of the pool and behind the garage sat a neat-looking cottage, about the size of his own flat, clearly the servant's quarters. No doubt it had a fully furnished interior, with a bathroom containing feminine things and a wardrobe full of clothes. Almost certainly, the kitchenette would include a well-stocked fridge. All this he'd figured out from that one thing Stuart had confessed. It struck him that just a few weeks ago, before he'd met Gail, he would have been oblivious to such suspicions. No longer the naive White man.

Stuart opened the door of the main house. "Come in, Ed, by all means." They walked through the entrance hall toward a doorway. A gasp greeted them as they stepped into the huge lounge.

"It's okay, Thabi," said Stuart. "This is Ed Brent. Ed—Thabisa."

She cowered away from him and hung her head. She wore shorts and an oversized T-shirt tied in a loose knot in front, with slops on her feet at the bottom of extremely long and shapely legs, her skin shiny and smooth. She was the most beautiful Black woman he had ever seen. Thabi had straightened her thick hair into several short tufts at the top and sides of her head, held with narrow ribbons, emphasising the high cheekbones of the Zulu race. He blinked. Sure, he'd seen attractive Black girls, but only on movie screens, with large round afros. South African Black women were servants in cheap uniforms, usually with scarves tied around their heads, or sometimes carrying babies on their backs.

Ed held out his hand. "Hello, Thabisa, pleased to meet you."

Her face came up, much darker. Ed remembered how Africans turned darker the way Europeans turned red. Her dark, intelligent eyes held him for a moment, making him think of exotic and proud Zulu princesses. No wonder Stuart had fallen in love with this woman. Who wouldn't? The poor girl moved back, cowering. He kept his hand out. At a nod from Stuart, she reached out a hand slowly, but as Ed took it, she turned her face away. Her palm felt cold and sweaty.

"How are you?" Ed didn't know what else to say. She pulled away and fidgeted with her hands.

"Fine…thank you, baas."

Stuart chuckled. "Come, Thabi, I told you. There's nothing to fear, and he's not your boss. He's married to a Coloured."

She turned her head back to Ed. "*Haau!*" She closed a hand over her mouth. "You married a Coloured, *Mnumzane?*"

Ed nodded and smiled, and her eyes met his for the first time. She grinned, showing her teeth, startlingly white, as he'd come to expect from the Zulu race. She turned back to Stuart and covered her mouth once again.

Ed dropped his gaze and stopped smiling. "But she is in prison, and I'm here to see if Stuart can rescue her."

"Ow, yebo. He must rescue her." Her shoulders relaxed. "I'll fetch some tea." She hurried off through a far door.

Stuart led him down into the L-shaped sunken room filled with sofas, chairs and pouffes, ideal for entertaining. "I see you're surprised?" He grinned. "She's not only gorgeous but bright, creative, compassionate, and a million other things. I take it, from the state of your jaw as you walked in, that you've never seen a Zulu woman just being herself?"

He'd seen Zulu women in their natural state in the Valley of a Thousand Hills, a popular day drive for tourists from ships docked in Durban. Mothers with their kids strapped to their backs, effortlessly carrying huge bundles of wood on their heads, and young topless Zulu girls wearing short skirts made for a favoured excursion. On the other hand, a "natural state" could also be living in tin shanties in overpopulated ghettoes with no electricity and little water.

He'd never been to one of these. It was too dangerous, but he'd seen enough photos and newsreels to know what they were like.

"Guilty as charged. It's good to see. But, Stuart, what if I'd been a cop?"

"Good point, it is a risk. By the way, I'm not the vulture you probably imagine I am. We hired her as a legitimate servant before my wife left me. I kept her on. We became friends and eventually fell in love. She still works for me, and we keep the servant's quarters looking lived in. We think we're relatively safe here, but none of us in our position really are, right? Still, we do have a plan which, for obvious reasons, I can't explain."

"Of course."

"Anyways, to business. Sadly, there's no good news to tell you. Van Greuning is playing the deceit game. Gail is not in the Coloured correctional at all. He claims," Stuart made finger quotes in the air, "he never gave orders to have her arrested, knows nothing about any arrest. As to that, I got a written statement from him, but there are no records."

Ed snorted. "He's lying. There are people at the house who witnessed her being snatched by the thugs who've been keeping watch."

"We both realise that. I'm working on it, but I'm afraid it will take a jury and a judge, and you wouldn't believe how long these things can take. Even if you did know, you'd be judging by White standards. In her case—"

"How about if we bypassed the courts and took a shortcut?" Ed slipped an envelope out of his pocket.

"What have we here?" Stuart's eyes gleamed.

"Gail has been at work herself. Let's not underestimate her." He handed over the contents of the envelope.

Stuart snatched it and read the letter.

Dear Ed or Mark,

I am safe. Hopefully, they didn't get you too, Ed.

I have made a deal with the bearer of this note.

She will deliver messages, but she is terrified.
Be careful. I hope everything is okay. I
would've <u>liked soap</u>.

Solvere sollicitat,
Gail

"It doesn't say much." Stuart returned the paper. "Too bad she didn't tell us where they took her, but I'm glad she's safe. Your lady is very erudite, Latin and all."

"That's what interested me more. Unfortunately, I only had one year of Latin, in standard six, and the only thing I remember is how to decline *mensa*. You are a lawyer."

"With limited knowledge of Latin, I'm afraid. Here, let me take another squiz at that," said Stuart, taking the note back and frowning. "Solvere sollicitat. Let's see, clearly solvere is to solve."

"Obviously, a message to work out?"

"Yes, you're right, something in this paper." He flipped it over and, seeing nothing, turned it back. "I can't remember what sollicitat means."

At that moment, Thabisa returned. She'd put on a medium-length jacket with Zulu patterns, which nevertheless exposed a good deal of her legs. She carried a tray with teapot, cups and saucers, and a plate of Marie biscuits.

When Ed jumped to his feet, reaching for the tea tray, Thabi's mouth dropped and she turned away. "*Cha cha mnumzane*, it's my job."

Stuart looked up from the couch. "Relax, Thabi, Ed's just showing his good manners. This isn't your job anymore."

She released the tray to Ed and stood, shoulders hunched, hands clasped under her neck.

Stuart smiled at her. "Thanks for the tea, my love."

"Yebo." She smiled at Ed. "Please, help yourself, *mnumzane*."

Stuart thanked her. "*Ngiyabonga*, Thabi. Oh! I wonder if you'd bring me a book from my office, it's a Latin dictionary, under L."

"Of course." She flashed her teeth in a smile for Ed and wiggled away.

"Help yourself to biscuits, Ed, and I'll pour you a cup."

But Thabisa returned within seconds, he had hardly lifted the teapot, and handed him the dictionary. He gave her hand a kiss and then opened the book.

"Here we go. Sollicitat. Puzzle. That's it, she's given us a puzzle to solve."

Ed frowned. "What sort of puzzle, where?"

"It has to be on the page. She's written some kind of message for us."

Ed peered over Stuart's shoulder and reread the letter. "Wait a minute, she's asking for soap. Why does she say she would've liked soap?"

"Hmmm. All this intrigue for a bar of soap. You're right. And why is that underlined?"

Thabi hurried across to a sideboard while they were scratching their heads and returned with a Scrabble box. She chuckled at their faces. "It's an anagram."

Stuart slapped his brow. "Of course! Your wife is quick-witted and smart. Solving the anagram will tell us where she is."

Ed agreed. "Right, soap is something she could ask for without suspicion. I guess this Susanne is too thick to know about the anagram."

"Well then, let's start with just liked soap. There's no J for jail, so it's a name only."

Stuart took the box and emptied the letters. "Thanks, Thabi, you love Scrabble. Join us."

They quickly took out the needed letters, and all three searched for syllables.

"I've got D-A-L," said Ed.

"Great. There're lots of places ending with dal."

They stared at the remaining pieces. I-K-E-S-O-P.

Three vowels. "Let's start with one consonant and go through the vowels," said Ed, taking the S and forming SIK and SIP.

178

Stuart shook his head. "No luck there, let's start with K then. Let's see, KIS, KIP. I guess not."

Thabi grabbed his hand as he was on the point of sweeping the pieces away. "Stop. It may be Afrikaans. If you use an O, Kop is head."

"Yes," said Ed. "And also a land feature, koppie, a small hill. And that uses a P. No, that can't be right, koppie has two P's."

Stuart slapped his forehead. "Give Gail a break, she had to figure this out. Without the extra P, we've got kopie, and that leaves only an S."

Thabisa clapped her hands together. "Koppiesdal. My grandmother lives there."

"Of course, you've got it!" Stuart gave her another kiss. "Brilliant. It's near Cato Ridge, and it has a jail, Koppiesdal Jail. Van Greuning, the crafty devil, he's hiding her there, well out of town." He stood up. "Let's go get her."

"What makes you think they'll release her?" Ed stood, too.

"Because I made Van Greuning sign an affidavit that he had nothing to do with Gail's incarceration. He can't suddenly claim he'd arrested her. They have no grounds for holding her at Koppiesdal Jail. This is nothing less than a kidnapping."

"*Hhayibo*," Thabi said, eyes wide as she stared at the men standing. "You can't go away. Hauw! First, you must drink the tea."

They sat down and he enjoyed the tea. In spite of the urgency, it turned into a comfortable tea break with Thabi joining the conversation. Ed listened to her accent and found it attractive. He realised he'd never thought that before. This was completely new to him, an African bringing him tea in the house where she actually lived. A cultured and beautiful Black. One with whom Stuart chose to live and who would surely be his wife if the law allowed it. He couldn't help staring. This should have been a perfectly normal scene, unremarkable, but instead it seemed surreal. A feeling of warmth washed over him; due to his choosing Gail, he belonged to this strange new world.

"Thank you so much," he said, as she refilled his teacup and held the plate of biscuits for him.

"*Akunandaba,* don't mention it, *mnumzane.*"

*****

Gail gripped the bars, her mouth tight, and frowned at Susanne.

"There isn't anything for me?" This wasn't possible. Couldn't they figure out the importance of the Latin message? *Didn't Ed notice I included Mark, who knows Latin?*

Susanne shook her head. "Your Ed wasn't at work. They said he had this morning off."

Gail frowned. "But you did hand him the message you took in yesterday?"

Susanne's face turned red. "Yes, miss. Honestly, I did. I told him I'd be back yust this morning. Truly, I did." She twisted her hands together, and tears flowed from the corners of her eyes.

"Yesterday, I said if he was not there, to leave it with Mark. Did you ask Mark today?"

"I did, as true as Bob, but the man called Mark said he didn't know nothing about it."

"I suppose you didn't ask him when Ed would be back?"

Susanne shook her head.

Of course not. She shouldn't be too upset. She still needed Susanne. Wait. She said Ed took the morning off. Maybe this afternoon? No, she couldn't send Susanne again. This place was far from town, and the woman had her job to do—the job of guarding her.

"Please, Miss Gail, does this mean you won't do my hair and makeup?" The tears were flowing now.

She sighed. "Don't worry, Susanne. I'll keep my word."

Back to the waiting game. She was quite aware of what happened to non-White people who broke political laws...and yes, immorality laws. Her jaw clenched. What's immoral about being with someone you loved more than life?

The dying rays of the afternoon sun found their way through the small, barred window of her cell. It was getting late. They had taken her wristwatch, together with her clothes, when she'd arrived, and she wore the shapeless grey prisoner's tunic they'd given her.

Gail turned to the *Huisgenoot* article she had yet to read, about applying makeup the most effective way. Certainly, this would be useful if and when she got to repay Susanne for her services.

Some noises from the office area distracted her from reading. A banging door, voices. Angry voices, coming this way.

"Ed." She rushed to the bars and so did he. His gaze swept over her, warming her body, and his eyes glistened with tears. His arms reached through the bar openings to hold her gently. She leaned her face to the bars, and his lips met hers in a passion. She didn't want it to stop despite the cold and hard metal between them. All the anguish, the fears, the despair were fading and turning to hope and pleasure as he pressed harder.

Loud voices made them break apart. Ed turned away and faced two men who strode in from the main office. The younger, taller one looked distinguished in a dark suit. The loudly protesting one behind him wore a rumpled prison guard's uniform. "I can't, I tell you. I have my orders from Sergeant Van Greuning himself."

The suited one stopped and faced him. "I need a copy of those for the court. Otherwise, Van Greuning's got nothing to do with this. He told me so himself. Here's a court order for her release and a letter from him." He waved them in front of the guard's face. "An affidavit, confirming he has no knowledge of Mrs. Brent's incarceration. Copies for you, so you won't get into trouble."

The guard pulled a pair of glasses from his top pocket, snatched at the papers, and started reading them.

The younger one pointed to the cell, waiting. "Open up, please."

Slowly, the guard pulled a keyring from his belt and walked to the cell.

"Gail, this is Stuart Albright," Ed told her. "He's a lawyer. Van Greuning raided Mrs. Cahill's flat and locked me up, too. Stuart got me out."

Stuart held out his hand. "Hi, Gail. Pleased to meet you."

The guard unlocked the cell door and headed out to the offices.

"Come, my sweetheart," said Ed, putting his arm round Gail's shoulders and urging her towards the hall.

She spotted Susanne cowering in the corner, her face tear streaked. "Ed, give me a sheet of paper from your notebook and your pen, and you go ahead."

While Ed walked on, casting a puzzled look over his shoulder, she held the paper on her knee and scribbled a note, then hurried to where Susanne stood. She pressed the folded note into Susanne's fist. "I haven't forgotten," she whispered. "Thank you. You did your job, and I'll do mine as your beautician."

Susanne read the address and broke into a quivering smile. Looking into her grateful, smiling face, Gail couldn't help believing her task was already half done.

CHAPTER
TWENTY-FIVE

Gail hurried to join Ed, and they walked outside, where Stuart stood on the pavement.

"Stuart. I can't thank you enough," said Ed.

"Me too." Gail was indeed grateful and hoped she had seen the last of that dreadful jail cell. Could it possibly be over? Stuart was certainly a clever lawyer, and he had got them off this time. But what now? So far, they had broken no laws. Still when they did—she couldn't imagine otherwise, for it would mean staying apart forever.

"I recommend discretion and caution for a while, Ed," Stuart said. "Would you, if possible, stay apart until Van Greuning gets off your case?" He held his car door open for her, and she climbed in and scooted past the steering wheel to sit in the middle, sinking into leather cladded luxury. Ed entered from the other side and sat next to her.

As the luxurious car sped back toward Pietermaritzburg, she leaned her body against Ed's. He had his arm around her and nuzzled her hair with his lips. She was too worried to enjoy it, especially as she hadn't had a bath since her imprisonment.

Stuart turned off the freeway and immediately slowed. "Looks like the traffic's snarled up, maybe an accident."

Ed frowned. "Or a roadblock."

She looked ahead and caught sight of a police car. Her heart raced. It was a roadblock. An officer in the distance was waving the cars through. They merged into one lane only and a slow start-stop queue developed. The time it took to creep, inch by inch, toward the police, passed entirely too quickly for Gail's state of terror, though the severe discomfort of her pounding heart and sweaty brow made it seem forever.

Three to go, two. Finally, it was their turn. The officer signalling the cars stopped and held his hand up, palm out. Two other uniformed men appeared from nowhere.

"Pull over to the curb, please," said the first, unclipping a radio from his belt and holding it to his mouth. "We've got them."

Stuart pulled the car over and switched off the engine. A familiar anxiety gnawed at Gail's solar plexus. They were the only car that had been pulled over, perhaps this was for a traffic violation. Stuart's speedometer had read ninety miles per hour more than once on the hilly, winding freeway leading into Pietermaritzburg. A glance at the wristwatch they'd returned to her on leaving the prison showed they'd waited ten minutes on the side of the road, and still nobody had come. This was no traffic violation.

Further up the road, the door of a large police van opened. An officer walked toward them, slapping his baton on his palm. As he neared, she recognised him as Sgt. Van Greuning. He stopped outside Stuart's open window.

"*Nouja*," he said in his gravelly accent, still thumping the solid looking baton onto his palm. "Do you want to explain why you broke my prisoner out of jail?"

Stuart stuck his head out the window. "What prisoner is that?"

"Don't play games with me, Mr. Albright. Miss Rabe, the one who is sitting right next to you."

"What? This lady? She's not a prisoner. She was never arrested. I'm sure I don't understand what you mean, Sergeant."

"I believe she calls herself Mrs. Brent now, and I arrested her myself."

"You arrested her? I'm so sorry, Sergeant, but surely you're confused." He reached in his pocket. "I have a paper right here, signed by yourself, stating you never arrested anybody going by either name."

Van Greuning gave a momentary start, then recovered. "Let me see that." He snatched the document and opened it. "That's funny. I can't remember writing this paper, but I do remember arresting Miss Rabe. And I am going to take her back and also arrest you." With that, he ripped the paper, scrunched up the pieces, and scattered them to the wind. "Oh, I'm sorry. My hand slipped."

Gail gasped, but Stuart simply frowned at the torn paper and shook his head. "Don't you worry. These accidents happen. No need to apologise. It was just a copy. I locked the real letter up in my safe."

Van Greuning scowled at him. "I warn you, Albright."

"No, actually I'm warning you, Sergeant. You can't go around arresting people for no reason and then denying you did to the extent of writing letters to prove it. You're chancing your arm here, and that sort of thing can lead to your getting fired chop-chop, you know."

Van Greuning tapped his baton again and bit his lip.

"Another thing," continued Stuart. "You threatened to arrest me. Do you honestly want to arrest a criminal lawyer? Think about it." He held one hand up, splaying his fingers. "Let me see. False arrest." He counted the fingers. "Destruction of evidence, changing a prisoner's place of incarceration, holding up traffic…"

Van Greuning's face grew red, and his jawbone moved from side to side as he glared at Stuart. "Mr. Albright, you'd better be careful." He whacked his baton on Stuart's door. "You want to play games, *nê*? Let me warn you, that can be dangerous."

Stuart's voice turned serious. "You know your little games with the law can have serious consequences for you. *Nê?*"

"*Nouja, laat hom gaan,*" Van Greuning yelled to the other three policemen and stepped back.

"Thanks, Sergeant, ta ta for now." Stuart tipped two fingers to his forehead and pulled the car back onto the road.

Nobody in the car spoke for a while. Outside, it had turned dark. "Where are we going?" she whispered to Ed.

"To Cahill's, to pick up my car. Stuart picked me up there."

Gail sensed the tension in the car. What were the others thinking? Van Greuning was dangerous and unscrupulous. They might be safe for the time being, but who knew for how long? Van Greuning, though a police officer, clearly had contempt for the law.

The ride to Cahill's did not take long, and Stuart pulled up alongside the parking lot. While they were getting out and thanking Stuart, Gail heard a clumping noise behind them.

"Dolores?" Ed said. "What are you doing here so late?"

Dolores smiled tightly at Ed but threw a contemptuous glance Gail's way. "Good evening, Ed. It's stock-taking time. You know that, don't you? Some of us work while you go gallivanting around the country."

Ed turned with a small grin. "Now now, Dolores. I've done my share of counting stock. I finished days ago. I can't help it if the bookwork is still going on."

Dolores humphed as she unlocked her car door. "Well, I need to go home, can't hang around here talking."

"Of course, goodnight, Dolores."

"Goodnight."

Ed turned back to Stuart. "Thanks, Stuart, for everything. I'm really in your debt for returning Gail to me."

"Think nothing of it, Ed. Can you come and see me at the house before work tomorrow? There are a few things I want to go over with you regarding Gail's imprisonment. A pleasure meeting you, Gail."

"Me too, thank you so much," she answered. "It definitely was a pleasure meeting you."

"Well, I must be off. There are things to do." Stuart shifted up the gear lever.

"So I can imagine," said Ed. "Send my best to Thabi."

His car sped off.

Dolores's car followed, dangerously close to the curb, forcing Gail to hop back.

Ed caught her and glared after the car. "Are you okay?"

"Yes, I'm fine."

Ed held the door of his car for her, and he drove off.

Who is Thabi?" she asked.

"Um," he said, running a finger under his collar.

"It's a Zulu name."

"Er—yes. She's his servant."

She stared at him. "Ed?"

After glancing back, he let out a puff of air. "Okay. She's his live-in girlfriend, but please keep that under your hat."

"Of course." It was nice to know she wasn't alone.

What was Thabisa's part in this? Living her life in secret. They surely couldn't legally go out anywhere. If she went out, would she have to wear a servant's uniform? And what must it be like living a life of secrecy? Did she have Zulu friends? Did she have White friends? What happened when Stuart got visitors or clients? Did she go hide in her servant's quarters? This didn't make her feel better about her own situation, only worse.

*****

The shrill ring of Ed's alarm woke him with a start. He pushed in the button to stop the racket. Great! He'd set it back an hour because of Stuart's request. A whole hour less sleep after a rough day. What did Stuart want anyhow?

Half an hour later, he turned into Stuart's road but slowed the car as he neared his house. He could see Stuart's Vanden Plas R up at the top of his drive, but several police cars and vans were in the road. Maybe an accident. He hoped this wouldn't delay him. He drove on slowly, but as he approached, it became clear they were gathered directly in front of Stuart's house. All the blood in his face drained at once. He jammed his foot on the brake and tightened his grip on the wheel. This could only mean one thing.

As if to confirm his thought, the door to Stuart's house opened and a familiar figure stumbled out. Thabisa, he realised, had been pushed roughly by two police officers behind her. She stumbled and nearly fell down the steps. On the path, the officers stood on either side of her and forced her toward the gate. She held her head high, remaining silent while they pushed her toward one of the vans. She climbed in the back, turned, and saw Ed's car. Her eyes widened. She shook her head almost imperceptibly before sitting on the bench. The two officers climbed in after her and slammed the door.

Ed remained seated, tightening his grip on the wheel to a painful level. This was dangerous. He needed to get out of there. His thoughts raced as he grappled with the idea of jumping in the van to rescue Thabi. Impossible. The cops held their guns at the ready. Others were coming down the drive. He wouldn't have a hope.

To the left, a triumphant-looking Van Greuning led Stuart out by his arm, his hands obviously cuffed behind his back. Somehow, the police had found out about his illegal affair with his Black maid. Apparently, Stuart's "plan" for such an event had failed.

Any moment, Van Greuning might spot Ed or recognise his car. To his relief, another officer impatiently waved him on. He needed no second bidding and managed to pull away without spinning the wheels.

The hairs on his neck bristled as he drove off, thinking of the consequences this would have for Gail and him.

The moment he left Stuart's road, Ed gunned the motor, breaking almost every traffic rule in the books until he braked in front of Candy's house. His tyres screeched, leaving dark traces of tyre rubber in the road. He rushed through the gate and hammered on the door.

Leonard, a cup of coffee in his hand, opened the door.

"Quick, Leonard," Ed barked. We've got to get Gail out of here."

Gail rushed around the corner, dressed in a nightie.

"Van Greuning arrested Stuart and Thabi," he said, hurrying to her and wrapping her in his arms. "Quick. With Stuart out the way, he's free to lock you up again. Throw something on and grab what you need, quickly."

She vanished back around the corner without a word. At once, the house was busy. Leonard, Ria and Candy were rushing around, packing stuff, helping Gail.

"Leonard," he said. "Have they been watching the house?"

Leonard shook his head. "Nobody for a long time, *ek sê*."

"I need the phone." Before Leonard could reply, Ed lunged to it and dialled a number. "Chantal. I'm so glad you're there."

CHAPTER
TWENTY-SIX

Gail's heart hammered in her ears while she changed into a pair of jeans and a T-shirt, not caring whether they matched. She threw whatever of her belongings she could lay her hands on into her small suitcase and rushed back into the kitchen.

Ed was just putting down the phone. "Chantal's at work," he said. "She's going to get off and come to fetch you. She doesn't want me to bring you because she thinks the cops will be watching for my car. She's probably right."

Gail swallowed. "But we can't stay here. Without Stuart, the first thing Van Greuning's going to do is pick me up."

Ed chewed his lip. "My place is just as bad. I know. We can hide at Cahill's until Chantal comes."

"No. That would be the next place on their list, and what about Dolores? She would gladly point us out to them wherever we're hiding."

"Leave it to me." Ed dialled the phone again. "Mark, has Dolores arrived yet? No. Good, we need to come in. Can you organize an errand for her?"

Mark's voice blasted through the receiver loud enough for Gail to hear, sounding somehow both excited and amused, but she couldn't make out the words.

"We appreciate it, Mark." He replaced the receiver and looked at her. "He's taking care of it. We need to leave at once."

Leonard opened the door a few inches and looked through the gap. "I'll drop you off," he said.

Ed laid a hand on his shoulder. "Thank you, Leonard. We owe you." Taking Gail's hand, Ed hurried her to the car.

Gail's wristwatch said five past eight when Leonard dropped them at Cahill's front door. Still early. Mark stood in the doorway, beckoning them.

"First, into the studio. I need passport photos for both of you," he said.

Despite her protests about not being ready, Mark sat her down on the stool and told her to face the camera. Multiple flashes went off in her face. While she still saw spots, Mark pulled something like paper out the camera. He gently waved it in the air and after what seemed like ages, but probably only a minute, pulled a white card off and looked at it.

"Perfect. Okay, Ed."

Ed shooed her gently off the stool and sat down himself.

A couple of minutes later, Mark seemed satisfied with the two double pictures he held in his hand. "Quick, Ed, we're going to put you two in Mommy's office."

Mommy's office? It was the first room right next to the showroom. Surely, the first place they would search, but Ed made no argument as he rushed after Mark, pulling her behind him.

Mark stood at the door. "Lock the door behind you. If we give you the signal, put out the light. Dolores won't be back for an hour or so."

"How did you get rid of her for so long?" asked Ed.

Mark grinned. "Easy, I sent her to Mommy's house. "Dolores just loves being useful to her, as you know. I phoned Mommy to let her in on it, and she said not to worry, she could handle it."

"Mark, we appreciate this."

"Nonsense, old chap. Now go in there with your honey. I'm sure you two will think of something to do."

Ed pulled Gail through the doorway and closed and locked the door.

Gail pointed. "What about the window?" It was long, about six feet wide and a foot high, giving a clear view of the whole shop.

Mommy probably used it to keep an eye on what her staff were doing, right from her desk chair.

Ed turned to look at the window. "What about it?"

She sighed. "If we can see out, they can see in."

He raised an eyebrow. "Oh, that. For one, the light will be off, and two, it's a one-way mirror. So we staff never know whether Mommy is giving us the hairy eyeball. All we see is a mirror."

Yes, she remembered seeing a mirror at the back of the shop. "Are you sure?"

"With your face right up against the mirror, you can sort of distinguish a few things, but only if the light is on inside. When Mark signals, we'll put it off."

Her body relaxed a little, then tensed again. "Surely, he'll want the door opened."

"Mark has a plan." He bit his lip. "I hope."

So do I. She looked around. Numerous family pictures adorned the walls, which were panelled in wood. A wedding photo, one of a man, one of Mrs. Cahill, and then lots of kids. Near the back stood a huge kidney-shaped desk, with a polished wooden top, probably mahogany. It was more like a table. And behind the desk...an office chair, the like of which she had never seen. Huge, white, sumptuous, and so inviting.

Ed caught her eye. "Race you."

Gail dashed to the left of the desk, Ed to the right, snapping off the light on his way. They both made a dive for the chair at the same time, and she landed on his lap. Of course, she stayed there.

"Alone at last," he whispered into her ear.

"You turned the light off," she whispered back, giving him a glare. What was the use of that? He couldn't see her.

"Only to be safe." His breath felt hot in her ear. "Clearly, we wouldn't want Van Greuning to observe us, would we?"

"No. We certainly do not." Gail placed her palm on his cheek. It was rough from his stubble. Obviously, he'd been in too much of a hurry to shave this morning. She leaned into his neck. She heard his breath catch and sensed his arms fold around her and pull her in close. Their lips met, she marvelled at their softness as they explored her own. She closed her eyes and surrendered herself to the moment as their kiss deepened. At least they were together as disaster waited for them outside.

*****

Ed heard noises from out in the shop and groaned in frustration. Through the one-way window, he saw a bunch of uniformed policemen pouring through the entrance. With horror, he spotted Van Greuning himself. Mark approached the sergeant and the two talked briefly, though of course Ed couldn't hear what they said. Van Greuning gave orders to his men. Two rushed into the studio area, one walked to the right towards the clerical offices, and two more came straight towards their office.

Ed slipped off the chair with Gail and crawled under the table. Her whole body trembled in his arms, and he drew her in closer.

The door handle rattled, and someone banged loudly on the door. Gail's body trembled harder. He cradled her head against his shoulder.

Someone shouted right outside the door. "*Dit is geslote, meneer.*"

"Oh?" Van Greuning said. "Why is that? Why is the door locked?"

"This is Mrs. Cahill's office." Mark answered calmly. "Sorry, she isn't here."

"So that means she locks her door?" Van Greuning replied, voice skeptical.

"Of course," said Mark. "That's where the safe is, and Mrs. Cahill keeps her personal stuff here."

Ed could hear only a silence for several seconds.

"Mr. Brent is not in today, you say?"

"No. Actually, I got a phone call from him this morning," Mark returned. "He sounded very panicked…said he wouldn't be in today. Not for the foreseeable future, in fact. He was talking about flying to Joburg."

A long pause ensued, through which Ed held his breath. Mark was obviously offering a red herring. Would Van Greuning take it?

"I need this door unlocked."

"Mrs. Cahill has the key, and she isn't in. I'm sorry," said Mark.

Gail's whole body shuddered. Ed gritted his teeth. *Why did we come here?* Of course, this would be Van Greuning's next stop after Candy's house. And surely, a locked door would only increase his suspicions?

"There must be another key," Van Greuning snapped. "For emergencies. No doubt Mrs. Pieterse keeps one."

"Dolores?" said Mark. "She's on an errand to Mrs. Cahill's now, and she won't be back for several hours. Maybe she has a key here. We can search her office if you'd like."

Another long pause, an eternity. Eventually, he heard footsteps going toward the darkrooms, and Ed released his breath. Gail's body slowly relaxed so deeply he thought she'd fainted.

Perhaps a quarter of an hour later, the footsteps returned. Van Greuning said, "I need to make a phone call."

He heard Van Greuning ask for Mommy's number and then the sound of dialling.

"Mrs. Cahill? This is Sergeant Van Greuning, SAP. Yes, good morning. I have one question. Do you keep your office locked? You do? Uh-huh—Perhaps you have another key?—The only key, hey? And Mrs. Pieterse, she doesn't. Oh, she's with you now?—No, no. That won't be necessary, Mrs. Cahill." Van Greuning muttered his thanks and the receiver clunked back onto its cradle.

"*Kom, ons gaan na die lughawe.*"

The cops were going to the airport. Mark's red herring had worked. Ed, finally able to breathe again, held Gail until Mark knocked on the door and announced, "All clear."

Gail sighed, sounding relieved.

They crawled out from under the table, and he unlocked the door, opening it a few inches.

"He's left one of his goons on watch out front," Mark whispered. "He'll presumably stay till Van Greuning twigs on that you never were at the airport, then I imagine he'll raise a stink. You might want to be on your way to Chantal's before that happens."

"Thanks, Mark," he murmured. "I take it we'll need to go out the rear exit."

"Unless you think the two of you can sneak past our friend on the pavement outside without suspicion."

Ed Looked through the one-way glass at the constable pacing up and down. "By the look of him, I guess it would be a piece of cake." He chuckled. "But just to be sure, we'll take the back way."

Both Ed and Mark had used the "back way" on more than one occasion when it had been expedient to avoid someone. He took Gail's case, and they exited through the labs, where Candy and Pamela wished Gail farewell and hugged her. They continued out the back door, past the toilets, to the unroofed, walled enclosure. At the brick wall, he climbed on the chest-high rubbish bin, tossed her case over, and returned to help her up.

"Can you manage to climb over?" he asked her in concern.

"You forget I was at boarding school."

"Huh?"

She fixed him with a stare that he couldn't decipher. "Oh, Ed. Didn't you ever read *Schoolgirls' Own* boarding school stories? They were always breaking bounds. Watch me."

In a moment, she was sitting atop the wall, checking out her surroundings, then she dropped down the other side. With rising panic, he scrambled up the bin, breathing a sigh of relief when he saw her standing below, arms akimbo.

"You coming or what?" she asked, tossing her head.

Happily, he climbed down next to her. "Mark will tell Chantal where to pick us up. Let's go."

CHAPTER
TWENTY-SEVEN

They hurried through lanes and alleys to the parking building off Pietermaritz St. Gail expected to see a cop on every corner. Instead, she was rewarded by the sight of Chantal, waiting inside the building's entrance.

Chantal waved. "Gail."

She fell into Chantal's hug, and her tension dissipated. For a long time, the two remained together. Words were unnecessary. Chantal was the sister she'd never had. She needed her now.

Ed stood by, checking his wristwatch, shifting his weight from foot to foot. "Right," he said at last. "You two need to go before Van Greuning draws a blank at the airport."

She spun round. "What about you? Aren't you coming with us?" She grabbed his hand.

"Chantal doesn't have the room, and she's risking her neck as it is. We can't be together yet." He squeezed her hand and drew her into a hug with the other. "Don't worry, Mark organised a safe room for me. It's in a rough, Coloured area we think will be safe to hide in. We'll be making plans. Leonard is working on a false passport using the pictures we took this morning. Do you have a proper passport, Gail?"

"I do. Sometimes, I go to Swaziland, so I brought it with me."

"Oh, Gail, be safe, my darling," he said. She snuggled closer. He cradled her head and kissed her hard. His lips expressed the same desperation she felt as to their impending separation, one of undetermined length. They parted, but he held onto her hands and gazed into her eyes, his own telling her the things they hadn't enough time to say. "We'll be in contact the moment we've made plans. Look after her, Chantal."

"Of course." Chantal laid her hand on Gail's shoulder as if to pry them apart and tugged her toward her car while Gail kept turning round to keep Ed in sight.

Chantal unlocked the passenger door of her car and all but shoved her in. Gail said from the passenger seat. "Thanks so much, Chantal. I hate imposing on you."

"It's only a pleasure, Gail," she said before climbing in herself. She stomped on the accelerator, tyres squealing. Before exiting the building, she flapped her left hand for Gail to duck out of sight.

Chantal muttered as she waited to turn into the busy street. Finally, she entered with tyres protesting.

Gail looked around the interior. *Looks brand new.* She determined it was a Triumph GT6. A closed sports car. It lacked the space she'd experienced in the cars she'd been in recently. It was very low, with little room to keep her head hidden. The dashboard was full of instruments and switches. She found the speedometer and gasped at the speed it indicated. Chantal kept changing gears, clearly there were five. But despite the numerous instruments, the car lacked a clock, so she glanced at her wristwatch. Twenty past eight. That couldn't be, she must have forgotten to wind it.

"What's the time, Chantal?" she asked.

Chantal checked her watch. "Ten past ten."

Ten! Her entire body stiffened.

Chantal turned and her eyebrows shot up. "Gail! Whatever's the matter? You're as white as a sheet."

At any other time, she'd be happy to hear that, but now..."Chantal, I completely forgot an appointment."

Chantal frowned as she braked for a red robot. "An appointment. Now?"

"No, actually ten minutes ago." She shivered as an icy feeling gripped her heart.

Chantal huffed. "That isn't what I meant. Appointment? Seriously? For a dentist, doctor, hairdo?"

"Not for me, for Susanne." How could she explain?

The light turned green, and Chantal pulled off so rapidly she must have had her pedal on the floor.

"Susanne was my jailer," Gail continued. "I promised to do her hair and makeup if she took a message to Ed, which led to my being freed."

"Okay, so considerate of you Gail, but I don't think we have time for—"

"You don't understand, I promised. I must keep my word."

Chantal sighed heavily. "Fine. Where's this appointment?"

"At Candy's house, where I was staying."

"Candy's house? But…"

"Sure, I realise they are watching it, but what can I do? I can't betray her. Besides, she might still be useful."

Chantal frowned at her. "You are serious, I suppose."

At Gail's nod, Chantal pushed the turn indicator and swung the wheel. The car spun around within the width of the road. "Good job this car turns on a tickey, hey?" she said and headed toward Candy's.

They pulled up at the house where a dejected looking Susanne was walking away. Her head hung down, and her face was red and wet with tears. Gail dashed out the car and put an arm round her.

"I'm waiting here," Chantal called. "Keeping an eye out for the police."

Gail waved and returned to the house with Susanne, who smiled at her in relief.

Inside Candy's room, Ria gave her makeup supplies, together with a hairdryer, curling tongs and brushes. Gail covered Susanne's body with a sheet and got to work.

After half an hour, Gail was making progress. She'd done the hair and had just finished with the lipstick when Chantal poked her head around the door. One look at Susanne and her jaw dropped. She took a deep breath, motioned Gail to the door, and pulled her into the hall. The door closed with a thud. "Gail, what do you think you're doing?"

Gail gaped at her. "What do you mean? Didn't I tell you, I was—"

"I know what you told me, but…honestly, Gail, the poor girl."

Gail coloured. "I know. Her face is unfortunate, but we mustn't judge."

Chantal scratched her forehead and stared at Gail. "It isn't her face that's unfortunate…it's her beautician." Her mouth relaxed into a grin. "Sure, we mustn't judge, Gail, but where did you learn your… um…beauty parlour skills? You're repaying her by giving her clown cheeks and racoon eyes. And parting so much of her hair to the side, with her face!"

Gail dropped her head. "That bad, huh? Maybe I should practice more on myself first."

"You are beautiful enough without makeup. This girl isn't. Shame man, people will laugh at her. She needs someone who knows what she's doing."

Gail bit her thumbnail. "She'll hate me. This is how I repay her for what she did for me."

Chantal put her arm around Gail's shoulders. "Come, Gail." She led her to the kitchen window and looked out. "See that mountain?"

"Yes, part of the Drakensberg."

"That is how big your heart is. Now, look at that pebble on the pathway?"

Gail looked.

"That pebble represents your beautician skills."

Gail lifted a corner of her mouth. "Thank you for your honesty, but…" She peered at Chantal hopefully. "You mean you'll do it for me? For her?"

Chantal laughed out loud. "Me? Talk about going from bad to worse. No. While I was here for your wedding, I had a complete makeover. Lucy's got skills, I'm telling you. I'll see if she's free. It'll definitely be quicker than if we tried to sort out your mess."

Chantal made a quick phone call and came back. "Let's go. Lucy can take her now. She's a magician."

When Chantal walked back to the bedroom, Gail stood and chewed her lip.

"What now?" Chantal asked.

"I doubt I can afford it. My bank balance is—"

"Stop. This is on me." Chantal took her hand and dragged her to the door. Inside, Chantal explained to Susanne that Gail was stressed out, nervous, missing supplies, and wasn't doing the best job she could, so they were taking her to a professional. Susanne took a peek at her face in the dressing table mirror and didn't seem to mind in the least.

Roughly ninety minutes later, Susanne sat in front of the mirror, perky and happy. Lucy had curled back her lanky, straight hair at the top and sides in bold waves, with thick waves descending past her shoulders. The coverup Lucy had applied transformed her pale, tear-stained face into unblemished smoothness, a touch of eyeshadow accentuated her blue eyes, and a sweep of pink emphasised her cheekbones. Susanne turned to the mirror for another look and smiled in a way Gail had never seen before.

"Susanne, you're...you're...beautiful," Gail said.

Susanne hugged her and Gail squeezed her back.

"How can I mos thank you?" said Susanne.

"Don't worry. You earned it."

"I'll do whatever I can to protect yous from him," Susanne promised.

They dropped Susanne off at the station, where she happily waved them off.

"Thank you, Chantal. You're the best friend ever," said Gail after they'd started on their way to Durban.

Chantal simply flipped her hand. "A pleasure, but now let's get you to safety. I'd better put foot."

She certainly did. The busy, hard-pressed engine, with a noisy exhaust note, ate up the miles to her flat.

Gail took her suitcase from the boot and followed Chantal, nearly bumping into her as she suddenly halted. Chantal was staring at the door. Gail spotted gouge marks on the doorframe. Someone had broken in.

"The police have been here," someone said from behind them.

Gail swung round. A very tall, lean young man with red hair walked up to them.

"Eric." Chantal introduced him as her neighbour, then turned back to him. "The police?" Chantal pointed at the lock. "Did you see them?"

"A whole gang of them. What have you been up to now?" He grinned at her with a wink.

Chantal ignored the remark. "When did this happen?"

"Not much after eleven."

"Thanks, Eric. Come, Gail," she said, as she dashed to the car. "Do you realise we would've been here, inside, at exactly the time the cops broke in." She gave Gail an impromptu hug. "To think I was mad at you for wanting to keep your promise to Susanne. Imagine if you hadn't."

Gail agreed, feeling a tingling in her spine. It sure was close. And how did the police know about Chantal? "But what now?"

Chantal furrowed her eyebrows, tapping her finger on her chin. The door swung open after she twisted the door handle. She rushed into her flat, emerging again a minute later with a large bag. "Nurse uniforms," she explained. "We're going to the hospital."

*****

The noise of the buzzer filled the room. Ed ran up the steps, crawled out the skillfully hidden entrance to the basement, and made his way to the front door where he peered through the peephole as a matter of course. Ragamuffin boys often played tok-tokkie, ringing the bell and running off. He confirmed that Mark and Leonard stood outside, looking tense. He slid the latch, turned the key in the lock, and cracked the door open.

"I've got bad news," said Mark, pushing the door which opened a few inches before being held by a chain. Ed unhooked it and Mark burst in, followed by Leonard. "They're onto Chantal."

"So I heard," said Ed. Chantal had called him from Durban earlier. "She got into the hospital with Gail disguised as a nurse, and Dr. Spence has got her hidden in his office."

Mark let out a breath. "Thank goodness. She also called me from a phone booth before they drove there."

"Mark, we need to get them out of there. Van Greuning will find out where Chantal works and have the whole hospital searched."

"That's why we're having this meeting. We must work fast. Leonard's organising the false passports. A pal of his is pretty good."

Leonard held up his thumb. "The best. He's expensive hey, but he's good."

"You gave him the photos we took today?" Mark asked.

"Yes. It will take time. They need laminating and a seal."

"There isn't much time," Ed broke in. "Van Greuning's only a step behind us. If he gets Gail—" He couldn't complete the sentence. His whole body shuddered, and he sensed the blood drain from his face.

"Gail has her genuine passport, right?" Mark raised an eyebrow. Ed affirmed she did.

"We may need to go with the real ones," said Mark.

"The ones with our actual names." He grimaced; just how many lists were those names on?

"I'm aware you're between a rock and a hard place, Ed. I'm sorry, but the longer we wait, the harder it will be."

Ed agreed, there was sense in that.

"So let's talk about where y'olls going," said Leonard. "I know some okes who've gone to Botswana."

"Fine, but Botswana's so far." Ed chewed his lip. Suddenly, it came to him. "I know! This morning, Gail told me she had a passport because she used to go to Swaziland. Maybe we should go there?"

Mark frowned. "Also a long way, and they may not let you in. Some sort of refugee problem. Our best bet is probably to head for Basutoland, or whatever they call it now… Lesotho."

"You mean up the Sani pass?"

"Yes. It is certainly the closest border and the quietest road."

"The worst is, none of our cars will make it up there. We need four-wheel drive."

Mark's expression turned sombre. "How can we find a Land Rover quickly, Leonard?"

Leonard squinted and scratched his head. "Wait! Naidoo, he's y'oll's friend, isn't he, Ed? He's got one."

"Careful, he's also under Van Greuning's observation," said Ed. "But I do trust him."

"Fine. Let's ask him then. It's the best we can do, right, Ed?" said Mark.

Ed agreed.

"You know," said Mark, "the *Hesperus* is steaming across the Indian Ocean right now. Wouldn't it be delightful if you two simply got on board? Sail away to Senegal or Portugal, Holland or Britain, while eating three meals a day for free, enjoying the swimming pools, playing croquet on deck."

Ed smiled wryly. "Would that it were that easy. You think you can just walk up the gangplank?"

Mark sighed. "Pity though. I've considered taking the trip lots of times."

"And that's another thing. After paying for our false passports, the engagement and wedding rings and what not, do you really imagine I could afford a luxury cruise on an ocean liner?"

"That, unfortunately, is what stopped me. A trifle under two hundred pounds, one way."

Ed whistled. "Four hundred pounds."

Mark winked. "Meals included."

"Right. Now, let's discuss our run to Lesotho."

TWENTY-EIGHT

Gail sat at the desk in Dr. Spence's office, still in a nurse's uniform and wearing a mask, just in case someone walked in, as both Chantal and Dr. Spence had warned her.

After reading the medical posters on the walls three times, they still made no sense to her. Too much medical talk. The only other things to read were pamphlets. Sure, there was a notebook and fountain pen, and, of course, the doctor wouldn't mind if she drew pictures or wrote something, but Gail was not in the mood. She sat tapping the pen for a while and then pushed herself away from the desk. The chair had rollers. Goodie. A few laps around the large adjoining room was the very thing she needed. She grabbed the armrests and pushed off with her legs.

Chantal had long since left, needing to do her job. She'd changed shifts in order to pick Gail up in Pietermaritzburg. Now was payback time.

There was a short rap on the door, and Doctor Spence peered round it. His eyes twinkled after tracking down her position on the rolling chair at the far end of the room. "Ah! Taking a sightseeing trip round the conference room, are we? I can always put you to work taking blood pressure if you're bored."

Her face grew hot. It seemed ages since she'd sneaked into the hospital, making a fool of herself pretending to be Ed's nurse. "If only I could. I know how to do it now. Did you hear anything? I'm going out of my mind waiting."

He shook his head. "Sorry, things are so busy. I haven't even seen Chantal."

"Things are busy? Please, let me help. Really, I remember how to take the readings." She clasped her hands together under her chin.

He pursed his lips. "Now now! You know I couldn't do that, for your own protection. You're not supposed to be in here at all." He rummaged through a pile of journals, folders and binders all over his desk. "Ah, here it is." He lifted a pile of folders and grabbed a book. "I hope you'll pardon me for the mess. I'm lucky I can even find my desk. Dorothy is out on an—"

"Oh, please," Gail broke in. "Let me sort these things out for you, I beg you. I'm so bored."

While he stared at her, she reached out and gently tugged at the folders.

He frowned, holding onto them as a gentle tug o' war ensued. "You, um…you sure you can—?"

She glowered at him, tapping her foot, his surrendered folders in one hand and arms crossed up high.

"Uh. Oh, well er, yes, I see, I suppose you can," he said. "Thanks very much."

He gave her some instructions before departing. Gail set to work, starting with the folders, pulling out the top drawer, and checking the labels.

Dr. Spence paused at the door, one hand on the doorknob. "Look, Gail, I'm sorry. About everything. I mean, everything you've been through. Things must change, as I believe they are, and my wish is I will still be around when you can legitimately work in a White hospital or be a patient in one."

"Yes, I'd love to see that, too. I doubt it, though. Either I'll be gone or in prison by that time. But thank you, Doctor Spence."

He left, closing the door. Gail set to work, grateful at last for having something constructive to do, but it didn't take her long. She had just sat at the desk, starting to write a poem, when the door opened again. A grey-haired lady with a wrinkled but jolly face entered, carrying a huge bundle of documents under one arm.

"Oh, hello. I'm Dorothy Pearce. How do you do? Dr. Spence told me you were doing some clearing up for me. I truly appreciate it." She stared at the clean desk and looked around at the shelves, bookcases and cabinets. "It does look like you know what you're doing. I'm indebted to you."

Gail smiled. "Don't mention it. I was only too happy to be of use, Mrs. Pearce. Um… I could do those for you if you like." She stared at the papers and licked her lips at the idea.

"What? Oh, how sweet of you. There is a lot of work to do, so that would be a great help. I need these sorted into date order."

"Sure. I'd be glad to do that for you."

"Thanks. You're amazing, Gail." She handed the documents over, smiled broadly, and left the room.

Gail started at once, pleased at being able to occupy herself whiling away the hours. What was happening, what decisions were being made, how long would she have to wait? Chantal had assured her beds were available in the hospital for both of them, so it might be days. Gail was used to working quickly, so the pile dwindled. She would ask Mrs. Pearce if she had more, so she could keep her mind off Ed.

The thought made her pause. When would she see him again? He'd said he was at a safe house, making plans. That could take ages. She wished Ed had suggested she stay with him, maybe help with their planning. But she supposed the men wouldn't bother themselves with anything she'd have to say. She was just a woman—a Coloured woman. What use was she to them? Her eyes stung, and she blinked back the tears. It wasn't true. She was a woman, but a smart and well-educated one and could most certainly be of use. Why, she'd even been at one of their own most reputable schools. Of course, she should be with them, sitting around a table, planning their escape.

The pile diminished all too quickly. Carefully, she opened the door, hoping to catch sight of Dorothy. All she saw was an empty corridor, a long one, with doors all along both sides. Which was Dorothy's? It wasn't possible to try them all, anybody might be behind them. She remembered Chantal telling her how lucky it was that Dr. Spence, and not Dr. Swanepoel, was the one who had attended Ed in the hospital and seen through her disguise. Dr. Swanepoel would have called the police on her immediately. And he—or any of tons of people like him—could now be on the other side of any of these doors. With a heavy sigh, she stepped back into hiding.

It was four o' clock. Five minutes after the last time she'd checked the wall clock, ten since the time before. It was as if she'd been in the room for two days rather than a few hours.

Chantal burst into the room. "Let's go." Her face glowed and the fidgeting of her hands and feet revealed her excitement. "We're meeting them in Merrivale. Gather your stuff, change out of the uniform, and make sure you've got your passport."

Gail needed no urging, asked no questions, and was ready in less than a minute. Dr. Spence and Dorothy came in and wished her well. She gave each of them quick hugs and thanked them, effused in fact, but Chantal dragged her out the room. They dashed the same way they'd entered, through thinly populated corridors and passages, and out emergency exit doors to where Chantal's Triumph waited.

"Get in," said Chantal. She threw Gail's suitcase in the back as she climbed in and drove off with wheels spinning.

"You said Merrivale?" Gail knew the small town on the way to Howick, but—

Chantal gave her a quick glance and a smile. "Your new home."

Gail gaped at her. "Merrivale?"

Chantal chuckled. "All bluffs! Gail, your face! Don't worry, it's the junction for the Underberg road. You're off to Lesotho."

Gail stared forward, not flinching when the car drifted around a bend into Smith St. So her new homeland was to be Lesotho. Well, anywhere, so long as she was with Ed, though she did wish she'd had some choice in the matter. It was her future, too. Still, this was no time to pout. If they had come up with a plan that would work, she would be happy. Anywhere but this infernal country.

Chantal frowned. "Are you okay?"

Gail didn't reply. Her thoughts ran to what she would lose.

"Omigosh, Gail. I'm sorry, I can't begin to imagine what you're feeling right now, leaving your mom, your friends, without even seeing them to say goodbye. Then worrying about getting across the border. And I was so flippant."

Chantal reached across to squeeze her hand. Tears had formed on her friend's cheeks. She gave Chantal's hand a quick squeeze in return but took it and placed it on the wheel. "The way you're driving, you need both your hands there, Chantal."

*****

Ed's heart hammered in his chest at the sight of the sports car cresting the hill. Please, no more parting. I want to be with you every minute, forever. The car screeched to a halt in the parking space beside the Land Rover. Before he reached the car door, Gail flung it open and threw herself into his arms. He held her tight and showered her with kisses. His mind focused on Gail only, not caring where he was or where he was going, provided she was in his arms. She looked relieved and happy despite his own apprehensive emotions. Her eyes swept closed, her long eyelashes fanning her tear-stained cheeks, and her lips parted, inviting his. He lowered his head till at last he sensed their softness against his own, then poured all his feelings into a long, deep kiss.

Mark coughed. "I'm sorry to interrupt, old chap, but we do have a long way to go."

"Agreed," Chantal said, hauling Gail's suitcase out of her car. "This road is long and slow, twisty and bumpy, and a Land Rover is not exactly fast. We need to get moving."

Gail shifted her gaze from the Land Rover and stared at her. "You mean you're coming with us?"

Chantal folded her arms and glared at her. "That doesn't deserve an answer, Gail."

Ed lifted his eyebrows. "Of course, you're not. Naidoo arranged picking up the Landie from Lesotho. We've got what we need, and we can make our farewells here." He held his hand out to Mark. "I don't know what to say, you're a friend in a million."

Mark placed his hands on his hips. "Whoa, hold on. You're not suggesting we stay behind?"

"Mark, you don't need to involve yourselves. If things go wrong, you would be implicated. We simply don't want to make trouble for you."

Mark looked at Chantal, who shrugged. "There's gratitude for you," she said. "After all the trouble we took."

"Only doing what friends do," he agreed. "Now, evidently we're to be dumped."

"Having served our purpose, no longer wanted, we're left crying at the side of the road." Chantal sniffed.

Ed looked from one to the other. "Listen you two, it isn't like that. Think of the danger. Being associated with us can get you arrested. We don't have the right, asking you to risk—"

Mark turned to Chantal, cupping a hand to his ear. "Do you hear something?"

Chantal took the handle of Gail's suitcase. "Yes, I believe I do. Some sort of whining, I'm not sure." She swung the suitcase into the back, a grin spreading across her face. "Let them sit in the back, Mark. Bags me driving first." She settled behind the wheel.

Ed stood and gaped at them. "But, I really—" He broke off as Gail yanked him toward the back seat.

As Chantal turned the Land Rover onto the Underberg road, Ed nuzzled his face into Gail's hair. If this kept up, the trip would zip by. The sound of Mark and Chantal's constant banter merged with the rumble of the Landie's tyres. For the next couple of hours, there would be nothing but each other for Ed and Gail.

CHAPTER
TWENTY-NINE

The Land Rover came to a shuddering halt and Gail woke up, her head still on Ed's shoulder. He was asleep, his head resting precariously on the seat back. She sat up and yawned, then heard the ratchety sound of the handbrake.

Chantal turned around. "Hi, you're awake."

Gail stretched as best she could without disturbing Ed. "Where are we? Is this Lesotho already?"

"Not quite," said Mark. "I'm glad you chappies got a bit of sleep. Seems you got bored with all the snogging back there."

Ed started at Mark's voice, opened his eyes, and blinked. It had grown dark, and there wasn't much to see apart from a glowing sign that read: "Customs/Doeana."

"What?" He sat up straight. "Are we here already? In Lesotho?"

"Not yet. This is the border post on the South African side. The Lesotho post is up at the top of Sani Pass, another five miles or more. I shall leave you to drive up it after we're finished here, Ed. I'm thinking of making use of the back seat myself." He eyed Chantal next to him.

Chantal returned his look and smiled a crooked smile. "He's trying to get out of his turn. I imagine because it's one of the worst roads in the world and it'll be at night. So everybody got their passports?"

The parking lot was empty except for two cars, probably workers. They saw no other travellers in the building when they entered. A duty officer sat behind the only open counter window. With a face devoid of expression, he waved them over.

"Can I see your passports, please?" said the official in a monotone. Chantal volunteered hers, and he peered at it. "What is your
business in Lesotho?"

Chantal smiled. "Sightseeing, travel."

"Do you know the king was deposed? There may be trouble?"
he said, with seemingly little interest in her answer. "Will you be
returning to South Africa?"

"Uh, yes, of course," she said.

"Are you all travelling together?" His eyes drifted to the others.
"Yes."

"Thank you." He stamped and returned the passport. "Next
one, please."

He took Mark's with still less interest, glanced at the picture
then up to Mark's face, pausing with stamp in hand, finally pressing
it to the passport with a sloth-like lack of haste.

"Next, please." His eyes focused on Gail, and a frown creased
his brow. She was used to frowns.

He took her passport and studied the main page, methodically
leafing through the other pages. "Swaziland? What is your interest
there?"

"I have friends in Mbabane," she managed to say, keeping her
voice as calm as possible.

"Do you also have…friends in Lesotho?"

She shook her head.

"You will need to fill in this form, with the address where you're
staying in Lesotho."

He motioned to Ed. "Your passport next, sir."

Gail took the form, together with her passport, and moved
along the counter.

Ed handed his over. The clerk studied it, then reached under
the counter. A short buzzing noise ensued, then another uniformed
man, taller than the first, pushed open a door and stepped through.
He took the passport and leafed through it.

"What is your purpose in visiting Lesotho?" he asked, frowning
at Ed.

"Business." Ed sounded confident.

"What is the nature of your business?" the taller officer asked Ed, but signalled to the first official, who stood up and left the room.

"A traveller in photographic equipment."

At least Ed had chosen a field he was familiar with, in case they asked questions. How he managed to stay so calm, while she was shaking? She didn't like the process one bit. Where had the other man gone? And what address was she supposed to put on the form?

The official asked no more questions and told them to have a seat while their passports were being verified—whatever that meant. Ed picked his up. The official frowned but said nothing further.

They found three chairs together. Mark shifted a large, metal first aid kit onto the floor and brought over a short bench. None of them talked. Obviously, their passports had been flagged. Their own names were on them, and both had been in jail. But what did these officials want with them? What was the holdup? Why not just refuse them entry through to Lesotho? There could be only one answer— Van Greuning. Had these customs officials phoned him? She looked at her wristwatch, almost quarter to eight.

She turned to Mark. "How long have we been waiting?"

"About a quarter of an hour," said Mark.

"We should leave," she said. "Surely, they phoned Van Greuning. Why should we wait for him?"

"He can't reach us here for another hour at least, Gail," answered Ed. "Even at flat-out speed. We may as well wait a little longer, just in case. We don't know for sure our passports have been reported to Van Greuning."

Ed, always the optimist. She disagreed. A feeling of dread had invaded her entire body. They ought to drive off in a direction different to the road they'd come on.

"I'm with you, Gail," said Chantal. "There can be no other explanation. Why wait around for that piece of rubbish to show up?"

Mark held up his hands, palms out. "If you don't mind, I'm appointing myself referee, but I agree with the lot of you." He looked at his watch. "Let's hold on till eight. If we still aren't cleared by then, we vamoose, *tout de suite*."

Ed folded his arms. "Fine."

Gail sensed the tension, dread crept over her. Even normally so jolly Mark showed an unusual number of crease lines on his brow. Nobody spoke, never so much as looked at each other.

The steady tock of the electric clock, once per second, was the only sound to punctuate the silence. The monotonous ticking hypnotised her for about ten minutes. She was aware of nothing else.

Tock...tock...toc...tocko...tocko...tocotocotoco. What was happening? The clock was speeding up and getting louder. The others were aware of it too because they jumped to their feet.

Chantal shouted above the din. "Helicopter."

Ed grabbed Gail's hand and followed Mark and Chantal to the side door.

Outside, the chopping sound swelled to a deafening level. Gail's eardrums throbbed in time to the ever-increasing din. A sudden gale whipped her loose hair violently about her face. Her skirt flapped noisily, as if being torn away. Ed pulled her in the direction of their car, fighting the wind.

The terrible and frightening noise subsided after the engine cut off, and the raging whirlwind subsided. A bright floodlight illuminated their bodies at the side of the Land Rover.

"Halt! Don't move, or I'll shoot," a now familiar voice shouted over the shrieking of slowing machinery. Van Greuning. Why hadn't they thought of the possibility he might arrive by air?

Two men hopped out the chopper, which wasn't very large, in spite of the noise, and strode toward the group.

"So." Van Greuning glared at them. "We made a good catch tonight, Piet. Two fugitives, unlawfully married, and their accomplices, hey." He faced Mark. "There will be charges for aiding and abetting a criminal, giving false information to a police officer, quite apart from sending us on a goose chase to the airport and lying to the officers. And you." He turned to Chantal. "Using your position as a nurse to hide and aide a criminal."

Gail's heart thumped loudly like a drum. This was entirely her fault. She had got them into this mess. She should never have gone out with Ed, knowing it was unlawful. Now three innocent people would be sent to prison. Van Greuning was yelling at Ed now. Ed could be in the most trouble of all, because of her.

"Please." She stepped forward. "I'm the one you want. The whole thing was because of me. I played White. It wasn't Mr. Brent's fault. And these others were just giving us a lift so we could start a new life in Lesotho."

Van Greuning faced her. "You're right. It was your fault, and they're in for serious repercussions. Happy now? Your people are scum. You tricked this oke here into taking you out. I bet he didn't even have a clue what you were, did he, Brent?" He leered at Ed. "I bet you didn't know her grandfather's a kaffir, hey? You want a bunch of Black brats?"

Without thinking, Gail swung at Van Greuning with all the force she could summon. He jumped at the loud clap of her hand on his cheek. The sergeant put his palm against his slapped face and stared at her, with eyes widening and jaw dropping.

"You'll be sorry for that, *kleurling*," he snarled, grabbed her by the hair with his right hand, and swung with his left.

*****

The moment he spotted Van Greuning's fist bunching up, Ed lunged forward, but before he managed to reach him, Gail had somehow grabbed Van Greuning's arm as it swung, rolled her body against his, and they both fell to the ground. Van Greuning yelled in pain and threw her off. His left hand hung limply at an odd angle. Clearly, Gail and her jiu-jitsu. Atta girl, Gail! But then he saw the intense hatred on Van Greuning's face and the surprised expression of the second officer.

With his uninjured hand, Van Greuning made a quick movement toward the leather holster on his hip, but Ed noticed and leaped at him. Gail took off at top speed for the dark, beyond the helicopter's spotlight. Van Greuning managed to unclip the holster and withdraw his gun. Ed rushed forward, but the second officer rugby-tackled him. In horror, he watched as Van Greuning held the gun up, pointing it at the shadows where Gail had vanished.

A deafening noise exploded in Ed's eardrums, followed by a scream—Gail's scream. Reflexively, he kicked and heard the satisfying crack of the second policeman's jaw breaking. But Van Greuning was in the process of levelling his gun and taking aim. Ed crouched and launched himself at the hand, grabbing the gun and pushing it upward just as the second shot exploded.

Ed got a good hold on the revolver and twisted, using his other hand to grab Van Greuning's throat. Van Greuning couldn't defend himself with a broken wrist. Ed sensed the gun loosen from his grip, and the inertia of the struggle sent both of them to the ground. Ed sprang to his feet and aimed the gun at Van Greuning's head.

"No, stop!" Mark screamed. "Listen. You're only wanted for breaking the Immorality Act, but if you shoot this piece of slime, you'll be guilty of murder. That will stick. Think, Ed. Don't do it."

Ed sobbed. "He killed my wife. I don't care if I hang for it. He's killed her."

"You don't know that for sure and Chantal's gone to her. What if she survives? They'll hang you, and she'll be a widow."

Ed's hand quivered, the gun still aimed at Van Greuning's head. It was a 38, like he'd carried at his bank job. This man's head could be obliterated at this range. His finger tightened on the trigger. Why not? Van Greuning was a danger, obsessed with them, merely because they had a mixed-race marriage. Only a gentle squeeze, a loud bang, and their troubles would be no more.

He eased his tension on the trigger. What if Gail had survived? What if he pulled the trigger and killed this man? Then he'd never see Gail again. A noose, growing ever nearer, tightened around his neck while Gail watched.

But Van Greuning had killed her. There was no longer a reason to live. He closed his eyes and pulled the trigger.

CHAPTER

THIRTY

Chantal yelled at Ed. "That's enough, don't waste those bullets. Mark, bring that first-aid box from the office. And, Ed, we must get Gail into the chopper. Move it, guys!"

She was alive? Ed's heart leaped into his throat at Chantal's words. Only pausing to deliver a knockout blow to Van Greuning, grateful he'd shot over his head, he raced in the direction Chantal had pointed. With his blood pounding, he searched around blindly. His fingers sensed something warm. Gail! Picking up her body, he raced towards the helicopter. "Please, Gail. Please don't die." The chopper was barely visible through a blur of tears.

Chantal snatched the gun, which still dangled from Ed's fingers and leveled it at the pilot. "Put that microphone down if you don't want to lose a hand. Quick, Ed, lie her down on the back seat on her right side. Mark, put the metal box on the floor and make sure it's open. Ed, you take this gun and persuade our pilot to head for Addington Hospital. Can you operate a radio?"

"Sure." He had used one once during overnight duty at the Automobile Association. He climbed through the front door and pointed the gun at the pilot. "Get this thing going," he said and turned to Mark, who had unloaded the kit. "You'll clean up and vamoose out of here?"

Mark assented, ducked down when the rotors commenced turning, and hurried off. Ed guessed he would sabotage communications at the customs office and ensure the police officers were securely bound. He would figure out a way to handle it, to buy them time. Ed kept his attention focused between the pilot and Gail at the back.

215

Chantal had removed Gail's top and was mopping up the blood on her back. "Speak to me, Gail," she said, pressing her wound with a cloth. "Ed," she yelled over the noise of the chopper. "Reach over and put something under her legs, raise them up, Quick, her blood pressure's falling."

Ed reached under his seat with one hand, keeping his gun pointed with the other. He pulled out a lifejacket, reached over the seat back, and manoeuvred it under Gail's legs.

"Thanks. I can still detect a strong heartbeat, but she's lost a substantial amount of blood. Are we close?"

Ed looked at the instruments and found the compass. Bearing 112 degrees east southeast. Air speed, 120 knots. He knew to add about 15 percent, so about 140 miles per hour. "Is this as fast as you can go?"

The pilot pointed at the rev counter. "Yes. I'm pushing the limit."

The needle hovered a fraction from the redline. "Push it some more," Ed ordered, and the revs increased audibly. He calculated about a hundred miles between Sani Pass and Durban, another forty minutes at least. "How's she doing, Chantal?"

"I'm worried, Ed. I'm stopping what blood flow I can. She's going to need a transfusion. Use the radio, try reaching Doctor Spence. Let's pray he's on night duty. He's the only one we can trust. If not, chances are, Gail won't survive. Without this helicopter, that would've been certain."

"Just keep going forty minutes, Chantal, please." He reached for the microphone.

"How do I reach Addington?" he shouted. A fine time to realise he didn't possess that much knowledge about radio, the Automobile Association's radio had been a single channel.

"Give me a few minutes." Chantal's voice sounded tense. "Stay with me, Gail."

The pilot held out his hand. "Here, I'll do it."

Ed hesitated.

"Eish, come on, you have a gun aimed at me," the pilot snapped, adjusting the radio controls, then snatching the microphone out of Ed's hand.

Ed stared at him.

"Addington Hospital?" The pilot identified himself as police and gave his call sign. A reply crackled over the radio, and he handed the mike back.

Ed realised the call sign could mean an unwelcome reception for them when they arrived at the hospital. He trusted that Mark would still be in charge of the situation at the border control, and Gail's condition left them no other option. "I wish to speak with Dr. Spence if possible. Over."

The reply crackled through the speaker. "Hold on. Not sure if he's on duty. We're on the intercom to his office."

A tense few minutes passed before the radio buzzed at last. "Hello. This is Dr. Spence. Over."

"I'll take it." Chantal leaned over from the back seat.

"Dr. Spence, this is Chantal. Gail's been shot. She's lost a considerable volume of blood, and I can't determine her type—"

"It's O positive," Ed said. "Pre-wedding blood tests."

Chantal relayed the information to Dr. Spence. "We'll need to take out the bullet lodged vicinity vertebrae T7 and 8. Severe blood loss. And she's in shock. Over."

"Got it." Dr. Spence's voice crackled. "We'll move her to my surgery as soon as you land. Can you drop your bird onto the beach opposite the entrance? We'll have a team waiting with the blood. Can you insert an IV? Over."

"Do my best."

"I don't know what supplies you're using, but if there is a bag of saline, put it on the drip. Are you being tailed or tracked? Can we expect trouble? Over."

"Negative. Mark is taking care of things. I must attend to Gail. Wait—"

The pilot gestured and tapped the clock.

"ETA is twenty-one hundred, over."

217

Ed handed the mike back to the pilot. "Can you find Addington Hospital?"

"Not a problem."

"Thanks for your help."

The pilot shrugged. "I saw what happened and heard what he said to this lady. I hope you can save her."

"Thanks. I suppose you'll go back for them after you drop us."

He grinned a half-grin. "Of course. Don't worry, it'll be slower going back, and I may have to stop for fuel, of course."

Ed murmured his appreciation and turned back to Gail. Her face was turned away from him, but what he saw of her back looked pale. This was the first time he'd seen her back exposed, or any part of her body not usually showing. Yet he was her husband, forced to be apart from her. For the second time that night, terror gripped his heart as he realized he could lose her forever. He twisted his body and reached over his seat. "Gail, Please hang on. Maybe another half hour and we'll have you all fixed up."

He stretched down, and the feeble response from her fingers reassured him. He pressed gently back and silently vowed to hold her hand the rest of the way.

"Good girl," Chantal said, then removed the cloth and peered at the wound. "The bleeding is slowing. Fight it, Gail. Don't let Van Greuning win. Hold this cloth, Ed. I'm going to put in some temporary stitches."

Ed choked with emotion at the glimmer of good news.

*****

Ed's voice. So far away. But it was night, she couldn't see, and that noise? They must be back in the Land Rover, but something must be wrong? It hadn't been that noisy. For some reason, she was lying down. She could feel Ed holding her hand but nothing else. No, her back and shoulder hurt. Too much. Things were going dark. "Ed?" Her head swam with a sudden dizziness, then all sensation faded.

*****

Ed heard a weak sound from the back seat. Gail was awake, alive, but she made no further sound.

"She may be recovering." Chantal used the stethoscope. "Her heartbeat's still there, weak, but there's still hope. The blood flow has stopped, and the saline is helping. She might go in and out of consciousness. Keep talking to her, Ed, keep squeezing her hand."

"Speak to me, Gail. Stay with us. I love you. I won't let you go."

"The beat is weakening. Keep talking. I'm going to give her some oxygen, but your voice is doubtless the best medicine. Don't stop."

*****

Gail trekked to town from school, accompanying her best friend Jane, arm in arm. It was a lovely warm winter's day. She couldn't be happier. No, ahead stood Melanie with her friends and a couple of boys. The warmth changed to a bitter cold. Melanie had that grin on her face.

"Hello, Gail. Where's your boyfriend?"

"Leave her alone, Melanie." Jane tugged Gail's hand. "Just ignore her. Let's go."

Laughter pealed from both the girls and the boys.

"Don't go, Gail." Melanie leered and caught Gail by the shoulder. "We've found someone perfect for you. There he is."

A Black man, obviously walking to work. Bare toes stuck out from the holes in his shoes, and he wore baggy pants showing the dust and a T-shirt with faded colours. As he passed, he raised his hat and gave a half-bow. "*Sawubona* misses." He gave them a toothy grin.

"*Sawubona*," Gail answered. "*Unjani?*"

"*Haau. Kulungile, ngiyabonga.* I am very well, thank you, miss." He bowed several more times before walking on.

Melanie and her cronies burst out in loud laughter. She pointed at his receding figure. "Hurry, Gail. Go after him. He's your last chance."

Jane pulled Gail's arm. "Come on, Gail. Don't let her sort bother you. Melanie, why don't you and your little group go and play in the traffic?"

Gail, refusing to be pulled, squared her shoulders and faced Melanie. "You mock that man for his poverty. Why? Because you were lucky enough to be born to a rich White family. He's a Black man, but he's a better person than you, Melanie."

This brought more laughter from all the girls and their boyfriends.

Melanie pointed at the man. "Go with him then. Go live with him in his kraal."

This time, Gail allowed Jane to pull her along. "Don't even listen to them, Gail. You're way better than any one of them." She squeezed Gail's hand.

"I am? What exactly am I, Jane? I'm not White. I'm not Black like him. I'm a Coloured, but I'm here in this White school, learning to be and act like a White person."

"Well, I hope you won't learn from those particular Whites."

"No. I'll learn from you and almost all the others. You're decent White people, but I'm not certain any more what I am, Jane. It's like I don't belong anywhere."

Jane put her arm around her. "You belong with us at our school. You'll fit in everywhere and have a brilliant future. I see you happily married somewhere, married to the ideal man."

The ideal man? At this her woozy feeling returned, like she was about to faint. Someone held her hand. Jane? No, not Jane.

"Stay with me, Gail."

A voice, but she couldn't fathom where it came from. She stopped and whirled around a few times, not seeing anybody. The voice, she recognised it. A hand squeezed her own. The noise came back, but so did the pain. Then the queasy motion stopped along with the noise slowing to a rhythmic whooshing sound.

Suddenly, bright light flooded her dark world. She opened her eyes, but the light made her squint. Hands were on and under her, lifting and carrying her. She was placed on the ground, then felt herself lifted again onto something. It moved, giving her a bumpy and uncomfortable ride. The bright light faded, and she was once more in the darkness, then inside something, a building. However, through it all, one thing remained—the sense of a hand holding hers.

"We're here, baby, you're going to be all right."

That voice. Ed's voice. The ideal man. Then all went blank.

CHAPTER
THIRTY-ONE

Ed paced the floor outside the operating theatre. What was taking them so long? Surely, Chantal could send him a message. He stared at his wristwatch again, a quarter past twelve. They'd been due to arrive at nine, but he hadn't checked the time then. Surely, they'd finished. He remembered Chantal attaching the blood bag to the IV as Gail was being carried on the stretcher, and she'd been rushed here directly. *What can they be doing in there?*

"Ed." The blood drained from his face when Chantal exited the theatre, exhausted and emotionless.

"Relax, Ed, we got the bullet out. Sure, it was a close call, but she'll be fine."

Slowly, he exhaled. "In that case, can I see her?"

She restrained him with a hand on his arm as he moved forward. "All in good time, Dr. Spence is still sewing her up. We've sent for someone we can trust to take her to—" She glanced over his shoulder, her mouth tightening.

Ed turned and saw the reason, another doctor strode toward them.

"Dr. Swanepoel," said Chantal.

"Dr. Spence is in here, is he?" Striding unswervingly past Chantal, the older man pushed through the doorway of the theatre, in spite of Chantal's protestations. She followed him in, while Ed tagged along.

Pausing only to pull his mask across his face, he walked straight to the operating table and peered at Gail's face. "Spence, so what I overheard was right…it's a good thing I came to check." He faced Dr.

Spence. "Apparently, my information is correct. This is a Coloured. You're operating on a Coloured woman."

Dr. Spence faced him. "And you, sir, should know better than to enter an operation room without proper attire and preparation. But you are correct, in fact, this lady arrived via police helicopter, and I performed emergency surgery."

Dr. Swanepoel sniffed. "Why didn't they take her to a Coloured hospital?"

"I haven't the foggiest idea. Only that there was a patient needing emergency surgery, and I attended to her. For an answer, you need to ask the police why they brought her here."

Dr. Swanepoel looked from him to Gail and spotted Ed standing in the doorway. "What is your business here?"

Before he could answer, Dr. Spence stepped forward. "This man accompanied her in the helicopter and was not present during the surgery, so I don't believe it's our business to worry about who he is. Now, if you don't mind, I need to have her moved."

"Well then, I suggest," Dr. Swanepoel's eyes narrowed, "that you transfer her to Wentworth Hospital immediately, where she'll occupy none of our White beds."

"I'm sorry, Dr. Swanepoel, no can do, since I cannot move this patient in her present condition. That is doctor's orders."

Two orderlies arrived and Dr. Spence pointed to where Gail was lying and murmured instructions.

Swanepoel glared. "When doctor's orders clash with laws, we have a problem."

Dr. Spence folded his arms and squared himself against Swanepoel. "Same old, same old, doctor. But this time, you've got it exactly. This woman is in critical condition, and therefore we're moving her to a private room and no further. Moving her across town could trigger an irreversible effect. If she dies because of your orders or actions, Swanepoel, you will be guilty of murder. Quoting your own words, 'When doctor's orders clash with laws, we have a problem.' Is that understood?" He reached out an arm and swept Swanepoel aside, allowing the orderlies to push the stretcher trolley out.

Ed's heart pounded violently at the words, *if she dies*. Did that mean she was still at risk?

Swanepoel glowered at them. "Very well, she stays in the room, but I shall have the police put a guard at her door."

"The police? None of them escorted her to this hospital. No officers accompanied her into the building, so I don't see why you'd treat a shooting victim as a criminal?"

"Why would I? Because I suspect something's going on, that's why." He turned and glared at Ed. "If this bloke isn't a police officer, what's he doing here with her? She's a Coloured, and he's White. Who exactly are you, sir?"

Dr. Spence tugged at Ed's shoulder as he passed. "Go with her."

Ed needed no second bidding. Ignoring Swanepoel, he rushed to the trolley. Her left hand rested on the white hospital blanket bed covers, and he took it gently in his, keeping pace with the cart.

Swanepoel's booming voice still echoed in the hallway. "I'm phoning the police now, as I know you're hiding something, Spence, and I mean to find out what it is."

Dr. Spence ignored him and caught up with Ed and the trolley. "He means it, I'm afraid. We'll need to get her out of here before he brings the likes of Van Greuning to this hospital."

Ed turned as Chantal caught up with them. "You were telling me of someone you trust—" he said.

She pursed her lips and shook her head, flicking her eyes toward the orderly in front of the cart.

They filed into the lift behind the orderlies, and Dr. Spence pressed the button for the twelfth floor. "We're doing our best to hide her location," he whispered to Ed. "We'll need time in case Swanepoel brings the coppers here."

The lift stopped and they exited. Dr. Spence instructed the orderlies to push the trolley into the second room. "Thanks, chaps, that'll do fine," he said.

They watched the two men return to the elevator and the doors closed. The moment the numbers above indicated the lift had reached the ground floor, Dr. Spence said, "Right, Ed, go push the button. We're changing floors."

The moment the doors opened, Chantal and Dr. Spence rolled the trolley out the room and back into the lift. "Down to the tenth, Ed."

At the end of the long corridor on floor ten, Dr. Spence led them through a set of double doors and into a booth. After they shifted Gail onto a bed, Chantal pulled the green curtain around them, providing instant privacy.

Dr. Spence slapped Ed's back. "This is the safest I can manage, Ed, I believe they'll be looking for a room, not this. Don't look so worried. She'll be woozy till the anaesthetic wears off, but your wife will make it. Thanks mainly to Chantal here, who'll be watching her. First-class job, Nurse Breyers." He faced Ed. "You can leave her in our care now, and you might want to make yourself scarce."

Ed looked at Chantal. "What about you? You pretty much hijacked the chopper."

Chantal grinned. "Didn't I, though? Talk about adrenalin flowing. Anyway, I have my job to do, Ed, and that is to take care of Gail."

He started to protest, but she held up a hand. "I know, it's your job, too, but yours is also to arrange a secure place for her, like the one you guys already set up for yourselves." Her eyes lowered as she bit her bottom lip. "Let's face it. Things are already hot for Gail. They may get hotter and soon. In which case, you need to come up with a plan, chop-chop."

Dr. Spence pulled out a bunch of keys, searched through them, and twisted one off the ring. "This is for my sixty-three Volkswagen, which I hardly ever use. It's in the staff parking. I'll expect you to park it somewhere well away from your safe house. Hide the key inside and slam-lock the car." He grinned. "Nobody will notice you in an elderly Volksie, I'm sure."

Ed thanked him and crossed to Gail's bed, where he bent down and paused his head close to her face. She looked at peace, and… and…beautiful. Earlier tonight, he had been sure he had lost her forever. Emotion overwhelmed him. She was still alive, thank God, but still in danger. *Won't it ever be over?* Her lips were embedded against the pillow, but he carefully placed a kiss on her cheek.

*****

As she was running, something hit her back, thrusting her forward. She screamed and tumbled onto the ground, where she lay motionless. Intense pain invaded her entire body, and she realised she'd been shot. Panic gave way to the realization that this was the end. Ed would have no more worries. He'd easily attract a nice White girl and fall in love with her, more than he ever was with her. After a while, he wouldn't miss her. Indeed, why should he? A Coloured, just a source of trouble. He'd certainly marry and have children, exactly what she always hoped for. A little girl just like herself, and a boy with Ed's black hair and blue eyes. Only they couldn't be blue if he'd married her, could they? She imagined a picture of his little girl. *Wait, she looks like Chantal.*

The thought made her lift her head. What was that smell? Familiar, somewhat like Dettol and bleach. She sensed something soft under her tummy, not the hard ground anymore, maybe some kind of bed. She pressed her fingers against the softness and raised her head a little, then her shoulders. A stab of pain struck her back and she gasped. It was awful. She plopped her head back down on… was this a pillow?

"Gail." A voice, it sounded like Chantal, calling her from above. What was she doing here? With Ed. She'd just seen their little girl.

"Gail, don't worry. You'll be okay, just take it easy. You've been hurt."

It was definitely Chantal's voice, but that meant…she twisted her head around, confirming it was Chantal. Her senses trickled back, and she realised she was lying in a bed where Chantal was holding her hand. The odour, she recognized it now—hospital.

Her lips were thoroughly dry, she tried to lick them, but her tongue felt like sandpaper.

"Here, drink this." Chantal held a glass to her lips, and she gulped at the feel of wetness in her mouth.

"Chantal," she croaked.

"Yes, Gail. You gave us a great big scare. Now, you just take it easy. Come back to us slowly. The bullet got you, but you'll pull through."

Gail let out a breath. "I'm still alive. Where's Ed?" She tried getting up, but the pain drove her back.

"Ed has been at your side all this time. But as soon as he knew you were going to recover, he hurried to locate a hiding place for the two of you."

Gail tensed, fully awake, the sense of danger and despair rushing back. "What happened? Where's Van Greuning?"

"He's injured, but he'll be back. You were unconscious for over twenty hours, so it's urgent we get you out of here, now that you're finally awake. We've been hiding you, and Dr. Spence has claimed he sent you to the Coloured hospital. Pandemonium will soon break loose when our local snoop, Dr. Swanepoel, discovers Dr. Spence lied, and Van Greuning will resurface. Mark or Ed should be back soon to take you to a safe house."

A face peered through the gap between curtains. She could move her head enough now to see Dr. Spence.

He beamed and stepped inside. "Well, good morning, awake at last. You really didn't want to wake up, did you?" Turning, he raised an eyebrow at Chantal.

Chantal gave a thumbs up. "Her vitals are good, and her memory seems fine. She even asked for Ed and fully remembers Van Greuning."

"That's good." He stepped to Gail's bedside. "I wonder if you'll let me inspect your wound."

She grunted an assent and sensed him lightly peeling something off her back. It hurt. He mumbled, "Okay…good…uh huh," and finally, "excellent! Clean this up and put more of the muthi on it, Chantal, then we should be able to remove her from here before Van Greuning pokes his ugly head in."

"Van Greuning, hey?"

Chantal gasped and whipped round at the sound of the unfamiliar voice.

Straining her neck, Gail saw a man's head poking through the curtains. "Well, a fine ring-a-rosie you led me, Spence," it said. "But it wasn't that difficult finding where you were hiding her, hey?"

"This is my patient, Dr. Swanepoel," Dr Spence said, "therefore, I'd thank you if you kept your nose out of her room."

"No problem. I know him, and from what I understand, he would be most interested to learn where you're keeping her, which, by the way, is not Wentworth Hospital." He swished shut the gap in the curtain, and Gail heard him walking away, but almost immediately, the footsteps paused and returned. Again, the curtains burst open. "Another thing, Spence. In case you have any plans of moving her, I shall ensure a police officer will be here, watching her."

"Nonsense. She's Coloured, so you know I can't keep her here. I'm moving her to a Coloured hospital. That is what you wanted, isn't it?"

"We'll see." Swanepoel left again. His footsteps faded and didn't return.

CHAPTER

THIRTY-TWO

The next day, Gail walked back from the shower room feeling a lot better. Despite the powerful painkillers, her back still hurt. At Dr. Swanepoel's insistence, they had moved her to a private room for security reasons. Van Greuning was due to pick her up later today. When she got back to her room, the police guard accompanying her sat back down on his chair. At least he hadn't followed her into the shower; she could be thankful for small mercies.

In the distance, Chantal approached along the corridor, so Gail hurried inside and ran a brush through her hair. Poor Chantal, Dr. Swanepoel had made clear, after his conversation with Van Greuning, that she was also due for arrest for her role in hijacking the police helicopter. And that was by no means the sole charge. Chantal could have taken advantage of this time to escape but had chosen instead to remain with her despite all her protestations. After all, Dr. Swanepoel had no powers of arrest. He couldn't even detain her.

"Well, hellooo there."

It was Chantal's voice, low and sultry, quite unlike her normal way of speaking, coming from the hallway. Curious, she opened the door a crack and peered out.

Chantal was standing in front of the young man, who had jumped to his feet. "How are you doing, Officer?"

"I…er. Fine, thanks," he said, a red colour spreading from his neck all over his face.

"When do you get off duty?" Slowly running her finger along the rim of her stethoscope, Chantal peered up through her lashes.

"Um…after my senior officer gets here in about an hour."

"Hmmm, and then you'll be free. Isn't that glorious?" Chantal tucked her chin into her shoulder and angled her head toward him.

Gail watched her flutter her eyelashes, so unlike Chantal.

"Don't go away now, handsome." Chantal gazed at him with lowered lashes, her lips pursed into a tight cupid's bow. "What's your name?"

His face turned red as a tomato. "Uh. It's uh… Dirk."

As Chantal backed toward the door, Gail silently closed it and heard Chantal's knock. "Time for your morning vitals' check, Miss Rabe."

Chantal opened the door and entered, still with her back to Gail. "Spot you later… Dirk." She closed the door slowly, giving Gail a wink and continuing loudly, "Have you seen your adorable guard? What a hunk." She turned round when the door clicked and leaned backwards on it, puffing out a breath and rolling her eyes at Gail. "Hi, Gail. Flirting with guards is not part of my job."

Gail couldn't resist a giggle. "Still, you do it so efficiently." They hugged for several moments. "I take it you have a reason?"

"Indeed. I suppose you heard what he said. Van Greuning will be here in an hour or less. We have a plan. My part is purely distraction." She opened the door a few inches, waved her fingers, and giggled. "Don't you go away now."

Gail winked. "Hmmm. You take the role to heart."

Chantal cleared her throat. "That was merely practice, a test, if you will. The real part comes later, when I put my dimples to work in earnest. Now, I'm here for checking your vitals." She connected the stethoscope to her ears, placed the diaphragm on Gail's chest, and glanced at her watch. She flapped her hand dismissively. "They're fine. Now, to our plan. Here's your part."

It was simple. A storybook escape, but perhaps a bit too simple?

Chantal checked her watch. "Time enough. The Gail-escape-plan-number-one begins."

Gail followed her to the door, which Chantal opened and peered around. "Still here, Dirk? I'll be back. Don't you go away now."

He stood. "Don't you worry about that. Um… I, uh…maybe we can do lunch?"

"I can't wait," she replied. Lifting her hand high, she slowly ran her fingers through her hair, pausing when her hand reached her neck, simultaneously fingering a button on her blouse. Slowly, she turned and walked away, giving him an over-the-shoulder look.

Several minutes later, Dr. Spence rapped on the door and opened it. Chantal stood next to him, but her eyes were on Dirk.

The doctor gave Gail a broad wink. "I hear you're feeling better, Gail, and I know you're leaving us soon, but here's a visitor for you." He stood aside, revealing… Dorothy.

Dr. Spence's office clerk, for whom she'd spent hours sorting papers, looked a lot different, much older, with significantly greyer hair, almost white, and a bent-over posture. She held a large brown paper bag in a tight grip, rolling and unrolling the edges with her nervous hands. "Gail. How lovely to see you."

Gail opened her arms for a hug, following Chantal's plan. "Aunty Dot."

"Aunty Dot," wide eyed, took a shaky step forward, freed one hand and pulled Gail against her.

Gail stepped aside, the first to break. "Please come in, Aunty."

Dorothy, in her haste to comply, stumbled and let go of the paper bag which dropped, spilling some of its contents just outside the door. A sudden silence fell, Chantal's flirty tones ceased, and everyone's eyes riveted on the bag. Dorothy dropped to her knees and quickly shoved back the grey and furry thing that had dropped out. Dorothy stood, Chantal resumed stroking Dirk's sideburns, and Dr. Spence picked up the rest of the contents.

"Thank you, Dr. Spence. Come, Aunty Dot." Gail gently pulled her into her room and closed the door.

Dorothy gave her another hug. "Gail, dear. Delightful to see you, and I'm sorry about everything that happened to you. So awful."

Gail patted her back. "It's sweet of you to help us, or should I say, try to help us." She bit her bottom lip and sighed.

"Now, chin up, Gail. This is going to work. Have some confidence."

"You're right. Fine, let's go for it."

Fifteen minutes later, Gail stood by the door, wiping the sweat beads which had developed all over her brow. She pushed the handle down, waiting a few seconds, Chantal's signal to turn up the heat with Dirk.

It worked. Gail eased open the door, and all she could see was Chantal's back as she sat on Dirk's lap. "Oooh! Your eyes are such a pretty aqua green. Open them wider and let me see." Her head completely blocked Dirk's from view.

This was the cue. Gail opened the door fully.

Dirk squirmed behind Chantal's head. "Hey! What's going on?" He sat up straight, shoving Chantal aside. "You! Stop! Come on, Chantal, get off me."

At the sound of his loud voice, the grey-haired figure walking down the corridor sped up.

"What do you mean, what's going on?" Chantal cooed. "Relax, baby." She stroked the side of his head.

"Stop." He jumped up, tumbling Chantal off his lap. "A trick!" He glared down. "Nice try. I'm disappointed in you, thinking you could outsmart me. You can forget that date."

Chantal sat on the floor where she'd landed, legs out and resting on her hands. "What do you mean, Dirk? What trick?"

"The old changing clothes trick. Seriously? Also, I didn't miss that grey wig. I wasn't born yesterday, you know." With a final glare, he took off at speed after his quarry, who had just darted around the first corner.

Chantal stared after him until he also vanished round the corner. Then she sprang to her feet and darted in through the doorway.

"Hurry, Gail. He fell for it. Grab your things and let's go."

Gail, already dressed in an outfit from the bag and the grey wig Dorothy had accidentally spilled, grabbed the bag with her few belongings. After looking left and right at the doorway, Chantal pulled her out into the corridor. "Now, let's slow down, as befits an old lady." She grinned at Gail. "You can rely on Dorothy to give our Dirk a hard time following her. She knows the hospital inside out. She'll disappear and reappear till we're long gone from here." After a pause, she sighed. "A pity, though. He was kind of cute."

Gail giggled and tugged at her arm. "Concentrate, Chantal."

"Okay, okay, if you insist. My only regret is we won't be here to see Dirk's face when he finally catches up with his escapee and finds out it's Dorothy."

Gail grinned. "I actually feel sorry for him. I'm imagining Van Greuning's face when Dirk tells him he let me go."

"Now that would be an expression worth sticking around for. Van Greuning's going to be livid."

*****

Mark's words crackled over the intercom from the front door. "Hot enough for June, isn't it?"

Trust Mark, choosing as a password the famous line from the movie with the same name. Always the comic. Ed clambered out of the hidden den and hurried to the front door, double checking by peering through the spyhole. Long black hair and matching beard, with dark glasses and a trench coat. That would be him, all right.

"Greetings, old sport," said Mark, sidling through the narrow opening. "I've got something for you. Let's go into your little den."

Mark crawled through the narrow opening, then straightened. He wiped his brow, pulled off the black wig and beard, and struggled out of the heavy winter trench coat. Pulling an envelope from one of the pockets, he placed it on the table, dropping the coat on the floor.

"A little belated wedding present for you and Gail, from Chantal, and others. Mrs. Cahill was very generous, as she can afford to be, but so was little Candy in proportion to what she earns, bless her heart. Her parents also contributed, of course, and our friend Naidoo. We also had a whip around among the staff at Cahill's, though I regret saying we had to shamelessly keep it a secret from Dolores. Let me think. Was that all? No. One other, yours truly."

Ed stared at the envelope. "This is very generous of you—and everybody else. We do appreciate it, Mark, but I'm afraid money isn't much use. We'll be doomed to spending our lives here. Much like Anne Frank and her family. At least I'll be able to live with Gail, at last, but I don't know what use we'd have for money other than compensating you guys for everything. Especially you and Chantal, you've gone way beyond duty, Mark and—"

"Yes, yes, yes. I know all that. Open it."

Ed tore the envelope and pulled out the contents. "Tickets for the *Hesperus*. So incredibly good-hearted of you guys, but what's the use? They'll never let us on board. Our passports must be as hot as the sun."

"Your passports would certainly spontaneously ignite. However, if you'll delve deeper into the package—"

Ed stared at the documents with their pictures and somebody else's names. "Swaziland passports?"

"Yes. Leonard's friends came through. They're well done."

"They are, but we're on record now. Even you are, and Chantal, we're all criminals. Gail and I are Bonnie and Clyde. We'll raise suspicions the moment we board the boat together."

Mark sighed and shook his head. "Not together, dear boy, separately. Incidentally, they only had two tickets left, luckily for you. Unlucky is that you will share a four-berth inner cabin with three other geezers, and Gail will be in a cabin on the other side of the boat with three girls. Until the boat departs, you had best remain strangers."

"It's a port of departure, Mark. They'll expect us to leave the country. They'll post spies at every train line that crosses a border, every airport, every port."

Mark shrugged and started putting the passports and tickets back into the envelope.

Ed grabbed his wrist. "Wait. Why do you think this would work?"

Mark breathed in and exhaled audibly. "The alternative is living here, as you say, like Anne Frank. You know that Chantal and I will be hiding out, too, most likely with you in this room. There's a price on our heads, and we need shelter till Mrs. Cahill's lawyer can locate someone else like Stuart to clear our records."

"The Franks got away with hiding for quite a few years."

"Obviously, you need to read the book and not only the diary part."

Yes, he knew the outcome; surely, the saddest story he ever read. He and Gail would not be sent to a gas chamber if they discovered them here. At least things hadn't gone that far, yet, but their fate

234

would not be pretty. He shuddered at the thought of what might happen to Gail.

Why? What had been the purpose for his falling in love over the phone? If he'd first met Gail in person, he probably wouldn't have given her a second glance. Well, a second perhaps, but...he rubbed his forehead. Life in the shop would be like it always had been if he hadn't fallen in love. Mark would be safe. Chantal would be an unknown nurse in Durban, not wanted by the law. Stuart and Thabisa would be free and well. Dolores would simply be an annoying woman, not a vile and treacherous traitor. It was even possible he would've taken a trip on the *Hesperus* himself one day, with no worries.

He shook his head as if waking from a dream. It was too late for regrets, and he had none of those about falling in love with Gail.

Mark laid out the tickets. "I take it your silence means that you're considering using these. But here's the thing. I'm not sure you looked at the date on them."

"The date?"

"The *Hesperus* departs from Durban harbour tomorrow afternoon."

Plenty of time for making arrangements then. Ed folded his arms, unfolded them, lifted his passport, and flipped it open.

"Wait. This photo—"

Mark coughed. "The general opinion was that the alerts would focus on a White man and a Coloured girl. We thought two separate Coloured people from Swaziland would raise less attention."

He studied the photo which had apparently been copied and doctored in the lab. His hair was close cropped and curly, his complexion darker.

"How exactly will this work? I don't look like my passport photo."

"You will. Chantal has someone who will do some work on you."

Ed gave a sceptical grunt. "Fine. I hope she can change my blue eyes to brown."

CHAPTER

THIRTY-THREE

Gail was sure Chantal was mindful of her still shaky condition, in spite of the speed with which she urged her along the hospital passageways.

Chantal looked back as she pulled Gail round a corner. "Dr. Spence said to look for an ambulance in the indoor parking lot. We'll switch to my own car in Pinetown."

"How did it get to Pinetown?"

"Sorry, you don't know the story, do you? Mark only stayed at the border post long enough to check on the condition of Van Greuning and the other cop and to sabotage the phone lines of the building before clearing off in the Landie. He parked it in Merrivale and brought my car to a parking lot in Pinetown. Your things are still in it. Dr. Spence is taking us there in an ambulance."

Despite the gravity of their situation, all this sense of adventure appealed to Gail. She had never been in an ambulance. It reminded her of *On Her Majesty's Secret Service*, the spy movie she'd seen last year. She pictured Ed's face instead of George Lazenby's as James Bond.

But this was real life.

They marched towards an exit into the parking garage. "He said it's just inside here," Chantal said, as she pushed the doors open. It was. A huge white one, with blue and red lights across the front and top, sat waiting. She opened the passenger door and froze as a figure stepped around from the other side.

"Well, well, Chantal. Good to see you."

"Dirk?" Chantal stared at him. He had his gun in his hand, pointed at Gail.

"The same." He winked. "Not quite so stupid, hey? You must've thought I was as thick as two bricks. I soon put two and two together and gave up the chase. Then I spotted the two of you and followed."

Gail stepped away from the ambulance door.

"Uh-uh, lady," he said, waving his gun at her. "I heard about your kung fu."

Gail shook her head. "Jiu-jitsu. Well, now what?"

"Now, I simply hand you over to him," said Dirk, motioning with his head to the right.

Gail's entire body went cold.

Van Greuning, his left hand in a sling, sauntered out from behind the ambulance and strode toward them. Two uniformed officers stood behind him." *Baie dankie*, Mr. Botha. Good job. I'll take over from here. Sorry I'm so early, ladies."

They'd been so close. Now all was lost. Just when she thought she'd be with Ed again. Was he still safe?

Van Greuning signalled to one of his uniformed men, who circled around behind Gail's back. The cold steel of the handcuffs dug into her wrist. He yanked her other arm behind her. Gail smarted at the sudden pressure on her wound. Crossing to Chantal, he did the same to her, before marching them to the open doors of a Black Mariah, which the ambulance had concealed.

After he shoved them into the van, Van Greuning shouted to the driver. "To Koppiesdal Jail. I'll be there after I speak with Doctor Swanepoel." He faced them in the van. "Ladies, we'll meet again very soon. It will be an interesting visit. I promise you that." He slammed the doors and stepped back.

The van pulled out of the parking lot. Gail peered through the small window and noticed they steered toward Smith Street. So she was going back to Koppiesdal Jail, but this time she had company. She lifted her eyes to Chantal, who sat opposite. "I'm so sorry I got you into this mess. You should never have come with me. Now that Van Greuning's got you, too, you'll have a criminal record, maybe even go to prison. I wish…"

Chantal sighed and stared at her, or perhaps it was a glare. "Oh, Gail. Do dry up," she said. "It isn't all because of you. I chose to help you and Ed. So I got caught. I'm White. There are laws protecting me. I'm entitled to a lawyer and a fair trial. You're the one I'm worried about. Because of these horrible racist laws, they can put you away for years without trial, quite apart from what you did to Van Greuning. And here you are worrying about me. Come on, Gail!"

Gail bit her lip. It was true. Though Stuart was no longer available, she was sure Mark had the initiative to organize another lawyer. Mrs. Cahill had lots of contacts. But as far as her and Ed's marriage was concerned, it seemed all was lost. They would never see each other again, and she'd forever be separated from him and her family.

Chantal leaned toward her. "I know there is cause to worry, but I'm entitled to my one phone call, and I'll use it for you. Somehow or other."

Too choked up to answer, she wished she could hold Chantal's hand, but both of them were still handcuffed.

The van arrived at the jail approximately half an hour later. The same man who'd been there before came out the office building to meet them, but there was no sign of Susanne.

When the van doors opened, he stared. "Two this time?" he asked the driver. "There are only two cells here. They need to share one."

He led them through the entrance. The cell area was devoid of people, except for a woman locked up in one of the two cells. Gail recognized the cell she'd occupied before, small, with only a pad for a bed, but being with Chantal would be a blessing.

No sign of Susanne. Odd. Their jailer looked around and muttered, before returning through the doorway to the office area. A few seconds later, Gail heard a thump, the door banged open, and Susanne stepped through. Her face lit up momentarily but immediately became serious.

Susanne took Gail by the arm. "Quick, go into the cell. We must hurry, my father will be here soon."

Her father? Van Greuning? Gail's mind whirred. She'd had no idea. If she had known that she'd never have attempted her previous plan to contact Ed. The cell door slammed behind them with a clang, making them both jump.

Susanne smiled. "Sorry." She still had the hairdo they'd arranged for her. A little odd with her drab uniform, but she still looked pretty.

Gail stared wide eyed. "You're his daughter? Sergeant Van Greuning's your dad?"

Susanne coloured, moving closer, out of view of the second cell. "My father is a very cruel man, and he hates you. You're in danger, listen." She gripped the bag she was carrying while taking furtive peeks toward the main doorway. "I'm yust supposed to get you to strip and put on these jail clothes." She shook the sack and prison uniforms fell out. "This is where I unlock your handcuffs, and you change into these, but I'm sommer changing plans, hey." She chuckled with another nervous look toward the entrance. "You're going to escape."

Gail took the bag and peered into it. "Escape? You can't do that. You'll get into trouble."

"Um, Gail," said Chantal. "If Susanne wants to arrange an escape for us, I think we shouldn't disappoint her, right?"

Susanne smiled at Chantal. "That's why you must lock me up, or else my father will beat me. You yust escaped and locked me in the cell, okays? Then he won't hit me so hard."

Chantal frowned. "You poor thing. But our escaping is impossible. Your dad would never believe it? What will your story be?"

"Gail must do her thing on me what she did to my father."

Gail held out her palms. "My jiu-jitsu? What? No, never. I couldn't possibly do that to you."

"You must, Gail. You can say you sommer did it when I unlocked your cuffs, okays? And you threw me into the cell."

"I could never hurt you. No, I can't do it."

Chantal looked from one to the other. "I don't think we've time for arguments about this."

"Well, you do it," said Susanne.

Chantal shrunk back. "Me! I'm a nurse. I fix people. I don't break them."

Susanne pulled her mouth tight. "Chantal's right. There's no time to argue. Turn round. I'm taking off your cuffs." There was a click and Chantal was free. Susanne tucked something into her hand. "This is the key for the chief's Opel Kadett outside."

Gail heard a click and felt the relief of the cuffs loosening. She rubbed her wrists.

"Now, Gail. Do your jo—joot—whatever it is."

Gail bit her lip, holding her arms behind her back. "Jiu-jitsu." She sighed. "I'm sorry, I just can't."

"Okay, yust get out of here." Susanne pushed Gail and Chantal out the cell before slamming the door and locking it. "Take these keys and throw them in the office. My chief is inside, knocked out. I sommer did it," she ended proudly.

Chantal took the keys and urged Gail toward the exit.

Susanne pleaded. "Please, when my dad comes, he'll find the keys and let me out, but he'll be so mad if he thinks I let you go. You must injure me. Even if you just break a finger."

Gail squeezed Susanne's hand, tears oozing onto her cheeks. How she wanted to help, but she was incapable of hurting anyone she liked.

Chantal took her arm and tugged her toward the office. "We can't afford to stay longer, Van Greuning will be here any moment. Let's go. Sorry, Susanne, really, and thanks for what you've done."

Gail got a glimpse of Susanne's shocked expression, but she simply didn't have it in her to injure anyone. As Chantal tugged her, she only had time to catch sight of Susanne reaching through the bars, wrapping her left arm tightly around them and gripping her wrist.

"Oh, just sommer go!" she said, before throwing herself sideways. The loud crack caused bile to rush to Gail's throat. But Chantal didn't allow her time to react, racing them into the office. Chantal bent over the still unconscious chief, putting her fingers on his neck. Evidently satisfied that he was alive, she took hold of Gail and rushed through the exit to the Opel, parked outside.

*****

In Lucy's Beauty Shoppe, Mark peered round the door of the private room where Ed sat, covered entirely, except for his head, by a white sheet.

Mark stared at him and broke into one of his characteristic chuckles. "Perfect. You look exactly like your passport photo. Well done, Lucy."

"Thank you, Mark." Lucy squinted at Ed's face. "You don't think I made his skin too dark, do you?"

"No, just like Gail's. Marvellous. He'll pass. Hey, Ed, are you ready for your new role?"

Ed studied his face in the mirror Lucy held up. She'd cropped his hair and made tight curls close to his scalp. He had to admit it, Lucy had done an effective job, but his blue eyes stared back at him from the mirror. "You couldn't've spray painted my eyes, I suppose?" He grinned at Lucy.

"I stock some sunglasses that should do the trick," she said. "But they may ask you to take them off before you go through passport control. Sorry, Ed, there isn't anything we can do about those eyes."

Mark laughed. "Now I've seen everything, a blue-eyed White guy playing Coloured."

Ed inspected his face in the mirror some more, then stood and stretched with a groan. "Yes, let's hope they'll be so confused they'll let it go. Playing Coloured has got to be unique in this country."

Mark reached into his pocket and pulled out a twenty and a ten. "Here, Lucy. Thank you so much."

"Aw shucks, that's more than generous, Mark. Thank you. The phone, excuse me one moment." She picked up the receiver. "Certainly, hold on a jiffy. It's for you, Ed."

Ed took the phone. "Ed, this is Leonard. Dr. Spence phoned. His plan's gone wrong, hey. Van Greuning's got both of them."

CHAPTER

THIRTY-FOUR

Gail clutched the armrest so hard her knuckles turned white as Chantal threw the Kadett around the bends and turns of Koppiesdal.

Chantal had to yell above the screeching tyres. "The moment Van Greuning arrives at the jail, this car will be hotter than a corrugated iron roof in February."

Gail shut her eyes and held the grab handle as the car did a four-wheel drift, narrowly missing a curb. "So are you planning to make it unrecognisable by rolling it?" She slid back into the door, the armrest jabbing into her bandaged ribs. She winced at the pain shooting through her back.

Chantal shot her a concerned glance. "Oops! Sorry, I'm forgetting you're still tender. Hang on, the freeway's not far."

"Are we going to Ed's? Won't this lead them right to him?"

"Relax, we're not going there yet. Remember, we have to pick up my car in Pinetown. You'll need your belongings in the boot."

Of course, Dr. Spence had planned on taking them there in the ambulance. The road was straightening out, making the ride more comfortable, though Chantal pressed her foot harder on the accelerator, all the way to the floor.

"Here's the ramp, hold on tight." She changed to second, spun the wheel and stomped on the accelerator, and the little car tore down the slope and entered the freeway.

"You should be a grand prix driver, Chantal."

Chantal grinned. "I used to spend quite a few afternoons at Westmead track. Fun over, now I must put foot and go. But I do wish the prison chief's car was a Jag."

Chantal showed impatience with the fading speed. Freeway or not, lots of steep hills forced her to change gears frequently. She muttered at the slower pace, the engine screaming at full revs, until they began the long downhill bends of Field's Hill. Here, the car had nothing holding it back. With mounting panic, Gail checked the speedometer. The needle hovered at the ninety mark.

Chantal took an exit and braked hard. They turned into Knowles parking lot, where Gail could breathe normally for the first time since they'd left the jail.

Chantal drove round to the rear of the supermarket and pulled in under some trees. She patted the car's fascia. "There, you won't be easy to see, will you, baby?" She turned her attention to Gail. "Right, time for a switch, but first, we must make a phone call."

They hurried round and into Knowles, where Chantal found a pay phone, dialled a number, and waited. Gail heard a ringing tone, but nobody picked up. After a minute or more, Chantal clucked her tongue, muttering, "Where could they be?"

Gail waited, rubbing her hands together under her chin. Surely, it was Mark Chantal was phoning, or Ed. Were they safe? Why didn't they answer?

Chantal tried once more, unsuccessfully, then folded her arms and chewed her bottom lip. "One more try, then we'll drive to 'Maritzburg. I really don't fancy hanging around here while there's a hot car out back. Maybe two."

Chantal tapped a foot and peered at the watch pinned on her uniform. Gail paced up and down. Each second was an eternity. Was Ed safe or had they found him? With a final stamp, Chantal tried the phone again. After waiting a whole minute listening to the *brrr brrr…brrr…brrr…brrr…brrr*, she banged the handset down full force. "Let's go."

Chantal's Triumph sat parked beyond the Kadett and the trees, tucked in behind a large rubbish container. "Still here, right where Mark said you'd be," she remarked, opening the boot to check on Gail's small suitcase and the bag from the hospital.

Gail breathed easier when she saw seat belts in the new Triumph. She found the buckle and snapped it into place.

At the sound of the click, Chantal looked sideways at her. "Oh, dear, you wasted no time buckling up, Gail. Sorry, I've been driving like a maniac, haven't I?"

"Don't worry, Chantal. You're only doing what you need to do." She looked across and winked. "All right, I admit it. I'm happy your car has seatbelts."

Chantal fastened her own and gripped the wheel, not starting the engine. "I've been selfish. I was keeping something from you for a surprise. But I never gave a thought how it might affect you. Still, it's given me an idea."

"Surprise? Good or bad?"

"Both, I'm sure. Mark's managed to book you on an Australian ocean liner bound for Southampton in England. She sails tomorrow from Durban."

Gail's jaw dropped. An ocean liner. England. It was too fantastic to be true. "They'll never let us board. It's a thoughtful but doomed idea."

"Fine then, let's tell Mark it's a no go…by the way, what's your plan?"

Excellent point, she had none. Van Greuning would have each port under surveillance, and every exit was dangerous. She shrugged and emitted a deep sigh. "All right then."

"Don't be like that. It'll work. I feel it in my bones. Forget raising Mark or Ed. They're bound to have heard about our capture, so they'll be out looking for us. We can't raise them, and they can't call us. And if all this does work, you won't see your mother again. Perhaps forever. Which is why I thought of a perfect solution."

That was right, she already missed Mom. "You're planning on going to my house, aren't you? Isn't that the first place they'll look?"

"It'll be too obvious? Well, we just have to be very careful." She started the engine.

Gail gave her directions, then spent the rest of the drive in contemplative silence. She was too overwhelmed by everything that had happened, to think of her mom. What if the scheme, crossing into Lesotho had succeeded? She would have been able to visit her and Ed once in a while. But would she ever have the means to travel as far as England? Perhaps if they got well-paid jobs, they could send her money. But she'd heard they had unemployment problems over there?

Chantal didn't park right at the house but not too distant either. Good thinking! It might look suspicious if Gail walked a long way with a White nurse. A short distance might actually be advantageous since she could be bringing a nurse for her sick mother.

But Gail's mom wasn't ill. With strong, healthy arms, she grabbed Gail into a tight hug. Their tears merged and ran down Gail's cheeks. Chantal asked if she could use the phone, then hurried out the room. Gail held onto her mother for another long minute, then stepped back and dried her cheeks. "If Mark's plan works, Momma, it means we'll be leaving, and…never allowed to come back. I'm so sorry." Her eyes welled up again.

"Now you just stop that, Gail. I realise now that Ed's a fine man, though I was suspicious of him at first. He's good for you, and this country of ours isn't. You'll have a better life somewhere else. Don't you worry about me."

Gail sniffed and gave her a wobbly smile. "Thanks, Ma, it's what we need to do, any chance we get."

"That's the spirit, Gail. Now come and help me make some Rooibos tea."

Chantal came back from the lounge and joined them in the kitchen. Her cheeks burned with a red glow, and she wiped them with the back of her hand.

Gail rushed to her side. "Are you alright? What's the matter? Are Ed and Mark safe?"

Chantal wiped the corners of her eyes. "Yes, they are. They've been hunting everywhere for us. They drove to Koppiesdal and saw Van Greuning outside, fuming, so they realised we'd escaped. Mark found my car gone from Pinetown, so they returned to the hideout, hoping to hear from me."

"So when do we go?" Gail clapped her fists under her chin.

"We don't. On nearing the safe house, Mark spotted some suspicious activity. They had to be exceedingly careful going back in unnoticed. He's not sure they know exactly where the house is. Still, there are no plans to leave before tomorrow, and they don't want us to risk going. So he wished for us to stay here tonight. You'll board separately, anyway."

That made sense, though Gail's heart ached at how awful it would be not being with Ed again till they were aboard. At least it gave her the opportunity to be with her mom one last day. That is, unless Van Greuning decided on rechecking the house.

"Is everything okay with Mark and Ed, Chantal? I fancied you were crying when you returned from the phone."

Chantal smiled. "Yes, it sure is."

"And Ed?"

"He's fine, and he can't wait to see you."

She could picture Ed's smile, knowing he was thinking as much about her as she was of him. "Me too. And Mark?"

"Mark? Mark is just perfect... I mean, perfectly well, thank you." Her blush flooded back and deepened two shades.

*****

Ed stared as Mark slowly replaced the receiver. "Is everything okay, Mark? What's wrong? You look weird."

Mark's face was a dark crimson red, a silly grin twitching the ends of his mouth. "Nothing at all, old chap, nothing at all. Everything's going just fine. Gail's happy with her mom, nobody's watching the house, and Chantal apparently has everything under control. Your wife is in expert hands, Ed. In exceptionally competent hands, yes. Extremely pretty hands, as a matter of fact."

Tense as he was, Ed couldn't help letting a chuckle escape. "I guessed as much. She smiles on you, huh? And you've taken a shine to her."

Mark coughed, turning a few shades darker. "What's not to like? Didn't you observe her in action?"

"And all this time I believed you were doing this for Gail and me. Brushing with the law, becoming an outlaw, smuggling humans over borders. All because of a pair of sparkling eyes, hey?"

"You should know, old sport. Remember, she has the same eyes as Gail."

"That, I remember distinctly. Seriously, Mark, I wish you two well." He lifted one eyebrow. "But we've no doubt been in your way. Let's hope tomorrow the two of you'll be able to concentrate on each other."

"The thought had crossed my mind. Still, you guys haven't yet escaped. Tomorrow will be tricky. Van Greuning may not have missed the fact that a ship presents a golden opportunity for his victims to escape his clutches forever. My hunch is, he'll be watching."

"You can count on it. We'll need to keep far apart till we set sail. It's not possible he'd know the names on our passports, and I'll wear my disguise and sunglasses. But how is Gail preparing?"

"Chantal's going to work on her with what she's got in Gail's mom's house. I don't know what she'll come up with, but if anyone can, it will be Chantal." His eyes glazed over as he stared into space.

Ed waved his hand a few inches from Mark's face. "Stay with us, Mark, you haven't seen us off yet."

Mark filled his lungs and sighed heavily. "To be honest, I can't wait to get rid of you chaps."

"Sure. Now. Supposing everything goes according to schedule and we wave goodbye from the deck before we sail into the sunset, what will you and Chantal do? No, focus, Mark." He snapped his fingers. "I'm referring to your being on the most-wanted posters."

"Oh yeah, that. Well, I spoke with Mrs. Cahill, and she believes she knows the right lawyer for us. Speaking of Mommy, she wants to see you off at the docks. My guess is, Candy will persuade her to take her along. Mommy did mention something about bringing along someone to keep a lookout for Van Greuning, and what's better than Candy's nose for sniffing out trouble?"

Apart from the various sensations going on inside Ed's stomach, he was reasonably optimistic. If they succeeded in passing through passport control with the fake passports and boarded the *Hesperus*, then they'd leave South Africa, perhaps forever. Other countries had difficult immigration policies. Would they succeed in seeking asylum? Mark had researched the United Nations High Commissioner regulations for refugees. That would be the last hurdle.

CHAPTER

THIRTY-FIVE

The elderly, grey-haired nurse pushed the wheelchair into the Port of Durban departures hall. In the chair sat a pale, sickly woman, wearing dark sunglasses and a cloth covering her head. At least Gail hoped that was the way it looked.

Despite the noise in the hall, Chantal bent to whisper in Gail's ear. "This looks extremely busy. I do believe we'll get away with it."

Gail agreed, with reservations. So many people were preparing to leave on a trip at sea, but they were White people. Without a doubt, she would be noticeable. And what about her nurse? Chantal wore the dilapidated grey wig, the same one they'd used in their hospital deception.

"Look, a free counter." Now her aged nurse propelled the wheelchair at a remarkable speed to arrive before the parents who were marshalling their family that way.

The young clerk greeted them with a friendly smile. "Good afternoon, ladies. May I have your ticket and travel documents, please?"

Grateful to be addressed ahead of her White "nurse," Gail returned the smile and reached up her hand with the papers.

The clerk scanned them quickly and returned them. "Thank you, these papers are in order, everything's fine. That suitcase on the back of your chair. Let us deliver it to your cabin for you."

She turned to Chantal, who waved her hand, palm out. "Oh, no, I don't have a ticket. I'm just here to accompany her on board. I'll be coming back."

"Certainly. You're welcome to stay until you hear the departure announcement. And you," the clerk turned back to Gail, "I wish you an enjoyable voyage. Just pass through those doors to the Department of Customs and Excise and be sure to have your passport and departure form ready."

Gail appreciated the pretty smile and thanked her. Chantal handed over the luggage before pushing Gail away on the chair. Travellers crowded the departure hall, but they found the shortest queue.

"Next in line." At last, they moved up to the Customs and Excise counter. The clerk stared with a bored expression at Chantal, ignoring Gail. "Your passports, please."

"This lady, Miss DuPreez, is the only one travelling," said Chantal, placing Gail's passport on the surface. "I will leave as soon as I've settled her in the cabin."

The young man opened the passport and leafed through it. He glanced at Gail. "Swaziland. Where do you live in Swaziland?"

"Manzini."

"What is the nature of your visit?"

Gail croaked in the feeble voice she deemed appropriate. "I have a condition." She gestured to the wheelchair. "I'm seeking medical treatment."

"Why not in South Africa? We have the finest doctors."

Yeah. If you're White. "I already made arrangements with a specialist in London."

He sniffed. "Will you be returning to South Africa?"

"Yes, but only in transit to Swaziland."

The clerk grunted and stamped the passport. Again, he looked only at Chantal. "You can use those doors over there where you'll find a lift for the wheelchair."

They murmured their thanks and departed through the doors. Once on board, Gail breathed easier, and Chantal let out a loud "Phew!"

"G'day, ladies." A man in a sparkling white uniform stood on deck at the handicapped entrance. He grinned at each of them in turn. "Welcome aboard the Hebrides, ladies. May I check your tickets, please?"

Gail handed him her ticket, explaining that Chantal would be deboarding after accompanying her to the cabin.

"No worries. Cabin 34 on C deck. The lifts are right this way. Fourth floor, right as you exit, and it isn't far from there."

They thanked him and proceeded along the deck and through the swing doors.

"This is so thrilling, Gail. How I wish I were going with you. Think, you and Ed will have such a glorious time."

"Yes...if he makes it. But I'm worried. I kept looking but saw no sign of him."

"Don't be. Boarding takes a long time. He may already be on the ship, and there's still more than a couple of hours before departure. Think positively."

"I'll try. But you and Mark, you're still wanted. Be careful."

"I will, but I'm confident I'm in capable hands. Mark will get us a lawyer."

They had no problem finding Gail's cabin.

"Since that crewman saw the wheelchair, you'll need to keep it hidden. There's no way I can let him see me go by with this thing. He'd expect you'll be needing it."

"I'll hide it some place. Hopefully, after I slip out of this disguise, he won't still be watching for an old woman in a wheelchair. We sure don't want him to worry and start searching."

Gail changed into something more comfortable but didn't worry about removing the makeup. "Come on now, let's go explore the ship."

*****

Mrs. Cahill negotiated the huge Dodge through the harbour passenger boarding area, skillfully slipping it into a passenger parking slot. She pulled the handbrake lever out, making a clicking noise.

"Yeslike, Ed." Candy fixed her gaze on the gigantic liner's bows peeking out from behind the terminal building. She whistled. "That's only a larney ship, hey. Y'olls so lucky, man."

Mrs. Cahill turned off the ignition and faced Ed. "Well, this had better be as far as I go since Van Greuning knows what I look like. Leonard, you should probably stay, too. We don't want too many of us going into the building."

Ed agreed. All five of them would be a dead giveaway, especially with their mixture of colours. Mark was bad enough by himself, still wearing his disguise. "Thanks for everything, Mrs. Cahill."

"Wait, I have something for you." Mrs. Cahill reached in her handbag and withdrew an envelope. "This is your last pay, plus leave, sick leave and a little something extra. Should you ever come back, your job will be waiting for you, and one for Gail as well."

"I don't know what to say. It's all been so sudden. Thank you so much."

"Please send my regards to Gail. She's such a fine girl." Mrs. Cahill reached across the wide seat and shook his hand. "Oh, come here." She hauled him across and pecked him on the cheek. "Now you'd better clear off out of here and board your ship before you witness Mommy cry."

From the back seat, Leonard stretched his hand over. "Ed, always a pleasure, ou. Exciting, but still a pleasure. Everything of the best hey."

"Thanks, Leonard, for all your help. We'd never have met were it not for Gail, but I'm glad we did." He gripped Leonard's hand tightly as they shook.

Mark exited the car and looked around. He reached out a hand for Candy. "Come on, our nosey little Mata Hari. Let's see to it that Ed doesn't mess things up at this stage in the game, and we'll need you to keep an eye out for our friend Van Greuning."

"Yeslike, you're right, ou." Candy winked. "That's me. Nothing will get by your little spy."

Hopefully not. He cringed at the spectacle the three of them made walking across the lot. He couldn't help but think their group was not exactly the most inconspicuous. First, a Coloured man with sunglasses concealing blue eyes. With him a White man with a long unkempt beard, matching moustache, dark glasses and a long great-coat with the collar raised. And accompanying them, a remarkably short brown girl staring all about her.

They entered the main terminal and gazed around. Crowds filled it to capacity. Fine, everybody was White. Now the conspicuous factor had increased a hundredfold. Not a sign of any other race. Of course, only the rich Whites could afford travel on a luxurious ship like the *Hesperus*. Mark led the way to join the smallest line.

"Good afternoon," said the uniformed clerk at the ticket counter. She smiled at Mark, who stepped aside and raised his palm to indicate Ed. The smile turned into a frown, perhaps more of a glare. Ed, surprised at first, quickly realised it was because he was now a Coloured. The clerk tapped her ballpoint pen against the counter. "Your tickets and travel documents?"

Ed handed over his ticket and papers. "I'm the only one sailing."

"I'll send on your baggage. You are in cabin number 252 D, and someone will be at the top of the gangway to direct you. Next, you'll need passport control through those double doors." She stared past him and smiled at the next passenger in line.

They moved on toward the entrance she'd pointed to.

"Well, old boy, this is it," said Mark. "You must go through those doors on your own and reconnect with your charming wife."

Ed looked around the hall again. "Whom I haven't caught a glimpse of yet. Let's hope she'll make her way here all right."

"She's no doubt sunning herself on deck as we speak. You two will have a marvellous time. Sorry again for the separate cabins, but you'll soon be away from all the nonsense. Remember, you've got several choices to jump ship if anything excites you. Dakar, Lisbon, Rotterdam, or obviously Southampton in your destination country."

"I don't have the words, Mark. Goodbyes like this are so permanent."

Mark rubbed his forefinger in his eye. "Don't go soft on me now. The moment you arrive on dry land, look for a pillar box, send us a postcard. My only regret is not being able to say farewell to your beautiful wife, too. Please give her my love."

"Of course, I will. She'll be sad she didn't see you, too."

"Don't worry, old boy. Soon, you'll settle someplace where you and your missus can live. Together, you'll produce the cutest children. Not because of you. If it were up to you they'd be ugly as sin, but that superbly cute creature of yours couldn't possibly give birth to anything less than dazzling."

"I appreciate that. And you, Candy. I will really miss our chats. Give Pamela my love and tell her I'm upset she couldn't be here."

Candy stepped up and threw her arms round his chest. "You bet, I'll miss our chit-chats, too. Specially the arguments. You know I always won, hey?"

"Of course, you did." He wrapped his arms round her shoulders and planted a kiss on her forehead. As she came out of the hug, her eyes flicked to something behind him. "Don't turn round, he's here."

His complete body chilled at once. No need to ask who she spotted.

"He's prowling around looking at people in the queues. Wait. Now he's going further into the room."

"Then that had best be my cue. Goodbye. My love to everyone."

Mark grabbed his arm. "Whoa. Van Greuning's here, and you're going?"

"Definitely. That's what my disguise is for. Now you two get out of here before you get caught."

He gave a final wave and walked directly toward the smallest queue. As he neared, a portly White woman with two kids in tow, dashed in front of him. He knew she'd seen him by the glare she sent him, and from the apology she gave to the White man in front, whom she'd bumped in her hurry to cut in. So this was what it was like to be Coloured. Did Gail put up with rude behaviour all the time?

Not too much later, he stood before the counter. The stern-looking clerk stared at him with a noncommittal expression. "Your passport, ticket and departure form."

"Good afternoon," Ed said with a smile. The clerk did not reciprocate.

The clerk opened the passport to the picture page. "Swaziland, hey? In what town do you live, Mr. Hendricks?"

Mark had grilled Ed for hours on this. Time to put it into practice. He didn't hesitate. "Mbabane."

The young man narrowed his eyes. "So I believe Swaziland is independent now."

"That is right, since 1968."

"And the name of your leader is…"

"King Sobhuza."

"Where do you work?"

"At the Havelock asbestos mine in Pigg's Peak, I'm a manager there. I commute from Mbabane."

"So you will return there?"

"Correct. I will be flying back."

His eyes fixed on Ed's face and narrowed. "Do you know a Miss Du Preez from your country?"

The question took Ed aback. He hadn't prepared for that one—Gail's passport name. "No, I don't believe so," he said quickly. "It's a small kingdom, but the population is quite large."

"I am aware of that, Mr. Hendricks." He reached for a stamp and poised it over the picture page. "I ask because there was a Miss Du Preez through here about half an hour ago." The stamp lowered, then stopped a few inches from the page. "Wait, I need you to take those sunshades off."

Ed whipped them off.

"Blue eyes? But you're a Coloured?"

Ed shrugged. "A present from my White father with some other genes added in. Literally, a one in a million chance." He replaced the glasses. "And not welcome. My eyes are very sensitive to the light."

"Very well." The man stamped and handed back the passport. "Proceed through the doors at the end of this corridor and turn right to the gangway. Next person, please."

Ed replaced his documents, looked up, then froze. Van Greuning had returned through those very doors the clerk had just pointed to.

So? This was no time to be coy. He looked straight ahead, took a deep breath, and marched towards the doors.

THIRTY-SIX

Gail hugged Chantal one last time when the speaker announced the last call for all non-passengers. "Please leave the ship now. This is your last call to disembark. The gangway will be removed in five minutes' time."

Gail wiped away the tears with the back of her hand, but it only brought more to the surface. Chantal's friendship, though brief, had been a lifesaver for her, literally in fact. And now the budding friendship was to be cut away.

"Gail." They both spun round at the sound of Ed's voice behind them.

He rushed to her, and she fell into his embrace. Their lips met, and she wrapped her arms around his neck. Her body shook as relief swept over her, warm and comforting, as if it had been years since they'd been this close. Tears ran down her cheek as they clung to each other in silence, the beating of their hearts the only conversation necessary. He was on board, meaning they would sail together—in just a few minutes—to safety.

"Let me look at you," said Gail, gulping for breath as they broke apart at last. Her jaw dropped, then she broke into giggles. "Oh, Ed, you're one of us, a true Coloured. Look at you, your hair—your skin."

Ed grinned. "Maybe I should rush to get reclassified as a Coloured citizen."

"Hmmm, you should have thought of that earlier." Her giggles turned to a groan of pleasure as his mouth found hers again.

"Hurmmm."

Gail opened one eye. Chantal stood, arms folded tightly, eyebrows arched, lips pursed. Gail stretched out an arm and so did Ed. No three-way hug could possibly have been tighter, of that she was certain.

Chantal broke apart, sniffed, then dabbed at her eyes with a tissue. "I better leave you to your journey and your future in each other's arms. I must get off this ship."

Ed faced Chantal. "You have to go now, but please, there'll always be a place for you in our future."

Gail took Chantal's hand and squeezed it. "Yes, wherever we end up, you must come and visit. Please. We haven't known each other very long, but it's a friendship I simply can't live without."

"I second that, for both you and Mark," Ed added.

Chantal reached for another tissue and coughed into it, then wiped her eye with a finger. "We will," she sniffed. "Wherever you wind up, expect a visit from us soon. Now, I must go. Those workers on the wharf are making intention movements, which means the gang plank will soon be moving. Cheers, Ed. Bye, Gail."

As Gail watched Chantal dash down the gangway, she heard a shout from the families and friends of departing passengers who crowded the open verandah of the terminal building. Gail scanned the faces until one in particular came into focus suddenly and vividly—Van Greuning. He was staring directly at Chantal, who was still on the wanted list. Hurry, Chantal, go. Run away as fast as you can. Next second, Gail's blood froze as she returned her gaze to Van Greuning and his face squarely turned towards her own. Their eyes locked for a mere moment, then he raised his toward the bridge.

"Stop. Stop the ship," he yelled. She wasn't sure anybody from above heard him. He ran back through the departures hall doorway, obviously headed for the wharf.

Ed glanced at his wristwatch. "We've got two minutes before they shift the gangway. Will he make it?"

So Ed had also seen him. Chantal had reached the last step on the gangway and spun for a final wave. Had she seen or overheard Van Greuning? Clearly, she had. She gave them a thumbs-up signal and sprinted for the parking lot.

Men had gathered at the ship's end of the gangway preparing to remove it, and others crowded at the bottom. Gail focused on the wharf's terminal entrance, holding her breath, expecting Van Greuning to arrive any second. Ed put his arm around her waist and held her other hand with a near painful grip. His eyes were pinned on the doorway, too.

After an impossibly long minute, Van Greuning's uniformed figure dashed out the door, accompanied by two other police officers, all yelling, and sprinted directly for the gangway, a good hundred yards away. A signal came from the top of the gangway, and the workers below began pulling it away from the ship's side. It had retreated about six feet by the time Van Greuning reached it and ran up the stairs, still shouting and waving his arms. Before he reached the top, the gap between it and the ship widened to ten feet. He grabbed the railing, only just preventing his fall to the concrete, and glared toward the bridge above, then cupped his hands to his mouth.

The ship's horn, making its loud and sustained note, instantly drowned out any sound he may have made. No music could have been as sweet to Gail's ears. The crowd on the viewing verandah threw streamers and confetti at the ship, and the passengers shouted raucous farewells. Simultaneously, Gail heard a noise of turbulent waters against the dock side start up, and the ship edged slowly away.

A red-faced Van Greuning gesticulated from the gangway before he ran down it and back towards the building again.

Ed frowned. "He's most likely going to radio the *Hesperus*… we're not clear yet."

"Can he? I mean, it's an Australian liner. Would he have the power to stop it just for us? Are we that important?"

"To him we are, but let's hope for some sanity. Don't you think it'd be downright expensive, delaying a ship like this? Let's not worry, Gail."

"I'll be happier when we pass between the north and south piers at the end of the Bluff and steam out to sea. I expect he'll be standing on the north pier, waving his fists at us as we go past."

Ed grinned. "I doubt he'd reach it before we do, and he couldn't stop us, anyway." He circled her shoulders and pulled her in close.

"Perhaps he'll dive in and swim after us. Come, relax, we're rid of him."

It was a nice thought, but she was uncomfortable still. Where could they go? Would they be accepted as refugees or be forced to return and serve their sentences?

The *Hesperus* sailed at a gentle pace, but soon they passed the piers, the slopes of the Bluff rising above them. There was no sign of Van Greuning, and Gail breathed easier. She rested her head against Ed's shoulder and wept. Ed held the back of her head and caressed her forehead with his lips.

The ship turned south and picked up speed. "Everything's going to be all right," he told her.

*****

Ed pushed open his cabin door to dress for dinner. The side walls had two bunks each, with a washbasin between them and built-in wardrobes beside the door. His suitcase lay on a rack near the bunks. He found his name tag on the top left bunk, on which lay a paper with all the information he needed, plus a bag containing some chocolates, toiletry items and his restaurant ticket with the menu and table number. How likely was it he'd get the same table as Gail? The odds were decidedly against him. Surely, he could arrange a transfer—the friendly staff would be flexible—and everyone would recognize the need, initially, of sorting diners into groups to avoid chaos the first night.

He wandered into the dining hall wearing a light blue jacket with a navy-blue tie and cream pants. Inside, a stewardess smiled at him as she handed him a name tag and pointed out his table. He made his way there, while looking all around for Gail without seeing her.

The table was at the far corner of the large dining hall. At the head, there was a portly Indian man, a pretty woman in a maroon sari sat by him, and along the side were a girl and boy between the ages of children and teenagers. At the other end sat a Coloured man, about Ed's age, but whose complexion was much darker than Ed's disguised skin. By his side sat a young, dark-complexioned Coloured woman. That left just two seats, and he claimed the one beside the woman. Everyone at the table introduced themselves. The Indian family were from Durban, the Coloureds a married couple from Swaziland. Ed had thought it more prudent going by his false Swazi name, Ben Hendricks, even though he might seem ignorant of Swaziland affairs during conversation. He wasn't ready to risk using his true identity yet.

Everybody was friendly, and the chatter flowed freely from the start. The Indian man, Mr. Ravi Moodley, was the one who brought up that one thing that surely was on everybody's mind.

"We were thinking, this is still like being in South Africa, isn't it?"

"A bit obvious, hey," added Frans Kleynhans, the Coloured man. "Even after we leave the country, we're segregated."

Everyone in the party murmured assent, and there was an immediate buzz of talk. Ed joined in and was animatedly questioning Aussie values together with Mrs. Audrey Kleynhans when he became aware of a lime green dress in his periphery. Gail. He jumped to his feet, his heart pounding, pulling the chair out for her, not know-ing yet whether to recognize her or pretend they didn't know each other. She was a member of their table, of course! Probably the only other non-White person on board. But never mind the racism—he couldn't believe his luck. She looked gorgeous in that long gown he'd never seen before, a matching band in her hair, which had been swept up somehow, leaving threads dangling alongside both cheeks. Her ring finger was bare, of course, seeing as she was playing the part of an unmarried woman. She flashed her smile around the table but quickly returned it to his face. His cheeks heated as the hubbub of chatter suddenly stopped—he reddened. Gail sat down and beamed around at the company.

Frans was the first to break the silence. "Well, Ben. Are you going to introduce us to your lady friend?"

There were chuckles all round, putting paid to the possibility of pretending they were unacquainted. He made the introductions, introducing her as Grace Du Preez. The table greeted her as if she were already part of the group. Gail sat down, and they all resumed their chatter, laughter, and banter. Ed loved the way they all took to Gail and made her welcome. He knew he'd enjoy this group and could see that Gail thought the same.

At this point, Shareena Moodley stared toward the doorway. "Oh, look. The captain."

An imposing white uniformed figure had entered the room, waving and smiling as he sauntered to the captain's table. His eyes roved toward Ed's group, and he stopped walking and frowned. He scanned the dining room, more than a flash of anger crossing his face. Not seeing the something or someone he was looking for, he strode toward Ed's table.

Ed's elation dropped like an anchor. The captain had seen them. Apparently, Van Greuning had contacted the captain and reported them. What would happen to them now? Would they lift them off the ship by helicopter? The ship's deck system, from what he'd seen, would not allow for that. But they would need something for medical emergencies. Then again, the captain was Australian, so he may not involve himself with internal South African affairs? And why so angry? What had Van Greuning told him?

Gail's hand gripped his arm. "Don't get stroppy with him, Ed. Just explain our situation." He squeezed her hand.

The captain's expression eased as he approached the table, but his frown remained. He nodded at each one individually. "Ladies, gentlemen. Good evening. I'm afraid I have apologies to make. This is deplorable. I assume you're all South African citizens?"

Frans half rose, a puzzled expression on his face. "Uh, we're, that is Audrey," he indicated her, "and myself, we're from Swaziland, and so are Ben and Grace."

"We are from Durban," said Ravi, also rising.

"Again, all of you, please accept my and the ship's most profuse apologies. The moment I find the imbecile who put you all together at one table, I'll have him drawn and quartered, I promise."

Ravi looked him in the eye, with a dead pan countenance. "Sorry, Captain, but what do you mean, put all of us together at this table? I don't understand."

A momentary silence followed. The captain hesitated, his face turning red and he loosened his collar. "I…mean because you, you are all…um."

"All what, Captain?" Ravi demanded.

Shareena punched her husband playfully on the arm. "Stop teasing him, Ravi." She turned to the captain. "Don't mind him, sir, he's impossible. We know what you meant."

The captain's face cleared as he stared around at the group for confirmation. "Thank you. You really had me going. Still, again I apologise, and I'll get that lunatic to reassign you to other tables."

Ravi was still standing. "As for me, Captain, and this time I am serious. My family and I prefer staying with this group—we've already become friends. Of course, I am speaking for myself."

"I'll second that." Frans glanced at Audrey, who agreed, smiling.

"Me too, I'll third it," said Ed, and Gail concurred.

The captain removed his hat and wiped his brow with a handkerchief. "Thank you so much, and if ever any of you should wish to change to another table, don't hesitate to ask me personally. Now, on behalf of the *Hesperus* and in view of the fact we have no official captain's table till after we leave Cape Town, I'm inviting the whole lot of you to join me tonight, now. That is, should you want…"

There was immediate accord, and the entire group rose to accompany the captain to his table, even though some officers would have to move.

CHAPTER

THIRTY-SEVEN

Ed and Gail roamed all around the top decks of the *Hesperus*. Ed had always liked to explore, but exploring with Gail tripled his enjoyment. He loved strolling with her hand in hand or with his arm wrapped around her shoulders. Gail took that little sharp, nervous intake of breath he loved so much, and he drew her closer. Close enough to sense her trembling like a cat's purr.

"Wait! You're cold, why didn't you tell me?" Indeed, the sun had long since gone, as had Durban's humidity. The air had turned chilly. "Come, let's go below. We can return tomorrow in the daylight."

She made a murmur of assent, which, together with her shivering, prompted him to bring both arms to surround her with as much of him as possible. They scurried toward the nearest door and descended a short flight of stairs.

"The cinema," he said. "That will be comfy and warm." It would also offer him the opportunity to turn this into a proper date. They entered and stood inside as their eyes adapted to the dark. Not many people. Ed led her to the back row.

They settled comfortably together, and Gail glanced at the screen. "Do you know what's showing?"

"Didn't I glimpse a poster outside for *Salesman* or something?"

"*Salesman*?" Gail made as if to rise. "Apparently, it's a real bomb."

Ed pulled her down. "Not exactly an emotion-exercising film or anything, I suppose, but who cares about the movie?"

She snuggled her head under his neck. "Hmmm. Yes. Who cares?"

Alone at last, well, almost. The few patrons were preoccupied with their popcorn and cold drinks, staring at the adverts. The Peter Stuyvesant movie ad finished and Pan Am's one for its new Jumbo Jet replaced it. An interesting new world. One where they could escape all the prejudice. A place for us. He shifted his attention to Gail as the feature film appeared on the screen. His arms were around Gail, perhaps for the first time since their dates at the Hi-Way Drive-In. Maybe not as comfortable as in his Rambler, not with the wooden armrest digging in his ribs, but he'd take it. Just so long as he was with his Gail, his wife. The notion flashed through his mind that they had not yet even consummated their marriage. The dim light from the screen reflected off her face. She tilted her head up, eyelashes resting on her cheeks, parting her lips, expectant. He lowered his head till those lips met his own, soft and welcoming, a wave of pleasure shuddered down his body.

Ed blinked as the lights came on and the curtains swished over the words "the end." Already? He hadn't even nearly had enough kissing yet. They kissed once more before they rose and made their way out.

Clutching both his hands, she said, "Thank you, Ed. What a marvellous date." She sighed. "I suppose I better go to my cabin."

Reality hit him. They had to part again, to sleep alone. It wasn't right. She was his wife; he should be taking her to their own cabin, just the two of them. Together.

He looked down at her sweet face, so close. It was going to be a long night. He sighed, slipping an arm around her shoulders. "I'll take you there," he murmured.

They walked in silence. Ironic, they were free from pursuit, free from the odious government that kept them apart, yet still doomed to sleep in separate cabins, with total strangers.

Ed took her hands at the door, feeling the warmth and velvety texture with his thumbs. "Soon we'll have an actual date. I'll take you dancing. There'll be nobody stopping us."

She smiled and looked up into his eyes. "I will certainly look forward to that. Will they have dancing while we're docked in Cape Town?"

He wasn't sure. There'd been no time to read the activities list.

"We might try someplace in District Six. We're both Coloureds now."

Gail gasped. "You mean, leave the ship?"

"Everybody else will. Cape Town. Haven't you ever been there?"

"Never in my life. Of course, I want to. I'd love to tour it by day and go up Table Mountain cableway, but this is still South Africa you know, and we're outlaws. Not to mention it'll likely be for Whites only."

"We can use our new Swazi identities."

"Still, let's get real, Ed. You watched him. Van Greuning knows we're here. Do you imagine he'll let it go? We'll be safer on board. Technically, we're on foreign soil here."

"Probably you're right. Safety first."

*****

Gail rose early before the others. She'd crept in last night to avoid disturbing the other three girls, but she'd switched her bunk light on and saw none of the night owls had yet returned.

This morning, they were all asleep, one snoring on her back, another curled into a tight ball, and the third lying completely nude on top of the covers. She scanned the page detailing the day's events, eased off her bunk down the ladder, then proceeded to the shower rooms at the end of the hallway.

When she came back, Ed was waiting for her outside the cabin door, wearing a blue and red board-striped shirt with blue shorts. He was starting to look less like a Coloured, his short curly hair straightening, and his colour dye fading. He had dressed for deck activities rather than lounge lizarding. Good.

"You look great." She slipped the ship's bath towel around his neck and yanked him toward her, pressing her lips against his. She released him and gasped. "Now, let me get dressed. I won't be long." She wiggled her fingers "goodbye" and sidled through the door.

The weather was perfect. Blue skies all round matching a deep blue ocean. In the distance were tall buildings of a city. Port Elizabeth possibly, as they should be approximately halfway to Cape Town. Gail leaned on the railing, observing the sea rush by. Ed stood behind her, holding her closely with his hands locked together at her waist. She leaned her head back as he pressed his mouth to her hair, which flowed freely in the breeze. She could stay this way forever.

"Grace. Yoo hoo, Grace."

At first, she didn't react to the call. Remembering her alias, she snapped her head round. A woman waved, it was Audrey, on the diving board of the main pool, evidently wanting them to come over.

Audrey grinned at her when they neared. "Hi, Grace. I've been calling and yelling. Your name is Grace, right?" Audrey raised one eyebrow.

"Sorry. I…er. It was windy."

"Yes. I did notice you were otherwise occupied." She winked at them. "Hello, Ben. How are you doing?"

"Just fine thanks. You're brave. Isn't the water freezing?"

"Well, this surely isn't Durban water, but we prefer it colder. Can't wait to swim at Clifton Beach tomorrow. It will be roughly fifty degrees there."

Gail shuddered. "I think we'll pass. Where's Frans?"

"There in the water."

He waved when Audrey pointed him out. He pulled himself out of the water, and the four sat on pool chairs.

The girls chatted like old friends and Frans turned to Ed. "So what's the story with you and Grace? Clearly, you know each other, yet last night you tried pulling off the idea you didn't."

Ed sighed. "I presume we're too transparent."

"Too transparent by far." Frans placed a hand on Ed's shoulder. "Like your attempt at passing as a Coloured. Nice try! You might fool the White okes, but not us. Now, out with it. Quite obviously, you're in love with her. Everyone at the table gathered that last night. Even the Moodley kids."

Ed sucked in a deep breath and blew it out.

Gail gripped his hand. "I trust them, Ed." She looked into his eyes, a question in her own.

He stared into hers and sighed. "We are a married couple, Ed and Gail Brent."

Audrey clapped her cheeks. "I knew it. I told you so, didn't I, Frans?"

Frans chuckled. "Yes, and another thing, there's no way you live in Swaziland. You're South Africans, and you're running away."

Gail tightened her grip on Ed's hand and lowered her eyes.

"Don't worry, sweetie," said Audrey, gripping her other hand. "We're on your side. We spoke of this last night. We see happiness in you but also fear. We want to help you if we can."

Gail blinked away sudden tears, too choked up to reply. She was about to make an attempt when a shadow fell over them.

"Miss Du Preez, is it?" A white uniform stood out against the sunlight. Gail stared at the man in it for several moments before inclining her head.

"I am sorry to disturb you, Miss Du Preez. The captain wishes to speak with you. If I may, I'll accompany you to his office."

Ed started to his feet. She took his hand and stood, too. Anxiety squeezed at her heart. Their time at the captain's table had been merry and entertaining. Perhaps it was nothing more than Captain Norton's wanting a furthering of their acquaintance. No need to worry. But Ed's face showed his uneasiness, too. He stood by her side.

The officer raised his eyebrows. "I assure you, there isn't any cause for alarm. If it's inconvenient, another time would do, and I can convey a message to him. But the captain did emphasize it had to be before we arrive at Cape Town tomorrow morning."

"Ja, well no fine." Gail made her excuses to Audrey and Frans, turned a pleading glance to Ed, who kept hold of her hand, and the three walked to the captain's office.

The officer knocked on the door and saluted after Captain Norton opened it.

"Ah, Miss Du Preez, thank you for coming." He acknowledged Ed. "I have a few questions for you, Miss Du Preez. It's entirely up to you if you want Mr. Hendricks to be present, I assure you."

Keeping her chin up, she looked the captain in the eye. "I would like him with me."

Captain Norton swept his hand toward two chairs in front of his desk and returned to his own behind it. "Let me reassure you I have made no inferences or decisions in this matter and only wish to hear your side." He rested his elbows on the desktop, fingers weaved together. "I have heard from a certain Sergeant Van Greuning." He pronounced the Van like the vehicle. "He claims that he has searched the travel details for our departure from Durban, and he has singled out the names of you two as being false ones. And the papers you presented were forgeries. Is there any truth in that?"

Suddenly, it was too much. Just as she'd begun to hope for a better future for Ed and herself, it was likely they'd be arrested. What they had done was against the law. There could be no excuses. She couldn't stop her tears. Ed pulled her against him.

"It was my idea, not hers," he said. "She's innocent. She had nothing to do with the arrangement."

"Easy, Ben," the captain hesitated. "I guess I should call you, Ed, shouldn't I?" He cracked a smile. "I assume you are actually South Africans?"

Gail slowly nodded.

"Do you have your genuine passports with you by any chance?"

"Yes," said Ed.

"First, I will need those. Then, I need the reason for the false papers."

"My name is Ed Brent, and Gail is my wife. We were married in church, but the law does not recognize the marriage in South Africa."

The captain sat up straighter. "Whyever not?"

"Because I am White, and Gail is Coloured."

"I see." He paused. "The sergeant also cited additional reasons for your being wanted." He reached for a paper in a desk drawer and looked at it. "Escaping from prison twice; attempting to flee the country; using counterfeit documents; injuring an officer of the law; hijacking a police helicopter. That's just your charges, Mrs. Brent."

Ed answered him. "Only because we wished to live together as man and wife, and Sergeant Van Greuning became obsessed with arresting us."

"Have you applied for asylum?"

"No. How could we? We weren't ever able to leave the country, especially with Van Greuning after us every inch of the way."

Captain Norton sat back in his chair, elbows on the desktop, fingers pressed together. "I cannot make any promises. Except one, that this officer will be waiting for you on the wharf in Cape Town. Having spoken with you two and to Van Greuning on the radio, I trust my own judge of character. The rest of the world is somewhat sympathetic to people in your predicament. I'll see what I can do. I shall send you further instructions.

"In the meantime, I want you to enjoy your time on board the *Hesperus*, knowing that I'm sympathetic to your cause. But I will need your passports." He winked at them. "Both."

CHAPTER
THIRTY-EIGHT

Ed called for Gail before dawn, not wanting to miss the scenic approach to Cape Town. They climbed the stairs for the top deck near the bow of the *Hesperus*. At first, it would seem they'd arrived too soon. There was nothing but ocean all around them, but Ed spotted a strip of land jutting out ahead of them. He cuddled her closer, wrapping his arms around her to protect her from the cool breeze. He pointed. "That will be Cape Point. Soon, we'll be in the Atlantic Ocean."

"I've never seen any ocean but the Indian." She looked ahead as they watched the strip come slowly nearer.

"The usually grey, sometimes blue Indian Ocean. Here, the Atlantic's green, more often than not. You're in for a treat."

She looked up at him. "When exactly does it become the Atlantic?"

"That portion you'll notice to the right is part of the coast of False Bay. Sailors back then believed they had arrived in the Cape and turned into the bay, hence the name. Around the next projection on the other side, Cape Point, is the Atlantic."

The ship sped towards the huge outjutting till it rose above them as an immense cliff. About halfway up, atop the steep banks stood the lighthouse. The ship obviously couldn't approach too close, because foamy waves crashed against the rocks below the cliffs.

"And voila! The Cape of Good Hope. Welcome to the Atlantic."

Gail laughed. "I can see the green. How long before we dock?"

"Two hours at least, I should say." He glanced at his watch. "A perfect time for breakfast. We really should be on deck for the last part, the approach to Cape Town."

Breakfast was a help-yourself, all-you-can eat affair. Ed took two trays and handed Gail one. "Just in case we succeed in getting into the city, you better fill up."

She frowned, then helped herself to a bowl of chocolate ProNutro. "Uh. I really don't think we should risk that. Van Greuning will be waiting for us."

"Yes, he will be." At the voice, they both spun around, Ed nearly spilling the milk he was about to pour on his cereal.

Captain Norton continued. "I imagine he's arrived, waiting at the docks. As for you, Gail, I don't want you on the ship."

The colour drained from Gail's face. She almost dropped the bowl, but the captain caught her wrist and stopped it in the nick of time.

"Relax, I meant for today only. I don't want you here while he's sniffing around, but I have a plan. After brekkie, you can view our arrival along the coastline. It's well worthwhile. But before we arrive, I want you both to hide under the lifeboats on the aft deck. I'll see your friend aboard and settled in my office, waiting." His lips twisted into a grin. "He'll have to be rather patient. Watch out for a biscuit-coloured Kombi on the wharf and keep an eye on it. You'll observe a man step out and wave the Australian flag…you know what that looks like—? Good. Go down the gangway separately, preferably when it's chock full of people. Stay away from each other till you're inside the Kombi. You're on a group tour and won't be back until late."

Ed closed his mouth, which he realized had been hanging open for some time. "I…we… I don't know…"

"No worries, mate. It's on us. The cabbie won't come back before it's safe. We still have to worry about tomorrow, but we'll sort out what happens then. Now, I must go."

Breakfast over, they decided on staying at the rear section of the ship, near their appointed hiding place. They leaned on the railing and gazed at the coast.

Ed's stomach somersaulted as the mountains of Cape Town came into view. He'd spent many of his childhood holidays on this stunning peninsula. It was a special part of his life, something he'd assumed would always be a part of him. But, the day after tomorrow, they would be torn from South Africa's mother city, never to be embraced by her friendly arms again. His throat constricted painfully.

The town they were passing was probably Kommetjie, confirmed a few minutes later when they passed Long Beach. Stunningly beautiful, with the whitest sand imaginable, separating the mountain range shooting up to lofty peaks and the startling green of the Atlantic Ocean.

Gail gazed toward the shore. Her eyes, already a beautiful hazel green, reflected the astonishing emerald hue of the ocean.

Gail, much absorbed in the scene, was blinking hard, too, and pressing her fingers against her lips. Those beautiful lips were brown, not red, and therefore forbidden. After today, Ed must either be torn from those lips or be torn from South Africa. What kind of choice was that? This was his country, his land of birth, his place of allegiance and patriotism, his source—until recently—of pride.

Gail's dazzling eyes and her lips turned to him, raising his pulse a hefty notch. The eyes won the contest, indisputably.

Those eyes filled with tears. "I hate this. Ed. Why should we have to leave this beautiful country? Why can't it accept how much we love each other and let us stay?"

South Africa, one of the most uniquely beautiful countries in the world, would have to wait for them to visit another time. His glance confirmed she was every bit a part of the country's beauty, yet they couldn't share it together. She must have been thinking similar thoughts. Her tears had wet her cheeks. He gently dried them with his thumb.

The two-mile length of beach gave way to mountains. Ed pointed to the road winding along the precipitous cliffs—Chapman's Peak Drive. It had always been his wish to drive this road in an open sports car. He pictured it now. Gail, leaning toward him as he steered the Spit a little too rapidly into the bends, her hair blowing in the wind while she stared at the sheer drop of over fifteen hundred feet.

Above them, the cliffs reached up another two thousand feet. "Do you know, in the space of less than six miles, there are some one hundred and fourteen bends."

He fell silent as the ship passed Hout Bay, soon to round the headland and sail toward Cape Town.

*****

Gail had always wanted to visit Cape Town, ever since she was a little girl. Her mom had been dead set against travelling by train, especially in third class, the only one available to non-Whites. She considered it too dangerous for women on their own. Unfortunately, by rail was the only way they could go while she was growing up. Mom could not afford to fly, and they'd never owned a car. It would have been heaven to come here with Ed. If only.

While leaning back into Ed, she admired the Twelve Apostle mountains gliding by, tall peaks in a perfect row, dropping precipitously to the Emerald Sea. He wrapped his arms around her, shielding her from the early morning chill.

The intercom crackled with an announcement they were sailing past Camps Bay, and that they'd soon pass Mouille Point into Table Bay. The names were familiar to her, both from her mother's tales of when she'd been here, and from reading about it.

Ed pointed. "That is Table Mountain from the edge. Look, can you see the upper cable station at the top and Lion's Head to the left?"

It was breathtaking, and she couldn't wait to see the famous mountain panorama from the front. Ed pointed out Clifton Beach. "If you wore your bikini there, you'd put all the other girls to shame."

"Izzit? That is, until I got arrested for being on a white beach, you mean."

He didn't answer. There was no need.

They reached Sea Point, nestled in front of Signal Hill. A rocky coastline replaced the white sand beaches. Ed showed her Robben Island in the distance. The island of exiles. In her childhood, she had read Lawrence Green's *Tavern of the Seas*, giving her a solid knowledge of Cape Town. The island was now home to political prisoners. She sighed. Black people fighting for freedom, only to lose every sense of it whenever it was briefly won.

The ship's horn blasted as they rounded the Point. There it stood, Table Mountain, like all the postcards, but now alive in all its magnificence. A perfectly flat-topped mountain with vertical, unscalable cliffs reaching to the top. She recognized the seventeenth century Castle of Good Hope on the left with its five prominent bastions. The castle echoed the mountain, she imagined the mountain as a fort with sloping sides at the base, and vertical walls at the top, from which they threw burning oil and rocks at the would-be attackers. It was ironic that now those same defenses should serve to prevent their inhabitants leaving.

Devil's Peak claimed as much a share of the scene on the left as it dared, rising to a sharp point at the same level as the tabletop. Lion's Head, the smaller peak on the right, successfully fought for attention.

Gail frowned. "Lion's Head? How on earth does it look like a head?"

Ed shrugged.

A lump formed in Gail's throat. Her tears instantly blurred at the magnificent scene. The ship weaved her way to her berth, and Gail's eyes cleared enough to note further landmarks, familiar from pictures she had seen. Modern buildings built on the foreshore, land reclaimed from the sea, were near them. The old city lay behind, crawling up toward the mountains.

A tugboat pulled alongside to assist the docking process. Ed tugged at her elbow. "It's time to go to our lifeboat."

They scurried to the first of the three boats in an area devoid of people. These offered the most hiding areas, well away from the gangway, yet close enough to see whatever was going on. Ed looked up, and Gail followed his gaze. There was a gap between the boat's canvas covering and the metal roof, big enough for both of them. From there, they could peer around the metal bulkhead in front of the boat.

Ed rubbed his jaw as he looked up and frowned. "Gail, are you able—"

Gail leaped onto a ledge on one of the large metal supports, jumped to the edge of the boat, and swung her legs over the top. She grinned down at him. "Are you coming or what?"

He gaped at her a few seconds, then attempted the same thing. She followed his clumsy attempts. Clearly, he found it wasn't as easy as it looked, especially getting onto the cover. She held out her hand to help him up, and together, they wiggled their way past the ridge of the canvas to a spot which hid them well.

The ship bumped against the tyres lining the dock, and a line was fed out to the workers there.

A small group of people waited on the wharf. Gail peeked around the side of the bulkhead and scanned the faces. Sure enough, as expected, Van Greuning stood between two other police constables. They were a short distance apart from some other people behind a barrier, probably waiting for disembarking passengers. They wouldn't be boarding the ship. Van Greuning, however, certainly would. A sharp intake of breath and a squeeze of her hand affirmed that Ed had spotted him.

What was it Captain Norton had said? A biscuit Kombi. Check. There, by a shed. A Coloured man stood next to it, looking toward the rear of the ship.

Several workers wheeled the gangway to the side of the *Hesperus* and locked it into place on the lowest deck. Immediately, a uniformed officer descended the steps. Gail recognized him as the one who had welcomed her on board the day before yesterday. At the bottom, he spoke to Van Greuning. A few seconds later, they both climbed up the steps, and they disappeared from Gail's sight onto the deck.

"Look out for the flag," Ed whispered, as she stared toward the Kombi.

Nothing happened for several minutes while the large group of passengers waiting to disembark pressed against the chain barrier at the top of the gangway. At last, a sailor unhooked the chain. The passengers, impatient for solid land, swarmed the gangway, making a loud clatter on the metal steps. Eager tourists made for the waiting Kombis and Hi Ace vans.

She could feel the sweat on her brow. She tugged on Ed's arm. "When will we be able to go?"

"Right now." Captain Norton again. He clearly had a habit of popping up unexpectedly out of nowhere. He stood with arms akimbo, gazing up at them.

"Van Greuning's safely waiting in my office, with my secretary bending his ear to keep him occupied. And there's your flag waving." He pointed toward the Kombi.

They both looked. Yes, the Coloured man was waving an Australian flag.

The captain held out a hand to help her down. "Hurry now, remember, only one of you at a time on the gangplank."

Ed gave her a gentle push in the back. "You first, and don't stop till you're in the van."

She needed no second bidding and rushed to the stairway leading down to the exit. She reached the head of the gangway where a large crowd still gathered, among them the two police officers. She kept her focus to the front, ignoring them, and they didn't stop her.

She found joining the crowd quite easy. A man in a suit stood by and waved his hand in front. "After you, ma'am."

Thanking him with a smile, she slipped into the queue. She wasn't used to such manners from White men, probably he was Australian. She reached the Kombi where the man with the flag greeted her.

"Mrs. Brent. Welcome, I'm Gavie," he said in a strong Cape Coloured accent. "Please step in the van."

She needed no extra persuasion, wanting to hurry out of view. From inside came a chorus of greetings. The Moodley family occupied the front row of seats, except for Nehri who sat in front, and Audrey and Frans were in the middle.

Audrey reached over, patting the seat behind her. "Welcome to the tour. Captain Norton's apologies for the lack of White people, but this was apparently so we can ride the cableway as a group. A car all to ourselves, and we get to bypass the queue."

Frans's wide grin showed his lack of upper teeth. "And this way, we're all allowed on, if you know what I mean."

Gail hadn't given that a thought. Of course. Whyever would Coloureds be allowed to ride the cableway? Something she'd wanted to do ever since she read about it. She took in a nervous breath. But where was Ed?

Shareena, seated at the window, read her mind. "He'll be here just now, don't you worry. There, he's in the middle of the gangway. He's reached the cops. Wait, one's looking at him…"

Gail stopped breathing.

"No. Here he comes."

Gail started breathing again.

THIRTY-NINE

Gail watched as Ed rushed to the waiting Kombi, nodded at Gavie, and piled through the door, taking his seat beside her. She slipped her hand into the crook of his arm.

He greeted all the others from the table. He was the only White person, though admittedly he still wore his Coloured disguise.

Gavie introduced himself to Ed, climbed in and turned to face the group. "Hellos, hey. Welcome to Cape Town, y'oll. There's a hang of a lot of things to see. We'll mos do the cableway first, the captain says. Have any of y'olls been up?"

Ed raised his hand. His was the only one. Of course, the cableway was doubtlessly for Whites only.

Gavie grinned. "Well, y'oll's lucky today. Y'olls getting y'olls own cable car, hey. That is number one, then anything y'olls want."

After a short drive, Gavie pointed out the Castle, the oldest building in the country, but he seemed more interested in what lay beyond. "Over there on the left, y'olls can see some of the streets of District Six. Y'olls know that it was declared a White area four years ago, hey? And they've been moving us Coloureds out since then. I used to live there, hey, but they sommer moved me to a place hang and gone from here. My home, the bulldozers sommer pushed it away while I watched hey. Okay, I know it's a slummy area, and lots of crime, but now they're gonna build larney homes for White okes only. Sorry, Mr. Brent, hey, but that's how it is. Now I have a hang of a long commute from the Cape Flats to get to work every day."

Ed looked very serious and didn't say anything. She squeezed his hand. It wasn't his fault. The Kombi steered into Heerengracht Street, where Gavie pointed out the huge Sanlam Building, apparently the tallest in South Africa at three hundred and six feet. Gail peered up at it as they passed. She'd seen nothing so tall in real life before. The letters of an electronic news display constantly crawled across the top floor. Gavie told them they were driving on land reclaimed from the ocean, so this part of the city was new, hence the broad streets and giant traffic circles, and the buildings so modern and tall.

Certainly, this had to be one of the most modern cities anywhere, surpassing even her own Durban. South Africans were no doubt proud of both cities, but she couldn't help comparing it to the area where she lived, far from the city itself, and typical of a third world country, so unlike what she was seeing. And the home where Gavie was living now was probably worse than the one that was bulldozed before his eyes.

Gavie pointed out the enormous new and modern-looking railway station, with large paintings of vintage railway engines on the outside façade, before turning sharp right into the old part of the city. The city was just turning three hundred and eighteen years old, he told them. From here, the road curved up between the mountains.

Gail peered through the window, taking in the vista of Table Mountain, spread out before them and growing ever larger as they approached. They turned onto the road leading to the lower cable station, negotiating sharp bends, twisting their way up ever steeper slopes, until at last they stopped beside the large white cable station.

Gavie double-parked, jumped out, and held a gate open. "We can mos sidestep the queue here." He ushered them past a long queue of White tourists to a door at the end of metal steps. Gail couldn't help noticing the frowns and head shakings of the White tourists as they passed. Could Ed have been one of them, outraged at seeing a group of Coloureds and Indians bypassing him while he stood in a long, slow moving queue. She gripped his hand tighter.

A stony-faced man at the gate took the strip of tickets Gavie handed over, and they passed through between metal railings, emerging into a room. From here, the enormous opening faced the crest of Table Mountain. On the left, she saw a gigantic wheel spinning, guiding a thick cable passing through the opening.

Ed pointed out the upper station atop the vast, flat-topped mountain. It was similar to the lower station, but so far off it looked like a miniature.

He pointed upwards. "Here she comes."

The two cable cars were crossing halfway up, looking tiny in the distance. As the descending car approached, Gail sensed her hand trembling in his. Four minutes later, the car slowed and came to rest with its floor exactly level with and a mere inch from the concrete platform on which they stood. The far door slid open, allowing the descending riders to exit before their own door opened.

They surged into the car, the children darting to the open window facing the mountain. Their group were the only occupants.

A loud ringing sounded, and the cable car smoothly began its journey upwards. For a small bunch of people, they sure made a lot of noise, all pointing different things out, such as the ground below, the ever-diminishing lower station, and the looming mountain above. Shareena stood in the middle looking nervous, likely because there was no glass in the window openings all around the car. Amaya yelled excitedly that the other car was approaching. The group surged to the left side and waved and called to the descending passengers, who responded in like manner, until some of them stopped. Obviously, they'd noticed the car was filled with non-Whites. She saw a mother smacking down the waving hand of her small child, who grinned at them.

There were lots of oohs and pointing as the car glided really close past the cliffs.

Shareena held a hand over her eyes. "We're going to crash!"

The kids stuck their arms out and leaned over so far that Ravi grabbed their arms and pulled them back. The car rose almost vertically as it glided into the upper cable station. From here, they climbed up steep steps before exiting to the mountain itself.

The group had a quick discussion on what to do, with no consensus, so decided to split up. Agreeing on a return time, Ed took her hand and they set off.

Gail squeezed his hand tightly as they walked along the path leading toward the edge. "I just can't believe we're here. Durban's nothing to this. I love it. Don't you wish we lived here?"

Ed grinned. "Wait till you see the view from the absolute edge of the cliff."

She slowed her steps. "You mean over there where the ground suddenly ends?" Not a chance.

"Yes, but I won't let you fall." He tugged at her to urge her closer toward the cliff.

When they approached within a few feet, she stopped. She'd always thought she'd follow Ed anywhere, but there had to be limits. "No ways. Not on your life. You won't get me any nearer than this."

"Okay, you don't have to." He crouched, then crawled to the edge. "Do it like this, on your stomach, until your head is over the ledge." Now his head dangled over the brink, looking straight down the cliffside, a sheer drop of about eighteen hundred feet, if she remembered correctly. Turning, he beckoned her.

Gail dropped to her knees and edged closer till she was prone. She wiggled her way forward on her elbows, muttering all the way. "Ed Brent, if this is your way of ending our problems…"

"Come now, you can do it." Her entire body trembled, and he pulled her closer. She peered down, hearing a sound somewhere between terrified and awestruck. It was her own voice, hardly recognisable. He laid his arm across her shoulders and pulled her tight. "Look, do you see the Sanlam building? You can read the messages at the top." He then pointed out the *Hesperus*, resting in the quiet waters of the docks.

"Over there on the left," he pointed. "Lion's Head. I could never see the shape of a lion's head, to tell you the truth."

Gail stared at it for a few moments, frowning, tilting her head all ways. "Wait! I do. It isn't supposed to look exactly like a head, I think, but see the hill on the right?"

"Yes, Signal Hill."

"Whatever. It looks like a lion lying down, with his tail toward the bay, and Lion's Head, well, that's his head. It's exactly the way they look when they're resting."

"Hey! I get it now. Of course, that must be how they saw it. They should have called Signal Hill, Lion's Body." He slapped his forehead. "Gail, you're brilliant."

His remark gave her enough confidence to sit up and stretch her legs forward, inching them closer till they dangled over the brink. He put his arm around her and pointed out all the many landmarks in the panorama.

All this, their heritage, their homeland, and yet it wasn't theirs. Not if they were to remain a married couple. Even sitting here, heads together, was reason enough to be arrested and forever separated. She turned her face back to him and felt a tear rolling down her cheek. His head came closer, and she opened her lips, a moment later accepting his in a kiss. Their home together would be somewhere, anywhere. But not here, where two of the country's citizens were forbidden to be together. They sat quietly, keeping as close to each other as possible.

*****

Ed squeezed Gail's hand as they sat silently in the Kombi. He imagined she couldn't believe they had to leave this. This should be a visit. Cape Town on holiday as husband and wife, perhaps every year. How their children would love the cableway.

At the end of the road, Gavie turned left and drove between Lion's Head and Table Mountain on Kloof Road, navigating down twisty turns and through forests. Suddenly, they were far away from the bustle of the city. The sunrays gently filtered through the tall pine trees and fell on the winding road. Somehow, everything about Cape Town seemed beautiful. The Friendly City, they called it, but not for mixed-race couples.

Gavie announced their arrival at Clifton Beach. "It's good, hey, and famous, so it's worth having a squiz at it. But if you want to swim, it's sommer better you wait for Camp's Bay. It's not far." This implied Coloureds were not welcome here.

After enjoying the beauty of the beach with surrounding cliffs, they did move on to Camp's Bay, another White beach, with a long strip of sand and many rocks, the breakers crashing around them sending foamy spray into the air.

Audrey stripped off her clothes down to a purple bikini and stood on the sand. "I hope y'olls brought your cozzies, too. Last one in is a pampoen." She took off toward the sea, but Frans was the only one who accepted the challenge and ran after her, perhaps afraid of being turned into a pumpkin.

Gavie grinned at Ed. "How'z about y'oll, come on, just for mos, hey?"

"No fear, not me," said Ed. "This water is freezing." The notably small number of people backed up his words. Few tourists came to Cape Town in June. "But I'm glad it's winter. I'm sure the crowds of Whites in summer wouldn't be pleased to see us on their beach."

The water was chilly enough to discourage even Audrey, who quickly returned, shivering, and wrapped herself in a towel.

Gavie drove a short distance and pulled into parking near a wharf. His face glowed with excitement. "Hout Bay. Everybody out, it's lunchtime! These okes got the best fish and slap chips in the world, hey."

He passed her a serving wrapped in newsprint. Ed could well believe his claim when he opened his, and the smell of fresh snoek and vinegar mixing with the ozone of the ocean hit his nostrils. Both ate while they wandered the quay, looking at the fishing boats. Gail pointed to a rock full of seals and hurried along the quay, towing Ed behind. It was fun to observe them playing, diving and swimming, so close their noise was loud and the smell quite overpowering. They returned to the shopping area and stopped to watch a gang of Black boys performing a gumboot dance with high kicking and much stamping. Ed tossed all his loose change into the hat on the ground.

When Gavie gathered them together, he pronounced it time to drive round the mountain, starting with the spectacular Chapman's Peak Drive they had noted from the ship. Ed sensed Gail was thankful for the strict speed limit here, since Gavie had been driving the Kombi like a racing car, and these bends were extremely tight. Sitting next to the window, she often slid towards Ed after looking straight down the cliffs to the rocky sea a thousand feet and more below.

The road ascended, and they had another sighting of the enticing white sands of Longbeach, swept into folds by the tide, growing to large dunes at the base of the cliffs. Screeching seagulls circled and swooped down to the water before soaring back to the beach with their prey.

They met the sea again after a further drive, and Gavie announced they were approaching the seaside town of Fish Hoek on False Bay. Here, he had everybody climb out and board a train for Simonstown, telling them the ride was one they would never forget.

Gavie apologised for the third-class tickets, but only Whites were permitted in the first and second classes. They didn't mind. Once the train pulled away from the station, it ran right along the rocky beaches, so close to the sea they were practically in the water, and they all stuck their heads out the windows.

The wind played with Gail's dark curls, sweeping it over her face. "Isn't this breathtaking?"

Ed agreed. He gazed at her beautiful profile; her lips were curved into a smile of childlike joy. Her face, glowing with pleasure and excitement, really did take his breath away. He had seen the view from the train many times, but this was the first time she'd been part of it, and the better part. It also struck him that he'd never travelled or had even been allowed in third-class before.

The day wore on. They explored Simonstown on foot, viewed Muizenberg from Boye's Drive high above, following the green waves flowing to the beach from afar in extremely shallow waters. Gail's eyelids drooped, and she snoozed against Ed's shoulder as the Kombi continued the drive.

Back in Cape Town, they viewed the castle from outside, shopped in the stalls at the marketplace opposite city hall, and walked the entire length of Government Avenue to look at the beautiful government buildings of this, the legislative capital city of South Africa. Gail clearly enjoyed feeding the squirrels in the gardens.

It was late and growing dark. Everyone looked weary, but Gavie insisted they had to view the city lights from Signal Hill before returning to the boat. Although worn out, they agreed. Gavie parked at a suitable spot, with a view of the length of Table Mountain between Devil's Peak in the distance and Lion's Head to their right, with the city in front of them. The first lights began to twinkle as they sat on the grass or leaned on the van, waiting for darkness to fall.

The sight was so pretty they didn't want to leave. Appearing much closer than they were stood the floodlit buildings, the windows of the skyscrapers, and the still busy news display of the Sanlam Building. The lights continued as far up the slopes of Table Mountain as people had dared to build. From there, it was dark except for the floodlit lower cable station and the upper one much higher. Ed couldn't overlook the symbolism it brought to him. They were leaving Cape Town into a dark, unknown future. Somewhere out there was their own light beckoning them. If only they could find it.

Billions of points of light continued as far as they could see, twinkling like stars in the distance. They even outlined Table Bay, curving gracefully round to the left.

Gail didn't want to go back to the ship, so Ed had to pull her to the Kombi. There, she laid her head on his shoulder, and he soon became aware she had dropped off to sleep. He gently woke her when they arrived at the dockside. Everybody piled out in high spirits and tipped Gavie, who stood by, grinning widely.

The gangway was quiet, and Ed's worst fear eased from his mind since Van Greuning was nowhere in sight. A deckhand met them soon after they reached the top, with a message from the captain, asking if they could stop by his office sometime.

They decided to eat first and found tables with finger food and hors d'oeuvres as the *Hesperus* had no dining service whilst in dock. About twenty minutes later, they knocked on the captain's door.

The captain greeted them. "Ah. I'm delighted you came, come on in." He opened the door wide and stood aside. "I told Van Greuning that the couple he sought had gone on a tour and would return at about six o'clock. Well, that was quite a while ago, and he hasn't showed up. Either he's given up, or he'll be back tomorrow before we leave. I still have my plan, though. If you've a moment, why not sit down and tell me about your day tour?"

They needed no second bidding. Ed liked the captain and was sure Gail did, too. They chatted like old friends for a while, then an abrupt knock sounded. Captain Norton walked to the door. "Who is it?" he asked without opening it.

"A sergeant Van Greuning to see you, sir."

CHAPTER
FORTY

Van Greuning. Here, right outside the captain's cabin door? Gail jumped to her feet, heart pounding, her eyes looking for an emergency exit. There were none. Why hadn't they just hidden somewhere safe? She grasped Ed's arm.

With his hand on the door handle, Captain Norton pointed at the only other door.

Ed opened it and pulled her into the captain's sleeping quarters. Opposite the door lay a single bed, to the right flimsy, half-open doors showed a small wardrobe, but the other wall had another door. She tugged at Ed's hand and whipped open the door, squashing into the cramped space of the toilet. Ed turned the latch and held her close. She pressed her face into his chest, barely daring to breathe as they heard the cabin door opening.

"Sergeant Fan Grewning." Captain Norton had pronounced the name correctly minutes before. "You're rather late, aren't you? I told you the group was due back at six."

Van Greuning's voice came to them through the thin walls. "Only making sure they'd be back."

"Well, have a seat. I suppose you do understand the ship's entrance will shut for the night and all visitors have to leave by that time."

A chair scraped, a door opened, and the captain called out." Mr. Cairns, please check if the couple are in Room 356 B? If they are, make my apologies and bring them to me."

Someone answered, the door clicked closed, and the captain said, "You realise they might be anywhere on the ship. Cairns is a fine man. He'll do his best to track them down, but there are no guarantees. Tomorrow might be a better time since you missed your appointment."

Gail held her breath. The captain didn't sound pleased with Van Greuning. How long would they have to wait here till he'd gone? And why had the captain sent Cairns to the wrong room? Ed enfolded her in his arms, raised her chin with a finger, and looked into her eyes with a look she knew all too well. She shook her head. Kissing in the toilet, no chance!

At the words, "May I use your toilet, please?" Ed tightened his arms around her. She gulped. This was not good.

"Afraid not," the captain answered. "The thing leaks water everywhere. I had to shut it off. I've been waiting days to get it repaired. I don't want you stuck in here when the *Hesperus* closes. There's one on the right at the end of the corridor."

She heard Van Greuning grunt, the door bang closed, footsteps, and, after a brief interval, a soft tapping on their door.

The skipper whispered through it. "No worries. Cairns will return soon. Hang on a little longer."

Shortly, the captain invited someone to come inside, and she heard sounds of new voices and scraping chairs. The captain murmured a few pleasantries then, not much later. "Ah, you're back, Sergeant. Excellent. We've got them. Miss Du Preez, Mr. Hendricks, this is Sergeant Fan Grewning. He asked for you."

"But...but... I," stammered Van Greuning.

"Sergeant?"

"Those aren't, I mean..."

The captain sounded surprised. "Those aren't what?"

"These are not the ones I was looking for. Are you Grace Du Preez?"

"That is me, yes." It sounded like Audrey.

"There...there's been some mistake."

"A mistake? You had me bring these people here, and they're not whom you're seeking?"

"Do you have your passports?" Van Greuning did not sound apologetic.

Someone gasped. It sounded like a very indignant Frans. "What? You want us to prove we aren't someone else. Captain?"

The captain's voice was soothing. "I do apologise, Mr. Hendricks, Miss Du Preez, I'm so sorry. Evidently, the sergeant made a serious error. Please accept the apologies of the line."

Angry mutterings from Audrey and Frans and more cooing from the captain.

Ed grinned at her, and Gail pressed her face into his chest to suppress a giggle.

The door slammed. "Well. That settles that, Sergeant, those are clearly not the people on your wanted list."

"But I saw her face. On the deck, in Durban. I know she's here."

The captain sounded placating yet authoritative. "Perhaps it was because of your determination to find her. You imagined the face you wanted to see."

Several seconds of silence ticked by, as if Van Greuning was considering the possibility. "No! That isn't possible. It was her face. I may be mistaken about the passports, which the Swaziland authorities assured me were fake. So it's their fault, unless..."

"It's always a possibility Mr. Hendricks and Miss Du Preez are travelling under false pretences. I'll investigate that. Why are they sharing a cabin if they're not married? I shall let you know. Now, if you'll excuse me, I'm a busy man. You'll want to disembark before you get locked on board."

"Ja well no fine, but I'll be back. I want to meet each non-White passenger. Have you got that? Every Coloured, curry muncher and kaffir. All of them. If you'll see to that Captain Norton, I'll be obliged."

"I cannot possibly identify my passengers by colour. Good night, Fan Grewning." The door slammed. A few quiet seconds later, it opened again, and the captain said, "Mr. Cairns, please be sure that officer goes down the gangway."

Their own door opened after a knock on it. The captain looked at Gail with a shake of his head. He frowned. "I'm sorry you had to witness that. I'll need to think this out again. He will be back."

Gail had no doubts of that. Why did this man pursue them with so much zeal? Didn't he have others to chase? Well sure, there was that little thing about a broken arm, a stolen helicopter, breaking out of jail…

*****

Ed escorted Gail to the Moodley's cabin after breakfast next morning, where Captain Norton had sent them, since it was the biggest and most suitable for hiding.

Ravi held the door wide. "Come on in. Frans and Audrey are already here."

Shareena beckoned them over to the table in the centre of the room. "Captain Norton told us to sit tight here and wait. You'll be safe, and Nehri is keeping watch for us outside."

Frans waved his hand. "So here we are, every non-White on the boat."

Ed grinned at them. "Including this honorary non-White." He looked round at the room, evidently one of the largest suites with two bedrooms, a complete bathroom, a large porthole and this dining table.

"True, hey?" Audrey slapped him on the back. "I think you like being one of us, ou?" She peered intently at his face and leaned in closer. "Though you could do with a touch up here and there. These little curls are going straight, and your skin is getting whiter every minute."

Frans rolled his eyes. "My wife, the makeup artist. Look, after we leave Cape Town, who cares? Ed can be a White again, but he'll still be one of us, hey?" He looked at Ed for confirmation.

Ed agreed. It was true. He really was enjoying the difference; the accents, the humour, the camaraderie after spending so much time with them.

Gail had chosen to sit on his lap as there weren't enough chairs for the entire group. "What's the news?" she asked. "Was Van Greuning here?"

Ravi chewed his bottom lip. "Bright and early. He asked us, even our daughter and our lightie, to present ourselves, and of course, he was introduced to Audrey and Frans last night."

Audrey and Frans laughed out loud. "You mean Ben and Grace, don't you?"

Gail lifted an eyebrow and looked hopeful. "Then, he's gone?"

Ravi breathed in deeply and let it out in a huff. "Unfortunately not. He knows you're here somewhere, but he hasn't a clue as to your alias."

"Because she's me." Audrey winked, grinning widely. "We've got that guy so confused he doesn't know whether he's Arthur or Martha, hey?"

Gail giggled, and Ed laughed along with her. Seeing Audrey and Frans in the captain's cabin last night must have really confused Van Greuning, who obviously believed he and Gail were using fake passports. But then he sobered. Van Greuning clearly would have had time to confirm the passports were fake, so then Frans and Audrey might be accused of fraud.

"What if he chased after you and Frans? He'll surely be suspicious."

Shareena shook her head. "He won't, don't you worry. And my little spy, Amaya, is on the job of watching him." She gave him a broad wink.

He pictured the Moodley's daughter tailing Van Greuning from the shadows. It must be a tricky job but also perilous for her. The police could easily spot an Indian child with dark skin.

"I should do that job," he said. "My own Coloured makeup is fading, and with my blue eyes, it'll be safer for me to take over."

Audrey, wide eyed, shook her head. "No, Ed, don't be a fool. You're a wanted man. That monster will spot you a mile off."

Further muttering and indignation met his suggestion. Gail grasped his arm. Still, he'd give anything to know what was going on? He glanced at his wristwatch. Nine o'clock. An hour before departure time.

The door swung open, and Amaya slipped through it. "That policeman's gone bananas. He's trying to force the captain to line everyone up on deck. He's got other police searching everywhere, and he's yelling and swearing at everybody at the top of his voice."

Shareena put her arms around her and purred. "Okay, no more spying for you, my love. It's too dangerous. They might notice and follow you."

Feet pounded down the hallway, and Nehri banged the door open. "Dad, they're coming."

Ravi gripped Ed's shoulder and pointed at the door. "You must go. Hide somewhere. Quick."

Ed clutched Gail's hand and bolted for the door.

Breathless, Nehri pointed left. "They're coming along the hall that side."

"Thanks," Ed muttered, grabbed Gail's hand and dashed along the opposite corridor with her in tow. He peeked around the corner and then took off aft at speed. At every intersection he stopped, their backs to the wall, gingerly peeping round the corners. The corridor ended at a stairwell.

Gail took the lead and pulled him up the stairway at the run. "Let's try for the lifeboats. This isn't far from where we were yesterday. At least we're familiar with that area."

"Right." He raced after her up the stairs, four flights, three steps at a time, swinging past the corner posts without slowing. The next landing bore a door on either side, each with a porthole. Gail swerved to the starboard side, and they peeped through. They couldn't see anybody.

Gail pointed. "Over there, the lifeboat. Quickly."

It was only a few yards from the door. Gail, then Ed, dropped and crawled under it to the railing side.

Ed grappled with the canvas covering. "This is too tight. I can't budge it."

"Can we go up on top?" Gail squinted upwards. His eyes tracked her gaze. The boat's tarpaulin arched up to a ridge a couple of feet below the metal roof, perfect for hiding if they made it to the space. Ed cupped his hands and squatted. Gail needed no further urging. Her foot hardly touched his hand as she launched herself onto the cover. Of course, Ed grinned, the skill she'd learned scaling her boarding school walls. He remembered how rapidly and skillfully she'd got over the back wall at Cahill's. After hauling himself up by a rope, he wiggled over the crest of the boat's tarp, Gail helping by pulling one of his arms. From here, they'd be hidden from anybody on the ship, though somebody might spot them from the wharf.

Two cops ran along the deck towards them. Ed ducked behind the ridge in the cover while keeping them in sight. One of them pushed through the door he and Gail had exited less than a minute ago. The other continued running.

Everything was quiet again, and Ed checked the time. A quarter past nine. Three quarters of an hour to go—before they could sail to freedom. Three quarters of an hour was an eternity.

As time passed, he risked frequent peeks. Passengers passed below them from time to time, and uniformed police popped up often. How many were there? The whole ship was crawling with them, but there couldn't have been that many. For what seemed like hours he lay, his arm tucked round Gail's body, not daring to move. At last, he risked a glance at his watch. Fifteen more minutes. A long breath escaped, and his body relaxed. Gail trembled under his arm. Reassured, he raised his head for another look.

Three cops passed their hideaway marching toward the bows. Another was coming their way. There was no mistaking the figure, Van Greuning, his face red with fury. He swore at his men and swung his baton, forcing them to duck as they hurried past to follow his orders. For some moments, he stood glaring at them, then suddenly whirled round, eyes exploring.

Ed ducked his head, but not before Van Greuning's eyes locked on his own.

FORTY-ONE

Gail's trembling transferred to his own body the moment he'd uttered the name, Van Greuning. Her arms tightened around his waist while they lay on the lifeboat's tarpaulin. So close, with just fifteen minutes before sailing time. Fifteen minutes. Then he would haul them off and throw them into separate jails. The likelihood of ever being together again was minimal, if not impossible.

"Get down from there at once." Van Greuning, by now Ed really hated that voice which was now calling for backup. In no time, a group of khaki clad fuzz surrounded the lifeboat.

Not hurrying, dawdling, Ed let his body slide down the tarpaulin and landed on the wooden deck in front of Van Greuning, who stood with a gun pointed at him.

"You too, *Kleurling.*" He scowled up at Gail, sneering in triumph as she inched along the slope.

Van Greuning had finally won, after all this time, within the last quarter hour. Fate could be cruel. Van Greuning barked orders to two of his khaki clad minions. One of them spun Gail around roughly and fastened handcuffs behind her back, while the other turned Ed with practiced ease, and the metal cut into his wrists. The loud click signalled the end. There would be no escaping from jails in their future. He twisted his neck to look at Gail. The tears seeping from her red eyes broke his heart. Was this to be his last memory of that sweet face?

Van Greuning grinned widely, regarding them. "You're finished. We have a jail here in District Six you'll never escape from. You can abandon all hope, hey."

He reached out and gripped Ed's arm, spinning him towards the exit. "Now, march, let's get off this boat before it sails. *Maak gou, julle.*" He hurried his men in the vicinity and sent two of them to gather the others.

The group marched along past the lifeboats toward the exit. Ed couldn't get anywhere near Gail, who was forced into a quick march between two men in front, while they mercilessly pulled him along at the rear. In between them, the motley crew of khaki-clad men grinned and slapped palms together. Van Greuning triumphantly led the parade.

As the group neared the exit, Ed spotted a bunch of *Hesperus* sailors blocking the gangway.

One of them stepped forward. "Stop where you are, Fan Grewning."

A familiar voice, one that gave Ed an inkling of hope.

Van Greuning stopped and glared. "We're getting off your boat, Norton," he said. "Please stand aside."

"Yes, you are indeed Fan Grewning, but not with these two." The captain waved a sheaf of papers. "I've been busy while you've been trying to locate these two…refugees."

"Refugees? Nonsense. They are wanted criminals, Norton. Move."

"Refugees first. They committed their crimes out of fear since they were being persecuted. If you will allow me to read from these laws in the United Nations convention relating to the status of refugees." He opened the pages and began. "A refugee is someone who… owing to well-founded fear of being persecuted for reasons of race, religion, nationality, membership of a particular social group or political opinion, is outside the country of his nationality and is unable or, owing to such fear, is unwilling to avail himself of the protection of that country; or who, not having a nationality and being outside the country of his former habitual residence as a result of such events, is unable or, owing to such fear, is unwilling to return to it.

"You see, Fan Grewning, fact is, these two are on Australian territory now, in fear of returning to their home country. They are refugees and intend to apply for asylum in Australia."

Van Greuning swore and muttered some inaudible, but obvious oaths. "That's mumbo jumbo. I don't care, Norton. Let me pass. I'm taking these two to South Africa, if you don't mind." He signalled to his troupe with his good hand, "*Kom julle*." He marched straight up to Captain Norton.

The captain's hand on Van Greuning's chest arrested his movement. "But I do mind," said the captain. "You work for the law, so I'm assuming you won't break it. Now if you'd be so kind as to remove those cuffs and turn these two people over to me."

Ed held his breath as Van Greuning's face ran through several shades of red.

"Never!" said Van Greuning, attempting to push the captain out of the way. "You can't stop me. I have been after them for a long while. I won't let anything or anyone stand in my way."

"How exactly is that?" The captain didn't move, even when Van Greuning shifted to within inches of his face. "Do you want to shoot me? Perhaps you don't care for your laws at all. I believe murder is still illegal."

Van Greuning sneered. "It isn't necessary to shoot you. I have enough trained policemen. We can force our way past. What can you do to stop me? For the last time, out of my way."

"Suit yourself." Captain Norton stood aside and bowed with a theatrical sweep of his arm. Van Greuning hesitated.

"You see, Fan. There are people in your country who still protect laws, and I have, of course, contacted them." He jerked his thumb toward a canvas backed military lorry and several cars on the dockside. Both police and soldiers stood in groups, armed with rifles. "Just a caution, you understand, seeing as I anticipated your disapproval."

Van Greuning paled at the sight of the vehicles, but still defiant, he returned his gaze to the captain. "I'm not through with this. I will appeal. These people are guilty of serious felonies. He"—he turned and glared back at him and Gail—"seriously injured me, and they stole a police helicopter."

"Crimes committed in self-defence, out of dread. And you haven't followed the proper protocol, you've been using your position to conduct a personal vendetta."

"That accusation would never stand up in court."

"Maybe not. We'll never know, because, as I said in the first place, these people are asylum seekers on Australian property and, if you'll forgive my reminder, your troop is trespassing. You've crossed the line of international law, and you need to be off my ship, which should have departed ten minutes ago. Time is money, Mr. Fan Grewning, and if you insist on staying, it will be to your account."

Van Greuning folded his arms and glowered at Captain Norton through narrowed eyes. "I refuse to leave."

"Right, your decision." The captain turned to one of his officers. "Mr. Holmes, notify the gangway crew and the bridge we'll be departing in five minutes." He turned back to Van Greuning. "I hesitate to have your country's own troops take you off. Shooting is dangerous for my passengers. On the other hand, evacuating you while we are at sea is terribly expensive. I'm sure you wouldn't want to be stuck with the bill."

*****

Gail watched the confrontation between Captain Norton and Van Greuning, scarcely daring to breathe. Other passengers had shown up, curious but tentative, increasing in numbers by the minute. As the captain gained control of the argument, they pressed in closer. In her periphery, she recognised their new friends.

The arguing stopped and the captain and Van Greuning began a staring match. She held her breath. The outcome of the match could mean the difference between life and death for Ed and her. Literally. She'd read of so many accidents in South African prisons, which defied any statistical probability. Would one of those one day be her or Ed? Or would the captain win? Was he just bluffing? Would Van Greuning simply march them off the ship to their doom?

The two men were still glaring at each other, their faces mere inches apart. Then Van Greuning motioned with his hands at his men. "Kom julle," he grunted, pushing the captain aside and striding toward the steps.

Gail caught her breath. Was he really leaving? Did this mean they'd remain on the *Hesperus*? "Stop, Sergeant Van Greuning," she called. "The handcuffs."

He stopped dead, slowly turning, converting her insides to ice. Never had she seen the kind of hate displayed by his features. His jawbone tensed, his eyes bored into her like drills. For several moments, he stood, projecting all his scorn, all the evident racism, the fury from his thwarted plans. He stepped up and thrust his face so close she could smell his pipe tobacco. He swore under his breath.

"You can keep the cuffs, kaffir." He swung his hand full-force across her cheek.

She glimpsed the blur of Ed racing forward, hands still cuffed behind his back. He headbutted Van Greuning, who stumbled backwards, recovered, and hurried down the gangway, followed by his troupe.

Ed rushed back, frowning as he inspected her face close-up. "Gail, you're hurt?"

She nodded, her cheek smarting and wet with tears, the cuffs biting into her wrists as she attempted to free her arms so she could hold him. She forced a grin. "If only my wrists were free, it would be Van Greuning who's hurting." Though desperate to be in Ed's arms, she had to settle for his head pressed against hers.

Captain Norton stood by her side, snapping an order to one of his men to fetch a toolkit. "Never fear, Miss Rabe. Sorry, Mrs. Brent. Come, let's get you to first aid and check for damage. We'll have those cuffs off in a jiffy."

She mumbled her thanks and buried her head on Ed's shoulder, perfect for crying on.

At once, her friends surrounded her, all commiserating and congratulating her at once. Her teeth chattered. Was she actually safe? Would the ship still sail with Ed and her aboard?

A loud blast sounded. The ship's horn, a symphony to her ears, sweeter than any she had heard before, signalling their escape, their freedom. Yesterday, she'd dreamed of living forever in this enchanting city with Ed. Today, she wanted that mountain out of her sight as soon as possible.

The man with the toolkit arrived, panting hard. A few moments later, she was free and reaching for Ed before his arms could reciprocate. Her friends awaited their turns for hugs and congratulations.

At last, Ed's fingers touched her face, anxiously examining the marks Van Greuning had left, eyes still seething with anger.

*****

Gail exited the first aid room, feeling much better though she still smarted from a bruised and cut cheek from Van Greuning's blow. Though a bit puffy, he'd caused no lasting harm.

Ed inspected her face. "I just want one more chance for revenge."

She frowned and shook a finger at him. "Don't even think of it. I never wish to see him. Not ever again."

"I can't argue with that." He tilted his head, folded his arms, and rocked from side to side.

"What is it? I know you too well. You want something."

"Um, are you up to viewing Cape Town dwindling? I always wanted to do that. It's apparently well worth watching."

A shiver ran down her spine. Leaving South Africa, their home, her mom, Chantal and Mark. Her last look at her home country. She blinked away the tears that were forming. But then—"Yes, please. Let's do it. The further it gets, the better I'll be."

They ran aft, already seeing the entire, recognisable front view of Table Mountain, with the city sprawled at its base, the white sands of Blauuberg Strand to the left. What a magnificent view. In spite of herself, more pangs gnawed at her solar plexus. They were leaving it all. The land of her birth, where her mother still lived. She blinked, would she ever see Mom again?

And Chantal. She and Mark still had to face criminal charges. Perhaps Van Greuning, in his sheer rage, would pursue them with renewed energy. She and Ed had always been the fugitives, yet here she was, worrying over the future of her two dear friends.

A voice came over the ship's speaker announcing they had reached their full cruising speed of twenty-four knots and would shortly pass Robben Island. She leaned back against Ed's chest as they watched the home of political prisoners go by. People who wanted to change the odious laws of South Africa and turned to violence as the only way to achieve their goals. A shudder travelled through her body. Would the country ever be free and peaceful for all its citizens?

The panorama of Table Bay and Table Mountain steadily diminished till it dissolved in the haze. South Africa's coast would still be visible on their right for a thousand or more miles before they'd see the last of it, but there would be no more stops till they reached the port of Dakar. Still Africa, but a completely different nation, over four thousand miles away.

Gail shuddered.

"I felt that, Gail, what are you thinking?" said Ed.

"I'm wondering, what if nowhere else takes us in as refugees? We'd never be allowed off the *Hesperus*, and it'll return this way to Australia. What if they drag us off in Cape Town?"

"You know what?"

"What?"

"You worry too much."

"Hmmmm." She couldn't say a thing. His lips were in the way.

CHAPTER
FORTY-TWO

Ed returned to his cabin long after saying goodbye to the coast of South Africa, possibly for the last time ever. He examined the contents of his suitcase and South African Airways overnight bag. Fifteen more nights before reaching Southampton, and his suitcase held a meagre supply of clothes. Turning up at the dining room table every night wearing the same things could present a problem. He needed to check the ship's clothing shops. Besides, he had promised he would take Gail dancing. Dressed like a tramp?

The content of his wallet didn't exactly encourage him, roughly a hundred rand in total. There'd been no time to arrange travellers' checks anyway, too risky for a fugitive. For the same reason, he'd shied away from going to his bank to make withdrawals. He might arrange a bank transfer once he settled somewhere, but that was impossible while on board.

Wait! Of course. He dived into his overnight. There it was, the envelope from Mrs. Cahill. He slit it open and found three cheques. His last paycheck included time he hadn't even been present. A tad over two hundred rands. The other two were for unused leave and sick leave, which made over four hundred in total. Good, he'd certainly cash them at the purser's office, unless Van Greuning had somehow managed to freeze his funds. No, these came from the Cahill's business account. Three cheques. Plenty for clothes, but probably not for something else he desperately wanted—a camera. He sighed. How he'd missed having one on his Cape Town tour with Gail. The only pictures of the two of them together were their wedding photos, which he'd had to leave behind.

Then he remembered the "little something" Mrs. Cahill had mentioned and dug into his bag. He found an envelope and pulled out the contents. Wow! Another hundred note, clean, crisp and brand new. Thanks, Mommy! Now they had over six hundred. Obviously, he shouldn't splurge. They had no expenses on the boat, but what about when they disembarked somewhere? Without money, they'd starve, and what if they couldn't find work? He visualised the Pentax camera flying away on wings. Well, maybe a Kodak Instamatic at least. Better than nothing, marginally better. Hey, at least it took pictures.

He stuffed the cheques and money into his wallet and set off to pick up Gail.

*****

Gail held the dress up and shook the creases out as best she could. This was the best she had? Her lips tightened into a twisted line. Ed wanted to go dancing. One glance at her in this and he'd waltz away with one of the other, appropriately dressed, women.

It was not as though she'd had much chance to go shopping for clothes of late. Being hunted down by police, making for the border or being shot all made it difficult. In any case, what need had she for fancy clothes at work, stuck in the storeroom, and taking phone calls? Or when Ed had taken her on dates. Precisely how much did you need to dress up for the drive-in? Okay, there ought to have been more clothes, but they'd left in such a hurry she and her mom had hastily thrown things into a suitcase. And now Ed wanted to take her dancing.

Well. She examined herself in the mirror while holding the dress in front of her and smoothing it down. It would just have to do. Perhaps Audrey or Shareena could make it look nice. Gail had no such skills in her repertoire. Or perhaps she could find a dress shop? She and Ed had seen shops during their explorations but hadn't gone inside. Even from outside, they seemed extremely larney, so likely way too expensive. She replaced the dress on its hanger in the wardrobe, already full with the possessions of four young women.

Her mood didn't lift much when she opened her purse. What little money they had between them wouldn't go far after they got off the boat somewhere.

Through the door came Ed's signature knock to the beat of "People Will Say We're in Love."

"Let them," she said, whipping the door open and falling into his arms.

In his unique manner, Ed huffed, then chuckled soundlessly, followed by chortling heartily with open mouth and teeth showing. Her heart warmed, his teeth rarely showed lately. This was the old Ed, the one she'd come to love so much. It seemed years since they'd first seen each other, years since he'd recovered from his shock. No. She ran over a few quick mental calculations. It had been a mere fifty-eight days.

He cleared his throat and suggested they should go shopping.

"So long as it's window shopping, we can't afford any other kind." Nothing new to her and the only kind she and her mother had generally done.

She thought back to the days she and her mother used to go window shopping in Smith and West streets during the Christmas season. So many delightful things in all the windows. The streets decorated with a million Christmas lights. Her face pressed against shop windows, ogling countless beautiful toys, dolls and books, especially books, which adorned the windows. She had wanted so many things; what she got were little ones, filling the pillowcase her mom hung at the end of her bed. Father Christmas had always been a fictional character for her, but if she humoured her mother, she would get extra presents. Maybe a useful trick to try on Ed next Christmas.

Ed looked at her sideways, a silly grin stuck on his face. She knew that expression; he wanted to buy something. Most likely expensive. She tightened her mouth. "Very well, what is it you want?"

He acted like a puppy waiting for a titbit. "Well, I'd love a camera."

Not a bad idea. "That sounds like fun. To keep memories of our sea cruise, I guess you can buy a box camera."

"A box camera? They don't actually make them anymore. And even if they did, I wouldn't be seen dead with one. The closest is a Hanimex, and honestly...no."

"Ja well no fine, Ed. Only teasing, hey, but don't go spending on frivolous things. We'll need our money to survive wherever we end up." She took her handbag, pulled and locked the cabin door, then they made their way up to the shopping complex. The key area comprised one vast showroom, resembling a sort of OK Bazaars, with a wide variety of things to buy.

They stopped here and there, looking at displays, exhibits and fancy presentations. She pointed. "I think I see a Kodak sign. Yes, look, a picture of those five cute kittens. They're so sweet."

"True," he said. "We had a copy at our shop. Fabulous shot."

"It sure is—" Not the kittens though, from the corner of her eye, she caught sight of a large glass case. Fabulous.

Ed's eyes followed her gaze. His jaw dropped, as had hers.

A dress. No, that wasn't the right word. A gown, a robe, regalia, shamefully draped on a headless, shapeless window dummy despite its own life and beauty. Rather than a specific colour, it shimmered in silver, bouncing the light outwards in a vast multicoloured array. The pearl-coloured bodice, as if itself bedecked in pearls, seemed to sing to her. From the top, it tapered to a broad, blue belt at the waist, then spread gradually in a graceful curve to the hemline where the gentle waves flowed, yet never moved. The whole dress yearned to be on the dance floor. From its glass cage, lit with a delicate though invisible fluorescent light, the gown beckoned her, pleading yet dignified. She revered the gown. No, not a mere gown. Something that called out to her. One which had found its wearer. Its one shimmering long sleeve rose in a majestic gesture, beckoning. Come to me. In a daze, she crossed straight to the case, pressing her hands to the sides, staring.

"Fine!" said Ed behind her.

She turned to him. "No, we can't. It must cost the earth."

"Hello, you two." Audrey said, walking up with Shareena, both loaded with parcels. Audrey stopped dead as she noticed the dress. Her mouth slowly formed into an O. "Gail! You'll look like an angel in that."

Shareena clearly agreed. "This will suit you to a T. You haven't tried it on yet?"

Gail bit her lip and peered up into Ed's face. Panic beat at her breast. No way in the world could they afford this.

Ed pointed at the blurb and price tag at the bottom of the case. One hundred and seventy-five Australian dollars. Her heart froze. That settled that. She turned from the cabinet, aiming a faltering smile at the two women.

Ed turned her gently back to the cabinet. "Go ahead."

A lady in a ship's uniform materialised from nowhere. "May I help you?"

Gail opened her mouth and closed it again.

"We have only one of these, but I'm certain it will fit you as is. I can tell you love it. Allow me to get it out of the case for a fitting."

Shareena, wearing an impressive sleek silk sari herself, clapped her hands enthusiastically. "They designed this just for you, Gail."

Without waiting for Gail's answer, the saleslady opened the cabinet and now held out the dress. "Follow me this way, ladies."

*****

Clearly, being women, they'd take quite a while in the dressing room, so Ed decided to explore the camera shop. Lots of photographic equipment sat in glass showcases against the walls. A quick glance confirmed they stocked the Pentax reflex camera and even a shamefully expensive Zeiss. Way outside his range now, of course.

Gail would want to buy that dress, and he'd not disappoint her for the world, but now he'd have to set his sights much lower. Looking at the less prominent areas, he found a reasonable Voigtländer with a built-in flash. Well-made, reliable, an excellent lens. *This will do nicely.* He reached for the cabinet sliding door. Locked! Every one of them, locked. Nobody in attendance at the shop. Perhaps the poor guy worked on his own and needed a toilet break. He let out a sigh. Gail could be a while changing, but not forever, so he should sort this out right away. He didn't want any sales pitch. He just needed to buy it with some film and go. They had a good supply of films, all sizes and speeds, excellent choices, but also locked up. He looked around, gazed at his wristwatch, and tapped his foot repeatedly on the floor.

A young lady arrived and stood at his side. "I'm so sorry, sir. Nobody is in attendance at the photo shop. Please accept the line's apologies."

Since she seemed genuinely contrite, he managed a friendly smile. "Quite all right. I don't need any help. I'd just like to buy this camera and films. Do you have a key?"

She chewed her lip. "I'm dreadfully sorry, really. I don't have one."

"What? It will be closed all the way to Southampton?"

Great. A trip of a lifetime with the woman he loved, and he couldn't take so much as a single snap.

The young lady looked as though she wished to be transported off the ship.

"It isn't your fault," he muttered.

"No, it's mine."

Ed turned at the sound of the voice. The captain, a frown creasing his forehead, stood behind him. "I should never have employed him. The rat jumped ship in Perth and made off with every penny of our takings."

"I'm sorry," Ed said. He meant it but more for himself. He wondered if the "rat" took the key with him.

"I do have the key," said the captain, as if reading his mind. "I shall open for you, of course, as long as you know what you want. Me, I have zip knowledge about photography." The captain, still frowning and muttering something about chaining the rat up in the brig, withdrew a bunch of keys.

Ed pointed at the Voigtländer. "No problem. This is what I want thanks, and some films with it, of course."

The captain picked his way through the keys, trying several without luck until finally, a satisfying click resulted in a smile.

Much relieved, Ed took the camera and put it through its paces, winding and releasing the shutter several times, making sure the rewind released and checking the rangefinder.

Captain Norton stood by, observing Ed's examinations with eyes wide. "You apparently know what you're doing."

Ed chuckled. "I should. I've been doing it for six years. It's my job."

Captain Norton lifted an eyebrow.

Ed continued. "I worked at Cahill's Photoshop as a salesman and general dogsbody, of course."

The captain stroked his chin. "So you've a lot of experience with cameras?"

Ed agreed, though feeling modest. "Pretty much everything. It's been my hobby most of my life."

"Your hobby, cameras?" The chin stroking turned into a more vigorous rubbing.

"Cameras? Well, I did take a few old ones apart to see what makes them tick, or should I say click." He grinned. "But no, I meant I used them. I always loved taking photographs since I got a box camera for Christmas at about eight years old."

"And I suppose you still do." He stared at the camera. "What kind of photos do you take?"

"A bit of everything, portraits, scenery, modelling shots of girls."

"That is interesting, Ed. And this Cahills, did they do photography?"

"Oh yes, of course. They had a studio and darkrooms. Everything."

By now, Captain Norton's hand was butchering his chin and cheeks. "But did you do photography there, professionally?"

"Mainly weddings, I did many when Will and Mrs. Cahill were fully booked. Over the years, I must have done close to a hundred. Occasionally, I did the odd portrait in the studio. Not bad at all, though I do say so myself."

"Did you ever work in the darkroom?"

"Not as part of my job, but I spent lots of time there whenever I got the chance. I loved making enlargements and transforming my pictures."

"So you're able to develop the negatives and make prints or enlargements as well as take the snaps?"

"Snaps?" He cringed. "None of us took snaps."

"No, of course not. Sorry, photographs?"

"Yes, all the way through."

"And, of course, they used four by fives at Cahill's?"

"Yes, we used Speed Graphics with Metz electronic flashes for the weddings, a Homrich four by five enlarger in the darkroom, and a Linhof view camera in the studio."

"Well, like I said, I know zip about photography, but I know those names. I'm sure you don't realise this, but the ship has a darkroom with similar equipment. And cameras, we have a Speed Graphic, too, and a Mamiya twin-lens reflex, whatever that means. Thank goodness they're still here. The rat didn't smuggle them off the ship."

"I'd never have expected you'd have that on the ship."

"A good man worked for us for years. Unfortunately, he retired, and I needed to employ this other bloke at short notice." He took a deep breath, opened his mouth to speak, but immediately his jaw slackened. He stared over Ed's shoulder, his eyes riveted on something.

"Hello, Ed," came the sweetest voice in the world. He spun round and gasped.

Gail stood before him gleaming, eyes sparkling, smile wide with beautiful white teeth, dimples deeper than he'd seen. A stunning vision, her face, but his eyes drifted downward. The gown matched her ideally. Her dark hair fell to her bare shoulder and over part of the pearl bodice. The outfit complemented her skin colour to an hypnotic degree. He became aware of other people's eyes in the store through the periphery of his own, staring, ogling, admiring.

Gail's focused only on his. "Do you like it?"

"No."

The smile vanished, and her eyes widened.

"Like isn't the word," he said.

Her smile returned, though quivering.

"I love it. No, that's not nearly adequate, either. Adore, worship, idolise. The term hasn't been invented yet." He took in the captivating picture again. "We need to photograph you in this gorgeous dress with my new camera." He held it up. "If there's anyone who'll sell it to me."

Gail's smile faded. "Ed, we're spending so much money. What will we live on? I shouldn't…"

"Stop right there. Not buying that dress for you would be sacrilege."

A small admiring crowd had formed around her. She reddened and hurried back to the change room and the grinning faces of Shareena and Audrey.

FORTY-THREE

The captain remained next to him, staring after her. "That is one remarkably beautiful woman. You are so lucky."

Really lucky. Being shot at, imprisoned, constantly on the run. But in the end, yes, being Gail's husband made him the luckiest man alive. Yet they'd never lived together. Was it possible to be the luckiest man yet the unluckiest at the same time?

"By the look of that delicate dress," the captain said, "she'll take a while to change back. Seeing as you have a moment, may I show you something?"

Ed tore his eyes from Gail. "Why, of course."

He followed the captain through a door between two glass cabinets. They emerged in a narrow passageway with the showroom on the left and a row of doors on the right. Pausing at the first, the captain again fiddled with his bunch of keys and inserted one in the lock. He pushed the door wide with a triumphant gesture, revealing a sizeable room. Ed's attention fell immediately on the Homrich enlarger prominent on its metal stand in the corner, the lamphouse almost reaching the ceiling. An assortment of processing equipment lay beside the enlarger, and above that hung a shelf with various cameras. Against the opposite wall stood a drying rack—a contraption made up of crisscrossed wires—an enlarger and a bench with three large developing trays.

He made directly for the Speed Graphic and took it tenderly in his hands. A similar model to those at Cahills, but he could tell this one was practically unused. Almost brand new. He cocked and released the shutter several times on the slow speeds, confirming this. Obviously, a well-stocked photo shop but barely used. What potential.

The captain grinned at him. "Impressed?"

"You're not kidding. This is quite a setup. Do you ever use all this stuff?"

"Alas, no. Certainly not the joker who jumped ship, but even the original photographer only took portraits of guests or photos of them dressed up for balls or dinner. His favourite was the little camera." He indicated the Zeiss Contarex sitting on the shelf attached to a Metz Pro electronic flash.

Some little camera! The Contarex felt like holding a brick. Ed gazed around the shop again, like a kid in a toyshop. When he looked back at the captain, he saw first a frown, followed by a small smile and a raised eyebrow. What they meant, put together, he had no idea.

"Ed, what are your plans after we dock in Southampton?"

"I haven't the faintest notion. We'll face that one when we get there."

The captain wrinkled his forehead more. "You need to find a place of asylum, which can be a long and difficult process. I…" he tapped his finger on his chin, "wondered, whether you would, um… perhaps work for us, in this photo shop and studio." He raised a hand. "Not now, you understand. You're a fare-paying passenger and need to enjoy the trip. After which, we start a series of cruises, and by that time I would like this shop in operation. The studio too."

"Well, uh…"

"No need to decide now. I will mention that we'd also employ your wife somewhere. We prefer married couples, who live aboard, to both work. There are some double cabins. Not so large or luxurious as the twin cabin you're in now, of course, but—"

"Wait! Our cabin?" Ed held up both hands.

Captain Norton's frown deepened. "Uh, yes."

"You realise we are sleeping in separate four-person cabins with roommates."

The captain looked shocked. "You…you're in separate cabins?"

"We booked too late for anything else and, as you know, we were posing as unacquainted, single travellers."

"But that is preposterous. You're not together? I should fix that right away, but every one of the twin and family units are full."

"I'll be more than happy to accept your job offer right now. It doesn't matter if I'm a paying passenger. I really want that crew cabin."

*****

Both Shareena and Audrey were making an awful fuss. Everything had to be just so. Still, Gail had to admit that Shareena had performed miracles with her hair, making it smoother than ever, cascading in gentle waves over her bare shoulder. Short, loose curls reached from her fringe, framing her eyes and forehead. Audrey had worked on Gail's face, darkening her brows and eyelashes, applying a delicate blue-green eyeshadow that brought out her eye colour. She'd also lightened Gail's skin and gave her cheeks a rosy blush. Or maybe they simply glowed with happiness.

Whatever they'd done had resulted in making Gail happy. As happy as she'd been on her wedding day. The first part, that is, before Van Greuning turned up. The memory made her grimace. But not for long, thanks to her two joking and teasing friends. She grinned. In the mirror, her white teeth contrasted with her bronze-red lipstick. She approved. *I think Ed will like me looking like this.*

"Perfect," Shareena announced, fluffing Gail's hair again with those creative fingers. "Only just in time. Ed will be here for you any minute."

As if she'd waved a wand, someone knocked to the rhythm of "I Could Have Danced All Night." Ed.

"He's here," squealed Audrey. "Oh no! I almost forgot—the earrings." She whirled back to the desk.

"Not to worry." Shareena produced a silver box between her fingers. "We'd hardly forget these."

Shareena winked at Audrey as she quickly passed the box over. But then she stumbled, and the box plunged under the desk.

Shareena grumbled, dropped to her knees, and felt around for it. She mumbled from below. "One of them's gone from the box. You go with Ed. I'll bring them to you. Putting them on won't take a jiff."

Audrey grabbed Gail's wrist and tugged her to the door.

Ed stood in the doorway, staring wide eyed at Gail, sending a shudder through her body all the way to the floor. He wore a new three-piece suit. Evidently, he'd spent more of their money. Still, he looked far too good in it to scold him. She placed her white gloved hand in the crook of his arm. He squeezed it against his side, never lifting his eyes from her face.

"There! But it's hard to reach," came Shareena's muted voice. "You two go ahead. I'll bring you the key before you go into the ballroom."

Silently, Gail handed over the cabin key to Audrey and walked out with Ed. She suddenly realised this would be their first proper date after he had proposed.

*****

Couples crowded the dance floor for the first hour or two. Just as well, Gail hadn't danced at all since high school. Very few of the guys from the boy's school had asked her to dance at the end-of-year social. She'd made do with her own few wallflower friends.

Ed apologised for his own lack of skills. She didn't mind. The busy, elbow-bumping crowd drove her deeper into Ed's arms, where she wanted to be more than any place in the world. Where she belonged. If only their dates in Durban or 'Maritzburg had been this good.

The band played, and a singer crooned a familiar song, the very one Ed had tried to sing at the drive-in. "*Something Stupid.*" She smiled. Ed hadn't been able to remember the words, but they came back to her now as though they were still sitting in his Rambler. He'd been singing the last line, and then he'd forgotten the next three little words which she'd filled in for him. "I love you." Or maybe he just pretended he'd forgotten so that she'd say them.

She blushed. Had she really just said those words aloud? Sang them even.

"I love you, too." Ed's lips caressed her cheek till they came to rest on her own. The other dancers nearby circled around, grinning, whistling and applauding.

Suddenly, Ed hooked her arm in his and tugged her off the dance floor. "Come with me." He drew her back to their table, his jaw set. Instead of pulling her chair out for her, he thrust her handbag at her.

What had happened? Had the whistling audience embarrassed him? He'd never acted like this before.

Her voice shook. "Is something wrong, Ed?"

"No. I want to go." He squeezed her arm tighter and led her to the exit.

What was wrong? What had she done? Ed didn't say a word as he strode to a lift, never looking at her. Her eyes welled up and she wiped the tears with the back of her fist. When they entered the lift, his entire body tensed up. What had gone wrong? Only minutes ago, they had both been so happy, so in love. At least that's what she'd thought. The lift doors opened, and he hauled her out. She had to grip his hand to avoid stumbling.

He pulled her down a corridor toward the front of the ship. "This isn't our floor," she said. Instead of answering, he stopped in front of an unfamiliar door.

She sniffed and tried to swallow away the threatening sob. "Why are we here and why did we leave? Without even getting my key back from Shareena. I'd like to have danced until they closed. Why are you mad at me?"

Ed turned to her, studied her watery eyes, then caressed her wet cheek. He seemed uncertain, as if he hadn't known he'd made her cry. "Aww, Gail." He pulled her into his arms. "No. Mad at you? I never could be. I just couldn't take not being with you anymore. You're so incredibly beautiful, and dancing with you, so close. And I guess, knowing that this"—he nodded at the door—"is here, waiting. I got more than a little desperate. I'm so sorry."

Gail sniffed. "What are you talking about? You've no idea how anxious you've made me. What's this anyway?" She looked at the door, up and down.

He pulled back and gazed intently at her face. "I didn't plan it this way. I was too impatient. I just this minute realised how thoughtless I've been. I made plans, without stopping to consider your feelings."

She pulled back and stared at him, wiping away fresh tears. "Well, perhaps you'd better explain the plans."

He pointed to the door. "This is your cabin now. And mine. The captain offered me a job, and…well…we have our own home at last, right here. I thought I would surprise you, but now I feel cruel in not telling you."

Their own home? A cabin for themselves? Intense joy washed over her. But he'd not told her a thing. She'd had no say at all, no hint of what he was planning. She crossed her arms. "I don't have my things from my cabin."

"Oh. Yes, Audrey and Shareena packed up your things and moved them here. They pretended to lose your earrings to get your key."

She narrowed her eyes at him, tightened her folded arms, and tapped one foot. "So everyone was in on this except me."

Ed's face paled, then got redder by degrees. Droplets of sweat beaded on his brow.

Let him squirm.

"I'm so sorry, Gail. It was all so sudden. A golden opportunity. I imagined it'd be a pleasant surprise. Oh please, Gail." He fumbled in his pocket and pulled out a key, fiddling with the lock, and at last swung the door open.

She turned an icy stare to the room. A double bed stood in the centre, a tiny shower near the door, and a small desk at the side with a couple of chairs. Certainly, a lot better than her present one—a whole lot better. Quite cosy. Above all, it was theirs. Alone.

She turned back to him with a scowl, arms still folded. "Ed Brent. If you think for one second, I'll step through that door, you're mistaken." She glared her fiercest glare. But she couldn't keep it up for long and succumbed to a giggle.

Ed grinned in relief. He exhaled loudly and wiped his brow. "Phew, Gail! You nearly gave me a heart attack." He gestured to the doorway.

"No, I told you, I am not walking through that door. I mean it." She scowled dramatically, then fell to giggling again. "I do mean it, Ed."

Ed frowned, studied her for several seconds, before his face cleared. "Ahhhh, I understand." He bent and swooped her up into his arms. "Mrs. Brent, may I carry you across the threshold of our very first home together?"

"Hmmmm." She put her arms round his neck and peered into his eyes. "Mr. Edward Brent, you certainly may."

ABOUT THE AUTHOR

Ken Reynolds, a native of South Africa, started writing books at age six. Over the years he has written several books for children. *Colour* is his first book for adults.

He loves skating, travel, cartooning, photography, learning languages and playing the piano, and above all, ballroom dancing.

Ken started university at thirty-one, where he met and subsequently married his one and only, Linda. He taught at a primary school in South Africa for several years. When a new opportunity in America opened for him, he and Linda packed up their two small children, Phillip and Becky, and immigrated to Anchorage, Alaska. Years later, after a family reunion in South Africa, they adopted a little Zulu girl, Mbali. Today, he and Linda, along with their three children and two grandchildren, all live in Virginia, USA.

CPSIA information can be obtained
at www.ICGtesting.com
Printed in the USA
BVHW050148300622
641013BV00004B/25

9 781685 262